THE
DEVIL
COLONY

ALSO BY JAMES ROLLINS

THE DEVIL COLONY

A Σ SIGMA FORCE NOVEL

JAMES ROLLINS

WILLIAM MORROW

An Imprint of HarperCollins*Publishers*

Schematics provided and drawn by Steve Prey. All rights reserved. Used by permission of Steve Prey.

THE DEVIL COLONY. Copyright © 2011 by James Czajkowski. All rights reserved. Printed in the United States of America. No part of this book may be used or reproduced in any manner whatsoever without written permission except in the case of brief quotations embodied in critical articles and reviews. For information address HarperCollins Publishers, 10 East 53rd Street, New York, NY 10022.

HarperCollins books may be purchased for educational, business, or sales promotional use. For information please write: Special Markets Department, HarperCollins Publishers, 10 East 53rd Street, New York, NY 10022.

FIRST EDITION

Library of Congress Cataloging-in-Publication Data has been applied for.

ISBN 978-0-06-178478-1 (hardcover)
ISBN 978-0-06-199283-4 (international edition)

11 12 13 14 15   OV/RRD   10 9 8 7 6 5 4 3 2 1

To Dad,
because it's about time (and you are too often unsung)

"Science is my passion, politics, my duty."

—THOMAS JEFFERSON IN A LETTER
TO HARRY INNES, 1791

ACKNOWLEDGMENTS

As this book has been two years in the making, the debt of gratitude I owe on it is long overdue. So let's get started. First, I mention this group in every book, and it's still not enough. They're my first readers, my first editors, and some of my best friends. I wanted to take this moment to acknowledge those folks who've been my bedrock over all of these past years: Penny Hill, Judy Prey, Dave Murray, Caroline Williams, Chris Crowe, Lee Garrett, Jane O'Riva, Sally Barnes, Denny Grayson, Leonard Little, Kathy L'Ecluse, J. M. Keese, and Scott Smith. And again I owe an extra big thanks to Steve Prey for all of his spectacular help with the maps and some crafty handiwork with the Great Seal of the United States. Beyond the group, Carolyn McCray and David Sylvian have kept me upright and moving through the best of times and the worst. Somewhere I probably owe fellow scribe Steve Berry for something (so consider yourself covered, Steve). And, of course, I *do* know what I owe everyone at HarperCollins: Michael Morrison, Liate Stehlik, Seale Ballenger, Danielle Bartlett, Josh Marwell, Lynn Grady, Adrienne Di Pietro, Richard Aquan, Tom Egner, Shawn Nicholls, Joyce Wong, and Ana Maria Allessi. Lastly, of course, a special acknowledgment to the four people instrumental to all levels of production: my editor, Lyssa Keusch, and her colleague Wendy Lee; and my agents, Russ Galen and Danny Baror. And as always, I must stress that any and all errors of fact or detail in this book fall squarely on my own shoulders.

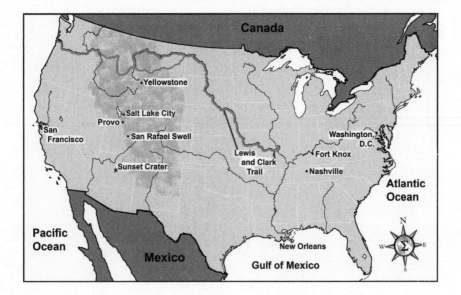

NOTES FROM THE HISTORICAL RECORD

Every schoolchild knows the name of Thomas Jefferson, the architect and scribe of the Declaration of Independence, the man who helped establish a nation out of a scatter of colonies in the New World. Volumes have been written about the man over the past two centuries, but of all the Founding Fathers of America, he remains to this day wrapped in mystery and contradictions.

For instance, it was only in 2007 that a coded letter, buried in his papers, was finally cracked and deciphered. It was sent to Jefferson in 1801 by his colleague at the American Philosophical Society—a colonial-era think tank promoting science and scholarly debate. The group was especially interested in two topics: developing unbreakable codes and investigating mysteries surrounding the native tribes who populated the New World.

Jefferson was fascinated to the point of fixation with Native American culture and history. At his home in Monticello, he put together a collection of tribal artifacts that was said to rival those held in museums of the day (a collection that mysteriously disappeared after his death). Many of these Indian relics were sent to him by Lewis and Clark during their famed expedition across America. But what many don't know is that Jefferson sent a secret message to Congress in 1803 concerning Lewis and Clark's expedition. It revealed the true hidden purpose behind the journey across the West.

Within these pages, you'll learn that purpose. For there is a secret history to the founding of America of which only a few have knowledge. It has nothing to do with Freemasons, Knights Templar, or crackpot theories. In fact, a clue hangs boldly in the Rotunda of the U.S. Capitol. Within that noble hall hangs the famous painting by John Turnbull, *Declaration of Independence* (a work overseen by Jefferson). It depicts each man who signed that famous document—but what few ever note is that Turnbull painted five extra men into that painting, men who never signed the Declaration of Independence. Why? And who were they?

For answers, keep reading.

NOTES FROM THE SCIENTIFIC RECORD

In this new millennium, the next big leap in scientific research and industry can be summarized in one word: Nanotechnology. In a nutshell, it means manufacturing at the atomic level, at a level of one billionth of a meter. To picture something so small, look at the period at the end of this sentence. Scientists at Nanotech.org have succeeded in building test tubes so tiny that 300 billion of them would fit within that one period.

And that nanotechnology industry is exploding. It is estimated that this year alone $70 billion worth of nanotech products will be sold in the United States. Nano-goods are found everywhere: toothpaste, sunscreen, cake icing, teething rings, running socks, cosmetics, medicines, even Olympic bobsleds. Currently close to ten thousand products contain nanoparticles.

What's the downside of such a growth industry? These nanoparticles can cause illness, even death. UCLA scientists have found that nano-titanium oxide (found in children's sunscreens and many other products) can trigger damage to animals at the genetic level. Carbon nanotubes (found in thousands of everyday products, including children's safety helmets) have been shown to accumulate in the lungs and brains of rats. Also, weird and unexpected things happen at this small level. Take aluminum foil. It's harmless enough and convenient for wrapping up leftovers, but break it down into nanoparticles, and it becomes explosive.

It's a new and wild frontier. There is presently no requirement for the labeling of nano-goods, nor are there required safety studies of products containing nanoparticles. But there's an even darker side to this industry. This technology has a history that goes back further than the twentieth century—much further. To find out where this all began and to discover the dark roots of this "new" science . . .

. . . Keep reading.

The skull of the monster slowly revealed itself.

A shard of yellowed tusk poked through the dark soil.

Two muddied men knelt in the dirt on either side of the excavated hole. One of them was Billy Preston's father; the other, his uncle. Billy stood over them, nervously chewing a knuckle. At twelve, he had begged to be included on this trip. In the past, he'd always been left behind in Philadelphia with his mother and his baby sister, Nell.

Pride spiked through him even to be standing here.

But at the moment it was accompanied by a twinge of fear.

Maybe that was due to the sun sitting low on the horizon, casting tangled shadows over the encampment like a net. Or maybe it was the bones they'd been digging up all week.

Others gathered around: the black-skinned slaves who hauled stones and dirt; the primly dressed scholars with their ink-stained fingers; and of course, the cryptic French scientist named Archard Fortescue, the leader of this expedition into the Kentucky wilderness.

The latter—with his tall bony frame, coal-black hair, and shadowed eyes—scared Billy, reminding him of an undertaker in his black jacket and waistcoat. He had heard whispered rumors about the gaunt fellow: how the man dissected corpses, performed experiments with them, traveled to far corners of the world collecting arcane artifacts. It was even said he had once participated in the mummification of a deceased fellow scholar, a man who had donated his body and risked his immortal soul for such a macabre endeavor.

But the French scientist had come with credentials to support him. Benjamin Franklin had handpicked him to join a new scientific group, the American Society for the Promotion of Useful Knowledge. He had apparently impressed Franklin in the past, though the exact details remained unknown. Additionally, the Frenchman had the ear of the new governor of Virginia, the man who had ordered them all to this strange site.

It was why they were still here—and had been for so long.

Over the passing weeks, Billy had watched the surrounding foliage slowly turn from shades of copper to fiery crimson. The past few mornings had begun to frost. At night, winds stripped the trees, leaving skeletal branches scratching at the sky. At the start of each day, Billy had to sweep and rake away piles of leaves from the dig site. It was a constant battle, as if the forest were trying to rebury what lay exposed to the sun.

Even now, Billy held the hay-bristled broom and watched as his father—dressed in muddy breeches, his shirtsleeves rolled to the elbows—cleared the last of the dirt from the buried treasure.

"With great care now . . ." Fortescue warned in his thick accent. He swept back the tails of his jacket to lean closer, one fist on his hip, the other hand leaning on a carved wooden cane.

Billy bristled at the implied condescension in the Frenchman's manner. His father knew all the woods, from the tidewaters of Virginia to remote tracts of Kentucky, better than any man. Since before the war, his father had been a trapper and trader with the Indians in these parts. He'd even once met Daniel Boone.

Still, Billy saw how his father's hands shook as he used brush and trowel to pick and tease the treasure out of the rich forest loam.

"This is it," his uncle said, excited. "We found it."

Fortescue loomed over the kneeling men. "*Naturellement*. Of course it would be buried here. Buried at the head of the serpent."

Billy didn't know what they were seeking—only his father and uncle had read the sealed letters from the governor to the Frenchman—but he knew what Fortescue meant by "the serpent."

Billy glanced away from the hole to survey the breadth of the site.

They'd been excavating an earthen mound that wound and twisted away through the forest. It stood two yards high, twice that wide, and ran two thousand feet through the woods and over the gentle hills. It looked like a giant snake had died and been buried where it fell.

Billy had heard about such earthen mounds. Embankments such as these, along with many more man-made hills, dotted the wilderness of the Americas. His father claimed the long-lost ancestors of the region's savages had built them, that they were sacred Indian burial mounds. It was said that the savages themselves had no memory of the ancient mound build-ers, only myths and legends. Stories continued to abound of lost civiliza-tions, of ancient kingdoms, of ghosts, of vile curses—and, of course, of buried treasures.

Billy shifted closer as his father unearthed the object, wrapped in what appeared to be a thick hide of skin, the black coarse fur still intact. A musky scent—a heavy mix of loam and beast—welled up, overpowering even the smell of venison stew from the neighboring cook fires.

"Buffalo hide," his father determined, glancing over to Fortescue.

The Frenchman nodded for him to continue.

Using both hands, his father gently peeled away a flap of the hide to reveal what had lain hidden for ages.

Billy held his breath.

Since the founding of these lands, many Indian mounds had been dug up and looted. All that had been found were the buried bones of the dead, along with a few arrowheads, hide shields, and shards of Indian pot-tery.

So why was this particular site so important?

After two months of meticulously surveying, mapping, and digging, Billy was still none the wiser as to *why* they had been directed to come here. Like the looters of other barrows, all his father's team had to show for their meticulous work was a collection of Indian tokens and artifacts: bows, quivers, lances, a massive cooking pot, a pair of beaded moccasins, an elaborate headdress. And, of course, they found bones. Thousands and thousands of them. Skulls, ribs, leg bones, pelvises. He'd overheard For-

tescue estimate at least a hundred men, women, and children must have
been buried here.

It was a daunting endeavor to collect and catalog everything. It had
taken them all the way to the edge of winter to work from one end of the
winding mound to the other, painstakingly stripping down the Indian
burial mound layer by layer, sifting through dirt and rock—until, as the
Frenchman said, they'd reached the head of the serpent.

His father unfolded the buffalo skin. Gasps spread among those
gathered here. Even Fortescue took a sharp intake of breath through his
pinched nose.

Across the inner surface of the preserved hide, a riotous battle had
been drawn. Stylized figures of men on horseback raced across the hide,
many bearing shields. Spears stabbed with splashes of crimson dyes. Arrows flew. Billy swore he could hear the whoops and war cries of the savages.

Fortescue spoke as he knelt down. A hand hovered over the display.
"I've witnessed such handiwork before. The natives would tan the buffalo
skin with a mash of the beast's own brains, then apply their pigment with
a hollowed-out piece of its own bone. But, *mon Dieu*, I've never seen such
a masterpiece as this. Look how each horse is different from another, how
each warrior's garb is painted in such detail."

The Frenchman's hand shifted next to hover over what the hide had
protected all these years. "And I've never seen anything like this."

The skull of the monster was laid bare. Earlier, they had excavated the
broken tusks of the beast, poking out of the hide-wrapped package. The
cranium, exposed now to the light of day, was as large as a church bell.
And like the buffalo hide, the bone of the skull had also been adorned,
become a canvas for some prehistoric artist.

Across its surface, figures and shapes had been carved into the bone
and painted so brightly they looked wet to the touch.

Billy's uncle spoke, full of awe. "The skull. It's a mammoth, isn't it?
Like those found over at Big Salt Lick."

"No. It's not a *mammoth*," Fortescue said, and pointed with the tip of his cane. "See the curve and length of the tusks, the giant size of its masticating teeth. The anatomy and conformation of the skull are different from the mammoth specimens of the Old World. Remains such as these—unique to the Americas—have been reclassified as a *new* species, a beast called a *mastodon*."

"I don't care what it's called," his father commented forcefully. "Is this the *right* skull or not? That's what I want to know."

"There is only one way to find out."

Fortescue reached and ran his index finger along the bony crest of the skull. The tip of his finger sank into a hole near the back. Over the years, Billy had dressed enough deer and rabbit carcasses to know the hole looked too clean to be natural. The Frenchman used that purchase and pulled up.

Another round of gasps spread outward. Several of the slaves fell back in horror. Billy's eyes widened as the top of the monster's skull split into two halves, opening like the doors of a cabinet. With his father's help, Fortescue gently pushed back the two pieces of the cranium—each two inches thick and as large as dinner platters.

Even in the meager sunlight, what lay inside the skull glinted brightly.

"Gold," his uncle choked out, shocked.

The entire inside of the skull had been plated in the precious metal. Fortescue ran a finger along the inner surface of one of the bony halves. Only now did Billy notice the bumps and grooves across the gold surface. It looked to be a crude map, with stylized trees, sculpted mountains, and snaking rivers. The surface was also inscribed with hen scratches that might be writing.

Leaning closer, he heard Fortescue mumble one word, full of awe and a flicker of fear. "Hebrew."

After the initial shock wore off, his father spoke at Billy's elbow: "But the skull is empty."

Fortescue turned his attention to the open cavity of the gold-lined cranium. The space was large enough to cradle a newborn baby inside, but as his father had noted, it was empty.

Fortescue studied the cavity, his face unreadable, but behind his eyes, Billy saw his mind churning on unfathomable calculations and speculations.

What had they expected to find?

Fortescue stood up. "Close it back up. Keep it wrapped in the hide. We need it ready for transport to Virginia within the hour."

No one argued. If word spread of gold here, the place would surely be ransacked. Over the next hour, as the sun sank below the horizon and torches were lit, men worked quickly to free the massive skull. A wagon was prepared, horses readied. Billy's father, his uncle, and the Frenchman spent much of that time with their heads bent together.

Billy crept close enough with his broom to eavesdrop on their conversation, pretending to be busy. Still, their voices were too low to pick out more than a few words.

"It may be enough," Fortescue said, ". . . a place to start. If the enemy finds it before us, your young union will be doomed before it has even begun."

His father shook his head. "Then maybe it best be destroyed now. Set a bonfire here. Burn the bone to ash, melt the gold to slag."

"It may come to that, but we'll leave such a decision to the governor."

His father looked ready to argue with the Frenchman, but then caught Billy hovering nearby. He turned and lifted an arm to shoo Billy off and opened his mouth to speak.

Those words never came.

Before his father could speak, his throat exploded in a spray of blood. He fell to his knees, clutching at his neck. An arrowhead poked from under his jaw. Blood poured between his fingers, bubbled from his lips.

Billy ran toward his father, regressing from young man to child in a dark instant. "Papa!"

In shock, his ears went deaf. The world shrank to include only his father, who stared back at him, full of pain and regret. Then his father's body jerked, again and again, and toppled forward. Feathers peppered his back. Behind the body, Billy saw his uncle kneeling, head hanging. A spear had cleaved clean through his chest from behind, its point buried in the dirt, its shaft propping the dead body up.

Before Billy could comprehend what he was seeing, what was happening, he was struck from the side—not by an arrow or spear, but by an arm. He was knocked to the ground and rolled. The impact also snapped the world back into full focus.

Shouts filled his ears. Horses screamed. Shadows danced amid torches as scores of men fought and grappled. All around, arrows sang through the air, accompanied by savage whoops.

An Indian attack.

Billy struggled, but he was pinned under the Frenchman. Fortescue hissed in his ear. "Stay down, boy."

The Frenchman rolled off him and flew to his feet as a half-naked savage, his face painted in a red mask of terror, came flying toward him, a hatchet raised high. Fortescue defended with his only weapon, as meager as it might be—his cane.

As the length of carved oak swung to point at the attacker, it parted near the handle. A sheath of wood flew from the cane's tip, revealing a sword hidden at its core. The empty sheath struck the savage in the forehead and caused him to stumble in his attack. Fortescue took advantage and lunged out, skewering the attacker through the chest.

A guttural scream followed. Fortescue turned the man's momentum, and dropped the savage beside Billy on the ground.

The Frenchman yanked his sword free. "To me, boy!"

Billy obeyed. It was all his mind would allow. He had no time to think. He struggled up, but a hand grabbed his arm. The bloody savage sought to hold him. Billy tugged his arm loose.

The Indian fell back. Where the hand had clutched his sleeve, a smeared handprint remained. Not blood, Billy realized in a flash.

Paint.

He stared down at the dying savage. The palm that had clutched him was as white as a lily, though some of the paint was sticking to creases in the palm.

Fingers clamped onto his collar and pulled him to his feet.

Billy turned to Fortescue, who still kept hold of him. "They . . . they're not Indians," he sobbed out, struggling to understand.

"I know," Fortescue answered with nary a bit of fright.

All around, chaos continued to reign. The last two torches went dark. Screams, prayers, and pleas for mercy echoed all around.

Fortescue hauled Billy across the encampment, staying low, stopping only long enough to gather up the loose buffalo hide, which he shoved at Billy. They reached a lone horse hidden deeper in the woods, tethered to a tree, already saddled as if someone had anticipated the attack. The horse stamped and threw its head, panicked by the cries, by the smell of blood.

The Frenchman pointed. "Up you go. Be ready to fly."

As Billy hooked a boot into the stirrup, the Frenchman vanished back into the shadows. With no choice, Billy climbed into the saddle. His weight seemed to calm the horse. He hugged his arms around the mount's sweaty neck, but his heart continued to pound in his throat. Blood rushed through his ears. He wanted to clamp his hands over those ears, to shut out the bloody screams, but he strained to see any sign of approach by the savages.

No, not savages, he reminded himself.

A branch cracked behind him. He twisted around as a shape limped into view. From the cape of his jacket and the glint of his sword, he could see it was the Frenchman. Billy wanted to leap off the horse and clasp tightly to the man, to force him to make some sense of the bloodshed and deceit.

Fortescue stumbled up to him. The broken shaft of an arrow stuck out of the man's thigh, just above the knee. As he reached Billy's side, he shoved two large objects up at him.

"Take these. Keep them bundled in the hide."

Billy accepted the burdens. With a shock, he saw it was the crown of the monster's cranium, split into two halves, bone on one side, gold on the other. Fortescue must have stolen them off the larger skull.

But why?

With no time for answers, he folded the two platters of gold-plated bone into the buffalo hide in his lap.

"Go," Fortescue said.

Billy took the reins but hesitated. "What about you, sir?"

Fortescue placed a hand on his knee, as if sensing his raw terror, trying to reassure him. His words were firm and fast. "You and your horse have enough of a burden to bear without my weight. You must fly as swiftly as you can. Take it where it will be safe."

"Where?" Billy asked, clenching the reins.

"To the new governor of Virginia." The Frenchman stepped away. "Take it to Thomas Jefferson."

PART I

TRESPASS

1

It looked like the entrance to hell.

The two young men stood on a ridge overlooking a deep, shadowy chasm. It had taken them eight hours to climb from the tiny burg of Roosevelt to this remote spot high in the Rocky Mountains.

"Are you sure this is the right place?" Trent Wilder asked.

Charlie Reed took out his cell phone, checked the GPS, then examined the Indian map drawn on a piece of deer hide and sealed in a clear plastic Ziploc bag. "I think so. According to the map, there should be a small stream at the bottom of this ravine. The cave entrance should be where the creek bends around to the north."

Trent shivered and brushed snow from his hair. Though a tapestry of wildflowers heralded the arrival of spring in the lowlands, up here winter still held a firm grip. The air remained frigid, and snow frosted the surrounding mountaintops. To make matters worse, the sky had been lowering all day, and a light flurry had begun to blow.

Trent studied the narrow valley. It seemed to have no bottom. Down below, a black pine forest rose out of a sea of fog. Sheer cliffs surrounded all sides. While he had packed ropes and rappelling harnesses, he hoped he wouldn't need them.

But that wasn't what was truly bothering him.

"Maybe we shouldn't be going down there," he said.

Charlie cocked an eyebrow at him. "After climbing all day?"

"What about that curse? What your grandfather—"

A hand waved dismissively. "The old man's got one foot in the grave and a head full of peyote." Charlie slapped him in the shoulder. "So don't go crapping your pants. The cave probably has a few arrowheads, some broken pots. Maybe even a few bones, if we're lucky. C'mon."

Trent had no choice but to follow Charlie down a thin deer trail they'd discovered earlier. As they picked their way along, he frowned at the back of Charlie's crimson jacket, emblazoned with the two feathers representing the University of Utah. Trent still wore his high school letterman jacket, bearing the Roosevelt Union cougar. The two of them had been best friends since elementary school, but lately they'd been growing apart. Charlie had just finished his first year at college, while Trent had gone into full-time employment at his dad's auto-body shop. Even this summer, Charlie would be participating in an internship with the Uintah Reservation's law group.

His friend was a rising star, one that Trent would soon need a telescope to watch from the tiny burg of Roosevelt. But what else was new? Charlie had always outshone Trent. Of course, it didn't help matters that his friend was half Ute, with his people's perpetual tan and long black hair. Trent's red crew cut and the war of freckles across his nose and cheeks had forever relegated him to the role of Charlie's wingman at school parties.

Though the thought went unvoiced, it was as if they both knew their friendship was about to end as adulthood fell upon their shoulders. So as a rite of passage, the two had agreed to this last adventure, to search for a cave sacred to the Ute tribes.

According to Charlie, only a handful of his tribal elders even knew about this burial site in the High Uintas Wilderness. Those who did were forbidden to speak of it. The only reason Charlie knew about it was that his grandfather liked his bourbon too much. Charlie doubted his grandfather even remembered showing him that old deer-hide map hidden in a hollowed-out buffalo horn.

Trent had first heard the tale when he was in junior high, huddled in a pup tent with Charlie. With a flashlight held to his chin for effect, his friend had shared the story. "My grandfather says the Great Spirit still haunts this cave. Guarding a huge treasure of our people."

"What sort of treasure?" Trent had asked doubtfully. At the time he had been more interested in the *Playboy* he'd sneaked out of his father's closet. That was treasure enough for him.

Charlie had shrugged. "Don't know. But it must be cursed."

"What do you mean?"

His friend had shifted the flashlight closer to his chin, devilishly arching an eyebrow. "Grandfather says whoever trespasses into the Great Spirit's cave is never allowed to leave."

"Why's that?"

"Because if they do, the world will end."

Right then, Trent's old hound dog had let out an earsplitting wail, making them both jump. Afterward, they had laughed and talked deep into the night. Charlie ended up dismissing his grandfather's story as superstitious nonsense. As a modern Indian, Charlie went out of his way to reject such foolishness.

Even so, Charlie had sworn Trent to secrecy and refused to take him to the place marked on the map—until now.

"It's getting warmer down here," Charlie said.

Trent held out a palm. His friend was right. The snowfall had been growing heavier, the flakes thickening, but as they descended, the air had grown warmer, smelling vaguely of spoiled eggs. At some point, the snowfall had turned to a drizzling rain. He wiped his hand on his pants and realized that the fog he'd spotted earlier along the bottom of the ravine was actually *steam*.

The source appeared through the trees below: a small creek bubbling along a rocky channel at the bottom of the ravine.

"Smell that sulfur," Charlie said with a sniff. Reaching the creek, he tested the water with a finger. "Hot. Must be fed by a geothermal spring somewhere around here."

Trent was unimpressed. The mountains around here were riddled with such baths.

Charlie stood up. "This must be the right place."

"Why's that?"

"Hot spots like this are sacred to my people. So it only makes sense that they would pick this place for an important burial site." Charlie headed out, hopping from rock to rock. "C'mon. We're close."

Together, they followed the creek upstream. With each step, the air grew hotter. The sulfurous smell burned Trent's eyes and nostrils. No wonder no one had ever found this place.

With his eyes watering, Trent wanted to turn back, but Charlie suddenly stopped at a sharp bend in the creek. His friend swung in a full circle, holding out his cell phone like a divining rod, then checked the map he'd stolen from his grandfather's bedroom this morning.

"We're here."

Trent searched around. He didn't see any cave. Just trees and more trees. Overhead, snow had begun to frost on the higher elevations, but it continued to fall as a sickly rain down here.

"The entrance has got to be somewhere nearby," Charlie mumbled.

"Or it could just be an old story."

Charlie hopped to the other side of the creek and began kicking at some leafy ferns on that side. "We should at least look around."

Trent made a half-assed attempt on his side, heading away from the water. "I don't see anything!" he called back as he reached a wall of granite. "Why don't we just—"

Then he saw it out of the corner of his eye as he turned. It looked like another shadow on the cliff face, except a breeze was combing through the valley, setting branches to moving, shadows to shifting.

Only this shadow didn't move.

He stepped closer. The cave entrance was low and wide, like a mouth frozen in a perpetual scowl. It opened four feet up the cliff face, sheltered under a protruding lip of stone.

A splash and a curse announced the arrival of his friend.

Trent pointed.

"It's really here," Charlie said, sounding hesitant for the first time.

They stood for a long moment, staring at the cave entrance, remembering the stories about it. They were both too nervous to move forward, but too full of manly pride to back away.

"We doing this?" Trent finally asked.

His words broke the stalemate.

Charlie's back stiffened. "Hell yeah, we're doing this."

Before either of them could lose their nerve, they crossed to the cliff and climbed up into the lip of the cave. Charlie freed his flashlight and pointed it down a tunnel. A steep passageway extended deep into the mountainside.

Charlie ducked his head inside. "Let's go find that treasure!"

Bolstered by the bravado in his friend's voice, Trent followed.

The passageway narrowed quickly, requiring them to shuffle along single file. The air was even hotter inside, but at least it was dry and didn't stink as much.

Squeezing through a particularly tight chute, Trent felt the heat of the granite through his jacket.

"Man," he said as he popped free, "it's like a goddamn sauna down here."

Charlie's face shone brightly. "Or a sweat lodge. Maybe the cave was even used by my people as one. I bet the source of the hot spring is right under our feet."

Trent didn't like the sound of that, but there was no turning back now.

A few more steep steps and the tunnel dumped into a low-roofed chamber about the size of a basketball court. Directly ahead, a crude pit had been excavated out of the rock, the granite still blackened by ancient flames.

Charlie reached blindly to grab for Trent's arm. His friend's grip was iron, yet it still trembled. And Trent knew why.

The cavern wasn't empty.

Positioned along the walls and spread across the floor was a field of bodies, men and women, some upright and cross-legged, others slumped on their sides. Leathery skin had dried to bone, eyes shriveled to sockets, lips peeled back to bare yellowed teeth. Each was naked to the waist, even the women, their breasts desiccated and lying flat on their chests. A few bodies had been decorated with headdresses of feathers or necklaces of stone and sinew.

"My people," Charlie said, his voice croaking with respect as he edged closer to one of the mummies.

Trent followed. "Are you sure about that?"

In the bright beam of the flashlight, their skin looked too pale, their hair too light. But Trent was no expert. Maybe the mineral-rich heat that had baked the bodies had also somehow bleached them.

Charlie examined a man wearing a ringlet of black feathers around his neck. He stretched his flashlight closer. "This one looks red."

Charlie wasn't talking about the man's skin. In the direct glare of the beam, the tangle of hair around the dried skull was a ruddy auburn.

Trent noted something else. "Look at his neck."

The man's head had fallen back against the granite wall. The skin under his jaw gaped open, showing bone and dried tissue. The slice was too straight, the cause plain. The man's shriveled fingers held a shiny metal blade. It still looked polished, reflecting the light.

Charlie swung his flashlight in a slow circle around the room. Matching blades lay on the stone floor or in other bony grips.

"Looks like they killed themselves," Trent said, stunned.

"But why?"

Trent pointed to the only other feature in the room. Across the chamber, a dark tunnel continued deeper into the mountain. "Maybe they were hiding something down there, something they didn't want anyone to know about?"

They both stared. A shiver traveled up from Trent's toes and raised goose bumps along his arms. Neither of them moved. Neither of them wanted to cross this room of death. Even the promise of treasure no longer held any appeal.

Charlie spoke first. "Let's get out of here."

Trent didn't argue. He'd seen enough horror for one day.

Charlie swung around and headed toward the exit, taking the only source of light.

Trent followed him into the tunnel, but he kept glancing back, fearing that the Great Spirit would possess one of the dead bodies and send it shuffling after them, dagger in hand. Focused as he was behind him, his boot slipped on some loose shale. He fell hard on his belly and slid a few feet down the steep slope back toward the cavern.

Charlie didn't wait. In fact, he seemed anxious to escape. By the time Trent was back on his feet and dusting off his knees, Charlie had reached the tunnel's end and hopped out.

Trent started to yell a protest at being abandoned—but another shout, harsh and angry, erupted from outside. Someone else was out there. Trent froze in place. More heated words were exchanged, but Trent couldn't make them out.

Then a pistol shot cracked.

Trent jumped and stumbled two steps back into the darkness.

As the blast echoed away, a heavy silence was left in its wake.

Charlie . . . ?

Shaking with fear, Trent retreated down the tunnel, away from the entrance. His eyes had adjusted enough to allow him to reach the chamber of mummies without making a sound. He stopped at the edge of the cavern, trapped between the darkness at his back and whoever was out there.

Silence stretched and time slowed.

Then a scraping and huffing echoed down to him.

Oh no.

Trent clutched his throat. Someone was climbing into the cave. With his heart hammering, he had no choice but to retreat deeper into the darkness—but he needed a weapon. He stopped long enough to pry the knife from a dead man's grip, snapping fingers like dried twigs.

Once armed, he slipped the blade into his belt and picked his way across the field of bodies. He held his arms ahead of him, blindly brushing across brittle feathers, leathery skin, and coarse hair. He pictured bony hands reaching for him, but he refused to stop moving.

He needed a place to hide.

There was only one refuge.

The far tunnel . . .

But that frightened him.

At one point, his foot stepped into open air. He came close to screaming—then realized it was only the old fire pit dug into the floor. A quick hop and he was over it. He tried to use the pit's location to orient himself in the darkness, but it proved unnecessary.

Light grew brighter behind him, bathing the chamber.

Now able to see, he rushed headlong across the cavern. As he reached the mouth of the tunnel, a thudding, tumbling sounded behind him. He glanced over his shoulder.

A body came rolling out of the passageway and sprawled facedown on the floor. The growing light revealed the embroidered feathers on the back of the body's crimson jacket.

Charlie.

With a fist clamped to his lips, Trent fled into the sheltering darkness of the tunnel. Fear grew sharper with every step.

Do they know I'm down here, too?

The tunnel ran flat and smooth, but it was far too short. After only five scared steps, it widened into another chamber.

Trent ducked to the side and flattened against the wall. He fought to control his ragged breathing, sure it would be heard all the way outside. He risked a peek back.

Someone had entered the mummy chamber with a flashlight. In the jumbling light, the shape bent down and dragged his friend's body to the edge of the fire pit. It was only one person. The murderer dropped to his knees, set down his flashlight, and pulled Charlie's body to his chest. The man raised his face to the roof and rocked, chanting something in the Ute language.

Trent bit off a gasp, recognizing that lined and leathery face.

As he watched, Charlie's grandfather raised a polished steel pistol to his own head. Trent turned away but was too slow. The blast deafened in the confined space. Half of the old man's skull exploded in a spray of blood, bone, and gore.

The pistol clattered to the stone. The old man fell heavily over his grandson's body, as if protecting him in death. A slack arm struck the abandoned flashlight, nudging it enough to shine directly at Trent's hiding place.

He slumped to his knees in horror, remembering the superstitious warning from Charlie's grandfather: *Whoever trespasses into the Great Spirit's cave is never allowed to leave.*

The tribal elder had certainly made that come true for Charlie. He must have somehow learned about the theft of the map and tracked them here.

Trent covered his face with his palms, breathing hard between his fingers, refusing to believe what he had witnessed. He listened for anyone else out there. But only silence answered him. He waited a full ten minutes.

Finally satisfied that he was alone, he pushed back to his feet. He looked over his shoulder. The flashlight's beam pierced to the back of the small cave, revealing what had been hidden here long ago.

Stone crates, each the size of a lunch box, were stacked at the back of the chamber. They appeared to be oiled and wrapped in bark. But what drew Trent's full attention rose in the center of the room.

A massive skull rested atop a granite plinth.

A totem, he thought.

Trent stared into those empty sockets, noting the high domed cranium and the unnaturally long fangs. Each had to be a foot long. He had learned enough from his old earth sciences classes to recognize the skull of a saber-toothed tiger.

Still, he couldn't help but be stunned by the strange state of the skull. He had to tell someone about the murder, the suicide—but also about this treasure.

A treasure that made no sense.

He hurried headlong down the tunnel, passed through the mummy chamber, and ran toward daylight. At the entrance to the cave, he paused, remembering the final warning from Charlie's grandfather, about what would happen if someone trespassed here and left.

The world will come to an end.

Teary-eyed, Trent shook his head. Superstitions had killed his best friend. He wasn't about to let the same happen to him.

With a leap, he fled back into the world.

2

Nothing like murder to draw a circus.

Margaret Grantham crossed the makeshift camp set up in a high meadow overlooking the ravine. She huffed a bit in the thin air, and the arthritis in her knuckles still throbbed from the cold. A gust of wind threatened to rip the hat from her head, but she held it in place, tucking away a few strands of gray hair.

All around, tents sprawled across several acres, broken up into various factions, from law enforcement to local media. A National Guard unit stood by to keep the peace, but even its presence only added to the tension.

Native American groups from across the country had been gathering steadily over the past two weeks, drawn to the remote location by the controversy, hiking or riding in on horseback. They came under the auspices of several different acronyms: NABO, AUNU, NAG, NCAI. But ultimately all the letters served one purpose: to protect Native American rights and to preserve tribal heritage. Several of the tents were tepees, constructed by the more traditional groups.

She scowled as a local news helicopter descended toward an open field on the outskirts of the camp, and shook her head. Such attention only made things worse.

As an anthropology professor at Brigham Young University, she had been summoned by the Utah Division of Indian Affairs to help mediate the legal dispute about the discovery in this area. Since she'd spent thirty years overseeing the university's Native American outreach program, local tribes knew her to be respectful of their causes. Plus, she often worked alongside the popular Shoshone historian and naturalist Professor Henry Kanosh.

Today was no exception.

Hank waited for her at the trailhead that led down toward the cavern system. Like her, he wore boots, jeans, and a khaki work shirt. His salt-and-pepper hair had been tied back in a ponytail. She was one of the few who knew his Indian name, *Kaiv'u wuhnuh,* meaning Mountain Standing. At the moment, standing at the trailhead, he looked the part. Closing in on sixty, his six-foot-four frame remained solid with muscle. His complexion was granite, only softened by the dancing flecks of gold in his caramel eyes.

His dog—a stocky, trail-hardened Australian cattle dog with one blue eye and one brown—sat at his side. The dog's name, Kawtch, came from the Ute Indian word for "no." Maggie smiled as she remembered Hank's explanation: *Since I was yelling it at him so much as a pup, the name sort of stuck.*

"So what's the pulse like out there?" Hank asked as she joined him with a quick hug of hello.

"Not so good," she answered. "And likely to get worse."

"Why?"

"I was speaking to the county sheriff earlier. Tox report came back on the grandfather."

Hank bit harder on the cigar clamped between his teeth. He never lit his stogies, just liked chewing on them. It was against Mormon practices to use tobacco, but sometimes concessions had to be made. Though full-blooded Native American, he had been raised Mormon, one of the north-western band of Shoshone who had been baptized back in the 1800s after the Bear River Massacre.

"And what was in the tox report?" he asked around his cigar.

"The old man tested positive for peyote."

Hank shook his head. "Great. That'll play right for the cameras. Crazed Injun hopped on drugs kills his grandson and himself during a religious frenzy."

"For now, they're keeping that detail under wraps, but it'll eventually come out." She sighed in resignation. "The reaction to the initial report was bad enough."

County law enforcement had been the first on the scene to investigate the murder-suicide of the young Ute and his grandfather. With an eyewitness—a friend of the murdered boy—the case had been quickly closed, the bodies shipped by helicopter to the state morgue in Salt Lake City. The initial coroner's report blamed the tragedy on dementia secondary to chronic alcohol poisoning. Afterward, op-ed pieces appeared in both local and national papers, weighing in on the abuse of alcohol among Native Americans, often reinforcing the caricature of the drunken Indian.

It wasn't helping matters here. Margaret knew the delicacy with which such issues had to be broached, especially here in Utah, where the history of Indians and white men was bloody and strained.

But that was only the edge of the political quagmire. There was still the matter of the *other* bodies found down in the cave, hundreds of mummified remains.

Hank waved toward the path down to the cave. His dog took the lead, trotting with his bushy tail high. Hank followed. "The surveyors compiled their report this morning. Did you see it?"

She shook her head as she joined him on the trail.

"According to the surveyors, the cave entrance is on federal land, but the cavern system extends under reservation territory."

"Effectively blurring the jurisdiction line."

He nodded. "Not that it'll make much difference in the long run. I read the brief filed by Indian Affairs. All this land, going back to 1861, was once part of the Uintah and Ouray Indian Reservation. But over the past century and a half, the borders of this reservation have waxed and waned."

"Which means Indian Affairs can still make a strong case that the contents of the cavern belong to them."

"That still depends on the other variables: the age of the bodies, when they were interred, and of course, if the remains are even Native American."

Maggie nodded. It was the main reason she had been summoned here: to evaluate the racial origins of those bodies. She had already conducted a cursory physical examination yesterday. Based on skin tone and hair color and facial bone structure, the remains appeared to be Caucasian, but the artifacts and clothing were distinctly Indian. Any further testing—DNA analyses, chemical tests—were locked up in a legal battle. Even moving the bodies was forbidden due to an injunction imposed by NAGPRA, the Native American Graves Protection and Repatriation Act.

"It's like Kennewick Man all over again," Maggie said.

Hank raised a questioning brow toward her.

"Back in 1996, an old skeleton was discovered along a riverbank in Kennewick, Washington. The forensic anthropologist who first examined the remains declared them to be Caucasoid."

Hank glanced to her and shrugged. "So?"

"The body was carbon-dated at over nine thousand years old. One of the oldest bodies discovered in the Americas. The Caucasian features triggered a storm of interest. The current model of North America puts early man migrating to the region across a land bridge from Russia to Alaska. The discovery of an ancient skeleton bearing Caucasoid traits contradicts that assessment. It could rewrite the history of early America."

"So what happened?"

"Five local Indian tribes claimed the body. They sued to have the bones reinterred without examination. That legal battle is still going on a decade later. And there've been other cases, other Caucasoid remains found in North America, and fought over just as fiercely." She ticked them off on her fingers. "The Spirit Cave Mummy of Nevada, Oregon's Prospect Man, Arlington Springs Woman. Most of these bodies have never been properly tested. Others were lost forever in anonymous Indian graves."

"Let's hope we don't end up with such a mess here," Hank said.

By now, they'd reached the bottom of the chasm. Kawtch waited for them, panting, tongue lolling, tail still high.

Maggie grimaced at the rotten-egg smell rising from the sulfurous spring that heated the valley. Her face had already beaded up with sweat. She fanned herself with one hand.

Hank noted her discomfort and hurried them toward the cave entrance. Two National Guard soldiers stood at their posts, armed with rifles and holstered sidearms. With all the publicity, grave robbing remained a major concern, especially with the reported treasure hidden in the cave.

One of the guards stepped forward—a fresh-faced young man with rusty-blond stubble. Private Stinson had been posted here all week and recognized the two approaching scientists.

"Major Ryan is already inside," he said. "He's waiting for the two of you before moving the artifact."

"Good," Hank said. "There's already enough tension up there."

"And cameras," Maggie added. "It won't look good to have someone in a U.S. military uniform seen absconding with a sacred Native American artifact. This has to be handled with some diplomacy."

"That's what Major Ryan figured." The private stepped aside—then added under his breath, "But he's getting impatient. Didn't exactly have kind words for what's going on here."

So what else is new?

Major Ryan had proven to be a thorn in her side.

Hank helped lift Maggie up to the raised entrance to the burial cave. His large hands clamped hard to her hips, triggering a flush of heat through her body, along with a surge of bittersweet memory. Those same hands had once run over her naked body, a short tryst, born of long nights together and a deep friendship. But in the end, such a relationship hadn't suited them. They were better friends than lovers.

Still, her cheeks heated to a fierce glow by the time he joined her, hopping easily up into the mouth of the cave. He seemed oblivious to her reaction, which made her both grateful and slightly hurt.

He ordered Kawtch to stay outside. The dog hung his head with disappointment.

They set off into the tunnel as a muffled shout echoed up to them.

Maggie and Hank shared a glance. Hank rolled his eyes. As usual, Major Ryan was not happy. The head of the unit had no interest in the anthropological importance of this discovery and plainly resented this assignment. Plus, she suspected there was an undercurrent of racial tension. She'd overheard a remark from him about the Native Americans gathered at the camp: *Should've driven 'em all into the Pacific when we had the chance.*

Still, she had to work with the man—at least until the treasure was secured. It was one of the reasons she and Hank had been given permission to move the totem artifact and ship it to the museum at BYU. It was too valuable to leave unguarded. Once it was gone, the amount of security could be scaled back, and hopefully some of the simmering resentment up above would calm down.

Maggie reached the main chamber, pausing at the threshold, again taken aback by the macabre spectacle of the mummified remains. Bright battery-powered lamps lit the space. Surveying strings and yellow crime-scene tape divided the chamber into sections. A cordoned-off path crossed the floor and led to the far tunnel.

She headed toward it, but her attention was again drawn to the bodies around her. Their state of preservation was amazing. The sustained geothermal heat had baked the fluid out of the remains, drying the tissues and concentrating the salts in the bodies, which acted as a natural brining agent.

For the thousandth time, she wondered why they had all killed themselves. It reminded her of the story of the siege of Masada, where Jewish rebels had committed suicide rather than succumb to the Roman legion at their gates.

Had something like that happened here?

She had no answer. It was one mystery among so many others.

A shift of shadows caught the corner of her eye. She tripped to a stop and stared toward a tangle of bodies in the far corner. A hand touched her shoulder, making her jump.

Fingers tightened reassuringly. "What is it?" Hank asked.

"I thought I saw—"

From the tunnel, a shout cut her off. "'Bout time you got here!"

A juggling light exited the far tunnel. Major Ryan appeared with a flashlight. He was in full uniform, including his helmet, which kept his eyes in shadow. His lips, though, were tight with irritation.

He beckoned with his flashlight and swung around, leading the way back into the tunnel. "Let's get a move on. I have the transport crate prepared as you ordered. Two of my men will assist you."

Hank mumbled under his breath as he followed. "Hello to you, too, Major."

Maggie paused at the mouth of the tunnel and glanced back over her shoulder. Nothing moved out there now. She shook her head.

Just a trick of light. Has me jumping at shadows.

"We've had a problem," Ryan said, drawing her attention. "A mishap."

"What sort of mishap?" Hank asked.

"See for yourself."

Concerned, Maggie hurried after them.

What is wrong now?

11:40 A.M.

Hidden in shadows, the saboteur watched the three vanish into the tunnel. She let out a slow breath of relief, fighting back a tremble of fear. She'd almost been spotted when she drew her pack farther behind a pair of bodies.

Doubts plagued her in the dark.

What am I doing here?

She waited in the shadows, crouched as she had been since early morning. Her chosen name was Kai, which meant "willow tree" in Navajo. As her heart pounded, she sought to draw strength from her namesake, to tap into the patience of the tree, along with its legendary flexibility. She slowly stretched a kink out of her left leg. But her back continued to ache.

It wouldn't be much longer, she promised herself.

She'd been hiding here since the crack of dawn. Two of her friends, pretending to be drunk and disorderly, had lured the guards a few yards away from the cave entrance. Using the distraction, she had ducked out of her hiding place and slipped into the tunnel behind them.

It had been a challenge to creep silently into position. But at only eighteen years of age, she was lithe, thin, and knew how to dance through shadows, a skill learned from tracking with her father since she was knee-high to him. He had taught her the old ways—before being shot while driving a cab in Boston.

The memory spiked a flare of bone-deep anger.

A year after his death, she had been recruited by WAHYA, a militant Native American rights group, who took their name from the Cherokee word for "wolf." They were fierce and cunning, and like her, they were all young, none over thirty, all proudly intolerant of the groveling of the more established organizations.

Hidden in the dark, she let that anger stoke through her and warm away her fears. She remembered the fiery words of John Hawkes, founder and leader of WAHYA: *Why should we have to wait to be handed back our rights by the U.S. government? Why bend a knee and accept bread crumbs?*

WAHYA had already made headlines with a few small events. They'd burned an American flag on the steps of a Montana courthouse after the conviction of a Crow Indian for using hallucinogenic mushrooms during a religious ceremony. Only last month, they'd spray-painted the offices of a Colorado congressman who sought restrictions on the state's Indian casinos.

But events here, according to John Hawkes, offered an even greater opportunity for exposure on the national stage. Drawn by the controversy, WAHYA would come out of the shadows and take matters into its own hands, mount a firm stand against government intrusion into tribal affairs.

A shout drew her eyes toward the deeper tunnel.

She tensed. Earlier—before the two new arrivals got here—a crash had echoed out of the back cavern, followed by a furious bout of cursing. Something had clearly gone wrong. She prayed that it didn't pose a problem for her mission.

Especially after waiting here so long.

Kai shifted her weight to her other leg, seeking patience, waiting for the signal. She reached out and rested one hand on the backpack full of C4 explosive, already embedded with wireless detonators.

It shouldn't be much longer.

11:46 A.M.

"What did you do?" Hank asked, his voice booming across the small cavern, full of outrage.

Maggie placed a calming hand on his shoulder. She recognized the problem immediately as she stepped into the back cavern.

Along the far wall had been stacked a pile of stone boxes, all identical, each a cubic foot in size. She had examined one yesterday. It had reminded her of a small ossuary, a stone box used to hold the bones of the dead. But until she got permission from the Native American delegation of NAGPRA, none of the boxes could be opened. Each was coated in oil and wrapped in dried juniper bark.

But circumstances had changed.

She stared down at the half-dozen boxes scattered on the floor of the cave. The one closest had broken in half, still roughly held together by its bark wrapping.

Hank took a deep breath and scowled at Major Ryan. "There's a strict injunction against touching any of this. Do you know how much trouble this will generate? Do you know the powder keg building up there?"

"I know," Ryan snapped back at him. "One of these numbnuts hit the stack with the corner of the transport crate when they were swinging it around. The pile came crashing down."

Maggie glanced to the two National Guardsmen in the room. Both soldiers stared at their toes, accepting the rebuke. Between them rested a plastic green trunk, hinged open, revealing a foam-lined interior, ready to secure and transport the room's singular treasure.

"So what do we do now?" Ryan asked sourly.

Maggie didn't answer. Her legs drew her to the broken stone box on the floor. She couldn't help herself. She knelt beside it.

Hank joined her. "We'd best leave it alone. We can record and document the damage, then—"

"Or we just take a peek inside." She reached to a fractured chunk of stone, bark still stuck on it. "What's done is done."

A warning rumble entered Hank's voice. "Maggie."

She picked loose the bit of stone and carefully laid it aside. For the first time in ages, light shone into the box's interior.

Holding her breath, she removed another piece of stone and revealed more of what was hidden inside. The boxes appeared to contain plates of metal, blackened with age. She leaned closer and cocked her head from side to side.

Strange . . .

"Is that some kind of writing on it?" Hank asked, curiosity drawing him down beside her.

"Could just be streaks of corrosion."

Maggie reached and carefully rubbed a thumb over a corner of the surface. The black oil smeared away, revealing a familiar yellowish hue beneath. She sat back.

"Gold," Hank whispered in hushed awe.

She looked to him, then to the wall of stone boxes. She pictured similar plates packed away in the containers. Her heart pounded faster in her throat. *How much gold is here?*

Maggie stood up, trying to fathom the extent of the treasure.

"Major Ryan," she warned, "I think you and your men will be spending a lot more time down here."

A groan escaped him. "So there's even more gold."

Maggie turned to the granite pillar in the center of the room. Atop it rested the massive skull of a saber-toothed tiger. All by itself, the prehistoric artifact was a valuable discovery, a spiritual totem of the slaughtered tribe—so important that the tribesmen had melted gold and coated the entire surface of the giant cat's skull.

She stepped in a slow circle around the precious idol. A trickle of fear seeped into her. Something was wrong about all of this. She couldn't put her finger on it but knew it to be true.

Unfortunately, she had no time to contemplate the mystery.

"Then at least get this skull out of here," Ryan ordered. "We can deal with the boxes later. Do you want my men to help you?"

Hank stood up rather sharply. "We'll do it."

Maggie nodded, and the two positioned themselves on either side of the gold totem. She held out her hands, her fingers hovering over the long golden fangs.

"I'll grab it from the front," she said. "You cup the back of the skull. On my count. We'll lift it and place it into the crate."

"Gotcha."

They both reached for the artifact. Maggie gripped the base of the fangs where they joined the skull. She could barely get her fingers all the way around the teeth.

"One, two . . . *three*."

Together they lifted the skull. Even covered in gold, it was far heavier than she had imagined. She felt something shift inside, sliding like loose sand. Curiosity sparked through her, but any further examination would have to wait. They sidestepped in a typical workmen's waltz over to the foam-lined open trunk and lowered the skull into the carrier. It sank heavily into the padding.

They both straightened, staring at each other. Hank rubbed his hands on his jeans and caught her eye. So he had felt it, too. Not just the shifting sands, but something even odder. As hot as it was in here, she had expected the skull to be warm. But despite the geothermal heat of the cavern, the surface had been cold.

Damned cold . . .

She read the unease in Hank's eyes. It matched her own.

Before either could speak, Ryan slammed the lid over the treasure and pointed toward the exit. "My men will carry the skull out of the cave. From there, it's your problem."

12:12 P.M.

Crouched low, Kai watched the parade cross the field of mummies. It was led by an older woman, her hair tucked under a wide-brimmed hat. A trio of National Guard soldiers followed. Two of them hauled a green plastic trunk between them.

The gold skull, she thought.

They were taking it out, just as she'd been instructed they would. Everything seemed to be going according to plan. With the skull gone, she'd have the cavern to herself. She'd plant the charges, wait for nightfall, then sneak off. Once the place was empty, they'd blow the cavern and rebury their ancestors. WAHYA would make its point. Native Americans were done asking for permission from the U.S. government, especially for such basic rights as burying their dead.

She stared at the tall figure who trailed behind the others. Irritation flashed through her. She knew him, most Native Americans did. Professor Henry Kanosh was a controversial figure among the tribes, sparking strong reactions. No one questioned that he was a staunch supporter of Indian sovereignty, and by some estimates, his labors alone had expanded reservation territory across the Western states by a full 10 percent. But like much of his ancestral band, he had taken up the Mormon faith, shedding the old ways to join a religious group that had once persecuted and slaughtered Indians in Utah. That alone made him an outcast among the more traditional members of the local Indian tribes. She had heard John Hawkes once refer to him as an "Indian Uncle Tom."

As the group reached the exit tunnel, Professor Kanosh pointed back. "Until we can get a handle on this, no one mention the gold we found in those boxes. Keep silent. We don't want to trigger a gold rush down here."

Kai's ears pricked at his words. *Gold?*

According to what she'd been told, the only gold down here was coating that prehistoric skull. WAHYA had been willing to let the totem be removed from here. The artifact was scheduled to be displayed at a Native American museum, so that was okay. Plus, if the explosion buried the golden skull with the mummified bodies, someone might be tempted to do a little digging to find it, disturbing once again the resting place of their ancestors.

But if there's more gold down here . . . ?

She waited until the others had climbed up into the tunnel, then stood and shouldered her pack. She stepped gingerly through the field of bodies toward the back chamber. She had to see for herself. If there was a stockpile of gold hidden here, that changed everything. Like with the skull, such a mother lode could lure a slew of treasure hunters to come digging.

She had to know the truth.

Rushing to the far tunnel, she dashed down its dark throat as another worry struck her. With a new stash of gold down here, the guards would certainly return to protect it, complicating her plans to escape. She could be trapped down here. If she were caught, how could she explain being found with a backpack full of plastic explosive? She'd spend years, if not decades, in jail.

Fear burned brighter, hurrying her steps.

Reaching the cave, she flicked on a penlight and swept the beam around the small dark chamber. At first, she saw nothing, just old stone boxes and an empty pillar of granite. But a spark of reflected light drew her eyes down to her toes. A box had shattered on the floor.

She lowered to one knee and shoved her penlight closer. The box held what looked to be a stack of half-inch-thick metal plates. A corner had been rubbed off the top one, revealing gold beneath a layer of tarnish. She sat back, stunned. She swept her penlight over the wall of boxes.

What am I going to do now?

Buried underground, she had no way to radio for help. She felt overwhelmed and trapped. This decision was hers alone. Sensing the press of time and fearing the return of the guards, she couldn't think straight. Her breathing grew harder. The darkness seemed to tighten around her.

A distant shout made her flinch. She swung toward the exit. More muffled voices followed. Someone screamed.

She sprang up.

What is going on?

Clutching her backpack, she sensed that WAHYA's careful plan was falling to pieces. Her heart hammered with a growing panic. Fear overtook reason. She bent down, tore open the stone box, and grabbed the top three gold plates, each about eight inches square. They were surprisingly heavy, so she tucked them into her jacket and zipped them snugly next to her body.

She needed proof for John Hawkes of why she had aborted the mission. He would not be pleased, but they might find a use for the gold, especially if there was some sort of government cover-up. She remembered Professor Kanosh's last words.

Keep silent.

She intended to do the same, but first she had to get out of here. She rushed headlong back to the main chamber. The angry voices outside grew louder. She had no idea what had triggered such a commotion but hoped it would help her escape. She knew she had to take the chance, or she'd be trapped down here when the soldiers returned.

That left only one hope, her best strength: her natural speed.

If I can bolt free and reach the woods . . .

But what stood in her way?

The booming voice of Professor Kanosh echoed down to her. "Back off!"

12:22 P.M.

Maggie stood only a couple of yards from the cave entrance. They hadn't gotten very far before the circus found them.

Bright camera lights pointed at her, pinning them all down. A step away, she recognized the chiseled features, white hair, and ice-blue eyes of an investigative reporter from CNN. The governor of Utah accompanied him. No wonder the National Guard hadn't stopped this news crew from coming down here. Nothing like a photo op to bolster the governor's re-election campaign.

Of course, along with the news crew came the usual suspects, dancing for the national spotlight and playing for the cameras.

"You're stealing our heritage!" came a shout from the mass of people.

She spotted the heckler, dressed in buckskin, his face painted. He had an iPhone raised and recorded the events. She expected she'd be on YouTube within the hour.

Maggie bit her tongue, knowing any response from her would only stoke the fires here.

Moments ago, as Maggie's group stepped from the cave and was spotted, the crowd surged past the governor, who was conducting an on-air interview. Several people were knocked down. Fights broke out, and a miniriot threatened. Major Ryan rallied a cordon of Guard soldiers, instantly stemming the tide and restoring a semblance of order.

In the meantime, Hank and the other guardsmen formed a wall between her and the pack of cameras and protesters.

Hank held up a hand. "If you want to see the artifact," he boomed out, "we'll show you. But then Dr. Grantham will be heading straight to BYU with it, where it will be studied by historians from the Smithsonian's National Museum of American Indians."

Another angry shout cut him off. "So you're going to do to this skull what they did to the body of Black Hawk!"

Maggie winced inside. It was a sore bit of Utah history. Black Hawk had been a Ute Indian leader who died during a conflict with settlers back in the mid-1800s. Afterward, his body had been put on display at various museums, then subsequently lost. It wasn't until a Boy Scout, completing an Eagle project, found the skeleton in a storage facility at the Mormon Church's historical department. The bones eventually were reburied.

Maggie had heard enough. Standing beside the green transport crate, she raised her arm. All eyes and camera lenses focused on her.

"We have nothing to hide!" she called out. "Clearly strong emotions surround this discovery. But let me assure everyone that all will be handled with the utmost respect."

"Enough talking! If there's nothing to hide, then show us the skull!"

This call was taken up by others and became a chant.

Maggie caught the gaze of the governor. He made a slight motion for her to obey. She suspected the golden totem had become a novelty for a majority of the crowd rather than an artifact of historical significance. So if this was a circus, she might as well be its ringmaster.

Turning her back, she bent down to the crate and struggled to undo the tight latches. Her arthritic fingers made it difficult. Plus, the mist in the valley had begun to turn into a thin drizzle. Droplets pattered against the plastic top of the crate. A hush fell over the crowd.

She finally freed the latches and hauled the top open. With the rain falling, she would not expose the artifact for longer than a minute. She stared down at the gold skull nestled in its foam cocoon. Even in the wan light down here, it shone brilliantly.

She stepped back to open the view to the cameras and the crowd, but she could not take her eyes off the skull. A misty haze coalesced over its surface. She watched a drop of rain strike the golden surface—then freeze immediately into an icy teardrop.

A collective gasp rose from the crowd behind her.

She thought they'd witnessed the event, too—then she heard a scuff of boot on rock. She glanced up to see a thin girl in black jeans and jacket come leaping out of the cave a yard away, her ebony hair fanning out like wings of a raven. She clutched an arm around her jacket, but something slipped from beneath it and hit the stone with a clanging thud.

It was one of the gold tablets.

Ryan shouted for the thief to halt.

Ignoring him, the girl turned, ready to flee toward the woods, but her foot slipped on the rain-dampened stone outside the cave. She stumbled, one arm pinwheeling for balance, sending her backpack tumbling. It rolled and came to rest near the crate. The girl came close to crashing down after it, but she gained her footing as effortlessly as a startled deer, turned on a toe, and leaped toward the edge of the forest.

Maggie remained fixed in place, crouched over the open crate to protect it. She stared down, making sure the artifact was safe. In that short time, more raindrops had fallen—and frozen—decorating the golden surface with beads of ice.

She reached and foolishly touched one, triggering a stinging snap. A painful jolt shot up her arm, but instead of being thrown back, she felt her arm pulled forward. Her palm struck the golden surface. With contact, the bones of her fingers suddenly ignited, burning through her flesh. Shock and horror clamped her throat shut. Her knees weakened.

She heard Hank shout at her.

Ryan bellowed, too.

One word cut through the agony.

Bomb!

12:34 P.M.

The brilliant flash blinded Hank. One moment he was shouting at Maggie, the next his vision went white. A clap of thunder tried to crush his skull, immediately deafening him. An icy shock wave knocked him back like a cold slap from God. He hit the ground on his back, then he felt a strange tug on his body, pulling him *toward* the explosion.

He fought against it, panicked down to the core. The sensation felt not only wrong, but fundamentally *unnatural*. He struggled against that tide with every fiber of his being.

Then it was over, as quickly as it had begun.

The inexorable pull popped away, releasing him. His senses snapped back. His ears filled with wails and screams. Images swirled into focus. He lay on his side, facing toward where Maggie had stood. He didn't move, too stunned.

She was gone—so were the crate, the skull, and most of the cliff, including the cave entrance.

He raised up to an elbow and searched.

There was no sign of her, no charred remains, no mangled body. Nothing but a blackened circle of steaming rock.

He struggled up. Kawtch shimmied closer on his belly, cowering, tail between his leg. If Hank had a tail, he'd have done the same. He placed a reassuring palm on the dog's side.

"It'll be okay."

He hoped it was true.

By now, the crowd had regained its collective footing. A panicked exodus began. The news crew retreated to higher ground, shuffled back by a cordon of National Guard. Two soldiers manhandled the governor up the trail, a precaution in case there was another attack.

Harry pictured the bag tossed by the girl. When it had landed by the crate, it had flapped open and its contents spilled out: cubes of yellowish-gray clay, embedded with wires.

Major Ryan had immediately recognized the threat.

Bomb.

But the warning had come too late for Maggie.

A knot of anger burned in the pit of his belly. He let it settle there as he pictured the attacker. From the girl's burnished copper skin, brown eyes, and black hair, she was definitely Native American. A homegrown terrorist. As if matters here weren't bad enough.

Numb with grief, he stumbled toward the blast zone, needing to understand. To the side, Major Ryan picked up his helmet and placed it back on his head.

"I've never seen anything like this," Ryan said, still dazed. "The force of this explosion should have taken out half the crowd. Including us." He held up an open palm. "And just feel that heat."

Hank did. It felt like a blast furnace. The air reeked of burning brimstone, turning his stomach.

As they watched, a large boulder crumbled apart within the blast zone, breaking down into smaller rocks. The face of the cliff began to do the same, disintegrating into a flow of boulders and sand. It was as if the hard granite had become loose sandstone, friable and weak.

"Look at the ground," Ryan said.

Hank stared at the blasted rock, steaming and awash with a swirl of mist. The drizzling rain hissed and spattered as it struck. Still, he didn't see what had Major Ryan so agitated. Then again, the man had much younger eyes.

Hank dropped to a knee to inspect the ground more closely. Then he saw it, too. He'd missed it through the swirl of steam. The stone surface wasn't solid, more like ground pepper—and it was *moving*!

The grains jittered and trembled as if they were drops of oil simmering atop a hot skillet. He watched a small pebble on the surface dissolve into coarse sand, then into a dusty powder. A drop of rain struck the ground and blasted a crater. Like a pebble hitting a still pond, ripples spread outward across the microfine surface

Hank shook his head in disbelief. Fearful, he studied where the blast zone ended and solid ground began. As he stared, the bordering edge of stone crumbled to sand, incrementally expanding the blast zone.

"It's spreading," Hank realized, and pushed Ryan back.

"What are you talking about?"

Hank had no answers, only a growing certainty. "Something is still active. It's eating away the rock and radiating outward."

"Are you nuts? Nothing can—"

From the center of the blast zone, a belch of water burst upward from below and coughed into a steaming column, rising several yards into the air. A scalding heat chased them farther off.

By the time they stopped, Hank's skin burned, and his eyes felt parboiled. He gasped and choked out a few words.

"Must've cracked into the geothermal spring . . . under the valley."

"What are you talking about?" Ryan pulled his jacket collar over his mouth and nose. The burning sulfur made even breathing dangerous.

"Whatever's happening here, it's not only spreading outward—"

Hank pointed to the minigeyser.

"—it's also heading *down*."

3

So much for dinner plans.

Though the explosion in Utah was only an hour old, Painter Crowe knew he'd be in his office all night. Details continued to flow in by the minute, but information remained sketchy due to the remote mountainous location of the blast. All of Washington's intelligence communities were on high alert and mobilizing to bear on the situation.

Including Sigma.

Painter's group operated as a covert wing for DARPA, the Defense Advanced Research Projects Agency. His team was composed of handpicked Special Forces soldiers—those whose IQs tested off the scales or who showed unique mental acumen. He recruited and retrained them in various scientific disciplines to act as field operatives for the Defense Department's research-and-development wing. Teams were sent out into the world to protect against global threats.

Normally, such a domestic attack as in Utah would not fall within his team's purview, but a few anomalous details had drawn the interest of his boss, the head of DARPA, General Gregory Metcalf. Painter might have still argued against utilizing Sigma's resources for such a messy business, but as a result of the controversy surrounding the blast, even the president—who owed his life to Sigma in the past—had personally requested their assistance in this delicate matter.

And one does not say no to President James T. Gant.

So Painter's barbecue plans with his girlfriend were put on hold for the night.

Instead, he stood with his back to his desk and studied the large flat-panel monitors mounted on the three walls of his office. They depicted various views of the blast. The best footage came from the CNN cameras that had recorded the event. The other monitors flowed with grainy video and photos captured from cell phones, the millennium's new digital eyes on the world.

For the hundredth time, he watched the looping feed from CNN. He saw an older woman—Dr. Margaret Grantham, an anthropologist—leaning over a green military transport crate. She undid the latches and lifted the lid. A commotion ensued, jittering the camera feed. The view swung wildly. He caught a glimpse of a figure behind the woman, fleeing away—then a blinding flash of light.

Using a remote control, he froze the footage. He stared into the heart of the blast. If he squinted, he could make out the shadow of the woman within that glare, a dark ghost within the blaze. He moved the image forward frame by frame and watched her shadow slowly consumed by the brightness, whittled away to nothing.

With a heavy heart, he hit the fast-forward button. From there, the footage became chaotic and jostled: trees, sky, running figures. Eventually the cameraman found a vantage point from which he felt safe enough to resume shooting. The view swung back to the steaming blast zone. Chaos still reigned as people fled the site. A handful of others remained below, cautiously examining the scene. Moments later, a steaming geyser erupted and chased even the stragglers away.

A preliminary report already sat on his desk from Sigma's resident geologist. He estimated the blast had cracked into a "subsurface geothermal stream."

Painter stared again at the geyser. It wasn't *subsurface* any longer. The geologist's assessment had included a topographic map dotted with hot springs in the vicinity. Even in the dry technical jargon of the report, Painter could sense the enthusiasm brimming in the young geologist, the raw desire to investigate the site firsthand.

While he appreciated such passion, the National Guard had the place locked down. A search was under way for the shadowy figure behind the blast. Using the remote control again, he froze the fleeting image of the bomber, blurry and indistinct, caught for less than a second.

According to interviews, it was a young woman. She had tossed a backpack full of C4, wired with detonators, then fled into the woods. The National Guard, local police forces, and agents from Salt Lake City's FBI field office were attempting to seal off the area, but the mountainous terrain, rugged and thickly wooded, posed a challenge to finding her, especially if she knew the area.

To make matters worse, eyewitnesses reported that the woman was Native American. If true, that would mean even more political tension.

Painter caught his reflection in the monitor and searched for his own ancestry. He was a half-blooded Pequot Indian, on his father's side, but his blue eyes and light skin came from his Italian mother. Most never pegged him as Native American, but the features were there, if you looked hard enough: the wide, high cheekbones, the deep black hair. But as he aged, those Indian traits shone more strongly.

Lisa had commented on it only last month. They had been spending a lazy Sunday in bed, reading the paper, finding no reason to get up. She had leaned on an elbow and traced a finger down his face. "You're keeping your tan longer, and these sun crinkles are deepening. You're getting to look a lot like that old photo of your father."

Not exactly something you wanted to hear when lounging in bed with your girlfriend.

She had reached and fingered the single lock of white hair behind his ear, tucked like a snowy feather against the field of black. "Or maybe it's just that you're letting your hair grow out. I could almost tie this into a warrior's braid."

In fact, he hadn't been growing his hair out. He just hadn't had a chance to get it cut for a couple of months. He'd been spending more and more time at Sigma Command. The covert facility lay buried beneath the Smithsonian Castle on the National Mall, occupying what had once been bomb shelters during World War II. The location had been picked for both its convenient access to the halls of power and for its proximity to the Smithsonian Institution's many research facilities.

It was where Painter spent most of his days. His only windows on the world of late were his office's three giant monitors.

He turned away and crossed back to his desk, contemplating the implication of a homegrown terrorist, one with a Native American background. He seldom gave his own heritage much thought, especially after spending most of his youth in a series of foster homes. His mother, suffering from depression, had stabbed his father to death after seven years of marriage and the birth of their son. Afterward, Painter continued to have some contact with his Native American roots, fostered through the extended family of his father's tribe. But after such a hardscrabble and chaotic upbringing, he'd grown to place more emphasis on the *American* part of his Native American ancestry.

A knock on his open office door interrupted him. He glanced up to see Ronald Chin, Sigma's geology expert, standing in the doorway. "Thought you should see this."

Painter waved the geologist inside, almost expecting him to have to duck through the doorway. Chin stood just shy of six feet, missing that mark only because he kept his head shaved to the skin. He wore a gray lab jumpsuit, zippered half down to reveal an Army Ranger T-shirt.

"What is it?" Painter asked.

"I was poring over some of the reports and came across something that could be important." He placed a file atop the desk. "It was from a debriefing of a National Guardsman on the scene, a Major Ashley Ryan. Most of the questions centered on the identity of the bomber, along with events leading up to the blast. But Major Ryan seemed mighty agitated about the blast itself."

Painter sat up straighter and reached to the file.

"If you look at page eighteen, I've highlighted the key passages."

Painter opened the report, flipped pages, and read what was marked in yellow. There were only a handful of exchanges, but the major's last statement sent a chill through his blood.

He read it aloud. *"'The ground . . . it looked like it was dissolving away.'"*

Chin stood with hands behind his back on the far side of his desk. "From the beginning, I thought there was something odd about that blast. So I consulted Sigma's demolition expert. He came to the same conclusion. For a detonation strong enough to break through bedrock and crack open a geothermal spring, the concussive blast radius should have been tenfold larger."

A gruff voice interrupted from the doorway. "That's right. Not nearly enough bang."

Painter turned to the doorway again. Apparently Sigma's new resident bomb expert had come to support Chin's assessment. The man leaned against the door frame. He stood half a foot taller than Chin, and outweighed his teammate by a good forty pounds, most of it muscle. His dark hair was stubble, but he still slicked back what little was there with gel. The man wore the same coveralls as Chin, but from the bared chest, it looked like he was wearing nothing underneath.

In his right hand, he kneaded a fistful of clay.

Painter grew concerned. "Kowalski, is that the C4 from the weapons locker?"

The man straightened with a shrug, suddenly looking sheepish. "Thought I'd run a test . . ."

Painter felt a sick lurch in his stomach. Joe Kowalski was ex-Navy, hired by Sigma a few years ago. Unlike others, he was more of an adoptee than a recruit. He had been serving as muscle and team support, but Painter sensed there might be more to this guy than met the eye, a vein of sharpness hidden beneath that dull exterior.

At least he hoped so.

Painter had reviewed the man's dossier since he'd joined Sigma—evaluating his aptitude and skills—and eventually assigned him to a field of study for which he seemed best suited: blowing stuff up.

Painter was beginning to regret that decision. "I don't think any explosives tests will be necessary." He tapped the file on his desk. "Have you read this field report?"

"I skimmed it."

"What's your take?"

"Definitely wasn't C4." He lifted his fist of explosive and gave it a squeeze. "The explosion was something else."

"Any thoughts?"

"Not without examining the blast field. Collecting some samples. Otherwise I have no clue."

He had to give Kowalski credit. It was a passable evaluation.

"Well, someone knows the truth." Painter leaned back in his desk chair and glanced to the screen with the frozen image of the bomber. "That is, if we can find her."

2:22 P.M.
Utah Wilderness

Kai hid in a dense thicket of mountain willows alongside a cold stream. She knelt, cupped the clear water, and drank. She ignored the nagging concerns of giardia or other intestinal parasites. Most of the flow here was fresh snowmelt. As thirsty as she was, she'd take her chances.

After drinking enough to wet her mouth and take the edge off her thirst, she covered her face with icy-wet palms. The cold helped her focus.

Still, even with closed eyes, she could not get the image out of her head. As she had fled the burial cave, she had glanced back in time to see the flash of brilliance, hear the thunderclap. Screams and cries chased her into the deeper woods.

Why did I drop my pack?

John Hawkes had sworn the C4 was safe. He'd said she could fire a bullet into one of the explosive charges, and nothing would happen. So what went wrong? Already scared, she came up with one frightening possibility. Had someone from WAHYA witnessed her flight out of the cave and telephoned in the detonation command?

But why would they do that, knowing people were around?

No one was supposed to get hurt.

She hadn't had any time to think. For the past two hours, she'd been running headlong through the woods, as fleet-footed as any deer. She kept hidden from the air as much as possible. She'd already spotted one helicopter as it skimmed past a ridgeline. It looked like a news chopper rather than law enforcement, but it still sent her diving for the thicket.

During the remaining hours of daylight, she had to put as much distance as possible between herself and any pursuers. She knew they'd be looking for her. She pictured her face being broadcast across the nation. She was under no illusion that her identity would remain a secret for long.

All those cameras . . . someone surely got a good picture of me.

It was only a matter of time before she was caught.

She needed help.

But whom could she trust?

4:35 P.M.
Washington, D.C.

"Director, it looks like we finally caught a break."

"Show me," Painter said as he stepped into the darkened room, lit only by a circular bank of monitors and glowing computer screens.

Sigma's satellite com always reminded him of the control room on a nuclear submarine, where the ambient light was kept low to preserve night vision. And like a sub's control room, this was the nerve center of Sigma Command. All information flowed into and out of this interconnected web of feeds from various intelligence agencies, both domestic and foreign.

The spider of this particular web stood before a bank of monitors and waved Painter over. Captain Kathryn Bryant was Sigma's chief intelligence expert and had grown to become Painter's second-in-command at Sigma. She was his eyes and ears throughout Washington and a savvy player in the internecine world of D.C. politics. And like any good spider, she maintained a meticulous web, casting strands far and wide. But her best asset was an uncanny ability to monitor each vibrating filament of her web, filter out the static, and produce results.

Like now.

Kat had called him down here with the promise of a breakthrough.

"Give me a second to bring up the feed from Salt Lake City," she said.

She winced slightly, placed a palm on her belly, and continued to type one-handed on a keyboard. At eight months along, she was huge, but she refused to go out early for maternity leave. Her only concession to her condition was that she'd abandoned her usual tight dress blues for a casual loose dress and jacket, and allowed the curls of her auburn hair to drape past her shoulders, rather than pinning them up.

"Why don't you at least sit down?" he said, and pulled out the chair in front of the monitor.

"I've been sitting all day. Baby's been doing a tap dance on my bladder since lunch." She waved him closer. "Director, you need to see this. From the start of the investigation, I've been monitoring the local news programs over in Salt Lake City. It wasn't difficult to hack into their computer servers and look over their shoulders as they readied their evening news broadcasts."

"Why?"

"Because I figured it's damn easy to hide a cell phone."

He glanced quizzically at her.

She explained. "From the number of people who witnessed the attack, the odds were good that someone got a picture or video of the bomber. So why no footage?"

"Maybe everyone was too panicked."

"Perhaps *after* the bomb, but not before. If you start with the proposition that a photo *was* taken, why wasn't it turned in to the police? I followed that line of reasoning. Greed is a strong motivator."

"You think someone hid footage of the bomber to make a few bucks."

"To be thorough, I had to assume that. It would be easy enough to hide a phone during the chaos. Or even e-mail the footage and erase the record. So I canvassed the broadcast logs for tonight's local news in Salt Lake City and came across a file at an NBC affiliate labeled 'New Footage from the Utah Bombing.'"

Kat hit a button on the keyboard, and a video started playing, another view of the same scenario he'd watched over and over. Only this time, the bomber was caught in full view, exiting the cave, still carrying the backpack. She was moving fast, but for a fraction of a second, she stared fully at the camera.

Kat deftly captured the image and froze it. The image was grainy, but she certainly looked Native American, as the eyewitnesses had reported.

Painter leaned closer. His heart began pounding harder. "Can you zoom in?"

"The resolution's poor. I'll need a minute to clean it up." Kat's fingers flew over the keyboard. "I thought we should be ahead of the curve on this. The broadcast is slated for the top of the six o'clock hour in Salt Lake City. I happened to read a draft of the accompanying copy. It's very inflammatory. Coloring the attack as a possible resurgence of Native American militancy. In the same broadcast folder, they posted archival footage of Wounded Knee."

Painter bit back a groan. Back in 1973, members of the American Indian movement waged a bloody siege with the FBI in Wounded Knee, South Dakota. Two people were killed and many others injured in the firefight that ensued. It took decades for the tension between the tribes and the government to subside.

"Okay," Kat said. "Program's done rendering the sample."

The image reappeared, a thousand times crisper. Kat manipulated the computer mouse to fill the screen with the girl's face. The detail was amazing. Her dark eyes were wide with fear, her lips parted in a panicked breath, her ebony hair billowing out and framing distinctly Native American features.

"She's certainly a looker," Kat said. "Somebody must know her. It won't take long to put a name to that pretty face."

Painter barely heard the words. He stared at the screen. His vision narrowed, fixed upon that frozen image.

Kat must have sensed something wrong and turned to face him. "Director Crowe?"

Before he could respond, his cell phone rang. He pulled it out. It was his personal BlackBerry, unencrypted.

Must be Lisa checking about the barbecue party.

He put the phone to his ear, needing to hear her voice.

But it wasn't Lisa. The caller's words came rushed, breathless. "Uncle Crowe . . . I need your help."

Shock choked him.

"I'm in trouble. So much trouble. I don't know—"

The words suddenly died. In the background, he heard the growl of a large animal, followed by a sharp, terrified scream.

Painter gripped the phone harder. "Kai!"

The line cut off.

4

Kai backed away from the dog.

Covered in mud, soaked to the skin, it looked feral, maybe even rabid. Lips rippled back in a menacing growl, baring all its teeth. It stalked toward her, head low, tail high, ready to pounce at her throat.

A shout behind her made her jump. "That's enough, Kawtch! Back down!"

She turned as a tall man in a Stetson rode through a thick stand of lodgepole pines atop a chestnut quarter horse. The mare moved with an easy grace, stepping nearly silently up the slope.

Kai pressed her back against a tree, ready to flee. She was sure it was a federal marshal, swore she even spotted a badge, but once he got closer, she saw it was only a compass hanging around his neck. He tucked it back under his shirt.

"You gave us quite the chase, young lady," the man said harshly, his face still shadowed by his wide-brimmed hat. "But there's no trail Kawtch can't follow once he's got his nose to it."

The dog wagged its tail, but its sharp eyes remained locked on her. A low growl rumbled.

The stranger slid out of his saddle and dropped easily to the ground. He patted the dog to calm it as he joined her. "You'll have to excuse Kawtch. He's still spooked by that explosion. Got him all on edge."

Kai didn't know what to make of the man's attitude. He was plainly not with the National Guard or the state police. Was he a bounty hunter? She eyed the pistol holstered on his right hip. Was that meant for her or merely a wise precaution against the black bears and bobcats that roamed the forests up here?

The stranger finally stepped out of the shadows, took off his Stetson, and wiped his brow with a handkerchief. She recognized his salt-and-pepper hair tied in a ponytail, the unmistakable hard planes of his Native American features. Shock made her momentarily dizzy. She had seen this same man in the mountain cavern only a couple of hours ago.

"Professor Kanosh . . ." His name tumbled from her lips, her voice half angry, half relieved.

One eyebrow cocked in surprise. It took him a moment to speak. He held out his hand. "I suppose, under the circumstances, Hank will do."

She refused to take his hand. She still remembered John Hawkes's description of the man. *An Indian Uncle Tom.* Of course, this traitor to his people would be working for the government to help track her down.

His arm dropped. He planted his hands on his hips, fingers brushing the top of his holstered pistol. "So what're we going to do with you, young lady? You've got yourself into a mountain of trouble. All the law on this side of the Rockies is out looking for you. That explosion back there—"

She had heard enough. "It wasn't my fault!" she blurted out, loud and angry, needing to lash out against someone. "I don't know what happened!"

"That may be so, but someone died during that blast. A dear friend of mine. And people are looking for someone to blame."

She stared at him. She read the well of sadness in the deep wrinkles at the corner of his eyes. He was telling the truth.

With his words, the anger inside her blew out like a doused candle. Her worst fears were now real. She covered her face, remembering the blast, the blinding flash. She slumped down the trunk of the tree and crouched into a ball. She had murdered someone.

The well of tears that had been building inside her chest since the explosion broke through the tight terror. Silent sobs rocked through her.

"No one was supposed to get hurt," she choked out, but her words sounded meaningless even to her.

A shadow fell over her. The old man knelt down, put an arm around her shoulders, and pulled her into his side. She didn't have the strength to fight it.

"I can only imagine what you intended with that backpack full of explosives," he said softly. "But you were right before. That explosion wasn't your fault."

She resisted the comfort of his words. Before her father died, he taught her right from wrong, instilled in her the importance of responsibility. It had just been the two of them most of her life. He took two jobs to keep food on the table and a roof over their heads. She spent more nights babysitting neighbors' kids than in their own apartment. They took care of each other as well as they could.

So she could not fool herself. Whether it was by accident or not, her actions had ended up killing someone today.

"I don't know what happened back there," Kanosh continued, his voice warm and full of reassurance, "but it wasn't your explosives that blew up the mountainside. I think it was that totem skull. Or something *inside* that skull."

A part of her heard his words and latched onto them like someone drowning. Still, lost in guilt and grief, she feared fully accepting what he was saying.

Perhaps sensing her resistance, he spoke quietly. "I read the reports before coming here, about the rumors concerning the cave, ancient stories shared by a handful of tribal elders. According to those stories, the burial cave was cursed, and any trespass would end in ruin for all." He let out a soft and sad snort. "Maybe someone should have listened. As much as I've studied our people's past, I've learned how often such stories have a hard kernel of truth inside of them."

The strength of his arms and the assurance of his words helped calm her. Tears continued to flow, but she found the strength to lift her head, needing to see his face as much as hear his words.

"So . . . so the explosion wasn't the C4 I had in my pack?"

"No. It was something much worse. It's why I came looking for you. To protect you."

She pulled straighter, out of his arms. He must have read her questioning look.

"That explosion helped set off the powder keg already brewing on the top of the mountain. When I slipped away, the activists gathered on the mountaintop were already beginning to skirmish with the National Guard. Everyone is accusing the other side of all manner of crimes and atrocities. But they're all certain about one thing."

She swallowed, guessing what that was. "They think I'm to blame."

"And they're all looking for you. And as much tension and confusion as is out there, I fear they may shoot first and ask questions later."

She shivered, suddenly cold. "What am I going to do?"

"First, you're going to tell me what happened. Everything. Every detail. The truth is often one's best shield."

She didn't know where to begin, wasn't sure she even knew the whole truth. But the old man's hand found hers and squeezed reassurance. She took strength from the iron in those strong fingers, so much like her father's callused hands.

Still, her words came reluctantly at first, but before long, her story came out in a rush, both as a confession and as an act of contrition. But deep down, she also knew she needed to unload her burden onto someone else's shoulders and share it.

3:08 P.M.

Hank watched the girl as much as he listened to her accounting of events. He kept his questions to a minimum, discovering more truth in the telling than in the facts. He saw the raw fear dim to embers in her eyes. As she told her story, he recognized her deep-seated sense of betrayal after the death of her father, needing to blame someone, to make sense of a senseless murder. Lost and scared, she found a new home, a new tribe with her militant fellow members of WAHYA.

It was a story he'd heard all too often among Native American youth: broken families, poverty, domestic abuse, alcoholism. All of it compounded and concentrated by the isolation of reservation life. It left young men and women lost and angry, looking to lash out. Many fell into lives of crime, others into profound hatred for anyone in authority. It was men like John Hawkes, the founder of WAHYA, who preyed upon those lost souls, who twisted that teenage angst to serve their own ends.

It was a path Hank knew all too well. In his teen years, he had begun selling drugs, first in school, then more broadly. He settled in with a hard crowd. It was only after one of his best friends had been killed by a strung-out junkie that he found his way back to his faith, back to the Mormon Church of his tribe. To many, it was a strange path to salvation for an Indian. He knew the disdain other Native Americans had for those tribesmen who joined the Mormon faith. But since finding his way back home, he had never been more content.

And since then, he refused to give up on anyone lost who fell across his path. It was one of the reasons he fought so hard to protect tribal rights, not so much for the tribes themselves, but to support and enrich the reservations, to build a better foundation for the youngest among them.

His own grandfather—long in his grave—had once told him: *The richest harvest comes from best-tilled soil.* It was a philosophy he attempted to live by every day.

As the girl finished her story, she unzipped her jacket, drawing back his full attention. She pulled out two paperback-sized plates of metal.

"This is why I left without setting the charges. I took these. As proof for John Hawkes. To show him there was more gold than just that cat skull."

Hank's eyes grew wide. She had stolen two of the gold plates. He had thought they were all lost, buried under half a mountain.

"May I see those?"

She offered one to him, and he examined it under a patch of sunlight. Through the black grime, he could make out lines of strange script etched into the gold. This was the sole surviving clue to the mystery of that cavern, of the mass suicide, of what was hidden so that blood had to be spilled to protect it.

But in truth, his interest went beyond the academic. His hands trembled slightly as he held the plates. While he was Native American, he was also Mormon—and as a scholar of history, he had studied his religion's past as thoroughly as his Native American heritage. According to his faith, the Book of Mormon came from translations of a lost language inscribed on gold plates discovered by Joseph Smith, the founder of the Church of Latter-Day Saints. Ever since that revelation, rumors of other caches of plates had been reported periodically across the Americas. Most of these discoveries were ruled out as hoaxes or frauds; others could never be found or substantiated.

He stared at the blurry writing, aching with both heart and head to study what was written there—but he had a more immediate concern.

The girl voiced it aloud. "What are we going to do?"

He passed the plate back to her and motioned for her to zip them both into her jacket again. He held out his arm once more, starting over. "Hank Kanosh."

She took his hand this time. "Kai . . . Kai Quocheets."

He frowned at her name. "If I'm not mistaken, Kai means 'willow tree' in Navajo. But from your accent and look, you strike me as someone from a Northeastern tribe."

She nodded. "I'm Pequot Indian. My mother named me. She was a quarter Navajo, and according to my father, she wanted me to carry a bit of her heritage."

Hank pointed down the mountainside. "Then let's see how well you live up to your name, young lady. The willow is known for its resiliency in the face of strong winds. And a storm is certainly brewing around you."

This earned him the shiest of grins.

Hank headed over to his horse. Though twenty years old, the mare was as sure-footed as any steed. He mounted up with a slight complaint from his hip.

He waved for Kawtch to lead the way. With the mountains being combed by armed hunters, he didn't want any more surprises. Kawtch would alert him if anyone came too close.

Turning in the saddle, he offered an arm to Kai. She eyed the mare with suspicion. "You've never ridden before?" he asked.

"I grew up in Boston."

"Okay then, grab my arm. I'll pull you up behind me. Mariah won't let you fall."

The girl took hold of his wrist. "Where are we going?"

"To turn you in."

Her smile vanished. The ember of fear flared brighter in her eyes. Before she could protest, he yanked her up, earning a sharp twinge from his shoulder.

"I'm sorry, but you'll have to face what you did."

She climbed into the saddle behind him. "But I didn't cause the explosion."

He twisted to face her. "True. But, aborted or not, you were still about to commit an act of violence. There will be consequences. But don't worry. I'll be at your side . . . along with a slew of Native American lawyers."

His words failed to dim the fear shining in her eyes.

There was nothing he could do about that. The sooner he got the child under custody, the safer she would be. As if it had heard his thought, the bell beat of a helicopter thundered out of nowhere. As he scanned the skies, a pair of scared arms circled his stomach. He never had a child himself, but the simple gesture warmed through him, igniting a paternal need to protect this frightened girl.

Off to the north, a small military chopper crested out of the neighboring valley and flew slowly over this one, dipping lower as it cleared the ridge, plainly searching. It looked like an angry and persistent hornet. Even without the military green of the craft, Hank recognized it as one of the Utah National Guard helicopters, even knew it was an Apache Longbow.

He took the name of the chopper as a good omen, not that either of them were Apache. He nudged his horse toward the edge of the pine forest, toward an open meadow.

Might as well get this over with.

Those arms tightened around him.

"Just stay low," he told her. "Let me do all the talking."

He kept Mariah to a slow walk, her flanks rolling as they headed toward the sunny spread of grass. He didn't want anyone being surprised. Even before they reached the edge of the dense forest, the chopper banked abruptly and swung toward them.

Must have infrared aboard. Picked up our body heat.

He walked the mare out of the forest and into the open glade.

The helicopter dove toward them, nose dipping, blades cutting the air with a deafening chop. The noise was so loud, he could only stare as twin rows of grass and soil blasted upward, silently chewing across the meadow toward their position.

At last, he heard the rattle of the chopper's chain guns.

What the hell . . . ?

Shock and disbelief froze him for a breath.

They were being fired at.

With a yank of the reins, he swung Mariah around.

A shout burst from his lips. "Hold tight!"

5

"Still no luck tracing your niece's cell," Kat announced as she stepped into Painter's office. "But we'll keep trying."

He stood behind his desk, checking the contents of his packed briefcase. The jet was set to take off from Reagan National in thirty minutes. It would get him to Salt Lake City in four hours.

He studied Kat's face. A single crease across her forehead expressed her worry. He shared it.

It had been over half an hour since his niece's frantic call had suddenly cut off. He'd been unable to raise her again. Had she dropped out of cell reception? Had she turned off her phone? Kat had attempted to track the cell's trace but clearly was having no better luck.

"And there's still no word of her being captured out in Utah?" he asked.

Kat shook her head. "The sooner you get out there, the better. If there's any news, I'll call you midflight. Kowalski and Chin are already waiting topside for you."

He snapped closed his briefcase. Before the desperate call, he had planned on putting a team out in the field in Utah. He wanted someone from Sigma on hand to determine the true nature of that strange explosion. Chin was the perfect choice—and Kowalski could certainly use some field time as a member of an investigative team.

But with that one phone call, matters had become personal.

He picked up his briefcase and headed toward the door. For the moment they were keeping knowledge of his niece to as few people as possible, maintaining a need-to-know basis. Kai already had a large enough target on her back.

As an extra precaution, Painter purposely neglected to inform his boss, General Metcalf, the head of DARPA. That slight was done to avoid a lengthy explanation as to *why* Painter was heading out into the field. Metcalf operated strictly by the book, an inflexible posture that continually tied Painter's hands. And considering the personal nature of his trip, Painter figured it was easier to ask for forgiveness from his boss than to get permission.

Plus he and Metcalf had not been on the best of terms of late, mostly due to a private investigation Painter had started six months ago, an investigation into a shadowy organization that had plagued Sigma since its inception. Only five people in the world knew about this secret research project. But Metcalf was no fool. He was beginning to suspect something was up and had begun to ask questions that Painter would prefer not to answer.

So maybe it was best to get out of D.C. for a while anyway.

Kat followed Painter into the hallway.

As they exited his office, a man stood up from a seat in the hall. Painter was surprised to see Kat's husband, Monk Kokkalis.

Given his craggy features, shaved head, and boxer's build, few suspected the sharp intelligence hidden behind that brutish exterior. Monk was a former Green Beret, but he'd been retrained by Sigma in the field of forensic medicine, with a secondary specialty in biotechnology. The latter came from personal experience. Monk had lost one of his hands during a prior mission. It had been replaced by a wonder of prosthetic sciences, employing the latest in DARPA technologies. Outfitted with all manner of countermeasures, it was half hand, half weapons system.

"Monk, what are you doing here? I thought you were running shakedown tests on that new prosthesis of yours."

"All finished. Passed with flying colors." He lifted his arm and flexed his fingers as proof. "Then Kat called. Thought you might need an extra pair of hands in the field. Or at least a hand and one kick-ass new prosthetic."

Painter glanced to Kat.

She kept her face fixed. "I thought you could use someone with more field experience joining you on this trip."

Painter appreciated her offer, especially because he knew how much Kat hated Monk being away from her side, especially now that she was about to give birth to their second child. But in this case, Painter refused for a more practical reason.

"Thanks, but with the escalating tension out on that mountain, I think a smaller, more surgical team might be best."

As he watched the crease in Kat's forehead relax, he knew he'd made the right call. While he was gone, he fully trusted Kat to fill in as the temporary director of Sigma—and he knew that with Monk nearby, she would remain focused. Her husband was both her anchor and the very water that kept her afloat. Monk slipped his arm around his wife's waist, resting his palm on her full belly. She leaned into him.

With the matter settled, he headed down the hall.

"Be careful out there, Director," Monk called to him.

Painter heard the longing in the man's voice. It seemed the offer to accompany him might not have solely originated from Kat. Likewise, Painter's decision to leave Monk behind was not entirely for Kat's benefit. While the man was certainly *her* anchor, he served that same role for one other, a teammate who was having a very tough few months.

And Painter suspected it would get worse.

5:22 P.M.

Commander Grayson Pierce did not know what to do with his mother. She paced the length of the medical exam room.

"I don't understand why I couldn't be there when the neurologist questions your father," she said, angry, frustrated.

"You know why," he replied calmly. "The social worker explained.

The mental acuity tests they're running on Dad are more accurate if family members aren't present."

She waved away his words as she turned and headed back across the room. He noticed her stumble, her left leg almost giving out. He shifted forward in his seat, ready to catch her, but she recovered her balance.

Leaning back into the plastic chair, Gray studied his mother. She had lost weight over the past couple of months, worn down by worry. The silk blouse hung from her thin shoulders, sagging enough to reveal one bra strap, a lack of modesty she normally would never have tolerated. Only her gray hair, done up and pinned back, remained perfect. Gray pictured her fussing over it, imagining it was the one bit of her life still under her control.

As she paced away her worry, Gray listened to the muffled exchanges going on in the exam room. He couldn't hear any words, but he recognized the sharper notes of his father's irritation. He feared an explosion from him at any moment and remained tense, ready to burst into the next room if needed. His father, a former Texas oil rigger, was never a calm man, prone to outbursts and sudden violence during Gray's childhood, a temper exacerbated by an early disability that left the proud man with only one good leg. But now he was even more short-fused as advancing Alzheimer's eroded away his self-control along with his memory.

"I should be with him," his mother repeated.

Gray didn't argue. He'd already had countless conversations about this with them both, trying to encourage moving his father into an assisted-living facility with a memory unit. But such attempts were met with stonewalling, anger, and suspicion. The two refused to leave the Takoma Park bungalow that they'd lived in for decades, preferring the illusory comfort of the familiar to the support of a facility.

But Gray didn't know how long that could be sustained.

Not just for his father's sake but also his mother's.

She stumbled again on a turn. He caught her elbow. "Why don't you sit down?" he said. "You're exhausting yourself, and they should almost be done."

He felt the frail bird bones of her arm as he guided her to a seat. He'd already had a private talk with the social worker. She had expressed concern about his mother's health—both physical and mental—warning that it was common for a caregiver to succumb to stress and die before the actual patient.

Gray didn't know what else to do. He had already employed a full-time nursing aide to help his mother during the day, an intrusion that was met with more resentment than acceptance. But even that was not enough any longer. There were growing issues with medications, with proper safety in his parents' older house, even with meal planning and preparation. At night, any phone call set his heart to pounding, as he suspected the worst.

He had offered to move into the house with them, to be there at night, but so far that was a Rubicon his mother refused to cross—though Gray believed her refusal was motivated less by pride than by a feeling of guilt about imposing upon her son in such a manner. And with all the rough water under the bridge between father and son, maybe it was for the best. So for now, it remained a private slow dance between husband and wife.

The exam room door opened, drawing back his attention. He sat straighter as the neurologist entered the room. From the doctor's stern expression, Gray anticipated that the assessment was grim. Over the next twenty minutes, Gray learned how grim. His father was sliding from the moderate stages of Alzheimer's toward more severe symptoms. From here, they could expect to see trouble with his ability to get dressed on his own, to use the toilet. There would be more issues with him wandering and getting lost. The social worker suggested alarming the doors.

As this was discussed, Gray watched his father sitting in the corner with his mother. He looked a frail shadow of the domineering man he once was. He sat sullenly, scowling at the doctor's every word. Every now and then a breathless "bullshit" escaped his lips, spoken so quietly only Gray heard him.

But Gray also noted his father's hand clutching tightly to his mother's. They held on to each other, weathering as best they could the doctor's prognosis, as if by force of will alone they could resist the inevitable decline and ensure that neither would ever lose the other.

Finally, with a rush of insurance paperwork and prescription revisions, they were set free. Gray drove his parents back home, made sure they had dinner for the night, and returned to his own apartment by bicycle. He pressed himself hard, pedaling quickly through the streets, using the exertion to clear his head.

Reaching his apartment, he took a long shower, long enough to use up all the hot water. Shivering as the water turned cold, he toweled off, slipped into a pair of boxers, and headed into the kitchen. He was halfway toward the refrigerator and the lone bottle of Heineken left from the six-pack he'd bought yesterday when he noted the figure sitting on his La-Z-Boy recliner.

He spun around. Normally he wasn't so unobservant. It wasn't a good survival trait for a Sigma operative. Then again, the woman, dressed all in black leather and steel zippers, sat as still as a statue. A motorcycle helmet rested on the arm of the chair.

Gray recognized her, but it did not slow his spiked heartbeat. The small hairs along his arms refused to go down. And with good reason. It was like suddenly discovering a she-panther lounging in your living room.

"Seichan . . ." he said.

Her only greeting was an uncrossing of her legs, but even this small movement suggested the power and grace stored within her whip-thin body. Jade-green eyes stared at him, taking measure of him, her face unreadable. In the shadows, her Eurasian features looked carved out of pale marble. The only softness about her was the loose flow of her hair, longer now, below her collar, not her usual severe bob. The left corner of her lips turned slightly up, amused by his surprise—or was it just a trick of those shadows?

He didn't bother asking how she'd gotten into his locked apartment or why she presented herself in such an abrupt and unannounced manner. She was a skilled assassin, formerly employed by an international criminal organization called the Guild—but even that name wasn't real, only a useful pseudonym to use in task-force reports and intelligence briefings. Its real identity and purpose remained unknown, even to its own operatives. The organization operated through individual cells around the world, each running independently, none having the complete picture.

After betraying her former employers, Seichan was left with no home, no country. Intelligence agencies—including those in the United States—had her on their most-wanted lists. The Mossad maintained a kill-on-sight order. But as of a year ago, she now worked for Sigma, recruited unofficially by Director Crowe for a mission too secret to be on any books: to root out the identities of the true puppet masters of the Guild.

But no one was fooled by her cooperation. It was driven by survival, not by loyalty to Sigma. She had to destroy the Guild before it destroyed her. Only a handful of people in the government knew of the special arrangement with this assassin. To help maintain that level of secrecy, Gray had been assigned as her direct supervisor and sole contact within Sigma.

Still, it had been five weeks since she'd last reported in. And then it had only been by phone. She'd been somewhere in France. So far, all she'd been hitting was dead ends.

So what is she doing here now?

She answered his silent question. "We have a problem."

Gray did not take his eyes off her. While he should be concerned, he could not discount a spark of relief. He pictured the beer bottle in the fridge, remembering why he had needed it. He was suddenly glad for the distraction, something that didn't involve social workers, neurologists, or prescriptions.

"This problem of yours," he asked, "does it have anything to do with the situation in Utah?"

"What situation in Utah?" she asked, her eyes narrowing.

He studied her, searching her face for any sign of deception. The bombing had certainly stirred up Sigma, and Seichan's sudden appearance struck Gray as suspicious.

She finally shrugged. "I came to show you this."

She stood up, passed him a sheaf of papers, and headed toward the door. Clearly he was meant to follow. He stared down at the symbol on the top page, but it made no sense to him.

He glanced up to her as she reached the door.

"Something's stirred up a hornet's nest," she said. "Right here in your own backyard. Something big. It may be the break we've been waiting for."

"How so?"

"Twelve days ago, every feeler I've been extending around the globe suddenly jangled. A veritable earthquake. In its wake, every contact I've been grooming went dead silent."

Twelve days ago . . .

Gray realized that this time frame coincided with the day the Native American boy had been killed out in Utah. Could there be a connection?

Seichan continued: "Something big has piqued the Guild's interest. And that earthquake I mentioned . . . its epicenter is here in D.C." She faced him from the door. "Even now, I can sense unseen forces mobilizing into position. And it's during such chaos that sealed doors get cracked open, just long enough for bits of intel to blow out."

Gray noted her eyes sparking, her breathing sharpening with excitement. "You found something."

She pointed again at the papers in his hand. "It starts there."

He stared again at the symbol on the top page.

It was the Great Seal of the United States.

He didn't understand. He flipped over the next pages. They were a mix of typed research notes, sketches, and photocopies of an old handwritten letter. Though the letter's ink was faded, the cursive script was precise, written in French. He read the name to which the letter was addressed, *Archard Fortescue*. Definitely sounded French. But it was the signature at the end, the signature of the man who wrote the letter, that truly caught Gray's attention, a name known to every schoolchild in America.

Benjamin Franklin.

He frowned at the name, then at Seichan. "What do these papers have to do with the Guild?"

"You and Crowe told me to find the true source of those bastards." Seichan turned and pulled open the door. He noted a flicker of fear pass over her features before she looked away. "You're not going to like what I found."

He stepped toward her, drawn as much by her anxiety as by his own curiosity. "What did you find?"

She answered as she stepped out into the night. "The Guild . . . it goes all the way back to the founding of America."

6

The data made no sense.

Jun Yoshida sat in his office at Kamioka Observatory. He stared at the computer monitor, ignoring the aching crick in his back.

The source of the data on the screen came from a thousand meters below his feet, at the heart of Mount Ikeno. Buried far underground, shielded from cosmic rays that could interfere with detecting the elusive subatomic particles, rested the Super-Kamiokande detector, a forty-meter-tall stainless-steel tank filled with fifty thousand tons of ultrapure water. The purpose of the massive facility was to study one of the smallest particles in the universe, the neutrino—a subatomic particle so small that it held no electrical charge and contained almost no mass, so tiny it could pass through solid matter without disturbing it.

Neutrinos continually shot straight through the earth from space. Sixty billion passed through a person's fingertip every second. They were one of the fundamental particles of the universe, yet they remained a mystery to modern physics.

Belowground, the Super-Kamiokande detector sought to record and study those elusive passing particles. On rare occasions, a neutrino would collide with a molecule—in the detector's case, a *water* molecule. The impact shattered the nucleus and emitted a blue cone of light. It took absolute darkness to detect that brief, infinitesimally small burst of light. To catch it, thirteen thousand photomultiplier tubes lined the massive water tank, peering into that pitch-black tank, ready to mark the passage of a neutrino.

Still, even with such a huge shielded facility, it was a challenge to find those particles. The number of neutrinos captured by the photomultipliers had held at a fairly steady pace over the course of the year—which was why the data on the monitor confounded him.

Jun stared at the graph on the screen. It displayed neutrino activity over the past half day.

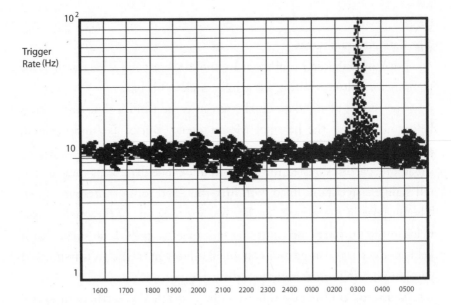

He ran a finger across the screen, tracing the graph. His fingertip spiked up as it reached the three o'clock hour this morning. It marked a sudden and massive burst of neutrinos that occurred three hours ago, a level never recorded before.

It has to be a lab error. A glitch of some kind.

For the past three hours, the entire facility had been troubleshooting every piece of equipment and electronics. Next month, his team was scheduled for a joint experiment with CERN, a Swiss facility.

If that had to be canceled—

He stood up to stretch his aching back and crossed to his window. He loved the light at this early hour, perfect for photography, a hobby of his. Adorning his walls were pictures he'd taken of Mount Fuji at sunrise, reflecting in Lake Kawaguchi, another of the Nara Pagoda set against a backdrop of fiery maples, or his favorite, a picture of Shiraito Falls in winter, with skeletal ice-encased trees scattering the morning light into rainbows.

Beyond his window was the less picturesque landscape of the observatory campus, but a small water garden lay below, alongside a raked and swept Zen garden, swirling around a tall craggy rock. He often felt like that rock, standing alone, bent-backed, swirled by life around him.

Interrupting his reverie, the door swung open behind him. A leggy blond colleague, Dr. Janice Cooper, a postgraduate student from Stanford, strode swiftly into the room. She was thirty years younger than Jun, as thin as Jun was round. She always smelled of coconut oil and carried herself as if she were about to bound away, too full of California sunshine to sit still.

Sometimes her simple presence exhausted him.

"Dr. Yoshida!" she said, out of breath as if she had been running. "I just heard from the Sudbury Neutrino Observatory in Canada and from the IceCube facility in Antarctica. They've all recorded massive spikes of neutrinos at the same moment in time as we did."

Clearly she wanted to say more, but Jun held up a hand, needing a moment to think, to let out a sigh of relief. So the data wasn't a glitch. That solved one mystery—but on its tail rode another more disturbing question: What then was the *source* for such a colossal blast of neutrinos? The birth of a supernova deep in space? A massive solar flare?

As if reading his mind, Dr. Cooper spoke again. "Riku asked if you'd join him down below. He believes he knows a way to pinpoint the source of the neutrino surge. He was still working on that when I left."

Jun didn't have time for the eccentricities of Dr. Riku Tanaka. With clear proof that the spike in neutrinos was not the result of a fault in their systems, he felt the mystery could wait a few hours. He'd been up all night, and at sixty-three years of age, he was no young man.

"He was insistent," Dr. Cooper pressed. "Said it was important."

"Everything's important with Dr. Tanaka," he mumbled under his breath, not bothering to hide his disdain.

Still, a bit of excitement entered Dr. Cooper's voice. "Riku believes the neutrinos might be *geoneutrinos*."

He looked sharply at her. "That's impossible."

Most neutrinos came from the background radiation of the universe: from solar flares, from dying stars, from collapsing galaxies. But some neutrinos—called *geoneutrinos*—originated from the earth itself: from decaying isotopes in the ground, from cosmic rays striking the upper atmosphere, even from the explosion of atomic bombs.

"That's what Riku believes," she insisted.

"Nonsense. It would take the equivalent of a hundred hydrogen bombs to generate a neutrino blast of this magnitude."

Jun crossed toward the door, moving too suddenly. Pain jolted up his right leg, a flare of sciatica.

Maybe I'd better get down there.

The desire came not so much from a need to find out if Dr. Tanaka was right, but from a wish to prove that the young physicist was wrong. It would be a rare failing, one Jun didn't want to miss.

Remaining behind to finish her own work, Dr. Cooper held the door for him. He did his best to hide his hobble as he marched out the door and headed for the elevator that descended from the topside offices to the subterranean labs. The elevator shaft was new. Prior to its construction, the only access to the mountain's heart was via a truck tunnel or mine train. While this approach was swifter, it was also unnerving.

The cage dropped like a falling boulder, lifting his stomach into his throat. Plagued by claustrophobia, he was all too aware of the meters of rock rising over his head. When at last he reached the bottom of the shaft, the doors opened into the main control room for the detector. Divided into cubicles and offices, it looked like any laboratory on the surface.

But Jun wasn't fooled.

As he stepped out of the elevator, he kept his back hunched, sensing the weight of Mount Ikenoyama above him. He found the shift-duty physicist standing beside a wall-mounted LED monitor near the back of the main hall.

Dr. Riku Tanaka was barely into his twenties, hardly over five feet in height. The wunderkind of physics held dual doctorates and was here working on his third.

At the moment the young man stood stiffly, hands behind his back, staring at a spinning map of the globe. Trails of data flowed in columns down the left half of the screen.

Tanaka held his head cocked, as if listening intently to some sound only he could hear, whispers that perhaps held the answers to the universe's secrets.

"The results are intriguing," he said, not even turning, perhaps catching Jun's reflection in one of the dark monitors to the side.

Jun frowned at the lack of simple courtesy. No bow of greeting, no acknowledgment of the hardship of his coming down here. It was said the young man suffered from Asperger's syndrome, a mild form of autism. But Jun personally believed his colleague was simply rude and used such a diagnosis as an excuse.

Jun joined him at the monitor and treated him as brusquely. "What results?"

"I've been gathering data from neutrino labs around the world. From the Russians at Lake Baikal, from the Americans at Los Alamos, from the Brits at Sudbury Observatory."

"I've heard," Jun said. "They all recorded the spike in neutrinos."

"I had those other labs send me their data." Tanaka nodded to the scrolling columns. "Neutrinos travel in a straight line from the source of their creation. Neither gravity nor magnetic fields deflect their path."

Jun bristled. He didn't need to be lectured on such fundamentals.

Tanaka seemed unaware of the affront and continued: "So it seemed a simple matter to use that data from various points around the globe and triangulate the primary source of the blast."

Jun blinked in surprise. It was such a simple solution. His face flushed. As director here, he should have thought of that himself.

"I've run the program four times, refining the search parameters with each pass. The source definitely appears to be terrestrial."

Tanaka tapped at a keyboard below the monitor. On the screen, a narrowing set of crosshairs fixed to the globe. First, encompassing the Western Hemisphere, then North America, then the western half of the United States. With a final few taps, the crosshairs sharpened and the global image zoomed into a section of the Rocky Mountains.

"Here is the source."

Jun read the territory highlighted on the screen.

Utah.

"How could that be?" he choked out, finding it hard to fathom these impossible results. He remembered his earlier words with Dr. Cooper, how it would take a hundred hydrogen bombs to generate a neutrino blast of this magnitude.

At his side, Tanaka shrugged, his manner insufferably calm. Jun restrained a desire to slap the man, to get a reaction out of him. Instead, he stared at the screen, at the topography of the mountains, with a single question foremost in his mind.

What the hell is going on out there?

7

Hank leaned low over the mare's withers, avoiding low-hanging branches as the horse raced downhill through a forest of Douglas firs, western spruce, and lodgepole pines. Still, he got battered and scraped. Behind him, clutching tightly around his waist, Kai fared no better.

He heard her sudden cries of pain, felt her bounce high out of the saddle they shared, but mostly he sensed her terror, her fingers digging into his shirt, her breath ragged.

Hank gave Mariah free rein, trusting her footing and eye for the terrain. He corrected her only with sudden tugs on the lead to keep her path within the shelter of the forest. His dog, Kawtch, kept up with them, racing low to the ground, taking a more direct path through the trees.

Behind them, the military helicopter gave chase, thundering above the treetops. The woodland canopy offered some protection, but Hank was growing more certain that the hunters were tracking them by body heat, using infrared.

Off to the left, a spate of gunfire shredded needles and branches from a spruce tree. Splinters stung his exposed cheek. The hunters' aim was getting better. As the roar of the chain guns died away, a sharp cry burst forth behind him.

"Professor!" Kai called out. She risked freeing an arm and pointed.

Ahead, a meadow cut across their path, bright with sunshine. It was wide and grassy, dotted by a few scraggly junipers and a handful of granite outcroppings. The forest continued beyond the meadow, but how to reach it? Out in the open, they'd be picked off easily.

As if sensing his worry, Mariah began to slow.

Someone else also noted their dire situation. A fresh rattle of gunfire tore into the forest behind them.

They're trying to drive us out of the forest.

With no choice but to obey, Hank spurred Mariah into a full gallop, faster than was safe in the dense woods. He whistled for Kawtch to keep at his side as they burst into the sunshine. Free of the forest, Hank aimed for the closest rocky outcropping. Gunfire pursued them, ripping twin lines through the grass as both of the chopper's guns let loose.

Hank ripped Mariah around the outcropping as if it were a barrel in a rodeo race. The mare cut sharply, hooves digging deep into the loose soil and grass. Hank leaned to keep balance, but he felt Kai's arms slip, caught by surprise by the sudden turn.

"Hold tight!" he hollered.

But she was not the only one who was surprised by the maneuver.

Rounds sparked off the stone that shielded them—then the chopper shot past overhead, missing its target. It spun, banking around, pivoting to come at them again.

Hank had not slowed Mariah. He aimed straight for the diving helicopter. As it swung to face them, he tugged his pistol from his holster. It was a Ruger Blackhawk, powerful enough to deal with the occasional wild bear. He didn't know if it was an act of war for a Native American to fire upon a National Guard chopper, but he had not started this fight. Plus his goal was not to kill, only to distract.

He pulled the trigger over and over again as he raced head-on toward the helicopter, emptying the clip. He saw no reason to be reserved. A few rounds even found their target, cracking off the windshield.

The attack caught the hunters off guard.

The chopper bobbled, a spate of return fire cut off abruptly, aborted as the vehicle jostled the gunmen. Hank used his heels to urge Mariah onward, ducking straight under the belly of the helicopter. It was so low now that Hank could have reached up and brushed his hand along the landing skids.

He spotted one of the gunmen hanging out an open hatch overhead, dressed all in commando black. They locked eyes, then Mariah cleared the helicopter. With the thunder of the engines and pound of the rotor wash, the mare needed no further urging.

Mariah shot for the woods again, diving back into the shadows.

Kawtch hit the forest's edge a few yards to the left.

The chopper's engines whined into a banshee's cry as it climbed again and spun after them.

This cat-and-mouse game could not last forever. They'd been lucky so far, but farther down the mountainside, the alpine forests would dwindle to a smattering of oaks and open fields. The hunters must have known the same. The helicopter sped after them. Their pursuers would not be surprised again.

Plus Hank was out of bullets.

A sparkle of silver drew his eyes to the right. A small stream, glacier-cut and flooded with snowmelt and rain from the passing storm, raced down a series of cataracts. He used his knees to guide Mariah toward it.

Once they'd reached the bank, he goosed Mariah with his heels. She leaped into the middle of the stream with a heavy splash—but from here, they would need to part ways.

Hank let loose the reins, grabbed Kai's wrist, and rolled out of the saddle downstream of the horse. With his other hand, he managed a fast slap to Mariah's rump, both as a good-bye and to get her moving.

She jumped out of the river as Hank and Kai hit the freezing-cold water. Kawtch splashed next to them. The current grabbed them all and spun them downstream. The last thing he heard before being dragged underwater was a sharp cry from the girl.

Kai scrambled for the surface, kicking wildly, striking a soft body with her heel. She had been too stunned to react when she was first pulled out of the saddle, but once the cold struck her, it loosed a scream, one trapped inside her since the explosion hours ago.

Then her mouth was full of water.

Out of breath from her yell, she choked as her body was flung around. Slick rocks battered her. Ice-cold water swamped her nose. Then her head was above water again. She coughed and cried. Arms scooped her and pulled her toward shore. She tried to scramble out of the river, but strong hands yanked her back into the water.

"Stay here," Professor Kanosh hissed. He looked half drowned, his gray hair plastered to his skull. His dog climbed onto a boulder, still standing belly-deep in the stream.

"Why?" she asked, her teeth already beginning to chatter, both from the cold and the terror.

He pointed up.

She searched and spotted the helicopter vanishing over a ridgeline to the west.

"Body heat," the professor explained. "It was how they were tracking us so well through the woods, why we couldn't escape. Hopefully they'll chase Mariah's big sweating rump deep into the woods. "

Kai understood. "And the cold water here . . . it helped hide us."

"A bit of sleight of hand. What sort of Indians would we be if we couldn't outfox a hunter in the woods?"

Despite the terror of their situation, his eyes smiled. She felt warmer for it.

"Let's go," he said, and helped haul her out of the frigid stream.

His dog clambered out after them and shook his coat, spraying water, as if nothing had happened.

Kai tried to do the same herself, shaking her hair, then her jacket, seeking to shed as much of the chill from her body as she could. One of the gold plates fell out of her jacket and struck the ground. Professor Kanosh's eyes fixed to the plate, but he made no move to take the burden from her. So she retrieved it and returned it alongside the other in her jacket.

Professor Kanosh pointed downhill. "We need to keep moving, keep warm."

"Where can we go?" she asked, her teeth still chattering.

"First, as far from here as possible. That trick will fool those hunters only until Mariah breaks free of the forest. Once they see her saddle's empty, they'll come backtracking, and we want to be long gone."

"Then what?"

"Back to civilization. Look for help. Get ourselves surrounded by people on our side."

He headed down the mountain, following a thin deer trail, but she read the worry in his face. She also remembered the call he had interrupted when he found her. Uncle Crowe was some bigwig in Washington, something to do with national security. He was not actually a close relative, but a half uncle on her father's side—whatever that meant. She had met him only a handful of times, last at her father's funeral. But all of the Pequot tribe was an extended family. The entire clan was a tangle of bloodlines and family relationships. She had a thousand aunties and uncles. But everyone knew if you were in big trouble, a call to Uncle Crowe could help smooth feathers.

"I know someone who might help us," she said.

As she walked, she reached into her pants pocket and removed her cell phone. Water dripped from it after the dunk in the stream. It wouldn't power up. She scowled and shoved it away. She doubted she could've gotten a signal anyway. She'd been lucky earlier to get a single bar when higher up the mountain.

Professor Kanosh noted her efforts. "Okay, then the first order of business is to reach a phone before the hunters regain the scent of our trail. Even if it means turning ourselves over to the state police or the National Guard."

She tripped a step. "But those were the ones who were trying to kill us."

"No. I got a look at their uniforms. They were certainly soldiers, but not with any National Guard unit."

"Then who?"

"Maybe it's still the government, or maybe a mercenary group looking to cash in on some bounty. Either way, I know only one thing for sure."

"What's that?"

His next words chilled her more than the dip in the icy stream. "Whoever they are, they want you dead."

8

"Did she at least leave a number?" Painter asked as he climbed into the passenger seat of a Chevy Tahoe with government plates. It sat on the tarmac near the private Gulfstream jet they'd flown from D.C.

Kowalski already sat behind the wheel, cranking the seat back to accommodate his large frame. Their third teammate, Chin, had transferred to a National Guard helicopter heading up to the blast site in the Rocky Mountains—but before Painter could direct his full attention to the anomalous explosion, he had another matter to address.

Kat's voice sounded tinny over the encrypted line. "That's all I could get out of your niece. But she sounded scared. And paranoid. She called from a disposable cell phone. But she did leave the cell's number and asked for you to call her immediately after you landed."

"Give me the number."

She did, but she had more news. "Commander Pierce also reported in." From the grimness of her tone, it didn't sound like good news. "He's with Seichan."

Painter's fingers tightened on the phone. "She's back in the U.S.?"

"Seems so."

Painter closed his eyes for a breath. He'd had no inkling that Seichan was back on American soil. But with her training and connections, he shouldn't have been surprised. Still, her sudden resurfacing suggested something major was afoot. "What's wrong?"

"She claims to have a lead on Echelon."

"What sort of lead?" He sat straighter in his seat as Kowalski kept the SUV idling. Echelon was the code name for the leaders of the shadowy terrorist organization called the Guild. He began to regret leaving D.C.

"Gray didn't elaborate. Only said that she needed his help to gain access to the National Archives. They're meeting with a museum curator this evening."

Painter scrunched his brow. Why was Seichan sniffing around the National Archives? The museum was a storehouse of America's historical manuscripts and documents. What could any of its contents have to do with the Guild? He checked his watch. It was half past nine, which meant it was after midnight in D.C. Late to be meeting with museum personnel.

"Gray said he'd call back if there was any breakthrough. I'll keep you informed."

"Do that. I'll see if I can't clear up this matter with my niece, then return to D.C. in the morning. Till then, keep holding down the fort."

Kat signed off, and Painter tapped in the phone number he'd memorized. It was answered on the first ring by a rushed voice.

"Uncle Crowe?"

"Kai, where are you?"

A silent moment stretched. He heard a gruff voice in the background, urging her to answer.

Still, her words came haltingly, balanced between tears and terror. "I'm . . . we're in Provo. On the campus of Brigham Young University. At the offices of Professor Henry Kanosh."

Painter squinted his eyes. Why did that name sound familiar? Then he remembered a report he'd read while en route from D.C. to Salt Lake City, a preliminary debriefing of the events up in the mountains. The professor had been a close associate of the anthropologist killed by the blast.

She gave him an office address, still sounding terrified.

He did his best to reassure her. "I can be in Provo in an hour." Painter waved for Kowalski to head out of the airport. "Stay put until I get there."

A new speaker replaced Kai on the phone. "Mr. Crowe, this is Hank Kanosh. You don't know me."

"You were a colleague of Margaret Grantham. You were at the site during the explosion." Painter shifted his briefcase up from the floorboard to his lap. He had a preliminary file on the man, along with files on many others who had witnessed the blast.

A pause indicated the professor's surprise at his knowledge, but the hitch in his voice suggested the hesitation was more than just surprise. "Maggie . . . she preferred to be called Maggie."

Painter softened his voice. "I'm sorry for your loss."

"I appreciate that, but you should know that your niece and I were attacked while escaping from the mountains. A helicopter bearing National Guard markings fired upon us."

"What?" He had heard no report from Kat about a sighting of the supposed terrorist, let alone someone shooting at her.

"But I don't think they were actually with the National Guard. They seemed more like a mercenary group, maybe bounty hunters who had access to a Guard chopper."

Painter wasn't buying that explanation, especially since the sighting and shooting hadn't been called in through proper channels. Someone else had tried to apprehend or eliminate the supposed terrorist. This raised a new fear. "Professor Kanosh, could you have been recognized by those hunters?"

Uncertainty wavered in his voice. "I . . . I don't believe so. We were mostly under tree cover, and I was wearing a hat. But if so, you think they might come looking for us here? I should've thought of that."

"No reason you should've." *Paranoia is part and parcel of my business.* "But as a precaution, is there someplace you and Kai can go that doesn't lead directly back to you?"

Painter could practically hear the gears turning in the professor's head; then he answered. "I wanted to check something over at the neighboring earth sciences building. We could meet there."

"Sounds good."

After getting all the information, Painter hung up. Kowalski already had them heading south on Interstate 15.

Kowalski commented around the chewed stub of unlit cigar. "Got about another forty miles to go to reach Provo."

Painter read the time estimate on the GPS. "Fifty-two minutes," he mumbled under his breath.

Kowalski rolled one eye toward his boss. "If need be, I can make that *forty*-two minutes." He gunned the engine and cocked a questioning eyebrow.

Painter sank deeper in his seat, his heart thudding harder as he considered the hunters already on Kai and the professor's trail. "How about making that *thirty*-two minutes."

Kowalski offered a crooked smile as he jammed the accelerator. "Always like a challenge."

Painter was thrown back as the SUV gained speed. While he should have been unnerved as the needle of the speedometer climbed toward the hundred mark, instead he was relieved that he'd come out to Utah. It was confirmation that his instincts hadn't grown stale during the time he'd been buried under the Smithsonian Castle.

Something major was afoot out here.

And maybe not just out here.

He remembered the call from Kat, reporting on Seichan's sudden appearance, coming to ground with a possible clue to the true leaders of the Guild. It was rare for any intelligence to leak out from the vaults of that organization. It would take something significant to get them to let their guard down.

Like this mysterious explosion.

He could be wrong, but Painter had little stomach for coincidences. And if he was right, he at least had one of his best men following those leads on the East Coast. Despite the late hour, he should be getting started.

That is, if the man could keep his focus.

9

Gray followed Seichan toward the massive pillared facade of the National
Archives Building. It was a cold spring night, a last blast of winter's chill
before D.C.'s boggy, humid summer started. Only a few cars moved along
the streets at this late hour.

Following Seichan's sudden appearance at his apartment, Gray had
donned black trousers, boots, and a long-sleeved Army T-shirt, along with
a knee-length wool overcoat. Seichan seemed oblivious to the cold, leaving
her motorcycle jacket open, exposing a thin crimson blouse, buttoned low
enough to catch a glimpse of lace underneath. The leather pants hugged
her curves, but there was no seduction to her manner. She moved with a
hard-edged purpose to her step. Her eyes took in every stir of windblown
branch. She was a piano wire stretched to the snapping point. Then again,
she had to be to survive.

They headed for the Archives' research entrance along Pennsylvania
Avenue. The access here was rather nondescript compared with the public entry on the far side of the building with its giant bronze doors. That
massive threshold led into the main rotunda of the Archives, a hall that
displayed the original copies of the Declaration of Independence, the
Constitution, and the Bill of Rights, all preserved in helium-filled glass
enclosures.

But those documents were not why they'd come for this midnight
visit. The building held over ten billion records covering the span of

American history, cataloged and stockpiled in the nine hundred thousand square feet of storage space. If they were to find the document they sought, Gray knew he'd need help.

As they approached the entrance, the door swung open ahead of them. Gray tensed until a slim figure stepped forth and waved to them brusquely. His face was fixed in a hard scowl. Dr. Eric Heisman was one of the museum's curators, specializing in Colonial American history.

"Your colleague is already inside," the curator said as greeting.

The man's hair was snowy white, worn long to the collar, with a trimmed goatee. As he held the door open for them, he fidgeted with a pair of reading glasses hanging from a chain around his neck. He clearly was not happy to be called from his home at this late hour. Summoned at the last minute, the curator was attired in a casual pair of jeans and a sweater.

Gray noted the emblem for the Washington Redskins—a profile of a feathered Native American warrior—sewn on the sweater. At the moment he found the symbol ironic, considering the subject matter he intended to broach. Dr. Heisman's historical expertise concerned the relationship between the burgeoning American colonies and the indigenous people the colonists had found living in the New World. It was just such an expert Gray needed to further his investigation.

"If you'll follow me," Heisman said, "I've reserved a research room near the main stacks. My assistant will pull whatever records you need." He glanced back at them as they crossed the entry hall. "This is quite unorthodox. Even clerks for the Supreme Court know better than to request records outside of regular hours. It would have been easier if you'd informed me about the specific matter that you required to be researched."

The curator looked ready to chastise them some more, but his glance happened to settle on to Seichan's face. Whatever he saw there silenced any further complaints. He swung swiftly away.

Gray looked at her. She met his gaze and lifted a single brow, her countenance innocent. As she turned away, he noted a small scar under her right ear, half hidden by a fall of black hair. He was sure it was new.

Wherever her investigations into the Guild had taken her, it had plainly been a hard path.

Following the curator through a maze of halls, they ended up in a small room dominated by a conference table and lined with microfiche readers along one wall. Gray found two people already waiting there. One was a young college-aged woman with flawless ebony skin. She could have stepped out of the pages of a fashion magazine. The black pencil dress that hugged her figure only accentuated her appearance. Her perfectly made-up face suggested she hadn't been lounging at home when she was suddenly called to work.

"My assistant, Sharyn Dupre. She's fluent in five languages, but her native tongue is French."

"Pleasure to meet you," she said, her voice silkily deep, tinged with a slight Arabic accent.

Gray shook her hand. *From Algeria,* he surmised from her lilting accent. Though the North African country had shaken off the yoke of the French colonists in the early sixties, the language still persisted among its people.

"Sorry to keep you waiting," Gray said.

"No trouble at all," came a gruff response from the far side of the table. The other figure waiting for them was well known to Gray. Monk Kokkalis sat with his feet up on the table, dressed in sweats and a ball cap. His face shone brightly under the fluorescents. He cocked his head toward the slender assistant. "Especially considering the company at hand."

The assistant bowed her head shyly, a ghost of a smile on her lips.

Monk had beaten them to the National Archives. Of course Sigma command was only a short walk across the National Mall from here. Kat had insisted that her husband join Gray this evening. Though Gray suspected the assignment had more to do with getting Monk out from under her feet than with offering backup for this investigation.

They all took seats at the table, except for Heisman, who remained standing, clasping his hands behind his back. "Perhaps now you could tell me why we've all been summoned here at such a late hour."

Gray opened the manila file in front of him, slipped out the letter, written in French, and slid it across the table toward Sharyn. Before she could touch it, Heisman swooped in and took it with one hand while securing his reading glasses in place with the other.

"What's this?" he asked, his head nodding up and down as he scanned the handful of pages. He plainly did not read French, but his eyes widened as he recognized the signature at the bottom of the letter. "Benjamin Franklin." He glanced to Gray. "This appears to be in his own handwriting."

"Yes, that's already been verified and the letter translated—"

Heisman cut him off. "But this is a photocopy. Where's the original?"

"That doesn't matter."

"It does to me!" the curator blurted out. "I've read everything ever written by Franklin. But I've never seen anything like this. These drawings alone . . ." He slapped a page on the table and stabbed at one of the hand-drawn sketches.

It showed a bald eagle, wings outspread, gripping an olive branch in one claw and a bundle of arrows in the other. Clearly it was still a work in progress. Hen-scratched side notes, indecipherable, pointed here and there at the figure.

"This appears to be an early rendition of the Great Seal of the United States. But this letter is dated 1778, years before this draft of the Seal appeared in the public record around 1782. Surely this is some sort of a forgery."

"It's not," Gray said.

"May I?" Sharyn gently retrieved the pages. "You said you've translated these, but I'd be happy to confirm the accuracy of that work."

"I'd appreciate that," Gray said.

Heisman paced alongside the table. "I'm assuming the content of this letter is what triggered this late-night meeting. Perhaps you could explain why something two centuries old could not wait until morning."

Seichan spoke for the first time. Her voice was quiet, but coldly threatening. "Because blood has been spilled to secure these pages."

Her words sobered Heisman enough to get him to sit down at the table. "Fine. Tell me about the letter."

Gray began, "It was a correspondence between Franklin and a French scientist. A man named Archard Fortescue. He was a member of a scientific group put together by Franklin. The American Society for the Promotion of Useful Knowledge."

"Yes, I'm familiar with the group," Heisman said. "It was an offshoot of the American Philosophical Society, but more specifically geared to the gathering of new scientific ideas. They were best known for their early archaeological investigations into Native American relics. In the end, they became almost obsessed with such things. Digging up graves and Indian mounds all across the colonies."

Sharyn spoke at the curator's elbow. "That is specifically what the letter seems to address," she said. "It is a plea to this French scientist to assist Franklin in mounting an expedition to Kentucky"—she translated the next with her brows pinched together—"'to discover and excavate a serpent-shaped Indian barrow, to search for a threat to America buried there.'"

She glanced up. "There appears to be some urgency to this correspondence." To prove her point, she ran a finger along a passage of the letter, while translating. "'My Dear Friend, I regret to inform you that the hopes for *the Fourteenth Colony—this Devil Colony—are dash'd. The shamans from the Iroquois Confederacy were slaughtered most foully en route to the meeting with Governor Jefferson. With those deaths, all who had knowledge of the Great Elixir and the Pale Indians have pass'd into the hands of Providence. But one shaman did live long enough, buried under the bodies of the others, to gasp out one last hope. He told of a map, mounted within the skull of a horned demon and wrapped in a painted buffalo hide. It is hidden in a barrow sacred to the aboriginal tribes within the territory of Kentucky. Perhaps such talk of demons and lost maps is the phantasm of an addled, dying mind, but we dare not take the chance. It is vital we secure the map before the Enemy does. On that front, we've discovered one clue to the forces that seek to tear asunder our young union. A symbol that marks the enemy.'"*

She flipped the page for them all to see. It depicted drafting compasses atop an L-square, all framing a tiny sickle-shaped moon and a five-pointed star.

She glanced up. "It looks to be a Freemason symbol, but I've never seen such a rendition like this. One with a star and moon. Have you?"

Gray remained silent as Dr. Heisman examined the symbol. The curator gave a slow shake of his head. "Franklin was a Freemason himself. He wouldn't disparage his own order. This must be something else entirely."

Monk leaned over to see the symbol. Though his partner's face remained stoic, Gray picked out the pinching of his nostrils as if he'd just smelled something foul. Like Gray, Monk recognized the mark of the Guild leadership. He met Gray's gaze, the question plain in his eyes: *How could such a symbol be found in a letter from Benjamin Franklin to a French scientist?*

That was the very question Gray wanted answered.

Monk voiced another mystery. "So how come ol' Ben was asking a Frenchman to help in this search? Surely there was someone closer at hand to lead such an expedition into the wilds of Kentucky."

Seichan offered one explanation. "Perhaps he didn't entirely trust those around him. This shadowy enemy he mentions . . . they could have infiltrated the government's inner circles."

"Maybe so," Heisman said. "But France was our ally against the British during the Revolutionary War, and Franklin spent a lot of time in Paris. More important, French colonists had developed close allegiances with Native American tribes during the French and Indian Wars, during which Canadian colonists fought alongside the region's natives against British forces. If Franklin needed someone to investigate a matter sensitive to the Indians of the time, it would not be strange to reach out to a Frenchman."

"The letter seems to confirm this," Sharyn said. She translated another few lines. *"'Archard, as confidant and bosom friend to the deceased Chief Canasatego—whose death by poison I still soundly believe was the dread work of our same Enemy—I could think of no one more fit to head such a vital exploration. This mission must not fail.'"*

Despite the words in the letter, Gray suspected the true answer to Monk's question lay in a combination of both theories. From the ominous tone, Franklin was wary and reaching out to a friend he knew he could trust, someone with close ties to the region's tribes.

"So who's this Canasatego guy?" Monk asked, suppressing a yawn with a fist, but from the sharp glint in his friend's eyes, Gray could see that the yawn was clearly feigned.

Gray understood Monk's interest. The letter suggested that Franklin's shadowy enemies had murdered this Indian chief—and if the symbol on the page was more than coincidence, possibly it was the same enemy against whom Sigma had been battling for years. It seemed impossible, but why else would the Guild have secured and hidden this specific letter, one bearing their mark?

Heisman took a deep breath and some of the officious coldness fell away. "Chief Canasatego," he said with the warmth of someone remembering a close friend. "He's a historical figure few people know about, but one who played a vital role in America's formation. Some consider him a lost Founding Father."

Sharyn explained a bit proudly: "Dr. Heisman has done extensive research on the Iroquois chief. One of his dissertations was vital in getting Congress to pass a resolution concerning the role Native Americans played in the country's founding."

Heisman tried to wave away her praise, but his cheeks grew rosy and he stood a bit straighter. "He's a fascinating figure. He was the greatest and most influential Native American of his time. If he hadn't been struck down so young, there is no telling how different this nation might look, especially regarding its relationship with Native Americans."

Gray leaned back in his chair. "And he was murdered like the letter said?"

Heisman nodded and finally took a seat at the table. "He was poisoned. Historians disagree about who killed him. Some say it was spies of the British government. Others claim it was his own people."

"Seems like ol' Ben had his own theory," Monk added.

Heisman eyed the letter with a hungry look. "It is intriguing."

Gray suspected there would be no further trouble convincing the curator to assist them with their research. The irritated sleepiness in his manner had drained away, leaving behind only avid interest.

"So why was this Iroquois chief so important?" Monk asked.

Heisman reached to the photocopied letter and flipped to the crude representation of the bald eagle with outstretched wings. He tapped the claw that held the bundled arrows. "That's why." He glanced around the table. "Do any of you know why the Great Seal of the United States has the eagle gripping a sheaf of arrows?"

Gray shrugged and shifted the page closer. "The olive branch in one claw represents peace, and the arrows in the other represent war."

A wry grin—his first of the night—rose on the curator's face. "That's a common misconception. But there's a story behind that bundle of thirteen arrows, one that rises from a story of Chief Canasatego."

Gray let the curator speak, sensing he'd get more by letting the man ramble on.

"Canasatego was a leader of the Onondaga nation, one of six Indian nations that eventually joined together to form the Iroquois Confederacy. That unique union of tribes was already centuries old, formed during the 1500s—long before the founding of America. After generations of bloody warfare, peace among the tribes was finally achieved when the disparate nations agreed to band together for their common good. They formed a uniquely democratic and egalitarian government, with representatives from each tribe having a voice. It was government like no other at the time, with laws and its own constitution."

"Sounds darned familiar," Monk added.

"Indeed. Chief Canasatego met with the early colonists in 1744 and presented the Iroquois Confederacy as an example for them to follow, encouraging them to join together for the common good."

Heisman stared around the room. "Benjamin Franklin was in attendance at that meeting and spread the word among those who would eventually frame our own Constitution. In fact, one of the delegates to the Constitutional Convention—John Rutledge of South Carolina—even read sections of Iroquoian law to his fellow framers, reading directly from one of their tribal treaties, which started with the words, 'We, the people, to form a union, to establish peace, equity, and order—'"

"Wait." Monk sat straighter. "That's almost word for word like the preamble of the U.S. Constitution. Are you saying we patterned our founding documents upon some old Indian laws?"

"Not just me, but also the Congress of the United States. Resolution

331, passed in October of 1988, recognizes the influence that the Iroquois Constitution had upon our own constitution and upon our Bill of Rights. While there is some dispute as to the degree of influence, the facts can't be denied. Our Founding Fathers even immortalized that debt in our national seal."

"How so?" Gray asked.

Heisman again tapped the eagle drawing. "At that gathering in 1744, Chief Canasatego approached Benjamin Franklin and gave him a gift: a single feathered arrow. When Franklin expressed confusion, Canasatego took back the arrow and broke it across his knee and let the pieces drop to the floor. Next he presented Franklin with a sheaf of thirteen arrows tied together in leather. Canasatego attempted to break the bundle across his knee like before, but joined as one, they would not break. He presented that bundle to Franklin, the message plain to all. To survive and be strong, the thirteen colonies needed to join together; only then would the new nation be unbreakable. The eagle in the Great Seal holds that same bundle of thirteen arrows in his claw as a permanent—if somewhat secret—homage to the wise words of Chief Canasatego."

As Heisman had been relating this story, Gray kept studying the drawing on the page, nagged by something that seemed amiss. The sketch was plainly crude, with cryptic notations along the sides and bottom, but as he stared closer, he realized what had been troubling him about this early rendition of the Great Seal.

"There are *fourteen* arrows on this drawing," he said.

Heisman leaned over. "What?"

Gray pointed. "Count. There are fourteen arrows clutched by the eagle in this drawing. Not thirteen."

The others stood and gathered closer around.

"He's right," Sharyn said.

"Surely this drawing is just a draft," Heisman said. "An approximate representation of what was intended."

Seichan crossed her arms. "Or maybe it's not. Didn't Franklin's letter mention something about a *fourteenth* colony? What was he talking about?"

A thought formed as Gray stared at the eagle. "The letter also hints at some secret meeting between Thomas Jefferson and the Iroquois nation's leaders." He stared over at Heisman. "Could Jefferson and Franklin have been contemplating the formation of a new colony, a fourteenth one, one made up of Native Americans?"

"A Devil Colony," Monk said, using the other name Franklin employed in the letter. "As in *red devils.*"

Gray nodded. "Maybe that extra arrow in this early drawing represents the colony that never was."

Heisman's eyes glazed a bit as he pondered that possibility. "If so, this may be the single most important historical letter unearthed in decades. But why is there no corroborating evidence?"

Gray put himself in the shoes of Franklin and Jefferson. "Because their efforts failed, and something frightened them badly enough to wipe out all record of the matter, leaving behind only a few clues."

"But if you're right, what were they hiding?"

Gray shook his head. "Any answers—or at least clues to the truth—may lie in further correspondence between Franklin and Fortescue. We need to start searching—"

The jangle of Gray's cell phone cut him off. It was loud in the quiet space. He slipped the phone from his coat pocket and checked the caller ID. He sighed softly.

"I have to take this." He stood and turned away.

As he answered the call, the frantic voice of his mother trembled out, distraught and full of fear. "Gray, I . . . I need your help!" A loud crash sounded in the background, followed by a bullish bellow.

Then the line went dead.

10

Major Ashley Ryan was guarding the gateway to hell.

Fifty yards from his command post, the site of the day's explosion continued to rumble, belching out jets of boiling water and gobbets of bubbling mud. Steam turned the chasm into a burning, sulfurous sauna. In just half a day, the circumference of the blast zone had doubled in size, eroding into the neighboring mountainside. At sunset, a large slab of the neighboring cliff had broken away, like a glacier calving an iceberg. The boulder had crashed into the widening pit. Then as night fell, clouds hid the moon and stars, leaving the valley as dark as any cave.

Now a worrisome, ruddy glow shone from the heart of the pit.

Whatever was happening in there wasn't over.

Because of the danger and instability of the site, the National Guard had cleared all nonessential personnel from the chasm, cordoning off the valley for a full three miles, with men patrolling on foot and a pair of military helicopters circling overhead. Ryan kept a small squad posted on the valley floor. The soldiers all had a background in firefighting and were turned out in yellow Nomex flame-retardant suits, equipped with helmets and rebreathing masks should the air get any worse down here.

Ryan faced the newcomer as he climbed into similar gear. "You think you can tell us what's going on here?" he asked.

The geologist—who had brusquely introduced himself as Ronald

Chin—straightened, cradling a helmet under one arm. "That's why I'm here."

Ryan eyed the scientist skeptically. The man had arrived fifteen minutes ago by helicopter, flown in from Washington, D.C. While Ryan had little respect for government bureaucrats who stuck their noses where they didn't belong, he sensed there was more to this geologist. From the no-nonsense way the man carried himself, along with his shaved head, Ryan suspected the geologist had a military background. After reaching the chasm floor, the government scientist had taken in his surroundings with a single hard-edged glance and began donning firefighting gear even before Ryan could insist that he suit up.

"I should go in alone," Chin warned, and collected a metal work case from the ground.

"Not a chance. While you're here, you're my responsibility." Ryan had been ordered to give the geologist his full cooperation, but this was still his operation. He waved one of his men over. "Private Bellamy and I will escort you to the site and back."

Chin nodded, accepting without argument, earning a tad more respect from Ryan.

"Then let's get this over with." Ryan led the way, thumbing on the LED flashlight mounted on his shoulder. The others followed his example, like a team about to explore an unknown cavern.

As they ventured into the dark woods, the air grew hotter with each step, stinging with sulfur. All three men quickly donned their helmets and masks. Still, the heat fought them like a physical wall. Steam condensed on their faceplates and clouded the view ahead. The canned air tasted metallic in his mouth, or maybe it was from his own fear. Stepping clear of the forest's edge, Ryan drew them all to a stop. He hadn't realized the deteriorating state of the blast zone.

Ahead, the valley floor dropped into a shallow declivity, roughly circular in shape, stretching thirty yards across and worn deep into the cliff face to the left. Closer by, the rocky edge still continued to crumble into gravel and coarse sand, slowly expanding the pit. Beyond the rim, the pit itself sloped downward, full of fine rock dust, until near the center it dropped precipitously into a deep, steaming hole.

Water boiled down that dark throat, aglow with subterranean fires. A tremor shook underfoot, and a geyser of superheated water and steam jetted into the night sky, accompanied by a sonorous roar. They all backed away warily.

Once the fountain died out, Chin crossed to within a yard of the crater. "The blast has definitely broken into the geothermal strata under our feet," he said, his voice muffled by his mask. "This entire region sits atop a volcanic hotbed."

Ryan followed with Bellamy to the rim of the pit. "Careful of the edge. It can give way."

Chin nodded, stepped warily to the lip, then dropped to a knee and opened his portable case. Inside, meticulously organized, was a slew of scientific tools and chemicals, along with rock hammers, containers, brushes, and picks.

The geologist spoke as he prepared a series of collection kits. "I need several samples of the detritus and silt, starting from the periphery and working toward the middle." He freed a hammer and chisel and held them out. "If one of you could chip a piece of granite near the lip, that would speed things up."

Ryan motioned for Bellamy to obey. "Why do you need a chunk of stone?"

"To use as a baseline for the composition of the local bedrock. Something to compare against the samples from the blast zone."

Bellamy took the tools and a small sample bag, crossed a few yards away, and set to work. The young black man had been a linebacker for the Utah State Aggies, but a knee injury had sidelined him. With a wife and a young daughter on the way, he had quit school and joined the Guard. He was a good soldier and knew how to work fast and efficiently.

Chin attached a glass vial to a telescoping aluminum pole. Bending down, he stretched the rod and scooped up a sample of the coarse sand closest to the edge.

While the geologist worked, Ryan stared across the pit. The debris grew even finer out there, becoming a powdery dust near the center, where it seemed to swirl in an hourglass shape, spiraling downward and disappearing into the throat of the steaming hole.

A muffled gasp drew his attention back to Chin. The geologist held his pole out over the pit. He'd been successful in scooping up a sample of the hot sand in the glass vial. Only now the jar's surface was covered in a web of cracks.

Had the heat shattered it?

As Ryan watched, the vial's bottom cracked off, spilling the sample back into the pit. As the chunk of glass hit the surface, it seemed to melt into the powder. No, not *melt*. In a matter of seconds, it dissolved away, vanishing into nothingness.

Chin straightened from his crouch. He still held aloft the pole with the remnants of the broken vial clamped at its end. As both he and Ryan stared, the rest of the container crumbled into a fine glassy powder and sifted into the pit. Even the tip of the aluminum rod began to disintegrate, working slowly down its length. Before it could travel more than a few inches, Chin tossed the pole into the pit. It impaled the powdery surface like a javelin—then continued to sink as if into quicksand.

Ryan knew it wasn't just sinking.

"It's denaturing," Chin said, amazement countering Ryan's terror. "Whatever's going on here, it's breaking down matter. Maybe at the atomic level."

"What the hell's causing it?"

"I have no idea."

"Then how do we stop it?"

Chin only shook his head. Ryan pictured the process continuing to spread like a cancer over the mountains, digging ever deeper at the same time. He remembered the geologist's words, describing what lay beneath his feet.

This entire region sits atop a volcanic hotbed.

As a reminder, the ground gave another violent shake, much worse than before. The geyser spouted again, reaching as high as the treetops, casting out a wall of superheated air.

Chin shielded his face with an arm while pointing the other man back toward the Guard post. "This is far too unstable! You need to evacuate this chasm. Retreat at least a mile."

Ryan had no intention of arguing. He yelled to Bellamy, who still stood a few yards away with a hammer and chisel. "Forget that! Get the men ready to move out! Gather all our gear!"

Before the big man could take a step, another boulder broke off the cliff face behind the private and crashed into the pit. Damp powder splashed outward. Several black splotches struck Bellamy on the lower right leg.

"Get back from there!" Ryan ordered.

Needing no urging, Bellamy trotted toward them. By the time he reached them, his face was a mask of pain. He hobbled on his right leg.

"What's wrong?" Ryan asked.

"Leg's on fire, sir."

Ryan glanced down. The flame-retardant trousers should have protected his skin against any burn from the splatter of hot powder.

"Get him on the ground!" Chin barked out. "Now!"

Ryan jumped, responding to the command in the geologist's voice. He reached for Bellamy's shoulder, but the private suddenly screamed, toppling as his right leg crumpled under him. The limb cracked midshin, breaking sideways.

Ryan managed to catch him and lower him to the ground.

"Fuuuuck," the private yelled, writhing in agony.

Ryan didn't admonish the cursing. He felt like doing the same himself. What the hell was happening?

Chin knelt by Bellamy's legs. He had a blade in hand, a military KA-BAR knife. He slit the private's trouser leg from knee to ankle, revealing an ugly compound fracture midshin. A splintered chunk of tibial bone poked out of his calf, stark white against the man's dark skin. Blood seeped, but not as much as Chin had anticipated.

"He's contaminated," Chin said.

Ryan struggled to understand what that meant—then as he watched, the sharp end of shattered bone began to turn to dust before his eyes. The skin along the edges of the wound retreated, dissolving away from the wound. Ryan pictured the splash of powder hitting Bellamy and remembered the word the geologist had used a moment ago.

Denaturing.

The powder must have eaten through Bellamy's suit and set to work on his leg.

"Wh-what do we do?" Ryan stammered.

"Get an ax!" Chin ordered.

It wasn't the force of command that got Ryan moving this time, but the fear in the geologist's voice. Chin had already cut away the stained piece of fabric, careful not to touch it, and tossed it into the pit. If Ryan had any doubt as to Chin's plan, it was dispelled when the geologist yanked off his belt and began preparing a tourniquet.

Bellamy also understood, letting out a low moan. "Noooo . . ."

"It's the only way," Chin explained to the private. "We can't let it spread up your leg."

He was right. As Ryan ran toward his camp, he remembered the question he'd posed earlier, picturing the expanding crater. *How do we stop it?*

He had his answer.

At great cost.

All they could do for now was damage control.

In less than a minute, he returned with an ax, collected from the camp's firefighting gear, along with two of his men. By the time they arrived, Chin already had his belt cinched around Bellamy's thigh. The private lay on his back, pinned at the shoulders by the geologist. Behind his mask, Bellamy's face shone with terror and pain.

Gasps rose from the other two soldiers.

Ryan understood. Bellamy's leg looked like a shark had taken a bite out of the calf. Only meat and skin still held the appendage together. The rest had been eaten away by whatever had contaminated him.

Chin met Ryan's gaze as the other two soldiers took his place. The geologist glanced from the ax to Bellamy. "Do you want me to do this?"

Ryan shook his head. *He's my man. My responsibility.* He hefted up his ax. He had only one question for the geologist. "Above or below the knee?"

He found the answer in the grim expression on Chin's face. They dared take no chances.

Heaving with all his strength, he swung the ax down.

11

Painter Crowe forced his fingers to loosen their death grip on the armrests of his seat. The race from Salt Lake City to the university town of Provo had challenged even his steely resolve. He had tried to distract himself by placing a call to his girlfriend, Lisa, to let her know he'd landed safely, but as they raced down the highway, dodging around slower traffic, often swerving wildly into the opposite lanes, he had wondered if perhaps that call had been premature.

Kowalski finally killed the engine on the Chevy Tahoe and checked his watch. "Twenty-eight minutes. That means you owe me a cigar."

"I should've listened to Gray." Painter shoved the door open and almost fell out. "He told me to keep you away from anything with wheels."

Kowalski shrugged and climbed out, too. "What does Gray know? Guy spends most of his time pedaling around D.C. on that bike of his. If God had wanted men to ride bikes, He wouldn't have put our balls where they are."

Painter stared over at Kowalski. Dumbfounded and at a loss for words, he simply shook his head and headed across the parking lot with Kowalski in tow. The larger man wore an ankle-length black duster, which allowed him to hide the Mossberg pump-action shotgun strapped to his leg. To blunt its lethality in the urban environment, the weapon was equipped with Taser XREP shells—wireless, self-contained slugs that delivered a paralyzing jolt of electricity into their targets.

It was a wise precaution, considering the man who was wielding that weapon.

At this late hour, the campus of Brigham Young University was quiet. A few students walked briskly down the sidewalks, bundled against the chilly wind blowing off the snow-crowned mountains surrounding the city. A couple glanced curiously their way, then moved on.

Ahead, streetlamps shone warmly along wooded walkways, and a tall bell tower loomed in the distance. University buildings, mostly dark, spread outward in all directions, while a few still glowed brightly with late-night classes.

Painter checked the campus map he'd pulled up on his cell phone. Professor Kanosh had asked them to rendezvous at a lab in the earth sciences building. Gaining his bearings, Painter led the way.

The Eyring Science Center was situated along a tree-lined path off of West Campus Drive. It was hard to miss the large domed observatory resting atop it. A wide staircase led up three levels to its massive glass facade.

Once they were through the doors, Kowalski frowned as he eyed the cathedral-like lobby, whose main feature was a giant Foucault's pendulum suspended from the ceiling, weighted down with a giant brass sphere. To the side a small café—closed at this hour—was shadowed by a giant life-sized allosaurus nestled amid tall ferns.

"So where now?" Kowalski asked.

"We're to meet at a physics lab in the basement."

"Why down there?"

That was a good question. It was an unusual place to meet a historian, but Professor Kanosh had mentioned something about some tests being run for him. No matter, it was still a remote and quiet place for them to meet. Painter checked a directory, then crossed to a stairway leading down. The Underground Physics Research Laboratory truly lived up to its name. The lab wasn't just in the building's basement; it was buried under the lawn on the north side of the building.

As they crossed into the complex, it wasn't difficult to find the specific lab, deserted as the facility was now. Raised voices echoed down the hall from an open doorway.

Painter hurried forward, fearing someone had already found Kai and Professor Kanosh. As he entered the room, he reached for the shoulder-holstered pistol under his suit jacket. He was on alert as he took in another man, who seemed to be threatening Professor Kanosh with a dagger—but Painter let his arm drop away from his holster as he fully absorbed the situation. The man with the knife was wearing a white lab coat, and the dagger looked old, possibly an archaeological artifact. Furthermore, Professor Kanosh was showing no fear, only irritation. Clearly the other man was a colleague, one who seemed determined to make a point.

"This may be the very proof we've been looking for!" he said, slapping the dagger on the tabletop. "Why are you so obstinate?"

Before Professor Kanosh could answer, the two men noted Painter's sudden arrival as he swept inside. Their eyes widened and grew even rounder as the hulking form of Kowalski followed him into the room.

The two colleagues were seated at a long table in the center of an expansive lab. A few lights glowed deeper in the facility, revealing an array of equipment. Some Painter recognized from his own background in electrical engineering and design: mass spectrometers, various solenoids and rheostats, resistance and capacitance boxes. One piece of equipment drew his eyes. In a neighboring alcove, the tall column of an electron microscope hummed alongside a series of glowing monitors.

"Uncle Crowe?"

The question came from the shadows alongside the microscope array. A young woman stepped tentatively into the light, her arms wrapped around her chest, her shoulders slumped. She stared up at him through a fall of long black hair.

It was his niece Kai.

"Are you all right?" Painter asked. It was a stupid question considering the circumstances.

She shrugged, mumbled something under her breath, and joined Professor Kanosh at the table. Painter tracked her. *So much for the warm family reunion.* Then again, it had been over three years since he'd last seen Kai. It had been at her father's funeral. In that short span of time, she had grown from a gangly girl to a young woman, but in her face, he could see that she had also grown harder, far more than she should have grown in only three years.

He could guess why. He recognized that guarded stare all too well, half challenging, half wary. Orphaned himself, he knew what it was like to be raised alone, taken in by an extended family that still held you at arm's length and shuttled you from one home to another.

It was that knowledge that tightened Painter's chest. He should have done more for her when he had the chance. If he had, maybe they wouldn't be standing here now.

"Thank you for coming," Professor Kanosh said, cutting through the tension. He waved Painter to the table. "Maybe with your help we can clear up this mess."

"I hope so." Painter eyed the professor's colleague, not sure how freely he could speak in front of him.

Recognizing his rudeness, the man held out his hand. Still, it was less a welcome than a challenge. While the man looked to be as old as Professor Kanosh, his gray hair had thinned to wisps atop his head, and where the sun had baked Kanosh's skin to hard leather, his colleague's face sagged and hung loose, bagging heavily under his eyes. Painter wondered if the man might have had a stroke in the past year or so. Or maybe it was simply a matter of being holed up in this basement lab for most of his working career, far from sunlight and fresh air.

Painter could relate to the wear and tear that put upon a body.

"Dr. Matt Denton," the man said. "Chair of the physics department."

They all shook hands. Painter introduced Kowalski as his "personal aide," which caused the big man to roll his eyes.

Professor Kanosh was polite enough not to question it. "Please call me Hank," he said, perhaps sensing Painter's guardedness. "I've explained our situation to Matt. I trust him fully. We've been friends since high school, going back to when we first served together on a church mission."

Painter nodded. "Then why don't you explain the situation again to me."

"First, let me assure you. I don't think Kai had anything to do with the blast. The explosive charges she dropped were not the source of that tragedy."

Painter heard the catch in his voice at the end. He knew the professor had been close to the anthropologist who had died. Kai placed a hand on the older man's arm, seeming both to thank him and to console him at the same time.

Kowalski rumbled under his breath, "Told you it wasn't C4 . . ."

Painter ignored him and faced the professor. "Then what do you think caused the explosion?"

The professor stared at him full in the face as he answered. "Simple." His next words were firm with conviction. "It was an Indian curse."

10:35 P.M.

Rafael Saint Germaine allowed himself to be assisted from the helicopter. Rotor wash flattened the spread of manicured lawn surrounding the landing site. While other men might blush at needing such help, he was well accustomed to it. Even the short hop from the height of the cabin to the helipad risked breaking a bone.

Since birth, Rafe—as he preferred to be addressed—had suffered from *osteogenesis imperfecta,* also known as brittle bone disease, an autosomal defect in collagen production, leaving him thin-boned and short in stature. Due to a slight hunch from mild scoliosis and a clouding of his dark eyes, most took him to be decades older than his thirty-four years.

Yet he was no invalid. He kept himself fit enough with calcium and bisphosphonate supplements, along with a series of experimental growth hormones. He also exercised to the point of obsession, making up in muscle for what he lacked in bones.

Still, he knew his greatest asset lay not in bone or muscle.

As he was lowered from the helicopter's cabin, he raised his eyes to the night sky. He could name every constellation and each star that composed them. His memory was eidetic, photographic, retaining all the knowledge that crossed his path. He often considered his fragile skull as nothing more than a thin shell enclosing a vast black hole, one capable of sucking in all light and wisdom.

So despite his disability, his family had had high hopes for him. He'd had to live up to those expectations, to make up for his shortcomings. Because of his defect, he had been mostly pushed aside, kept hidden away, but now he was needed at this most auspicious moment, offered a chance to bring great honor to his family.

It was said the Saint Germaine lineage traced back to before the French Revolution, and that much of the family fortune came from war profiteering. And while this continued through to modern times, the family company now extended into a multitude of businesses and enterprises.

Rafe, with his exceptional mind, oversaw the Saint Germaines' research-and-development projects, sequestered and isolated in the Rhône-Alpes region near the city of Grenoble. The area was a hotbed for all manner of scientific pursuits, a melting pot of industry and academic research. The Saint Germaine family had its fingers in hundreds of projects across various labs and companies, mostly specializing in microelectronics and nanotechnology. Rafe alone held thirty-three patents.

Still, he knew his place, knew the darker history of his family, of its ties to the True Bloodline. He fingered the back of his head, where, hidden under a drape of hair, there was a freshly shaved spot, still tender from a recently drawn tattoo. It inked his family's role—his pledge—to that black heritage.

Rafe lowered his hands, staring out. He also knew how to take orders. He had been summoned here, given specific instructions, reminded of the cold trail of history that had led to this moment. It was his chance to truly make a mark in this world, to prove himself and bring untold riches and honor to his family.

As the helicopter door closed behind him, he caught his reflection in the glass. With his black hair cut rakishly long and his fine aristocratic features darkened by a perpetual shadow of beard, some considered him handsome. He'd certainly had his share of women.

Even the strong arms that assisted him out of the helipad belonged to a member of the fairer sex—though few would call his caretaker "fair." *Fearsome* would be the better term for her. He allowed himself a shadow of a smile. He would share this observation with her later.

"*Merci,* Ashanda," he said as she let go of his arm.

One of his men came forward with his cane. He took it and leaned on it, waiting for the rest of his team to offload.

Ashanda stood stolidly at his side. More than six feet tall and with skin as black as shadows, she was both nurse and bodyguard, and as close a member of his family as anyone who shared the Saint Germaine bloodline. His father had found her as a child on the streets of Tunisia. She was mute, a result of having her tongue cut out; she'd been brutalized and sold for sex—until she was rescued by his father. He had killed the man who offered her to him as he passed along the street on business. After that, he stole her back to the family château outside the fortified French city of Carcassonne, where she was introduced to a boy in a wheelchair, becoming both pet and confidante to that fragile child.

A scream echoed over to Rafe. He stared across the rolling lawn to a dark mansion—on whose grounds they'd landed. He didn't know who owned this estate, only that it was convenient to his plans. The home sat on the slope of Squaw Peak overlooking the city of Provo. He had handpicked this spot because of its proximity to Brigham Young University.

A muffled gunshot silenced the cry from the mansion.

There could be no loose ends.

His second-in-command, a German mercenary named Bern, formerly a member of the special forces of the Bundeswehr, stepped before him, dressed all in black. He was tall, blond, blue-eyed, Aryan from head to toe, a mirror image to Rafe's darker self.

"Sir, we're ready to proceed. We have the targets isolated in one of the campus buildings with all access points watched. We can take them on your orders."

"Very well," Rafe said. He despised using English, but it had become the common language among mercenaries, fittingly enough considering the crudeness and lack of true subtlety of the tongue. "But we need them alive. At least long enough to secure the gold plates. Is that understood?"

"Yes, sir."

Rafe pointed his cane toward the campus. He pictured the girl and the older man, fleeing on horseback. While his team had been outfoxed by a clever ploy, it was only a momentary setback. From video of that hunt and by means of facial-recognition software, he'd identified the Indian on horseback. It hadn't taken long to determine that the historian had returned to where he felt the safest, to the bosom of his university. Rafe smiled at such simplemindedness. While the pair had escaped his snare once, that would not happen again.

"Move out," he ordered, and hobbled toward the mansion. "Bring them to me. And do not fail this time."

10:40 P.M.

"What do you mean by *an Indian curse*?" Painter asked.

Professor Kanosh held up a palm. "Hear me out. I know how that sounds. But we can't dismiss the mythology surrounding that cavern. For ages, the Ute elders, those who passed shamanic knowledge from one generation to another, claimed that anyone who entered that sacred burial chamber risked bringing ruin to the world for their trespass. I'd say that's pretty much how it unfolded."

Kowalski made a scoffing noise deep in his throat.

The professor shrugged. "I think there must have been a kernel of truth in those old stories. A proverbial warning against removing anything from that cave. I believe that something unstable was hidden there for centuries, and our attempt to transport it out caused it to explode."

"But what could it be?" Painter asked.

Across the table, Kai shifted in her seat. The answer to that question was plainly important to her, too.

"When Maggie and I first lifted the golden skull from its pedestal, I found it to be unusually cold, and I felt something shift inside it. I think

Maggie felt it, too. I suspect something was hidden inside that totem, something valuable enough that it was sealed inside a fossilized skull."

A corner of Kowalski's lips curled in distaste. "Why pick a skull for that?"

The professor explained: "In many Indian gravesites, prehistoric fossils have been found buried with the dead and were clearly revered. In fact, it was an Indian who first showed the early colonists the location of rich fossil beds, where the remains of mastodons and other extinct beasts sparked the imagination of the scientists of that era. There were heated debates among the colonists, some even involving Thomas Jefferson, about whether such beasts still lived out west. So if these ancient Indians needed a vessel to secure something they considered sacred—and possibly dangerous—a prehistoric skull would not be an unexpected choice."

"Okay," Painter said. "Assuming you are correct, what might that be? What were they hiding?"

"I have no idea. At this point, it has yet to be determined if the mummified bodies found in the cavern are even Native Americans."

At Painter's side, the physics professor cleared his throat. "Hank, tell him about the carbon-14 dating of the remains."

Painter's gaze shifted from one professor to the other.

When Kanosh was slow to answer, Professor Denton spoke in a rush, impatient and excited. "The archaeology department dated the bodies to the early *twelfth* century. Well before any Europeans ever set foot in the New World."

Painter didn't understand the significance of this information or why Denton seemed so worked up about it. The dating simply lent credence to the fact that the bodies were Native American.

Denton reached to the table and slid the old dagger toward Painter. He remembered the physics professor gesturing with the same blade earlier.

"Take a closer look at this," Denton said.

Painter took the knife and flipped it over in his hands. The hilt was yellowed bone, but the blade looked to be steel, with a handsome, almost watery sheen across its surface.

"The dagger was recovered from the cave," Kanosh explained.

Painter looked up sharply.

"The local boy who escaped the chamber after the murder-suicide fled with this knife in hand. Afterward, we confiscated it from him, as it's illegal to remove relics from an Indian burial site. But the unusual nature of the blade required further investigation."

Painter understood. "Because Indians of that time didn't have the technology to make steel."

"That's right," Denton said, staring significantly at Kanosh. "Especially this *type* of steel."

"What do you mean?" Painter asked.

Denton returned his focus to the dagger. "This is a rare form of steel, identifiable alone by its unusual wavy surface pattern. It's known as Damascus steel. Such metal was forged only during the Middle Ages in a handful of foundries in the Middle East. Legendary swords made from this steel were prized above all others. It was said they held the sharpest edge and were all but unbreakable. Yet the exact method of their forging was kept secret and eventually lost sometime during the seventeenth century. All attempts to replicate it failed. Even today—while we can produce steel as hard, if not harder—we still can't make Damascus steel."

"Why's that?"

Denton pointed to the towering electron microscope humming in the neighboring alcove. "To make sure my initial assessment was correct, I examined the steel at the molecular level. I was able to verify the presence of cementite nanowires and carbon nanotubes within the metal. Both are unique characteristics of Damascus steel and give the material its high resilience and toughness. Universities around the world have been studying samples of this steel, trying to figure out how it was made."

Painter fought to make sense of this news. He was familiar with nanowires and nanotubes. Both were by-products of modern nanotechnology. Carbon nanotubes—artificially created cylinders of carbon atoms—demonstrated extraordinary strength and were already being incorporated in commercial products from crash helmets to body armor. Likewise, nanowires were long, single chains of atoms that showed unique electrical properties and promised coming breakthroughs in microelectronics and computer-chip development. Already the nanotech industry had grown into a multibillion-dollar industry and was continuing to expand at a blistering pace.

All of which raised a question in Painter's mind. He pointed to the strange dagger. "Are you suggesting these medieval sword makers were capable of manipulating matter at the atomic level, that they'd cracked the nanotech code way back in the Middle Ages?"

Denton nodded. "Possibly. Or at least, *someone* knew something. Other traces of ancient nanotechnology have been found. Take, for example, the stained-glass windows found in medieval churches. Some of the ruby-colored glass in those old churches can't be replicated today, and now we know why. Examination of the glass at the atomic level reveals the presence of gold nanospheres, whose creation still defies modern science. Other such examples have been discovered, too."

Painter struggled to put this all together in his head. He picked up the knife. "If you're right about all of this, how could this dagger be found here in America, buried among bodies dated to the twelfth century?"

He noted a shared glance between Denton and Kanosh. The Indian historian gave the smallest shake of his head toward the physicist. The man seemed anxious to say more, his face reddening with the effort to remain silent. Eventually he glanced away. Painter recalled the angry words he'd overheard as he entered the lab: *This may be the very proof we've been looking for! Why are you so obstinate?*

It seemed the two scientists had further speculations on the matter, but for the moment they were reluctant to share them with an outsider. Painter didn't press the subject. He had a more immediate question to broach first.

Turning, he faced Kai. "So tell me more about the men who were hunting you. The ones in the helicopter. Why do you think they were trying to kill you?"

Kai seemed to shrink into herself. She glanced to the professor, who gave her a kindly nod of reassurance. When she spoke, there remained an edge of defiance in her voice.

"I think it's because of what I stole," she said. "From the burial cave."

"Show him," Kanosh said.

From inside her jacket, she slipped out two gold tablets, each about eight inches square and a quarter inch thick. One of the pair appeared to be freshly polished; the other remained coated in a black tarnish. Painter noted some writing inscribed on the surface of the plates.

Kanosh explained. "There appeared to be hundreds of such tablets in the cave, secured in stone boxes and wrapped in juniper bark. Kai stole three of the plates as she made her escape."

"But there are only *two* here."

"That's right. She dropped one as she fled the cave, in full view of the cameras."

Painter let that sink in. "You think someone saw it. And they came looking to see if she had more gold."

"If it is gold," the physics professor added.

Painter turned to Denton.

"Like the dagger, I examined one of the plates under the electron microscope. While the tablets appear gold in *color,* the metal is harder than it should be. Much harder. Normally, gold is a relatively soft, pliable metal, but these tablets are as hard as gemstones. Microscopic analysis of the metal revealed an unusually dense atomic structure, made up of macromolecular structures of gold atoms fitted tightly together like a jigsaw puzzle. And the whole matrix seems to be held in place by the same cementite nanowires found in the dagger." He shook his head. "I've never seen anything like it. Their value is incalculable."

"And apparently worth killing for," Painter added.

With those words, the lights suddenly went out. Everyone froze, holding their breaths. A few battery-powered emergency signs glowed from the hallway, but cast little light into the laboratory. A low canine growl rose from underneath the table, raising the hairs on Painter's arms. As his eyes adjusted to the darkness, he spotted a stocky, shadowy shape slip around the foot of Kanosh's chair, keeping guard.

"Hush, Kawtch," the professor warned in a soft voice. "It's all right, boy."

Kowalski let out a loud huff. "Sorry, Doc. But this time I think you should be listening to your dog. There ain't nothing *right* about any of this."

Kai crept from her own seat and circled to stand in Painter's shadow. He reached back and took hold of her wrist. Under his fingertips, he felt her pulse quicken as something loud crashed off in the direction of the stairwell, echoing down the corridors.

The dog, Kawtch, growled again.

Painter whispered to the physics professor. "Is there another way out of here? An emergency exit."

"No," came his hushed, scared response. "The lab is underground for a reason. All exits are by the stairwell and lead up to the main building."

So we're trapped.

12

May 31, 1:12 A.M.
Takoma Park, Maryland

"Take the next left," Gray instructed the cabdriver.

To Seichan, Gray's anxiety was plain to read. After getting that frantic call from his mother, he remained wound up tight.

Leaning forward from the back and pointing with an outthrust arm, he looked like he wanted to climb over the seat and take the wheel himself. His other hand still clutched his cell phone. He'd tried calling his parents' house several times during the ride from D.C. out to the Maryland suburbs, but there had been no answer, which only set him further on edge.

"Turn on Cedar," he ordered. "It's faster."

As he perched on the edge of his seat, Seichan stared out the window. The taxi sidled past the Takoma Park library and swung into a shadowy maze of narrow streets lined by small Queen Anne–style cottages and stately Victorians. A heavy canopy of oaks and maples turned the roads into leafy tunnels, whose bowers muffled the glow of the occasional streetlamp.

She watched the dark houses and tried to imagine the lives of the people inside, but such an existence was foreign to her. She remembered little of her own childhood in Vietnam. She had no memory of her father, and what she remembered of her mother she wished she could forget: of being ripped from her arms, of her mother being dragged out a door, bloody-faced and screaming, by men in military uniforms. Afterward, Seichan spent her childhood in a series of squalid orphanages, half starved most of the time, maltreated the rest.

These quiet homes with their happy lives held no meaning for her.

At last, the taxi turned onto Butternut Avenue. Seichan had been to the home of Gray's parents only once. At the time she'd been shot and fleeing toward the only man she could trust. She glanced over to Gray. It had been almost three months since she'd been this close to him. His face, if anything, had grown more gaunt, his features detailed in harsher lines, softened only by full lips. She remembered kissing those same lips once, in a moment of weakness. There had been no tenderness behind the act, only desperation and need. Even now, she remembered the heat, the roughness of his bearded stubble, the hardness of his hold on her. But like the quiet homes here, such a life was not for her.

Besides, the last she knew, he was still casually and intermittently involved with a lieutenant in the Italian carabiniere. At least, that was the case months ago.

Gray's eyes suddenly pinched in worry, revealing the deep-set creases at the corners. She faced forward. The street was as dark as the others in the neighborhood, but ahead, a small Craftsman bungalow with a wide porch and overhanging gable blazed with light, every window aglow. No one was sleeping there.

"That's the house," Gray instructed the driver.

Even before the cab pulled to a full stop, he was out the door, tossing a fistful of bills at the driver. Seichan met the cabbie's eyes in the rearview mirror. He looked ready to respond harshly at such rude treatment, but she stared him down, silencing him. She held out a palm.

"Change."

She left him a small tip, pocketed the rest, and climbed out.

She followed Gray as he hurried across the street, but his goal was not the front porch. To the side of the house, a narrow driveway stretched to a single-car garage in the back. The roll-up door was open, lights on, revealing two slight figures silhouetted in that glow. No wonder no one had answered the house phone.

Gray stalked quickly down the driveway.

As Seichan drew near the open garage, she heard the whining sound of a saw motor, the bite of steel into wood, smelled the cedar scent of saw-dust.

"Jack, you're going to wake the entire neighborhood," a woman begged plaintively. "Shut things down and come back to bed."

"Mom . . ." Gray hurried forward into the middle of the drama.

Seichan kept a few steps back, but Gray's mother still noted her with a pinch of her brows, trying to identify the stranger who accompanied her son. It had been two years since they'd last set eyes on each other. Slowly, recognition and confusion played across the older woman's face—and not unexpectedly a flash of fear.

Likewise, Seichan was shocked at how aged Gray's parents appeared, frail shadows of their former selves. His mother, her hair disheveled, was dressed in a housecoat, cinched at the waist, and slippers. His father, bare-foot, wore a pair of boxers and a T-shirt, exposing his prosthetic leg, belted at the thigh.

"Harriet! Where's my sander? Why can't you goddamn stay out of my stuff?"

Gray's father was standing at a workbench, his face red with fury, his brow damp with exertion. He struggled to secure a piece of wood into a vise clamp. Behind him, a table saw idled with pieces of oak cut into haphazard sections scattered on the floor beneath it, as if he'd been trying to construct the pieces of a wooden puzzle whose solution only he knew.

Gray stepped forward and unplugged the saw, then crossed to his father and tried to gently guide him away from the workbench. An elbow lashed out, striking Gray in the face. He stumbled back.

"Jack!" his mother yelled.

His father looked around, confused. Realization seemed to sink through whatever fugue state the man was in. "I'm . . . I didn't mean . . ." He placed a palm on his forehead, as if feeling himself for a fever. He reached an arm toward Gray. "I'm sorry, Kenny."

Gray's face flinched a bit. "It's Gray, Dad. Kenny's still in California."

Seichan knew Gray had a brother, his only sibling, who ran some

Internet start-up in Silicon Valley. Gray, his lip split and bleeding, approached his father more cautiously.

"Dad, it's me."

"Grayson?" He allowed his son to take his arm. Eyes, red-rimmed and exhausted, stared around the garage. A flicker of fear passed over his face. "What . . . where . . . ?"

"It's okay, Dad. Let's go inside."

He sagged, wobbling a bit on his bad leg. "I need a beer."

"We'll get you one."

Gray guided him toward the rear door to the house. His mother hung back, arms crossed tightly over her chest. Seichan stood a few paces off, unsure, uncomfortable.

His mother's gaze, brimming with tears, found her face. "I couldn't stop him," she said, needing to explain to someone. "He woke up all agitated. Thought he was back in Texas and was late for work. Then he came out here. I thought he was going to cut his hand off."

Seichan took a step toward her, but she had no words to comfort the distraught woman. Seeming to sense this, Gray's mother ran her fingers through her hair, took a deep steadying breath, seeming to draw a bit of steel into her back. Seichan had seen Gray do the same many times before, recognizing at this moment the true source of his resiliency.

"I should help Gray get him back to bed." She headed toward the house, crossing close enough to reach out and squeeze Seichan's hand. "Thank you for coming. Gray always shoulders too much alone. It's good that you're here."

His mother headed toward the door, leaving Seichan in the yard. She rubbed the squeezed hand, still warm from the touch. She felt an inexplicable tightness in her chest. Even this small bit of inclusion, this bit of familial closeness, unnerved her.

At the door, Harriet turned toward her. "Do you want to wait inside?"

Seichan backed away. She pointed toward the front of the house. "I'll be on the porch," she said.

"I'm sure it won't be long." With a small, sad smile of apology, she let the door close behind her.

Seichan stood a moment longer, then crossed back to the garage, needing to do something to steady herself. She turned off the light, pulled closed the door, then headed to the front of the house. She climbed the porch and sank onto a bench, bathed in lamplight from the front parlor. She felt exposed, her body limned against such brightness, but no one was about. The avenue remained dark and empty—yet so inviting. She had a momentary desire to flee. The streets were her only true home.

Eventually the lights in the house began to go off, one by one. She heard muffled voices but could not make out the words. It was the slow rumble of family. She waited, trapped between the emptiness of the street and the warmth of the home.

At last, a final light blinked off, sinking the yard into shadows. She heard footsteps; the door opened to the side. Gray came out, letting loose a long sigh.

"Are you okay?" she asked softly.

He shrugged. What else was there to say? He came and joined her. "I'd like to stick around for another half hour or so. Make sure everything stays quiet. I can call you a taxi."

"And go where?" she asked, letting a little black humor blunt the grimness.

Gray sat down next to her, leaning back. He remained silent for a long moment before speaking again. "They call it sundowner's syndrome," he said, plainly venting, or maybe he was trying to make sense of it himself, to give his pain a name. "Dementia symptoms get worse at night for some Alzheimer's patients. Don't really know why. Some say its hormonal changes that occur at night. Others that it's an unloading of the day's accumulated stress and sensory stimulation."

"How often does this happen?"

"Getting to be regular now. Three or four times a month. But he should be fine for the rest of the night. Outbursts like this seem to exhaust him. He should sleep well. And once the sun's up, he does much better."

"And you come out here every time?"

Again that shrug. "As often as I can."

A silence settled over them. Gray looked off into the distance, likely into the future. She suspected he was pondering how long he could keep it up on his own.

Sensing a distraction might do him good, Seichan turned the conversation toward their other problem. "Any word from your partner?"

Gray shook his head. His voice grew firmer; he was on steadier ground with this subject. "No calls. It'll probably take until morning for the archivists to do a thorough search. But I think I figured out why that letter—the one from Franklin to that French scientist—turned up amid all the Guild activity of late."

She sat straighter. It had cost her much, came close to exposing her, to retrieve a copy of that letter.

"According to what you told me," he said, "Franklin's note surfaced twelve days ago."

"That's right."

"That was just after the cave was discovered out in Utah."

"You mentioned that before, but I still don't see the connection."

"I think the crux comes down to two words found in Franklin's letter. *Pale Indians.*"

She shook her head, remembering the line from the letter. She'd read the translation enough times to memorize it.

With those deaths, all who had knowledge of the Great Elixir and the Pale Indians have pass'd into the hands of Providence.

She still didn't understand. "So?"

Gray shifted closer on the bench, as if physically trying to make his point. "Just after the discovery, an investigation began to identify the mummified remains found inside that cavern. Native American groups were claiming rights over the bodies, but ownership was in dispute, as the remains appeared more Caucasian in appearance."

"Caucasian?"

"*Pale* Indians," Gray stressed. "If the Guild—Franklin's old enemy—was involved in the past with some matter concerning white-skinned Indians, the sudden discovery of a cave full of such mummified remains, along with their relics, would certainly draw them out. Back then, Franklin and

Jefferson were clearly searching for *something*, something that they believed threatened the new union. Apparently their enemy was after it, too."

"And if you're right, they're *still* after it," she added. "So what do you think? Did the Guild cause that blast out in Utah?"

"I don't think so. But either way, I've got to brief Director Crowe. If I'm right, he's stepping into the middle of a centuries-old war."

13

As her eyes adjusted to the darkness in the lab, Kai slipped her wrist from her uncle's grip. A weak glow flowed in from the hallway, coming from illuminated emergency signs.

She searched the maze of the dark lab, ready to run. It was her first means of defense. Passed among foster homes, she had quickly learned to read the warning signs around her. It was vital to survival, to sense the mood, to know when to walk warily and when to stand your ground in homes where you were unwanted or barely tolerated.

Professor Kanosh rose up from one knee, where he'd been calming his dog, Kawtch. "Maybe it's just an ordinary power outage," he offered.

Kai latched onto that hope but knew it was desperation. She looked to her uncle for some reassurance.

Instead, Painter crossed to a desktop phone and lifted the receiver. Kai flashed to the old stereotype of an Indian pressing his ears to the ground to listen for signs of danger. This was a modern version of that.

"No dial tone," he said, and replaced the receiver. "Somebody cut the lines."

She crossed her arms, holding tightly. *So much for that hope . . .*

Painter turned to the big man he'd come here with and pointed to the lab's door. "Kowalski, watch the hall. Be ready to barricade the door if necessary."

The hulking man moved to the exit, sweeping aside his long jacket to reveal a shotgun strapped to his leg. Kai was familiar enough with guns from her hunting days with her father, but there was something odd about the weapon, especially the extra shells mounted on the gun's butt. They were spiked at one end. Still, the sight of the shotgun made the situation all the more real. Her heart began to pound harder in her throat, her senses stretching to a keening edge.

"What're we going to do?" Denton asked.

"We should hide," Kai blurted out, fighting back a tremble that threatened to leave her quaking on the floor. She took a step away, seeking the comfort of dark spaces.

Painter stopped her with a hand on her shoulder. He pulled her closer. She didn't resist, leaning against him, but it was like hugging a metal post. He was all hard muscle, bone, and purpose.

"Hiding won't do any good," he explained. "Clearly someone had you all under surveillance. Tracked you here and sent a strike team to flush you out. They'll sweep the place until they find you. Our only hope is that it'll take time to search the main building before they venture down to the underground facility. Until then, we need to find another way out of here."

Kai stared toward the ceiling, picturing the buried lab in her mind's eye. "How about *up*?" she asked, grasping for anything.

Painter gave her an appreciative squeeze. It did much to return some strength to her legs.

"What about that?" he asked the two professors. "Are there any air vents? Service tunnels?"

"Sorry," Denton said, his voice quavering. "I know the entire schematics of this place. There's nothing like that. At least not large enough to crawl through. Only thing above our heads is a foot of reinforced concrete and about a yard of soil, rock, and lawn."

"Still, the kid's idea is a good one." The gruff words came from the doorway, from the man named Kowalski. "How 'bout we make our own exit?"

He tossed something the size of a ripe peach toward her uncle, who caught it one-handed. She felt Painter flinch next to her, then swear under his breath.

11:35 P.M.

Painter stared down at what he held. Though his eyes had somewhat adjusted to the dark, it was still difficult to examine the object—but from the chemical smell and the greasy feel to the claylike substance, there was little doubt of its identity.

He fought through his shock to ask, "Kowalski, what are you doing with C4?"

Kowalski shrugged both shoulders. "Still had it with me from before."

From before?

Painter pinched his brows, thinking back; then he remembered. He recalled the man kneading a fistful of the plastic explosive in his office, as casually as someone squeezing a stress-relieving ball. And maybe it served that purpose for him, as he'd apparently never gotten rid of it.

Painter lowered his arm and shook his head in disbelief. *Leave it to Kowalski to be walking around with a pocketful of explosives.*

Which begged another question.

"I don't suppose you have a blasting cap to go along with it?" he asked.

Kowalski turned his back dismissively, focusing back on the hallway. "C'mon, boss. I can't think of everything."

Painter glanced around at the lab, trying to determine how he could improvise some type of detonator. C4 was notoriously stable. It could be burned, electrocuted, shot with a bullet, and it still would not explode. It took an intense shock wave, like the one caused by an exploding blasting cap, to set it off.

Denton stepped forward and offered a possibility. "The applied physics lab might have what you need. They work in conjunction with the region's mining operations. They keep percussion and blasting caps over there."

"And where's that?"

"Off by the stairwell."

Painter sighed inwardly. Not the direction he wanted to go. It would be dangerous, and risked exposure, but he had little choice. He studied Denton. He hated to involve a civilian, but the underground facility was a maze, and he didn't know where to begin looking for blasting caps in that other lab.

"Professor Denton, would you be willing to come with me? To show me?"

The professor nodded, but he was clearly reluctant.

Next, Painter crossed to Kowalski and handed back the balled-up chunk of explosive. "Find a place to plant this. A roof joist or someplace where we have the best chance to blast a hole to the surface. And get as deep as you can into this facility, as far from the science center as possible."

Painter imagined all the exits were being watched. If his plan worked, he wanted to pop out beyond whatever snare had been set around the building.

Denton pointed. "The rearmost lab is the particle accelerator chamber."

"I know where that's at," Kanosh added. "Straight down at the other end of the hall. Can't miss it. I can take him."

"Good. Bring Kai and your dog, too. All of you hole up down there until we return."

Painter sensed the press of time and quickly calculated in his head what he needed to pull this off. Denton helped him gather the necessary tools. He then crossed back to Kowalski and freed his SIG Sauer pistol from its shoulder holster. He traded his sidearm for the man's Taser-modified shotgun.

"Keep the others protected. Shoot to kill."

Kowalski scowled. "Like I shoot any other way."

Kai shifted to the shadow of the big man, but her eyes were huge on Painter. "Uncle Crowe, be careful . . ."

"That's definitely my plan." Still, he could not escape a feeling of misgiving as he pointed to the door. "Everybody move out."

11:36 P.M.

Seated in a leather desk chair in the mansion's library, Rafe watched his laptop's monitor. It carried live feed from the operation in the field, offering multiple viewpoints via cameras mounted on the black helmets of his mercenaries. It was a jumbling viewpoint that threatened to turn his stomach, but he couldn't look away.

He had watched the initial assault as power and telephone feeds were cut, all exits under close watch. Four shell-shocked students stumbled out of various doors, escaping the dark building. They were quickly dispatched, their bodies whisked into hiding. The assault team continued inside, searching floor by floor for their targets.

He was not surprised that the power loss had failed to flush out his targets as it had the few students. After the events in the mountains, his prey had grown more wary, but his men had been handpicked by Bern for both their thoroughness and ruthlessness. Their targets would be found.

On one corner of the laptop screen, Bern turned his camera toward his own face, indicating he wanted to report in from the field. His voice was a bit choppy from the digital feed. "Sir, all the upper levels are clear. That leaves only the basement. The team's heading down."

"Very good." Rafe drew his face closer to the screen, eager to watch.

So they fled into the cellars, like so many frightened rats. No matter. I've got the best rat catchers money can buy.

A whimper drew his attention to a wingback chair by the fire. Flames danced, casting shadows—but none darker than his black queen, Ashanda, who sat in the chair, holding a small boy, no older than four. The child's face was a ruin of tears and mucus. His eyes were wide with shock and fear. They probably should have moved the body of his mother from the room, but there'd been no time for such niceties. The woman lay on the Persian rug, her blood and brain matter ruining the subtlety of the wool pattern.

Ashanda stared into the flames and gently stroked the boy's hair. One of Bern's men had offered to alleviate the boy's suffering with the swift skill of his blades, but Ashanda had backhanded the muscular mercenary away as if he were a rag doll, in order to protect the child.

Ever the caretaker.

Rafe sighed. The boy would still have to be dealt with, but not when Ashanda was watching.

Until then . . .

He faced the screen, giving it his full concentration.

Back to the show.

11:38 P.M.

Painter worked quickly atop a small bench inside the applied physics lab as Denton held a penlight. The professor had guided him safely here, not far from the stairwell that led up to the main building.

Despite his qualms about involving a civilian, he was glad that Denton had accompanied him. The lab was tucked off the main hall, easy to miss. The long narrow room held a jumble of gear and equipment, dominated by a large cubic press with stainless-steel anvils used for high-pressure studies, as in the creation of synthetic diamonds.

But Painter's goal here was more priceless than any diamond.

Denton had guided him to a locked cabinet. After a breathless fumble of keys, he got it open and passed Painter a box of solid-pack electric blasting caps. "Will this do?" he had whispered, breathless with hope.

It would have to . . . but it still required some improvisation.

Painter concentrated on his work, using tweezers and needle-nose pliers, performing delicate surgery. These types of caps required a jolt of electricity to ignite, like from a cell-phone battery or some other source. And you didn't want to be close by when that cap exploded the C4. He needed a remote way of shocking the blasting cap from a distance—and with no cell-phone reception down here, that left only one other possibility.

With great care, he crimped the cap's fuse wires to the battery leads on the gutted XREP Taser shell. The shotgun shell was the same size as any twelve-gauge round, but its casing was transparent and packed with electronics rather than standard buckshot. Even with his background in electrical engineering and microdesign, Painter held his breath. Any misstep could blow off his fingers.

As he secured the last wire—checking to make sure he didn't disturb the device's transformer and microprocessor—a furtive noise drew his attention toward the lab's door. The telltale tramp of boots on stairs echoed over to them, followed by muffled voices, clipped and terse, definitely military. The search team was headed down here, confident, moving with minimal caution, thinking their targets were nothing more than frightened, unarmed civilians.

Painter quickly reassembled his jury-rigged shell, pocketed it, and grabbed the Mossberg shotgun from where it leaned against the bench. Turning, he whispered and motioned to Denton. "On my signal, you take off for the others. I'll buy us some time."

The professor nodded, but the penlight in his hand shook as he flicked it off.

Painter led the way back to the lab's door and crossed the few steps to the main hall. With Denton hovering behind him, he peeked around the corner. In the wan illumination of emergency signs, he spotted a clutch of men in black commando uniforms gathering at the foot of the stairs. With hand gestures, the team prepared to split: half to search the basement beneath the science building, the others preparing to enter the underground facility that extended north of the center.

Painter didn't have a moment to spare. With a finger to his lips, he waved for Denton to head down the hall, away from the gathering in \ the stairwell. Denton wouldn't be exposed for long. Fifteen feet away, the darkened hall turned abruptly to the left. Once around that corner, the professor had a clear run straight for the others.

Denton seemed to realize this. Hugging the wall, he hurried toward safety. Painter used the Mossberg's ghost-ring sighting system to keep a watch on the assault team. If any of them made an aggressive move in Denton's direction, he intended to drop the man with a sizzling jolt of a Taser round. The surprise of such armed resistance should drive the hunters into momentary cover, hopefully buying Painter enough time to make it around the same corner as Denton before the team regrouped.

Without taking his eyes off the assault team, he listened to the soft tread of Denton's retreating steps. When he reached the corner, a soft double cough sounded from that direction. Painter turned in time to see

Denton's body blown away from the corner and hit the far wall. He slid into a boneless slump, half his face gone.

Painter fought against reacting, going deadly calm, hardened by fury.

A large figure stalked into view from around the corner, a pistol fitted with a silencer smoking in his grip. The man wore black combat gear like the others, his helmet fitted with night-vision goggles. Unlike his teammates, there was nothing sloppy about his manner. The sureness of his movement spoke of command. He must have silently sneaked past Painter's position in the applied physics lab, taking point and scouting ahead on his own. From his wary posture, the fleeing professor must have caught him off guard. The soldier clearly didn't intend to allow that to happen again as he swung toward Painter's direction.

Whether he'd been spotted or not, Painter knew that his only hope lay in taking the offensive. He dove low into the hall. A pistol cracked in his direction—the man was fast, but in his haste, he shot too high.

Painter fired as he slid on one shoulder, the shotgun blast loud in the confined hallway. He hit the man in the upper thigh, marked by a bluish spark of electricity as the Taser ignited. The man gasped, going rigid with a violent tremble of his limbs. As he toppled toward the floor, Painter rolled on his back, pumping the Mossberg with one hand, ejecting the spent cartridge and positioning another.

Leaping to his feet, he fired blindly toward the stairwell and turned away. He heard a shocked cry from that direction, indicating he'd hit someone. He let that small victory fuel his flight down the hall. Reaching the corner, he vaulted over the twitching, agonized body of the ambusher.

As he passed, he caught a glimpse of Denton on the floor, knew he was dead. Guilt flashed through him. The professor had been under his protection. He should never have exposed him like this—but he knew why he had.

He pictured Kai's face, scared, wide-eyed as a doe, looking years younger than eighteen. He'd taken risks he normally wouldn't have dared to take—and another man had paid the price for his recklessness.

Still, for the moment, he had no time for remorse.

As he turned the hall's corner, gunfire spattered behind him. He ducked and fled out of the direct line of fire from the assault team—but such a reprieve wouldn't last for long.

11:39 P.M.

"Get up!" Rafe yelled at the screen.

Through the camera feed, he had watched Bern shoot some white-coated old man in the face, savoring that frozen look of surprise before it vanished in a fog of bone and blood. But that victory was short-lived. A moment later, his second-in-command was on his back. The camera feed revealed a twitching view of the ceiling—then a shadowy figure leaped over Bern's body, carrying a rifle or shotgun in one hand.

Rafe leaned close enough to bring his nose to the screen. He pressed to activate Bern's radio. "Get up!" he repeated.

He didn't so much care if Bern captured the shooter. He just wanted to see what was happening. He leaned back, a tight grin on his face. All of this was quite exciting.

11:40 P.M.

Painter sprinted down the hall. It was a straight run to reach the laboratory at the back of the facility. Ahead, a set of double doors creaked open. He spotted Kowalski spying out, his pistol pointing down the hall toward Painter. He must have heard the gunfire.

Painter yelled, "Get everyone back! Into cover!"

Obeying, Kowalski retreated, but not before he kicked the door wide, opening the way for Painter's headlong flight.

Every second counted.

As he ran, Painter pulled back the shotgun's pump, ejecting the spent cartridge. Cradling the Mossberg under an arm, he freed the jury-rigged shell from his pocket and fumbled it into the empty chamber. Once this was done, he slid the pump forward, pushing the block and firing pin into position.

He would have only one shot.

As he reached the lab door, the crack of a pistol sounded behind him. He felt a burning slice across his upper arm as a bullet grazed him. Glancing back, he saw the downed commando, limbs still twitching, haul himself around the corner. The pistol, wavering in his grip, fired again, but missed.

Painter grimly admitted the truth to himself: *That's one tough bastard.*

Reaching the lab, he dove inside and pulled the door shut behind him. Seconds later, the staccato rounds of an automatic rifle pounded the steel door as the rest of the assault team must have reached the hallway. The gunfire continued without pause.

He had no time.

To make matters worse, he was blind. With the door shut, the laboratory was pitch-black. He skidded deeper into the room, one arm in front to keep from crashing into something.

"Where?" he yelled above the ringing cacophony of the assault.

Ahead, a flashlight ignited, spearing the room with a dazzling brightness. It revealed the others hidden behind the heavy bulk of a Van de Graaff accelerator, part of a larger complex that extended deeper into the cavernous room.

Painter hurried toward them, scanning the roof for the C4.

"Behind you!" Kowalski yelled from his shelter. "Above the door."

Painter swung around and stared up. The flashlight's beam centered on a yellow-grayish glob of explosive crammed into a crevice above the door. It looked like an old stress fracture that had recently been patched. Kowalski had chosen a good spot.

He raised his shotgun—just as the double doors were yanked open in front of him. Gunfire strafed blindly into the room. Painter stumbled away and dropped to his back. A pair of commandos rushed into the lab under the cover of the barrage. Kowalski returned fire from his sheltered position.

Painter caught a glimpse of the soldier he'd Tasered out in the hallway. The guy pointed an arm, barking orders, clearly the leader.

Painter couldn't give him any more attention than that.

From the floor, he lifted his shotgun, centered his aim on the patch of C4, and pulled the trigger. The shotgun blasted, the XREP dart flew out, and a spat of electricity sparked along the roof as it impacted—but nothing else happened.

Kowalski swore, clearly girding himself for the pitched firefight to come.

What had gone wr—

—a deafening *boom* knocked the wind from Painter's lungs and flung his body against the bulk of the accelerator. As he flew back, he watched the two commandos in the room get flattened, pounded first by the shock wave, then buried under a tumble of cement, twisted rebar, and soil.

Smoke and dust rolled across the room, billowing deeply into the facility.

Dazed, he felt his body lifted off the floor. Kowalski had him under one arm, hauling Kai with the other. Ears still ringing, he struggled to get his legs under him. Ahead, slabs of broken debris blocked the doorway, cutting off the hunters. Painter craned up. In the smoke-choked darkness, light flowed down through the roof.

Moonlight, achingly bright.

They'd done it.

11:42 P.M.

Rafe stood before the desk that held his laptop. He folded his fingers atop his head, staring at the ruins of a hallway as his team retreated. He finally let out the long breath he'd been holding.

He lowered his arms, balling both hands into fists.

He glanced to Ashanda, as if silently asking her if she'd witnessed what had happened on the screen. She still sat with the small boy, who looked half comatose from shock.

Rafe could relate.

His heart pounded, firing his blood. While he was certainly angry, a part of him could not help but be impressed.

So our quarry found some help . . . a bodyguard with some skill.

If nothing else, Bern had gotten a good picture of the wily culprit from his helmet-mounted camera, just before the explosion dropped the roof. While the photo was grainy, the camera managed to capture a full view of his face. The new enhancing software and facial-recognition program developed by a Saint Germaine family subsidiary for Europol should make short shrift of identifying the man.

Over the radio, Bern's voice came garbled with digital dropouts. ". . . escaped on foot. Local law enforcement and emergency response teams are already arriving on-site. What . . . orders?"

Rafe sighed, damping down the fire in his blood. It was a shame. With the limits of his body, it wasn't often he got to enjoy such a heady rush of adrenaline. He spoke into his throat mike. "Clear out. The targets won't remain in the area. We'll pick up their trail again."

It sounded like Bern wanted to argue, furious at the loss of his teammates. It must be his Aryan blood, fueling that Germanic desire for immediate revenge. But Bern would have to learn patience. If there was one true source behind the wealth and power of the Saint Germaine family, it came from their knowledge of, appreciation for, and skill in *le long jeu.*

The long game.

And with his unique mind, there was no better player than Rafael Saint Germaine. For others this might be a mere boast, but he'd proven himself time and again. It was why he stood here now, assigned by the family to chase after a treasure going back millennia.

Was there any *longer* game?

After Bern signed off, Rafe crossed back to his laptop and brought up the image of the shadowy intruder into their affairs. Many primitive cultures put great stock in names, believing that to obtain such details granted special powers over others. Rafe believed this down to his crumbling bones.

He leaned on his fists atop the desk and stared at his adversary.

"Vous êtes qui?" he asked the man.

It was a question he desperately wanted to answer.

Who are you?

12:22 A.M.

From the passenger seat of the SUV, Painter watched the lights of Provo vanish into the distance in the rearview mirror. Only now did he let his guard down.

Slightly.

Against his better judgment, Kowalski was again behind the wheel of their rental, in this case, a white Toyota Land Cruiser. Where they were going, a four-wheel-drive vehicle would be needed. Painter wasn't up for the long drive himself. His upper arm still throbbed from the bullet graze, and his head ached from the concussive explosion.

Maybe I'm getting too old for this . . .

He flashed back to his couch at home, Lisa fingering the white lock in his dark hair, noting the gray notes elsewhere. What was he doing out in the field? This was a younger man's game.

Proving this, Kowalski seemed little fazed, nursing a thermos of coffee to keep him alert for the overnight drive. A glance to the backseat revealed Kai leaning on Professor Kanosh, with one hand resting on the old man's dog. Both were asleep, but a pair of canine eyes—one brown, one blue—stared up at him, wary, guarded.

He gave the dog a nod. *Keep an eye on her.*

This earned a weak thump of a tail.

He turned back around, still heavy-hearted. After their escape across campus, he'd had to break the news about the murder of Professor Denton. Kanosh had looked crushed, aging in seconds. He'd lost too many close friends in the span of a day. Only the need to put some distance between them and the hunters had blunted the anguish. So after a quick stop at a CVS pharmacy for first-aid supplies for his wound, they set out of town.

They were headed to some friends of Kanosh, a group of Native

Americans who were living off the grid. Painter wanted to get Kai somewhere safe. Plus he needed answers to his questions about what was really going on out here.

His cell phone vibrated in his pocket. Frowning, he fished it out, checked the caller ID, and raised it to his ear. "Commander Pierce?" He was surprised by the call at this late hour, especially from the East Coast, where it was two hours later. He kept his voice low so as not to disturb the others.

"Director Crowe," Gray said, "I'm glad you're okay. I heard from Kat about the attack. She asked me to give you a call."

"Concerning what?"

Painter had already reached out to Sigma Command. He'd briefed Kathryn Bryant on the events in Utah. She was helping with the aftermath of the blast at the university, while using her resources in both federal law enforcement and various intelligence communities to help identify the team who invaded the physics lab.

Gray explained, "I believe I might have some insight on the attack."

The words sharpened Painter's attention. The last he knew Gray was investigating some lead about the Guild. He had a bad feeling about this.

"What sort of insight?" he asked.

"It's still preliminary. We've barely scratched the surface, but I think some information Seichan obtained is tied to events out in Utah."

Painter listened as Gray told a story of Benjamin Franklin, French scientists, and the pursuit of some threat tied to *pale Indians,* to use Franklin's term for them. He leaned forward as the history unfolded, especially concerning a shadowy enemy of the Founding Fathers, one who used as their trademark the same symbol as the modern Guild.

"I believe the discovery of that cave ignited the Guild's attention," Gray said. "Clearly something important got lost long ago or was hidden from them."

"And now it's resurfaced," Painter added.

It was an intriguing thought, and from the sophistication and brutality of the night's assault, the attack definitely had all the earmarks of the Guild.

"I'll keep working the angle out here," Gray said. "See what I can dig up."

"Do that."

"But Kat wanted me to call you for another reason, too."

"What's that?"

"To pass on news of an anomaly that's reverberating throughout the global scientific community. It seems a group of Japanese physicists have reported a strange spike in neutrino activity. It's off the scales, from what I understand."

"Neutrinos? As in the subatomic particles?"

"That's right. Apparently it takes violent forces to generate a neutrino burst of this magnitude—solar fusion, nuclear explosions, sunspot flares. So this monstrous spike has got the physicists all worked up."

"Okay, but what does this have to do with us?"

"That's just it. The Japanese scientists were able to pinpoint the source of the neutrino spike. They know where the burst came from."

Painter extrapolated the answer. Why else would Gray be calling? "From the blast site in the mountains," he concluded.

"Exactly."

Painter let the shock wash through him. *What did this news mean?* He questioned Gray until they were talking in circles, getting no further. He finally signed off and sank back into his seat.

"What was that about?" Kowalski asked.

Painter shook his head, causing the dull ache behind his eyes to flare. He needed time to think things through.

Earlier, he'd talked to Ron Chin, who had been monitoring the blast site. He reported a strange volatility there, described how the zone remained active, spreading deeper and wider, eating away anything that it came in contact with, possibly denaturing matter at the atomic level.

Which brought Painter's thoughts back to the *source* of the explosion.

Kanosh suspected something hidden inside the golden skull, something volatile enough that just removing it from the cave had caused it to explode. He'd also found evidence that the mummified Indians—if they *were* Indians—possessed artifacts that indicated some sophisticated knowledge of nanotechnology, or at least some ancient recipe for manufacturing that allowed them to manipulate matter at the atomic level.

And now this news of a spike in neutrinos—particles produced by catastrophic events at the *atomic* level.

It all seemed to circle back to nanotechnology, to a mystery hidden amid the smallest particles of the universe. But what did it all mean? If his head wasn't pounding like a snare drum, he might be able to figure it out.

But for the moment he had only one firm sense, a jangling warning.

That the true danger was only starting.

PART II

FIRESTORM

14

"We should tell someone," Jun Yoshida insisted.

With his usual insufferable calmness, Dr. Riku Tanaka merely cocked his head from right to left, like a heron waiting to spear a fish. The young physicist continued to study the data flowing across the monitor.

"It would be imprudent," the small man finally mumbled, as if to himself, lost in the fog of his Asperger's.

As director of the Kamioka Observatory, Jun had spent the entire day buried at the heart of Mount Ikeno, in the shadow of the massive Super-Kamiokande neutrino detector. So had their Stanford colleague, Dr. Janice Cooper. The three of them had been monitoring neutrino activity following the early-morning spike. The source had been pinpointed to a mountain chasm in Utah, where some explosive event had taken place. But the exact details remained sketchy.

Was it a nuclear accident? Was the United States trying to cover it up?

He wouldn't put it past the Americans. As a precaution, Jun had already alerted the international community about the spike, refusing to let such knowledge be buried away. If this was a secret experiment gone awry, the world had a right to know. He glared a bit at Janice Cooper, as if she were to blame. Then again, her incessant cheeriness was reason enough for resentment.

"I think Riku is right," she said, speaking respectfully to her superior. "We're still struggling to pinpoint this new source. And besides, the pattern of this new burst doesn't look the same as the one in Utah. Perhaps we should hold off on any official announcement until we know more."

Jun studied the screen. A graph continued to scroll, like a digital version of a seismograph. Only this chart tracked neutrino activity rather than earthquakes—but considering what they'd found, it was *earthshaking* in its own right. For the past eighty minutes, they'd picked up a new surge in neutrino generation. Just as before, it appeared to be coming from earth-generated *geoneutrinos*.

Only Dr. Cooper was correct: this pattern *was* distinctly different. The Utah explosion created a single monstrous burst of neutrinos. Afterward it had died down to a low burble, like a teapot on a stove. This new surge of activity was less intense, coming in cyclical bursts: a small spike, followed by a stronger one . . . then a lull, and it repeated, like the *lub-dub* beat of a heart.

It had been going on for over an hour.

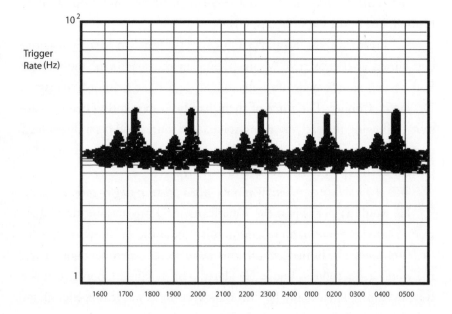

"This has to be related to the earlier event," Jun insisted. "It's beyond statistical possibility to have *two* aberrant neutrino surges of these magnitudes within the span of a day."

"Perhaps one *caused* the other," Tanaka offered.

Jun leaned back and took of his glasses. He rubbed the bridge of his nose. His first knee-jerk reaction was to reject such an idea—especially considering its source—but he remained silent, contemplating. He had to admit it wasn't a bad hypothesis.

"So you're suggesting the first spike ignited something else," Jun said. "Perhaps an unstable uranium source."

In his mind's eye, he pictured that initial burst of neutrinos radiating outward from the explosion, particles flying in all directions, passing through the earth like a swarm of ghosts—but leaving a trail of fire, capable of lighting another fuse.

"But neutrinos don't react with matter," Dr. Cooper said, throwing cold water on that idea. "They pass through everything, even the earth's core. How could they ignite something?"

"I don't know," Jun said.

In fact, there was little he understood about any of this.

Tanaka pressed ahead, refusing to admit defeat. "We know some mysterious explosion generated this morning's spike in Utah. Whatever that source was, it is very unique. I've never seen readings like this before."

Dr. Cooper looked unconvinced, but Jun believed Riku might be following the right thread. Neutrinos were once thought to have no mass, no charge. But recent experiments had proven otherwise. Much about them remained a mystery. Maybe there was an unknown substance sensitive to neutrino bombardment. Maybe the Utah explosion of particles had lit the fuse on another deposit. It was a frightening thought. He pictured a daisy chain of blasts, one after the other, spreading around the globe.

Where would it stop? Would it stop?

"This is all conjecture," Jun finally concluded aloud. "We won't know any true answers until we find out *where* this new surge is coming from."

No one argued with him. With a renewed determination, they set to work. Still, it took another half hour to finally coordinate with other neutrino labs around the globe to triangulate the source of these intermittent bursts.

They gathered around a monitor as the data collated. A world map filled the screen with a glowing circle that encompassed most of the Northern Hemisphere.

"That's not much help," Jun said.

"Wait," Tanaka warned tonelessly.

Over the course of another ten minutes, the circle slowly narrowed, zeroing tighter and tighter upon the coordinates of the new neutrino surges. It was clearly nowhere near Utah.

"Looks like we can't blame the United States this time," Dr. Cooper said with relief as the contracting circle cleared the North American continent.

Jun stared, dumbfounded, as the source was finally pinpointed, fixed with a set of crosshairs.

They all shared a glance.

"So *now* do we tell someone?" Jun asked.

Tanaka slowly nodded. "You were most right before, Yoshida-*sama*," he said, using a rare honorific. "We dare not wait any longer."

Jun was surprised by his reaction—until Tanaka motioned to the neighboring computer screen, the one with the digital graph mapping current-time neutrino activity. A small gasp escaped him. The spikes of activity were growing more frequent, like a heartbeat boosted by adrenaline.

His own pulse leaped to match it.

He reached for the phone and a private number left for him, but his gaze remained fixed to the screen, to the crosshairs centered on the Northern Atlantic.

Someone had to get out there before it was too late.

15

"Iceland?" Gray asked, shocked. He held the phone tighter to his ear, speaking to Kat Bryant. "You want me to head out to Reykjavik within the hour?"

He and Seichan were sharing the back of a black Lincoln Town Car. As a precaution, Kat had sent the car out to his parents' house once she got word of the attack on the director. At the moment they were headed back to the National Archives. Monk and his two researchers had found something of interest, something too important or involved to discuss over the phone.

"That's correct," Kat said. "On Director Crowe's orders. He wants you to take Monk, too. Pick him up on the way to the airport."

"We're headed there already. Monk texted me about some discovery at the National Archives."

"Well, find out what that is, but be at the airport in forty-five minutes. And dress warmly."

"Thanks, but what's this all about?"

"Earlier I told you about that burst of subatomic particles reported from the Utah blast site. I've just spoken to the head of the Kamioka Observatory in Japan. He's detected another surge. One that has him deeply troubled, coming from an island off the coast of Iceland. He believes the two neutrino surges might be connected, that the bombardment of subatomic particles from the Utah blast might have triggered this new

Icelandic activity, literally lit its fuse. Director Crowe believes it's worth investigating."

Gray agreed. "I'll pick up Monk and head out."

"Be careful," she said. Though her message was terse, Gray heard the underlying meaning. *Watch after my husband.* He understood.

"Kat, this mission sounds like something Seichan and I could do on our own. It might be best to leave Monk with the researchers who are pursuing the historical angle."

The phone went silent. He pictured her weighing his words. She finally sighed. "I understand what you're offering, Gray. But I'm sure those researchers don't need Monk watching over their shoulders. Besides, Monk could use a little stretching of his legs. With a baby coming—and Penelope heading for her terrible twos—the pair of us is going to be housebound for months. So, no, take him with you."

"Okay. But trust me, being housebound with you is not something Monk is dreading."

"Who was talking about *him?*"

Gray heard the exasperation in her voice, but also the warmth. He had a hard time imagining such a life, the intimacy of two sharing everything, of children, of the simplicity of a warm body beside you every night.

"I'll bring him home safe," he promised.

"I know you will."

After settling a few more details, they signed off.

Across the seat, Seichan leaned against the side door, arms crossed. It looked like she had been dozing, eyes closed, but he knew she'd overheard every word. This was confirmed when she mumbled, not bothering to open her eyes. "Road trip?"

"Seems so."

"Lucky I packed my sunscreen."

A short time later, the Town Car pulled up to the National Archives Building. Monk met them inside. He wore a wide grin, his eyes bright, and waved to them impatiently, plainly excited.

"Iceland," he said as he led them back to the research room. "Can you believe it?"

From his manner, he was clearly enthused about doing a bit of field-work. But there remained a mischievous gleam to his eye. Before Gray could inquire further, they'd reached their destination.

The research room had undergone a dramatic transformation since they'd last been there. Books, manuscripts, and maps, along with stacked file boxes, covered the surface of the conference table. All three microfiche readers along the wall glowed with pages of old newsprint or pictures of yellowed documents.

Amid the chaos, Dr. Eric Heisman and Sharyn Dupre had their heads bowed over one of the boxes, searching its contents together. Heisman had shed his sweater and rolled up his sleeves. He removed a thin dog-eared-looking pamphlet and added it to a pile.

"Here's another of Franklin's monographs about the eruption . . ."

They looked up as Monk returned.

"Did you tell him?" Heisman asked.

"Thought I'd leave it to both of you. You've done all the hard work. All I did was order pizza."

"Tell us what?" Gray asked.

Heisman looked to Sharyn, who still wore her tight black dress, but she had pulled a long white coat over it and had donned thin cotton gloves for handling fragile documents. "Sharyn, why don't you start? It was your inspired suggestion that opened the floodgates. Then again, your genera-tion is much more proficient with computers."

She smiled shyly at the praise and gave her head a slight bow of thanks before turning to Gray and Seichan. "I'm sure we would have found it eventually, but with a majority of the Archives' documents digitally copied, I thought we could sift through the records more efficiently by expanding and generalizing the search parameters."

Gray hid his impatience. He didn't care how they found it, only what it was. Still, he noted the amused twinkle in Monk's eye. His partner was holding something back.

"We did a global search for the combination of names Fortescue and Franklin," Sharyn said, "but we came up empty-handed."

"It's as if all records had been purged," Heisman said. "Someone definitely seemed to be covering their tracks."

"So I expanded the search beyond Franklin and tried all manner of alternate spellings for Fortescue. Still nothing. Then I simply tried putting in the man's initials, Archard Fortescue. A.F."

She glanced to Heisman, who smiled proudly. "That's where we found it." He picked up a sheaf of brittle yellow pages. "In a letter from Thomas Jefferson to his personal private secretary, Meriwether Lewis."

"Lewis? As in Lewis and Clark. The two explorers who crossed the continent all the way to the Pacific."

Heisman nodded. "One and the same. This letter to Lewis is dated June 8, 1803, about a year before the two left for that adventure. It concerns a discussion about a volcanic eruption."

Gray didn't understand where this was going. "What does a volcano have to do with anything?"

"First of all," Heisman explained, "such a discussion wasn't unusual— probably why this note drew no notice and wasn't expunged with the rest. Over the course of their relationship, Lewis and Jefferson often discussed science. Meriwether was former military, but he had been educated in the sciences and had great interest in the natural world."

Gray realized how much that sounded like any member of Sigma.

Heisman continued: "The two were very close friends. In fact, their families had grown up within ten miles of each other. Jefferson trusted no one more thoroughly than Lewis."

Monk nudged Gray. "So if Jefferson was keeping secrets, there's one person he'd surely take into his confidence."

Heisman nodded. "In this letter, one name comes up over and over, a man cryptically identified only as A.F."

"Archard Fortescue . . ." Gray said.

"Plainly Jefferson did not trust writing the man's name in full, which was very much in character for this Founding Father. Jefferson had a great interest in cryptography, even developing his own secret cipher. In fact, it wasn't until the last year or so that one of his codes was finally cracked."

"That guy was paranoid," Monk said.

Heisman glanced to him, offended. "If Franklin's earlier letter was accurate about some great enemy besieging the new union in secret, maybe he had reason to be. This same paranoia may have fueled Jefferson's purging of the Army during his presidency."

"What are you talking about?" Gray asked, growing intrigued.

"Just after Jefferson was elected president following a bitter campaign, one of his first orders of business was to reduce the standing army. He chose Meriwether Lewis to help him decide which officers were competent and which were not. Lewis communicated his findings back to Jefferson via a system of coded symbols. Some historians suspect this purge had less to do with *competency* than it did with *loyalty* to the U.S."

Monk glanced significantly at Gray. "If you wanted to weed out traitors, especially those leading armed forces, this would be a good way of going about it in secret."

Gray knew the difficulty Sigma had in purging Guild moles and operatives from their own fold. Were the Founding Fathers trying to do the same? He pictured Lewis's involvement in this affair. *Soldier, scientist, and now spy.* The man sounded more and more like a Sigma operative.

Seichan crossed to the table and took a seat, plopping heavily into it, looking bored. "All well and good, but what the hell does this have to do with volcanoes?"

Heisman seated his reading glasses more firmly on the bridge of his nose and spoke stiffly. "I was just getting to that. The letter addresses an eruption that occurred exactly two decades prior. To the day, in fact. The twentieth anniversary of it. The Laki eruption. It was the deadliest volcanic eruption of historical times. In its aftermath, over six million people died globally. It wiped out livestock, and crops failed around the world, leading to massive famines. It was said the skies turned bloodred, and the planet cooled enough to cause the Mississippi to freeze over as far south as New Orleans."

Sharyn interrupted, lifting one of the papers she'd been sifting through when Gray first entered. "Here's Benjamin Franklin's own words describing the eruption's effect. *'During several of the summer months of the year 1783, when the effect of the sun's rays to heat the earth in these northern regions should have been greater, there existed a constant fog over all Europe, and a great part of North America.'* Franklin became obsessed with this volcano."

"And apparently with good reason," Heisman added, drawing back Gray's attention. "According to this letter, Archard Fortescue was present at that eruption—even felt guilty about it, as if he'd caused it."

"What?" Gray couldn't keep the surprise from his voice.

Seichan spoke while he struggled to understand. "Excuse my lack of geographical prowess, but where is this volcano?"

Heisman's eyes widened, as if suddenly realizing he'd never told them. "In Iceland."

Gray turned to Monk, who wore a big, amused grin. This was the detail he'd been hiding. Monk shrugged. "Looks like we're following in that Frenchman's footsteps."

3:13 A.M.

As the others discussed the volcano's location using various maps spread on the table, Seichan sat to the side, fingering a tiny silver dragon pendant hanging from her neck. It was a nervous habit. Her mother had always worn one of the same. It was one of the few details she still remembered about the woman.

As a child, Seichan would often stare at the tiny curled dragon in the hollow of her mother's neck as she slept on a small cot under an open window. While night birds sang in the jungle, the moonlight reflected off the silver, shimmering like water with her mother's breathing. Each night, Seichan imagined the dragon would come to life if she just watched it long enough—and maybe it did, if only in her dreams.

With a flare of irritation at such sentimentality, Seichan let the silver charm drop from her fingers. She had waited long enough. No one seemed to be addressing the most obvious question in the room, so she asked it.

"Back to that letter, Doc." All eyes turned to her. "What did you mean when you said that the Frenchman felt *guilty* about the volcano blowing up?"

Heisman still had the sheaf of papers in hand. "It's here in Jefferson's letter." He cleared his voice, picked out a passage, and read it aloud. "*'We have at last heard from A.F. He has suffered greatly and carries a heavy heart after all that befell him during the summer of the year 1783. I am very mindful that it was in supporting our cause that he followed the trail marked on the map recovered from the Indian barrow, a prize he gained at much grievous personal injury due to the ambush by our enemy. A.F. yet bemoans the volcano he caus'd to be born out in those seas during that summer. He has come to believe that the great famines that struck his home shores following that eruption were reason for the bloody revolutions in France, and bears much guilt for it.'*"

Heisman lowered the pages. "In fact, Fortescue might be right in that last respect. Many scholars now conjecture that the Laki eruption—and the poverty and famine that followed in France—was a major trigger for the French Revolution."

"And from the sounds of it," Gray added, "Fortescue blamed himself. *'The volcano he caus'd to be born.'* What did he mean by that?"

No one had an answer.

"So then what do we know?" Seichan asked, cutting to the quick. "From that first letter, we know Franklin called on Fortescue to find a map buried in some Indian mound. From the gist of *this* letter, he succeeded."

Gray nodded. "The map pointed to Iceland. So Fortescue went there. He must have found something, something frightening or powerful enough that he believed it caused the volcanic eruption. But what?"

"It was possibly hinted at in the first letter," Seichan offered. "Some power or knowledge that the Indians possessed, knowledge they seemed willing to share, possibly in exchange for the formation of that mythical Fourteenth Colony."

"But that deal got screwed up," Monk said.

Heisman's assistant had been sifting through the piles of paper. "Here's the passage again," she said. "*The shamans from the Iroquois Confederacy were slaughtered most foully en route to the meeting with Governor Jefferson. With those deaths, all who had knowledge of the Great Elixir and the Pale Indians have pass'd into the hands of Providence.'*"

Gray nodded. "But now we know that one of the shamans lived long enough to reveal the location of a map, possibly a map to a fount of that knowledge. That's what Fortescue was sent to find."

"And apparently he succeeded," Monk added. "Maybe it was that *elixir* mentioned in the letter, or something else. Either way, he believed it was powerful enough to trigger a volcanic eruption. Afterward, he was racked with guilt."

"Until twenty years later, when Jefferson summoned him again," Heisman said.

Seichan turned to the scholar, realized she was fingering the dragon charm, and forced her arm down. "What do you mean?"

Heisman fixed his glasses and read again from the letter. "*'After such tragedy, I am loath to drag A.F. yet again into another search, but his warmth and high regard among the aboriginal tribes of this continent will serve us well for that long journey. He will join you in Saint Charles, well enough in time to secure what he will need to join your excursion to the West.'*"

Gray leaned forward. "Wait. Are you saying Fortescue joined the Lewis and Clark expedition?"

"Not me," Heisman said and shook the papers in his hand. "Thomas Jefferson."

"But there's no other record—"

"Maybe they were purged, too," Heisman offered. "Like the rest of this man's records. This letter is all we could uncover. After Fortescue leaves on this expedition, he's never mentioned again. At least as far as we can tell."

"But why was Jefferson sending him with Lewis and Clark?" Gray asked.

Seichan guessed the answer, sitting up straighter. "Maybe Iceland wasn't the *only* place marked on that Indian map. Maybe there was another spot. One out west. Iceland would have been closer, so they investigated that one first."

Gray rubbed a finger along the edge of his right eye, one of his habits when struggling to connect pieces of a mental jigsaw puzzle. "If there was another site, why wait twenty years to go look for it?"

"After what happened the first time," Monk said, "do you blame them for being more cautious? If Fortescue was right, their actions killed six million people and triggered the French Revolution. Of course they'd be more careful a second time."

Heisman interjected. "There's further support in the historical record that Lewis and Clark's mission wasn't purely for exploration. First, Jefferson all but admitted it."

"What do you mean?" Gray asked.

"Prior to the expedition, Jefferson sent out a letter in secret, meant only for members of Congress. It revealed the true reason for the trip: to spy on the Indians out west and to gather as much intelligence about them as possible. Second, Jefferson had also developed a private secret code with Lewis so that messages sent back could be read only by Jefferson or those loyal to him. Does that sound like a yearlong nature hike? Jefferson was clearly looking for something out west."

"But did he find it?" Seichan asked.

"There's no public record of anything like that. Then again, all records of Archard Fortescue were expunged. So who knows? But there is one intriguing detail that suggests something was being covered up."

Monk shifted closer. "What's that?"

"On October eleventh, 1809, three years after the expedition returned from the west, Meriwether Lewis was found dead in his room inside a Tennessee inn. He'd been shot once in the head, once in the chest. Yet for some reason his death was deemed a suicide, his body hastily buried near the inn. It's taken two hundred years for this cover-up to be exposed. It's now firmly believed that he was killed by an assassin." Heisman turned to them all. "Lewis had been on his way to Washington to meet with

Thomas Jefferson. Some believe he had valuable information or was carrying something vital to national security when he was killed. But from there the trail goes cold."

The room settled into silence. Seichan noted Gray still rubbing the corner of his right eye. She could practically hear the gears turning in his head.

Heisman checked his watch. "And that, dear gentlemen and ladies, is where we should stop for the night. I understand you have a flight to catch."

Monk stood, and they said their good-byes. Heisman and Sharyn promised they'd continue the search in the morning, but didn't sound hopeful.

Seichan followed the two men out to the street, where the Town Car still waited for them.

Monk eyeballed Gray. "You've got that worried crease across your forehead. What's up? Nervous about the trip?"

Gray slowly shook his head as a cold breeze swept down the street. "No. I'm worried about Utah. After what we learned about Iceland—and knowing the two places are both showing odd neutrino discharges—I think today's blast is the least of our problems."

Monk popped open the car door. "If so, we have someone keeping an eye on things out there."

Gray climbed inside. "That's what worries me most."

16

Major Ashley Ryan kept vigil with the geologist Ron Chin. The pair stood at the rim of the chasm. Dawn was not far off—and could not come soon enough for Ryan.

It had been a long, bloody night. He and his unit had managed to haul their injured teammate out of the steaming valley, where a helicopter had evacuated the man to the nearest hospital—missing most of his right leg, dazed on morphine, blood seeping through the pressure bandage on his stump.

Ryan had tried to take a nap afterward, but every time he closed his eyes, he flashed to the ax blade as it bit deep into the man's thigh . . . or he pictured Chin taking that severed limb and tossing it into the smoldering pit, as if throwing another log onto a bonfire. But Ryan understood. They couldn't risk contamination.

Finally giving up, knowing he'd never sleep, he had climbed out of his tent and kept watch on the valley with the geologist. Over the course of the night, the scientist had set up a whole battery of equipment: video cameras, infrared scanners, seismographs, something he called a magnetometer, used for measuring the strength and direction of the magnetic field. He knew his own men were reporting a growing interference with radios and cell phones. In the past hour, compasses all pointed toward the chasm. But worst of all, the tremors and quakes were rattling the mountain and were escalating in both frequency and severity.

"Unit's evacuated the area," Ryan said, glancing back to the open-air Jeep parked nearby. "We've pulled back to a base two miles down the mountain. Is that far enough?"

"Should be," Chin said, distracted. "Come look at this."

The geologist knelt beside a video monitor. It displayed footage from a remote camera left beside the pit. Chin pointed to a hellish glow radiating from the center of the old blast site, illuminating a dark column of ashy smoke rising into the air.

"The geyser hasn't blown in over forty minutes," the geologist said. "I think all the water from the hot spring got boiled away."

"So what's coming out now?"

"An outgassing. Hydrogen, carbon monoxide, sulfur dioxide. Whatever process is going on here, it must have drilled beyond the spring and into the volcanic strata underpinning these mountains."

As Ryan stared, a flash of fire shot through the dark column, then vanished. "What was that?"

Chin sat back, his face going pale.

"Doc?" Ryan pressed.

"I think . . . maybe a lava bomb . . ."

"What?" His voice rose to a girlish pitch. "Lava? Are you telling me that thing's starting to erupt?"

As they watched, another two flashes streaked out of the column and struck the floor of the pit. A molten gobbet of rock rolled across the surface, leaving no doubt as to what was happening.

"Time to bug out of here," Chin said, standing up. He ignored the equipment and began rapidly packing all the flash drives that held his data.

Ryan got in his face. After what had happened to Private Bellamy, he had questioned the geologist about this exact scenario. "I thought you said this wouldn't happen. That even drilling into a volcano wouldn't make it blow."

"I said that *usually* doesn't happen." He spoke in a rush as he worked.

"Occasionally deep-earth drilling has caused explosions when a borehole hits a superhot magma chamber, vaporizing drilling fluid and allowing lava to flow. Or take, for example, a case three years ago. In Indonesia, a drilling mishap gave birth to a massive mud volcano that continues to erupt today. So, no, it *ordinarily* doesn't happen—but there's nothing *ordinary* about what's going on here."

Ryan took a deep breath, remembering Bellamy's leg. The geologist was right. What was going on here was off the map and into the weeds. He needed to get his team evacuated even farther back.

He lifted his radio but only got a squelch of static. He spun in a circle, got a brief snatch of words, then lifted the radio to his lips. "This is Major Ryan! Pull back! Pull back now! Get the hell off this mountain!"

A garbled response came through, but he didn't know if it was acknowledgment or confusion. *Did they hear me?*

Chin straightened, snapping closed his metal briefcase. "Major, we must get clear of here. Now!"

Punctuating his words, the ground gave a violent shake. Ryan lost his footing and fell to one knee. They both turned to the video feed. On the chasm floor, the remote camera had been knocked over on its side, but the view remained on the pit.

The geyser had returned—but rather than steam and water, a jetting column of boiling mud and fiery rock now bubbled and splashed from the hole, heavily obscured by a churning cloud of smoke and ash.

Underfoot, the ground continued to shake, nonstop now, vibrating through the soles of Ryan's boots.

"Move out!" Chin yelled.

Together, they fled to the Jeep. Ryan leaped behind the wheel. Chin crashed into the passenger seat. With the keys already in the ignition, Ryan roared the engine to life, tugged the stick into reverse, and pounded the accelerator. With a yank on the wheel, he spun the truck around, throwing Chin against his door.

"You okay?" Ryan asked.

"Go!"

Earlier in the evening, his team had cleared a rough, winding road down the mountainside, but it still required a rugged four-wheel drive to traverse it, and it was best traveled at a snail's pace.

That wasn't the case now.

Ryan didn't slow, especially as the world exploded behind him. A glance at the rearview mirror revealed a brilliant fountain of lava dancing back there, shooting above the rim of the chasm. A glowing black column rose high into the sky, but the valley was not large enough to hold it. The fiery cloud spilled over the edge and rolled like an avalanche toward them.

That wasn't the only danger.

Red-hot boulders the size of small cars struck the forest and slopes around them, bouncing away, setting fire to trees and shrubs. They hit with the force of mortar rounds. Ryan now understood why they were called lava *bombs.*

One sailed past overhead, raining flaming ash. Cinders burned his cheeks, his exposed arms, reminding Ryan all too well that his vehicle had no roof.

He ignored the pain and focused on the road ahead. The Jeep bucked and rocked down the steep, rocky trail. His left fender crumpled against an outcropping, shattering the headlamp on that side. The Jeep lifted. For a moment he swore he was driving on a single wheel, like a half-ton ballerina. Then the vehicle crashed back down.

"Hold on!"

"What do you think I'm doing?" Chin had turned around backward, one arm hugging his headrest. "The pyroclastic flow is moving too fast down the mountain. We'll never make it!"

"I can't get any more speed. Not in this terrain!"

"Then turn around."

"What?" He risked taking his eyes off the road to glare at Chin. "Are you nuts?"

Chin pointed along a streambed that bisected their path. "Go that way. Upstream!"

Ryan again heard the raw command in the guy's voice, confirming his suspicion that the geologist had spent some years in uniform. He responded to that authority.

"Fuck you!" Ryan shouted, furious at the lack of options—still he hauled on the wheel.

Defying every instinct for survival, he made a right turn into the streambed and gunned the engine. He sped uphill, casting a rooster tail of water behind his rear tires.

"I really mean it, Chin. *Fuck you!* What the hell are we doing?"

The geologist pointed to the right, upslope, toward the peak's summit, where it overlooked the fiery chasm. "We have to skirt the cloud's edge and get higher. Pyroclastic flows are fluidized clouds of rock fragments, lava, and gas. Much heavier than air. They'll hug the mountainside and flow down."

Despite his pounding heart, Ryan understood. "We have to get *above* it."

But even that was chancy. By now, the surrounding woods were glowing with flames, while boulders continued to crash out of the sky, stripping branches, leaving a swath of fire. Worst of all, the world to the right of the Jeep ended at a towering wall of smoky fire, a witch's cauldron of ash and rock. The cloud rolled toward them, swallowing all in its path as they sped along below it.

The only consolation was that the streambed was wide and shallow, full of packed gravel and sand. Ryan jammed the accelerator to the floor. The Jeep sped higher, gaining ground, skipping around boulders with deft turns of his wrist. But the farther he went, the narrower the course grew. They were running out of stream.

Fifty yards ahead, a boulder hit with the force of a rocket. Water exploded into steam, gravel rained down on them.

End of the road.

"There!" Chin yelled, and pointed beyond the right bank.

Past a few trees, a steep high alpine meadow spread outward, rapidly being eaten away by the flow of fiery smoke.

Ryan hauled sharply on the wheel and sent the Jeep leaping over the bank, catching air, before it hit the meadow. Deep-treaded tires tore into the grassy soil, patched by snow at this altitude.

"We're not going to make it," Chin said, staring to the right, to where the world ended.

Like hell we aren't.

Ryan raced across the meadow as the cloud bore down on them. The heat of the approaching cloud burned like the breath of a dragon. Patches of snow began to melt around them.

At the end of the meadow rose a steep slope of raw granite. He aimed for it, hit it, and shot up its length. He climbed higher and higher, pressed back into his seat as the Jeep tilted precariously toward vertical. In the rearview mirror, he watched the cloud wash below them, erasing the world and replacing it with a roiling black sea.

Heat washed upward, blistering, searing his lungs, but he still cried out in relief. "We did it!"

Then the tires—all four of them—lost traction on the slick stone. The Jeep lurched, slipping sideways, falling backward. He fought against it, but gravity pulled them back toward the flaming sea.

"C'mon, Major!"

A hand balled into the collar of his uniform. He was yanked from his seat. Chin climbed over the windshield, dragging him along. Ryan understood and hit the hood beside Chin. Together, they shoulder-rolled forward as the Jeep slid backward under him.

Ryan hit the granite slope and scrambled to keep from following the Jeep down. Fingers latched onto his wrist and hauled him to a precarious lip of rock, enough for a toehold. Choking, coughing, the pair of them perched there like two little burned birds.

Ryan followed Chin's gaze over the valley. The fiery cloud continued down the dark mountainside. Closer at hand, the chasm below belched with fire and flowed with ribbons of lava.

"My men . . ." he mumbled numbly, wondering about their fate

Chin reached and squeezed his elbow, offering sympathy. "Pray they heard you."

17

Hank Kanosh greeted the dawn on his knees, not in an act of worship, but from exhaustion. He'd climbed the steep trail from the circle of cabins just before sunrise. The winding track led up through a maze of slot canyons and into a dry wash. Kawtch sat next to him, tongue hanging, panting. With the sun just rising, the morning was still cool, but it was a challenging trail and neither of them was young.

Still, he knew it was not the passing of years that weighed down his legs and made the climb so taxing. It was his heart. Even now, the feel of it pounding in his chest came with an upwelling of guilt, guilt for surviving, for not being able to doing anything when he was most needed. For the past day, while he was on the run, it had been easier to push aside the pain of his friends' deaths.

That was no longer the case.

He stared out over the broken landscape below. He and Maggie had made this same hike almost a decade ago, while testing the waters with each other. He still remembered the kiss they'd shared on this very spot. Her hair had smelled of sage; her lips tasted salty, yet sweet.

He savored that memory now as he knelt atop a slab of rock that jutted precariously over a deep gorge nicknamed the "Little Grand Canyon." The valley lay at the heart of the San Rafael Swell, a sixty-mile-wide bulge of sedimentary rock that had been uplifted here by geological forces over fifty million years ago. Since then, rain and wind had carved and chiseled the region into a labyrinth of steep slopes, broken canyons, and rugged washes. Far below, the San Rafael River continued the eroding process, snaking lazily across the landscape on its way to the Colorado.

The red-rock region was mostly deserted, home to wild burros, stallions, and one of the largest herds of desert bighorn sheep. The only two-legged visitors here were the more adventurous hikers, because entry to the remote area required four-wheel-drive vehicles to traverse its few roads. In the past, the Swell's nearly inaccessible maze of canyons and ravines had been the hideouts and escape routes for many outlaws, including Butch Cassidy and his gang.

And it seemed such was the case again.

Hank and the others had arrived here in the wee hours of the morning, crawling down a rock-strewn track from Copper Globe Road. Their destination was the family cabins of his retired colleagues, Alvin and Iris Humetewa. Hank's group had barged in without any warning, but as he had known, the couple had taken the intrusion in good-natured stride.

The small homestead of five mud-and-stone pueblos was half commune, half school for Hopi children who were taught the old ways by three generations of the Humetewa clan, all led by Iris Humetewa, matriarch and benevolent dictator.

At the moment there were no students.

Or almost no students.

"You can come out," Hank said.

A peeved sigh rose from beyond a boulder in the wash behind him. The slim figure of Kai Quocheets stalked out of hiding. She'd been trailing him since he'd left the cabins.

"If you want to see the sunrise," he urged her, "you'd best come up here."

With a sullen slump to her shoulders, she climbed to the overlook. Kawtch slapped his tail a couple of times against the sandstone slab in greeting.

"Is it safe out there?" she asked, eyeing the drop beyond the edge of the jutting rock.

"Stone's been here thousands of years, it'll probably last another few minutes."

She looked doubtful about his assessment but came forward anyway. "Uncle Crowe and his partner are putting together some sort of satellite dish tied to a laptop and phone."

"I thought he wanted to stay off the grid."

The Humetewas' cabins had no television or telephones. Even cellular reception was nonexistent in the labyrinthine canyons.

She shrugged. "Should still be safe. I heard him say something about encryption software. Probably acts as a scrambler or something."

He nodded and patted the stone. "You came all the way up here to tell me that?"

She sank cross-legged to the stone. "No . . ." There was a long pause, too long for the truth. "Just wanted to stretch my legs."

He recognized the waffling and could guess its source. He had already noted how she shied away from her uncle, circled him like a wary dog fearful of being beaten but drawn anyway. Still, there was no timidity to her. She kept her hackles raised, ready to bite. All this uncertainty must have made it too uncomfortable for her to stay below at the cabins, pushing her to follow after him.

He faced the rising sun as it crested fully and set fire to the red-rock landscape below. "Are you familiar with the *na'ii'ees* ceremony?"

"What's that?"

He shook his head sadly. Why was it that the most fervent of the Native American activists were so often ignorant of their own heritage?

"It's the sunrise ceremony," he explained, pointing to the blazing birth of the new day. "A rite of passage for girls into womanhood. It involves four days and nights of dancing and sacred blessings, imbuing the new women with the spiritual and healing power of the White Painted Woman."

Answering the questioning lift of an eyebrow, he explained the Apache and Navajo mythology surrounding this goddess, also known as the Changing Woman, named for her ability to shift appearances along with the seasons. He enjoyed how her gaze turned from dull to rapt with the telling, a sign of her thirst for such knowledge.

As he ended his description, she turned to the rising sun. "So do any tribes still perform the ceremony?"

"Some, but rarely. In the early twentieth century, the U.S. government banned Native American spiritual rites and practices, making the sunrise ceremony illegal. Over time, the practice slowly faded, only to return in a weakened version today."

Kai's face turned darker. "They've stolen so much from us . . ."

"The past is the past. It's now up to us to sustain our own culture. We only lose what we fail to nurture."

She seemed little mollified by this, her words bitter. "What? Like you're doing? Forsaking your own beliefs for the white man's religion. A religion that persecuted our people and incited massacres."

He sighed. He'd heard it all before, and once again tried his best to enlighten the ignorant. "Mistakes are made by stupid men. In the course of human history, religions have been used as excuses for violence, including among our own Native American tribes. But when it comes to *culture,* religion is only one thread in a vast woven rug. My father was raised Mormon, as was my mother. That is as much my history as my native blood. One does not negate the other. I find much in the Book of Mormon that gives me peace and brings me closer to God—or whatever you want to call that eternal spirituality that exists in all of us. In the end, my faith even offers another viewpoint on our own people's past. It's why I became a Native American historian and naturalist. To seek the answer to who we are."

"What do you mean by that? How does Mormonism explain anything about our people?"

He wasn't sure this was the right time to explain the history that was buried within the pages of the Book of Mormon, a testament of Christ's footsteps in the New World. Instead, he'd offer Kai some insight into the shadows that still clouded the earliest histories of the Native American tribes.

He stood up. "Follow me."

With a slight arthritic limp, he hobbled over to a neighboring scalloped-out dome of sandstone. Under a fluted lip of rock stretched a line of chipped stone blocks, marking the ruins of an old Indian home. Ducking his head, he stepped over the threshold and crossed to the far wall.

"There is much that we still don't know about our own people," he said, and glanced back. "Are you familiar with the prehistoric Indian mounds found throughout the Midwest—stretching from sites around the Great Lakes to the swamps of Louisiana?"

She shrugged.

"Some mounds date back six thousand years. Even tribes living in the area when Europeans arrived had no memories of those ancient mound builders. That is our heritage. One big mystery."

He reached the far wall, where some prehistoric artist had painted a trio of tall, skeletal figures in crimson pigments against the yellow sandstone. He lifted a hand over the ancient artwork.

"You'll find petroglyphs like this throughout the area. Some archaeologists have dated the oldest images here at eight thousand years old. And those are relatively new compared to the Coso Petroglyphs above China Lake's salt beds. Those go back *sixteen* thousand years, to the end of the last Ice Age, when the continent was still roamed by mammoths, saber-toothed cats, and monstrous Pleistocene bison." He turned to Kai. "That is how far back our history goes, with so little known."

He allowed the weight of ages to press down on her young shoulders before continuing. "Even the number of people who lived here has been vastly underestimated. Newest studies from the chemical composition of stalagmites, and the depth and breadth of charcoal deposits found throughout North America, put modern estimates of Native American populations at well over a hundred million. That's more people than were living in Europe when Christopher Columbus set foot in this New World."

Her eyes shone large in the shadowy space. "Then what happened to them all?"

He waved to encompass the ruins as he led the way back out. "After the Europeans arrived, infectious diseases like smallpox spread faster across the continent than the colonists, leading to the impression of a sparsely populated American wilderness. But that is a false history, much like the rest of it."

Kai joined him back on the rocky outcropping, along with Kawtch, who had his nose in the air. She wore a thoughtful expression as she stared out. The skies had shed the rose of dawn for the deeper blue of morning.

"So I get your point," she said. "We can't truly know ourselves until we know our own history."

He looked to her, sizing her up anew. She was far sharper than she let on—proving it again when she turned to him to ask, "But you never did say how the Book of Mormon offered insight into our history."

Before Hank could answer, Kawtch let out a low growl of warning. His nose was still in the air, sniffing. They both turned to the northeast, to where Kawtch's nose was pointing. The skies, lighter now, revealed a churning black smudge at the horizon, like thunderclouds stacking up toward a gully-washing storm.

"Smoke," he mumbled.

And a lot of it.

"A forest fire?" Kai asked.

"I don't think so." His heart thudded with a growing sense of dread. "We should head back down."

6:38 A.M.
Provo, Utah

Rafael Saint Germaine sat enjoying a tiny porcelain cup of espresso in the mansion's massive and extravagant kitchen. The absurdity of the room amused him. What the Americans considered to be the epitome of class struck him as ridiculous, living in homes of cheap modern construction, decorated to evoke faux–Old World charm. His family's château in Carcassonne dated back to the sixteenth century, surrounded by fortified walls atop which battles had been fought that changed the course of Western civilization.

That was the true mark of aristocracy.

He stared out the kitchen windows and across the sprawling lawns to the helicopter as a crew prepped it for departure. Across the table were reams of biographical data. He'd read them with his breakfast and saw no need to peruse them again. He could recite most of the details by rote.

On the top of the stack rested the photograph of the man who had thwarted his actions at the university last night. It had taken only a short time to put a name to the face. It ended up being someone well known to his organization. If the photo hadn't been so grainy and shadowy, he wouldn't have needed the facial-recognition software to identify him.

He whispered the name of his adversary, "Painter Crowe." *The director of Sigma.* He shook his head—both dismayed and amused—and stared down at the photo. "What are you doing out of your hole in D.C.?"

Rafe had not anticipated that Sigma would be so quick to respond to the events that had occurred here. It was an underestimation he intended not to repeat. But such a miscalculation was not entirely his fault. It had taken much longer to connect the pieces together. Their target—the lithe thief with such sticky fingers—was indirectly related to Crowe, sharing the same tribal clan. She must have called upon family ties to enlist his aid.

It was an interesting development. He spent the rest of the night, except for a short nap, incorporating this new variable into his equations and running various permutations through his head. *How best to play this out? How to turn this to his advantage?*

It had taken until this morning to tease out a solution.

Footsteps echoed from the hallway, passing through the butler's pantry to reach him. "Sir. We're ready to depart."

"*Merci,* Bern." Rafe tapped his Patek Philippe wristwatch. The timepiece included a tourbillon movement, the French word for "whirlwind." That's what they needed to be this morning. "We're running late."

"Yes, sir. We'll make up time in the air."

"Very well."

Rafe took one last sip of his espresso. He pursed his lips at the taste. It had gone lukewarm, bringing out a sharp bitterness. It was a shame, as the discovery of the coffee beans here, an expensive import from Panama, had been a pleasant surprise. He had to give the owners of this monstrosity some points for taste, if only for their beans.

He stood up, feeling generous.

"Is Ashanda still with the boy?" he asked Bern.

"They're in the library."

This elicited a smile. Without a tongue, she certainly wasn't reading the child a story.

"What do you want me to do with the boy after you leave?" Bern's manner stiffened, perhaps knowing what the answer must be.

Rafe waved an arm dismissively. "Leave him here. Unharmed."

Bern's brows lifted ever so slightly. For the stoic man, it was the equivalent of a gasp of surprise.

Rafe turned away. Sometimes it was good to act unpredictably, to keep your subordinates on their toes. Using his cane, he crossed through the house to collect Ashanda. The library was a two-story affair, filled with leather-bound books that were likely never read, only showcased as ostentatiously as everything else in the home.

He found Ashanda seated in a plush wingback chair. The child was asleep in her arms as she gently brushed her long, impossibly strong fingers through his blond curls. She hummed tunelessly deep in her chest. It was a comforting sound to Rafe, as familiar as his mother's voice. He smiled, drawn momentarily into the past, to happy summer nights, sleeping on the balcony under the stars, warmed by the presence of Ashanda next to him in a nest of blankets. He'd often heard her hum like that, holding him as he recovered from some break in his brittle bones. It was a balm that soothed most aches, even the grief of a child.

He hated to disturb her, but they had a schedule. "Ashanda, *ma grande,* we must depart."

She bowed her head, acknowledging the command. She rose smoothly, turned, and gently placed the boy onto the warm cushion, curling him into place. Only then did Rafe notice the bruising around the boy's thin throat, the odd canting of his neck. He had not been asleep after all.

She crossed to Rafe and offered him her arm. He took it, squeezing her forearm in sympathy. She had known what must be done, known what he would have normally ordered. She had acted as much for his benefit as the child's, granting the boy a swift and painless end. He did not have the heart to tell her it wasn't necessary—at least, not this one time.

He felt bad.

Am I truly that predictable?

He would have to prepare against that, especially today. He had been informed about the volcanic eruption in the mountains, confirming what was long suspected. Things had to move fast now. He checked his watch, noting the spin of the tourbillon.

Like a whirlwind, he reminded himself.

He could waste no time. They had to flush out the birds that had escaped his grasp last night, to pick up their trail again. It had taken most of the night to puzzle out a solution, one played out in the wild every day.

To bring down a frightened bird, it often took a hawk.

7:02 A.M.
San Rafael Swell

"How many dead?" Painter asked, the satellite phone pressed against his ear.

He paced the length of the central room of the largest pueblo. Embers glowed in the fire-blackened cooking hearth, accompanied by the bitter scent of burned coffee. Kowalski sat on a pine-log sofa, his legs up on a burl-wood table, his chin resting on his chest, dead tired after the long drive.

Ronald Chin's voice was raspy over the phone. Magnetic fluctuations along with particulate debris from the erupting volcano were interfering with digital reception. "We lost five members of the National Guard. But even that number is low only because Major Ryan was able to send out a distress call and initiate an evacuation. We're still uncertain about hikers or campers in the region. The area was already cordoned off and restricted, so hopefully we're okay there."

Painter stared up at the beamed roof. The pueblo had been constructed in a traditional manner with pole battens, grass thatching, and
a plaster made of stone fragments bound in mud. It seemed strange to be
discussing the birth of new volcanoes in such a conventional setting.

Chin continued, "The good news is that the eruption seems to be
already subsiding. I swept over the area in a helicopter just before dawn.
Lava has stopped flowing. So far, it remains confined within the walls of
the chasm and is already hardening. The biggest danger at the moment
seems to be the forest fire. Crews are hurriedly setting up firebreaks, and
helicopters are dumping water. It's about fifty percent contained already."

"Unless there's another eruption," Painter said.

Chin had already given his assessment of the cause. He believed some
process birthed by the explosion was atomizing matter and had drilled
down into a shallow magma chamber that heated the geothermic region,
causing it to explode.

"We may be okay there, too," Chin said.

"Why's that?"

"I've been monitoring the lava field over the blast zone. It's been
steadily growing thicker across the chasm. And I'm not seeing any evidence of renewed atomization. I think the extreme heat of the eruption
burned out whatever was disassembling matter down there. Killed it permanently."

Killed it?

Painter suspected Chin had some idea of what that might be.

"If I'm right," Chin continued, "we're damned lucky for that volcanic
eruption."

Painter didn't consider the loss of five National Guard soldiers to be
lucky. But he understood the geologist's relief. If that process had continued unabated, it might have spread across the Rockies, eating its way
across the landscape, leaving nothing but atomized dust in its wake.

So maybe Chin was right. Maybe it was lucky—but Painter didn't
place much faith in luck or coincidence.

He pictured the mummified remains that had been found in the cave, buried with such a destructive cargo. "Maybe that's why those dead Indians—or whoever they were—chose that geothermic valley to store their combustible compound. Maybe they kept it there as a fail-safe. If the stuff blew, the process would drill into the superhot geothermic strata below the ground, where the extreme heat would kill it before it could spread and consume the world."

"A true fail-safe," Chin said, his voice introspective. "If you're right, maybe the compound needs to be kept steadily *warm* to stop it from exploding in the first place. Maybe that's why the skull exploded when it was brought out of the hot cave and into the *cold* mountain air."

It was an intriguing thought.

Chin ran further with it. "All this adds additional support to something I've been thinking about."

"What's that?"

"You mentioned that the dagger taken from the cave was composed of Damascus steel, a type of steel whose strength and resiliency is the result of manipulation of matter at the nano-level."

"That's what the physicist, Dr. Denton, related before he got killed. He said it was an example of an ancient form of nanotechnology."

"Which makes me wonder . . . as I was watching the denaturing process occurring in the valley, it struck me as being *less* like a chemical reaction and *more* like something was actively attacking the matter and breaking it down."

"What are you getting at?"

"One of the end goals of modern nanotechnology is the production of *nanobots,* molecular-sized machines that can manipulate matter at the atomic level. What if these unknown people were adept not only in ancient *nanotechnology,* but also in ancient *nanorobotics?* What if that explosion activated trillions and trillions of dormant nanobots—birthing a *nano-nest* that began to eat and spread in all directions."

It seemed far-fetched. Painter pictured microscopic robots snipping molecules apart, atom by atom.

"Director, I know it sounds mad, but labs around the world are al-

ready making breakthroughs in the production and assembly of nanomachines. Some labs have even been positing self-replicating silicon-based
bots called *nanites* that can reproduce copies of themselves out of the raw
material they consume."

Painter again pictured the denaturing process described in that valley.
"Chin, that's a mighty big leap to make."

"I'm not disagreeing. But already there are countless nanobots found
in the *natural* world. Enzymes in cells act like little robot workhorses.
Some of the tiniest self-replicating viruses operate on the nano-scale. So
maybe someone in the distant past accidentally cooked up a similar nano-
bot, maybe a by-product of the manufacturing of Damascus steel? I don't
know. But the earlier issue of *heat* does make me wonder."

"How so?"

"One of the hurdles in nanotechnology—especially in regard to the
functionality of nanobots—is the dissipation of heat. For such a nano-
machine to function, it has to be able to shed the heat it produces while
working, a difficult process at the nano-level."

Painter put it all together in his head. "So an easy way to keep nanobots dormant would be to store them somewhere hot. Like in a geother-
mally heated cavern, where the temperature would stay relatively uniform
for centuries, if not millennia."

"And if there's a mishap," Chin continued, "this nest of nanobots—
spreading outward in all directions—would eventually eat their way down
to the geothermal levels and inadvertently destroy themselves."

Despite the impossibility of it at face value, the idea was frighteningly
feasible. And dangerous. Such a product would be a ready-made weapon,
but the bigger prize would be the technology behind its production. If *that*
could be discovered, it would be invaluable.

Nanotechnology was already poised to be the next big industry of the
new millennium, with the potential to become vital to all manner of science, medicine, electronics, manufacturing . . . the list was endless. Whoever took true and lasting hold of those reins could rule the world from the
atomic level on up.

But all this begged one huge question.

"If we're right about all of this, who the hell were the people mummi-fied in that cave?" Chin asked.

Painter checked his watch. The one person who might be able to answer that question should be here within the hour. He arranged a few more details with Chin over the phone, ordering him to remain on-site and keep monitoring that valley.

As Painter hung up, Kowalski spoke from the sofa, not bothering to lift his chin. "Causing volcanoes to erupt . . ."

Painter glanced his way.

"If that's what this stuff can do"—one eye opened and stared back at him—"maybe you'd better tell Gray to pack some asbestos underwear for his trip to Iceland."

18

Gray crossed the stern deck of the fishing trawler. Though the day was clear, a hard wind blew the sea into a stiff chop, causing the boat's deck to jar and buck underfoot. He found Seichan and Monk at the rail, bundled in waterproof coats against the salty chill of the breeze. The midday sun reflected brightly off the sea but did little to warm the air.

"According to the captain," Gray said, "we'll reach Ellirey Island in about twenty minutes."

Seichan shaded her eyes and looked to the east. "And we're certain that's the right island?"

"That's our best guess."

The three of them had landed in Reykjavik an hour ago and hopped a private plane to the chain of islands that lay seven miles south of Iceland's coast. The Vestmannaeyjar Islands were a fierce line of emerald-capped sentinels, riding a storm-swept sea—seas as turbulent as the region's history. The islands were named after Irish slaves, known as Westmen, who killed their captors in AD 840 and escaped briefly to these islands, until they were eventually hunted down and slaughtered, leaving behind only their names. Today, it took a hearty soul to live out here, clustered on the largest of the islands, sharing the bits of land with seabirds and the world's most populous colonies of arctic puffins.

Gray stared back at the picturesque harbor of Heimaey as it retreated behind them, with its brightly painted homes and shops set against a back-drop of green hills and a pair of ominous volcanic cinder cones. They'd landed at the island's small airport and wasted no time chartering the boat to ferry them to the coordinates supplied by the Japanese physicists—but the coordinates were admittedly *rough,* according to Kat. And there were a lot of islands out here. More than a dozen uninhabited islands made up the archipelago, along with countless natural stone pillars and wind-carved sea arches.

The entire chain was geologically young, born within the last twenty thousand years from volcanic activity along a fiery seam that stretched across the seabed. That firestorm was still ongoing. In the midsixties, an undersea volcanic eruption gave fiery birth to the southernmost island of the chain, Surtsey. In the seventies, the Eldfell volcano—one of two cones on Heimaey—exploded and buried half of the colorful harbor town in lava. Gray had noted the aftermath from the air as they swept down to-ward the island's airport. Street signs still stuck out of the lava fields; a few homes at the edges were being excavated from the rock, granting the town its other name: the Pompeii of the North.

"I think that's the place," Monk said, and pointed ahead.

Gray turned and spotted a towering black rock sticking out of the sea. This was no island of sandy beaches and sheltered harbors. Sheer black seawalls surrounded the island of Ellirey, which was little more than a broken chunk of volcanic cone protruding out of the waves. The top of the island was a scalloped stretch of emerald green—a high meadow of mosses, lichen, and sea grass, so bright in the sunlight it looked unnatural.

"How are we getting up there?" Monk asked as the boat churned steadily toward the towering rock.

"You climb, my American friends."

The answer came from the wheelhouse of the boat. Captain Ragnar Huld stalked onto the deck in an open yellow slicker, wearing boots and a heavy woolen sweater. With his thick red beard traced with gray, and grizzled, salt-aged skin, he could have stripped to fur and leather and easily been mistaken for a marauding Viking. Only the easy amusement spar-kling in his green eyes softened that impression.

"Afraid the only way up," he explained, "is by rope. But you all look fit enough, so that should be fine. Young Egg will bring the boat alongside the east shore of the island, where the cliffs are lowest."

Huld pointed a thumb toward the cabin, where his son, Eggert, twentysomething in age, shaven-headed with both arms sleeved in tattoos, manned the wheel.

"Don't worry," Huld said. "I bring hunters, even a few nature photographers, up here quite regularly. Never geologists like the lot of you. But I've never lost anyone yet."

He gave Seichan a coy wink, but with her arms crossed, she did not look amused. According to their cover story, they were researchers from Cornell University, doing a study on volcanic islands. It went a long way to explain their heavy packs and inquiries about this specific island.

Huld pointed at the rock as it drew ever closer. "There's a hunting lodge up top where you can rent a room, if need be. If you squint your eyes, you should be able to spot it."

Gray searched for a moment, then found it. Sheltered square in the middle of the scooped greensward stood a good-size lodge with a blue slate roof.

"Don't know if you will find much room up there, though," the captain said. "Late yesterday, another ferry took out a tourist group. Hunters from Belgium, I heard. Or Swiss, maybe they were. They're lodging here for a few more days. Besides the lot of them, you'll only have a few cattle and the usual gathering of puffins for company."

Just as well, Gray thought. He'd prefer to keep their search for the source of the neutrino emissions as quiet as possible.

Seichan suddenly jolted back from the ship's rail, jostling Gray, coming close to losing her footing before he caught her.

"What's wrong?"

Speechless, she pointed out to sea. A tall black fin crested high, splitting through the waves alongside the boat. As Gray watched, another fin rose, followed soon thereafter by a third, fourth, and fifth.

"More over here," Monk said from the opposite side of the trawler. "Orcas. A pod of them."

Huld puffed out his chest and waved an arm. "Not unusual. Our islands have the largest population of killer whales and dolphins in all of Iceland. They're just curious and enjoy riding our bow wake. Or maybe looking for a nibble. I'll often share a little of my catch with them, if I've had a good haul. Brings *gangi pér vel*—good luck—as they say around here."

After a time, with no free meal offered, the pod sank away, vanishing in unison upon some silent signal. Still, Gray noted Seichan kept a wary watch on the waves, plainly unnerved by the sight of the large predators.

Good to know something could shake up that iron resolve.

As the trawler chugged past the southern tip of the island, Gray studied their destination, noting the waves that were crashing into the dark depths of volcanic sea caves that peppered the cliffs. If some treasure had been hidden in those watery caves long ago, the tides and storms would have wreaked havoc on it. To find what they were seeking, their best hope lay in looking somewhere that was better sheltered, an inland lava tube or cavern.

But where to begin their search?

Gray turned to Captain Huld. "In order to set up our equipment, we're looking to get as deep into the island as possible. Any suggestions?"

The captain scratched his beard, eyeballing the towering rock faces. "Yes. Lot of caves and tunnels here. Take your pick. Place is practically a hardened chunk of Swiss cheese, carved by wind and rain. But there's one famous cave up there, gave the island its name. Ellirey cavern. Story goes some young lass fled here and hid in that cave from the rape and pillaging of invaders—Turks or Barbary pirates, depending on the storyteller. Anyway, once safely hidden, she had a child, a boy, and raised him here. That child acted as guardian to the islands and was said to have special powers, able to call the forces of fire and molten rock to protect our seas." Huld shook his head. "Of course, it's just wild stories, told around the hearth in the long winters here."

Gray caught a look from Monk. Maybe there was a kernel of truth in that old tale, some hint of an explosive power buried here long ago, hidden by someone seeking a desperate refuge.

"Can you tell me where this cave is?" Gray asked.

Huld shrugged heavily. "*Fjandinn* if I know. But there's a caretaker up at the lodge. Ol' Olafur Bragason. Call him Ollie, though. Quite a piece of work, that one. Been living out here for over sixty years, as crusty and sharp-edged as the island's rocks. But he knows every nook and cranny of this place. That's the man to ask."

By now, the trawler had cleared the southern tip and made a slow approach toward a broken section of cliff face. A thick rope, anchored in places to the jumble of rock, snaked down from above, marking a trail meant more for mountain goats than human traffic. It ended at a small tie-down. To reach the rope, they would have to row an aluminum dinghy from the trawler, but at least the place was relatively sheltered from the crashing waves.

Still, it took some crafty maneuvering by the captain's son to bring them in close. In short order, Gray was helping Seichan climb from the dinghy to the slick rock, where she shifted her pack and grabbed tightly to the rope. Staring up, Gray shouldered his backpack. It would be a hard trek. He suddenly found himself envying Monk's prosthetic hand. With the newly designed actuators, he could crush walnuts between his fingers. Such a grip would serve him well during the long climb.

Huld shared the dinghy with them, manning the small outboard at the stern. "Egg and I will keep close by, do a little fishing. When you are ready, radio us and we'll come fetch you. But if you decide to stay the night, let us know that, too. We can come out any time tomorrow to ferry you back."

"Thanks."

Gray stepped from the rocking dinghy onto solid ground. The volcanic rock, while damp, was coarse and sharp, giving good traction for the tread of his boots. The path up, while steep, had plenty of good footholds and shelves of rock. The rope added extra reassurance.

He stared up, appreciating the view. Seichan climbed steadily without resting, her thighs stretching her jeans and rising to the gentle curve of her backside. The pace she set made it clear that she was happy to flee the dark waters below.

A few yards down the rope, Monk must have noted the direction of Gray's gaze. "Don't let that Italian girlfriend of yours catch you gaping like that."

Gray scowled down at him. Luckily the winds ate away most of his words before they reached Seichan. He'd not seen Rachel Verona in over four months. Their occasional dalliances had dried up after her promotion within the carabiniere forces, locking her down in Italy, while his own issues with his parents made long weekend trips to Rome impossible. They still kept in touch by phone, but that was about it. Separated by a gulf far wider than the Atlantic, they both recognized that they needed to move on.

After one last haul, the group climbed clear of the cliffs and out onto a beautiful panorama of grasses and outcroppings painted in mosses and lichens in every shade of green. A slight mist clung within the sheltered scallop of volcanic cone, casting a prismatic glow across the landscape.

Monk whistled sharply. "Looks like we just stepped into some Irish folktale."

Seichan was not enchanted. "Let's go interview the caretaker."

She led the way toward the two-story hunting lodge nestled in the center of the meadow to the right. To the left, the summit of the island dropped in a series of large tiers and labyrinthine tumbles of black rock. Gray hoped the caretaker could help them narrow their search.

After a short hike, they reached the sole building on the island. Clad in wood with a few tiny windows, the hunting lodge looked more like a rustic barn, especially with the handful of cows, lowing pitifully, that were grazing farther up the green slope. A sickly spindle of smoke rose from the homestead's single chimney.

Passing through a fenced gate and across a small vegetable garden, Gray reached the front door and knocked. When no one answered, he tested the latch and found it unlocked. Then again, why wouldn't it be?

He pushed inside.

The main room of the lodge was shadowy and stiflingly warm after the cold trek. A scarred and stained plank table crossed before a low fire, making the space both a meeting hall and dining room. A single flickering oil lamp lit the tabletop, revealing a spread of topographic maps and sea charts. They were in disarray, clearly well thumbed through.

Gray unzipped his coat, freeing an easy reach to his holstered SIG Sauer. Seichan also tensed, a dagger appearing in her fingers.

"What's wrong?" Monk asked.

Gray searched around. The place was too quiet. The pile of maps looked more like a war room than the staging area for a casual hunt. A low groan rose from a room at the back.

He freed his pistol and hurried forward, sticking to the walls, leading with his gun. Seichan flanked to the other side. Monk took up a position at a window facing the front of the lodge, keeping watch.

With a quick peek into the back room, Gray spotted a wiry old man tied to a chair, his nose broken, his lip split and bleeding. It had to be Olafur Bragason. Gray swept the rest of the room before entering. No one else was there.

He moved over to the man, whose head lolled back, hearing Gray's footsteps. A bleary, dazed eye rolled over him before the man's chin fell back to his chest.

"Nei, nei . . ." he gasped softly out. "I told you all I know."

Seichan turned to Gray. "Looks like someone else knew about the neutrino emissions and beat us here."

She didn't have to mention a name. But how could the Guild know about this island? A twinge of suspicion flashed through him as he stared her way. Something must have shown on his face. Seichan's manner stiffened with anger, but he also saw the hurt in her eyes. She swung away to the door. She had gone a long way to prove her loyalty. She didn't deserve his suspicions.

Gray crossed to the door, touched her arm, offering a silent apology, but he had no further time for injured feelings. He waved to Monk. "I'm going to search the rest of the lodge. You help the caretaker. We need to be able to get him moving. Whoever's here surely noted our approach by sea."

A loud explosion burst across the island, rattling the windows. Gray rushed across the room. He recognized the crack of TNT. Out one of the windows, he spotted a dark smoky cloud rising from the jumble of rocks halfway across the island. A flock of black-and-white puffins took to wing, fluttering through the smoke, rousted and panicked. Someone was trying to blast their way deeper into the island.

Closer at hand, movement caught his attention. A line of eight men rose from the boulder line and stalked across the meadow, staying low, moving stealthily from outcropping to outcropping. They were armed with rifles, scopes sparking in the sunlight. Here were the hunters who had been described by Captain Huld.

Only apparently the true hunt was just beginning.

10:14 P.M.
Gifu Prefecture, Japan

Jun Yoshida must have fallen asleep at his desk. The knock on the door startled him awake. Even before he could compose himself, Riku Tanaka came rushing inside, drawing Janice Cooper in his wake.

"You must see this," Tanaka said, and slapped a fistful of papers on his desk.

"What? Has there been another neutrino burst?" Jun tilted straighter in his chair, earning a twinge from his aching back. He'd left the main lab below three hours ago to finish some paperwork in his office, which still lay untouched on his desk.

"No . . . well, yes . . . not really," Tanaka stammered, clearly agitated, and waved the question aside in exasperation. "Some minor ongoing blips. I've been tracking them, but they don't appear to be important."

Dr. Cooper cut him off. "That's not why we rushed up here, Dr. Yoshida." She turned to Tanaka. "Show him."

Tanaka came around his desk, invading his personal space. He shoved aside the pile of paperwork, replacing it with his own printouts. "We've been monitoring the surge in Iceland. Graphing the results. Look at how the neutrino spikes radiating from that island have grown steadily more frequent."

"You noted that before."

"Yes. I know." Tanaka's face reddened. Clearly he did not like to be interrupted.

Jun allowed himself a flicker of satisfaction. "Then what's this sudden invasion of my office all about?"

Tanaka traced the graph. "Over the past hour, I've been noting how the double beat of the Icelandic signature has been changing. The smaller bursts have been growing stronger, while the taller spikes have been getting weaker."

Dr. Cooper explained, "The changes have been slow. It took hours to recognize what was happening."

Tanaka set two graphs side by side. "This first graph is from four hours ago. The second one was taken within the last half hour."

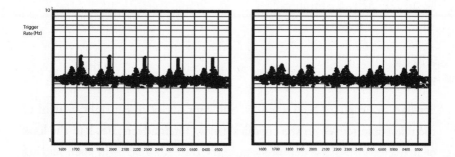

Jun picked up his reading glasses, secured them in place, and leaned over to see. Tanaka's assessment appeared to be correct. On the older graph, the paired bursts of neutrinos were of distinctly different amplitudes. In the latest readings, the pairings were nearly equal in size.

"But what does that mean?" Jun took off his glasses and rubbed his tired eyes.

Tanaka looked to Dr. Cooper, who nodded encouragement. It was rare for the man to show such insecurity. That small fact spoke to how truly upset Tanaka must be. Something had the man scared.

"I believe," Tanaka said, "that what we're witnessing is an approach toward critical mass. Once those two amplitudes match and come into alignment, it will trigger a massive chain reaction within the substrate that's radiating these subatomic particles."

"Like a nuclear reactor melting down," Dr. Cooper said. "Riku and I believe the escalating frequency and changes in amplitude are acting like a natural timer, counting down until the unknown substance in Iceland goes critical."

Jun's chest tightened. "There's going to be another explosion . . . ?"

"Only this time a hundredfold larger," Tanaka added.

"When?"

"I've performed my calculations over and over, extrapolating the time when the paired emissions will align."

"Just tell me when?" Jun pressed.

Dr. Cooper answered. "Within the hour."

Tanaka clarified, demonstrating his usual distaste for generalities. "To be precise, *fifty-two* minutes."

2:32 P.M.
Ellirey Island

Seichan stood guard by a window. She kept out of direct sight, fearful of the telescopic scopes on the enemies' rifles. Their adversaries had the look of mercenary soldiers, definitely military trained. The eight men had set up a perimeter across the front of the lodge, staying sheltered behind rocky outcroppings. She guessed they were awaiting orders as their superiors tried to identify the newcomers to the island. Someone must be trying to decide whether to kill or capture them.

Not that Gray's team had much say in the matter.

She clutched a pistol in both hands, holding the weapon at her knees, ready to shatter the window and defend their base. But she was under no illusions. They were outmanned, outgunned, and outpositioned. With the cadre of soldiers guarding the front of the lodge, the only safe exit was out the back. Then what? They would be exposed if they made a run for the cliff's edge. Even if they reached it, all that would earn them was a swift death on the rocks below the cliffs.

They were trapped.

Gray took up a position on the far side of the door by another window. He clutched a black SIG Sauer in one hand and held a cell phone to his ear in the other. He had managed to reach Sigma command, but the island was too remote for an immediate rescue. They were on their own until help arrived. Seichan could feel acid burning in her stomach, not so much at their predicament, but at Gray's reaction a moment ago when he'd realized they'd been ambushed. She had seen the flash of suspicion. He tried his best to quell it, to damp it down, but it had still been there.

She stared out the window. What did she have to do to prove herself to him? Dying might do it. Then again, maybe not.

She heard Monk talking in low whispers to the caretaker. He'd used smelling salts to revive the man enough to get him on his feet. Once free of the chair, the tough old codger rallied. Swearing a litany that came close to making her blush, he pulled a shotgun down from above the fireplace, ready to exact some revenge.

Gray's voice grew sharper as he spoke on the phone to Sigma command. "Forty minutes? That's how long we have to get clear of the island?"

Frowning, she stared out the window. What was that about? Any answer would have to wait. She watched the soldiers begin to move, shifting out of hiding. They must have received their orders. Whatever fate awaited them—capture or death—it had been decided.

Seichan lifted her pistol. "Here they come!"

19

Kai crept into the small guest bedroom at the rear of the pueblo. She found Hank Kanosh crouched over an open laptop, but he wasn't staring at the screen. He sat with his palms over his face, his posture one of grief. She felt horrible for intruding, considered stepping back out, but her uncle had sent her here.

"Professor Kanosh . . ."

He jerked in the seat, startled, and quickly lowered his hands. He stared at his palms as if he was surprised to find them there.

"I'm sorry for disturbing you," she said.

He reached and closed the laptop. She caught a glimpse of an open e-mail, something with strange writing inscribed in the body of the text, very much like the script she had seen on the gold tablets. He had obviously been trying to work, to keep himself busy.

Painter had allowed them access to the Internet, scrambled over an encrypted satellite feed. They could check their e-mail, peruse the news, but they were forbidden to reach out. *No sending e-mail, no Facebooking.* Though the prohibition on the latter of those two was directed more at her than the professor.

Kanosh took a deep, shuddering breath, collecting himself. "What is it, Kai?"

"Uncle Crowe asked if you'd join him in the main room. There's something he wanted to talk to you about before the others arrived."

He nodded and stood. "It's always something with your uncle, isn't it?"

She offered him a small smile. He squeezed her shoulder as he passed. She flinched from his touch, betraying her nervousness.

"I'll stay here," Kai said. "Uncle Crowe wanted to speak to you alone."

"Then I'd best not keep him waiting."

Once he was gone, she quietly closed the door. She eyed the computer. She'd been reluctant to check her e-mail, afraid of what she'd find. But a gloomy curiosity drew her to the laptop. She couldn't turn her back forever on the havoc she'd caused. She'd have to deal with the consequences eventually—but for now, exposing herself to the world in this small way was enough.

Slipping into the seat that was still warm from the professor, she opened the laptop and stared at the glowing screen. It was now or never. She reached out a hand, opened a browser, and called up her Gmail account.

As she waited for the connection to be made, she held her breath. She had to sit on her hands to keep from reaching out and slamming the laptop closed. What would it hurt to shut out the world for a little bit longer? But before she could act on that thought, the screen filled with lines of unread e-mails. She scanned the list, reading the subject lines. There were a few bits of spam and a few notes dated from before the explosion, but near the top, one message caught her eye.

She went cold all over, her skin prickling, and blindly reached to the laptop, ready to close it, regretting even attempting this. The e-mail address was jh_wahya@cloudbridge.com. She recognized the personal e-mail address for WAHYA's founder, John Hawkes. She didn't even have to open the note to know its contents. The subject line made that clear enough. It was only three letters: *WTF.*

Knowing there was no avoiding it, she tentatively clicked on the message and opened it. As she read the note, a heavy stone settled in her gut. Her friends and compatriots at WAHYA were her entire world. They'd taken her in when she'd aged out of the foster care system and was left to fend for herself. They supported her both financially and emotionally, offering a bond of family that had been sorely missing since the death of her father.

It made the bitterness in the letter so hard to read.

From: jh_wahya@cloudbridge.com
Subject: WTF
To: Kai Quocheets <willow3tree@gmail.com>

What have you done? All of WAHYA placed so much at stake in your honorable and peaceful mission, only to see it come to ruin, bloodshed, and shame. Your face is splashed across all the national news media, labeled as a terrorist and a murderer. It will not be long until your shame becomes ours. Yet, still we have no word from you, only a resounding silence. Were you paid by the U.S. government to betray us, to frame us? That is what is being whispered about you here.

I've done my best to urge patience, to discourage rash judgments, but without some explanation, some proof of your loyalty to our continuing cause, I cannot hold back the wolves from the door much longer. They demand blood, while I only ask for answers.

The WAHYA council has met this past hour. Unless you can clear your name in our eyes, we have no choice but to deny you, to denounce your actions as a rogue agent, to expose you as a true terrorist who subverted our good cause. You have until noon today to respond before we call a press conference.

JH

Kai closed the e-mail. Tears rose from deep inside. She pictured all of her friends, smiling, hugging her before she left for the mountains. She remembered lingering in the embrace of Chayton Shaw, one of the fiercest advocates in the youthful organization. Chay's name meant "falcon" in Sioux, a fitting name given his long black hair, loose to his shoulders, always seeming to lift with even the softest breeze. Two days ago—which seemed an eternity now—they had talked in the quiet of the night of becoming more than just friends.

She thought of him now, picturing him turning his back on her, shunning her. With a soft sob, she covered her face with her palms, hiding both her shame and her tears.

What am I going to do?

8:35 A.M.

Hank Kanosh sat at the table with his back to the hearth, appreciating the warmth of the last embers. Painter took a seat on the other side of the table. His large-boned partner snored softly from the couch.

From the circles under Painter's eyes, it looked like he could also use some sleep, but something was certainly troubling him. Hank suspected it didn't even relate to the matter at hand. The man was too slow to broach whatever subject he wanted to discuss, his manner distracted. Something else was going on. He'd been on the phone all morning. Maybe it had to do with the strange volcanic eruption, maybe another matter. All Hank knew: it had the man on edge.

Eventually Painter cleared his throat and folded his hands on the tabletop. "I'm going to be frank with you, and I hope you'll do the same. People have died, and more will, too, if we don't get a better understanding about what we're facing."

Hank bowed his head slightly. "Of course."

"I've spoken to our geologist, who's monitoring the volcanic activity at the blast site. We believe we have a rudimentary understanding of what was hidden in that cave. It involves the manipulation of matter at the nano-level. We also believe those ancient people created—whether deliberately or accidentally—an unstable compound, something active and explosive, that requires heat to keep it dormant. That's why it was hidden in a geothermal area, where it would be kept warm and safe for centuries."

A flare of guilt burned through Hank. "That is, until we removed it from that heat source."

"And it destabilized. In the wake of that explosion, it released what our geologist calls a *nano-nest,* a mass of nanobots, microscopic nanomachines that eat through matter, with the potential to spread outward indefinitely. But whether through luck or planning by these ancient people, the heat of the erupting volcano killed the nano-nest, stopping it."

Horrified, Hank closed his eyes for a moment. *Maggie . . . what did we do?* He spoke quietly. "That's why the old stories about the cave warned against trespassing there."

"And it may not be the *only* cave like that."

Hank opened his eyes and pinched his brows. "What are you talking about?"

"There may be another site in Iceland."

Iceland?

Painter went on to explain how neutrinos from the Utah blast may have lit the fuse on a potential second cache of this substance.

"The Iceland deposit is destabilizing as we speak," Painter finished. "We have other people in the field investigating it, but there's one key piece of this puzzle that we're missing."

Hank stared the man in the eye, waiting.

"We have some grasp as to *what* was hidden at these sites—but not *who* hid them. Who were these ancient people? Why did they appear Caucasian, yet wore Native American garb?"

Hank's mouth went dry. He had to break eye contact, staring down at his hands.

Painter pressed on: "You know something, Hank. I heard you arguing with Dr. Denton back at his lab. Such knowledge could be vital to fully understanding the danger we face."

Hank knew the man was right, but such answers trod a dangerous line between his blood heritage and his faith. He was reluctant to divulge what he suspected without further proof. Though maybe now he had that proof.

"It was just a theory," Hank said. "Matt may have been a physicist, but he was also a devout Mormon, like myself. Our discussion—Matt's conclusions—were fanciful, not worth mentioning at the time."

Painter cocked his head, fixing him with one eye. "But it is now."

"Your mention of Iceland does offer some support for Matt's theory."

"What theory?"

"To answer that, you have to understand a much-disputed section of the Book of Mormon. According to our scripture, Native Americans were said to be the descendants of a lost tribe of Israel, who came here after the fall of Jerusalem in roughly 600 BC."

"Hold on. Are you actually claiming Indians rose from a Jewish tribe who got exiled here?"

"According to a literal reading of the Book of Mormon, yes. Specifically they are the descendants of the Manasseh clan of Israelites."

"But that makes no sense. There's plenty of archaeological evidence that people were living in the Americas long before 600 BC."

"I am well aware of that. And while it seems contradictory, the Book of Mormon also does acknowledge those people, those early Native Americans. It even makes reference to people living here when that lost tribe of Israelites arrived out west." Hank held up a hand. "But let me continue and perhaps I can clear up that conflict through an interpretation of Mormon scripture that's less literal and more allegorical."

"Okay. Go on."

"According to a *direct* interpretation of the Book of Mormon, the band of Israelites who came to America consisted of two families led by a common father, Lehi. The two branches were the Nephites and Lamanites. I'll skip over the more complicated details, but in the end, around a thousand years later, the Lamanites slaughtered the Nephites and became the Native American tribes of today."

Painter looked unconvinced. "The story sounds more racist than historical. And I know there's certainly no DNA support for a genetic lineage of Native Americans back to European or Middle Eastern origin."

"I agree. Genetic studies have resoundingly shown Native Americans to be of Asiatic origin, likely crossing the Bering Strait and descending into the continent. Believe me, over the years, Mormon scientists and historians have bent over backward trying to link Native Americans to a Jewish heritage and only succeeded in embarrassing themselves."

"Then I don't understand where this is going."

"Today, most Mormons believe a more allegorical version of that part of our scripture. That a lost tribe of Israelites *did* come to America, that they encountered the indigenous clans—the Native American people." Hank motioned to both himself and Painter. "The Israelites settled among our tribes, perhaps tried to convert them, to bring them under the Abrahamic covenant. But the Israelites kept mostly to their own clan, becoming just another tribe among the many Indian nations. That's why there's no lasting genetic trace."

"Such an explanation sounds more forced than convincing."

Hank felt a flash of irritation. "You asked for my help. Do you still want it?"

Painter held up a palm. "I'm sorry. Go on. But I think I know where this is headed. You believe the mummified bodies in the cave were members of that lost Jewish tribe."

"Yes. In fact, I believe they were the scripture's Nephites, who were described in the Book of Mormon as being white-skinned, blessed by God, and gifted with special abilities. Does that not sound like those poor souls we found?"

"And what about those murderous Lamanites who wiped them out?"

"Perhaps they were Indians who converted or made some truce with the newcomers. But eventually something changed over the passing centuries. Something frightened the Indian tribes and drove them to wipe out the Nephites."

"So you're saying the history described in the Book of Mormon is a mix of legend and actual events. That the lost tribe of Israelites— the Nephites—came to America and joined the Native American tribes. Then centuries later, something scared a group of those Indians—the Lamanites—and they wiped out that lost tribe."

Hank nodded. "I know how that sounds, but there's additional support, if you'll hear me out."

Painter waved for him to continue, but he still looked unconvinced.

"Take, for example, the amount of Hebrew sprinkled among the languages of Native American tribes. Research has shown there to be more similarities between the two languages than can be attributed to mere chance. For example, the Semitic Hebrew word for 'lightning' is *baraq*. In Uto-Aztecan, a Native American language group, the word is *berok*." He touched his shoulder. "This is *shekem* in Hebrew, *sikum* in UA." He ran a hand down the bare skin of his arm. "Hebrew *geled*. UA *eled*. The list goes on and on, well beyond coincidence."

"Well and good, but how does this directly relate to the mummified remains in the cave?"

"Let me show you." Hank stood and crossed to his backpack. He opened it, retrieved what he wanted, and returned to his seat. He placed the two gold tablets on the tabletop. "The Book of Mormon was written by Joseph Smith. It came from a series of golden plates gifted to him by the angel Moroni. It was said that the plates were written in a strange language—some say hieroglyphics, others that it was an ancient variant of Hebrew. Joseph Smith was given the ability to translate the plates and that translation became the Book of Mormon."

Painter pulled one of the plates closer. "And the writing on this plate?"

"Before you arrived at the university last night, I had copied a few lines and forwarded them to a colleague of mine—an expert in ancient languages from the Middle East. I just heard back from him this morning. It intrigued him. He was able to recognize the script. It *is* a form of proto-Hebrew."

Painter shifted forward in his seat, perhaps growing more intrigued himself.

"A scholar, Paracelsus, from the sixteenth century was the first to name this proto-Semitic script. He called it the *Alphabet of the Magi.* He claimed to have learned it from an angel, said it was the source of special abilities and magic. All of which makes me wonder if Joseph Smith hadn't come upon a similar cache of such plates and translated them, learning the history of these ancient people—this lost tribe of Israelites—and recorded their story."

Painter leaned back. Hank could see that doubt still remained in his eyes, but it was less scoffing and more thoughtful.

"Then there's Iceland," Hank said.

Painter nodded, already putting that piece of the puzzle into place. "If these ancient practitioners of nanotechnology—scholars, magi, whatever—were indeed from a lost tribe of Israelites, if they were fleeing across the Atlantic with something they wanted to preserve but were unsure if they'd make the journey—"

Hank finished the thought. "Once they hit Iceland, a land of fire in an icy sea, they would have found the perfect warm place to secure at least a portion of their volatile treasure before moving on to America."

"Hank, I think you may—"

The crunch of tires on loose rock cut him off, sounding distant, yet coming fast. Painter swung around, a pistol appearing in his hand seemingly out of nowhere. He hurried to the door.

Kowalski sat up, belched, and looked around blearily. "What? . . . What did I miss?"

Painter checked the window, stared for a full minute as the road noise grew steadily louder—then visibly relaxed. "It's your friends Alvin and Iris. Looks like they found our last guest."

8:44 A.M.

The old dented Toyota SUV kicked up a swirl of sand and dust as it came to stop in the center of the stone cabins. Painter stepped out of the shade of the porch and into the blaze of the sun. Though it was barely morning, the light hammered the surrounding badlands into shades of crimson and gold. Squinting against the glare, he crossed to help Iris out of the driver's seat. Alvin hopped out on the other side.

The elderly pair, wizened by the sun and well into their seventies, looked like old hippies with tie-dyed shirts and faded jeans fraying at the hems. But their clothing was accented with traditional Hopi elements. Iris had her long gray hair done in a Hopi-style braid, decorated with feathers and bits of turquoise. Alvin kept his long snow-white hair loose, his bare arms fitted with thick wristbands of beaten silver holding shells and chunks of turquoise. Both had embroidered belts of typical Hopi design, but rather than ox-hide or buckskin moccasins, they wore hiking boots straight out of some urban outfitter's catalog.

"So at least you haven't burned the place down," Iris said, her hands on her hips, inspecting the homestead.

"Only the coffee," Painter said with a wink.

He stepped past her to the rear door of the SUV to help the final member of the party. Last night, Painter had sent word that he wanted to speak to one of the Ute elders, someone from the same tribe as the grandfather who had murdered his own grandson to keep the cavern secret. Clearly that old man had known something. Maybe other elders of his tribe did, too. He needed someone who could shed some light on the meaning of the cave, on its history. Alvin and Iris had fetched the old man from the bus station so that Painter and the others could keep their exposure to a minimum.

Painter reached for the door handle, ready to assist the elder—only to have it open in front of him. A young man barely in his twenties climbed out. Painter searched the backseat, but no one else was there.

The slim figure stuck out his hand. He was dressed in a navy suit, carrying his jacket and a loose tie over one arm. His white shirt was open at the collar. "I'm Jordan Appawora, elder of the Northern Ute tribe."

The absurdity of that statement did not escape the youth, who offered a shy, embarrassed grin. Painter suspected that shyness was not a habitual trait in the kid. His handshake was hard and firm. There was some muscle hidden under that suit. When he withdrew his hand, he swept his lanky black hair out of his eyes and looked around at the circle of pueblos.

"Perhaps I should clarify," the young man said. "I'm a de facto member of the council of elders. I represent my grandfather, who is blind, mostly deaf, but remains sharp as an ax. I warm his seat at council meetings, take notes, discuss matters with him, and cast his vote."

Painter sighed. That was all well and good, but this young Ute was not the elder that he'd been hoping to question, someone steeped in ancient stories and lost tribal knowledge.

"From your expression," Jordan said, his grin growing wider and warmer, "I can tell you're disappointed, but there was no way my grandfather could make this long trip." He rubbed the seat of his pants with one hand. "As rough as those roads were, he'd be heading to his next hip replacement by now. And considering that last mile, I might need my first."

"Then let's stretch our legs," Alvin said, proving the wisdom of his own years. He waved them toward the pueblo's porch, but he hooked an arm around his wife and nodded to a neighboring cabin. "Iris and I'll see about rustling up a real breakfast at our place while you settle matters."

Painter recognized that the two were making themselves scarce so that his group could talk in private, but considering how matters had changed, this wasn't necessary; still, he wouldn't turn down breakfast. He led Jordan up to the shaded porch. Kowalski was already there, kicked back on a chair, boots up on the rail. He rolled his eyes at Painter, plainly as unimpressed with the so-called elder as Painter was.

Kanosh joined them on the porch with Kai. His stocky cattle dog came, too, sniffing at the newcomer's pant leg.

Jordan made his introductions again—though a bit of that shyness returned as he shook Kai's hand. She also stammered, her voice going soft, and retreated to the opposite side of the porch, feigning a lack of interest, but the corner of her eye often found Jordan through a fall of her hair.

Painter cleared his throat and leaned back on the rail, facing the others. "I assume you know why I asked you to come all the way out here," he said to Jordan.

"I do. My grandfather was good friends with Jimmy Reed. What occurred—the shooting at the cavern—was a tragedy. I knew his grandson, Charlie, very well. I was sent to offer whatever help I can in this matter and to answer any questions."

It was a politician's answer. From the kid's clipped and restrained response, Painter suspected Jordan had spent at least a year in some law school. The young Ute was here to help, but he wasn't going to open his tribe to any further involvement, potentially damaging involvement, in the tragic events that had occurred in the mountains.

Painter nodded. "I appreciate you coming, but what we truly needed was someone—like Jimmy Reed—who adhered to the old ways, who had intimate and detailed knowledge of the cave's history."

Jordan looked unperturbed. "That was clear. Word reached my grandfather, who pulled me aside privately and sent me here without anyone else knowing. As far as the Ute tribe is aware, we refused your request."

Painter shifted, fixing the youth with a sharper gaze. *Maybe this wasn't such a waste after all.*

Jordan didn't shrink from Painter's attention. "Only two elders even knew that cave existed—preserved on a scrap of tribal map that marked the cave's location on Ute lands. It was my grandfather who told Jimmy Reed about the cave. And last night, my grandfather told *me.*"

A flicker of fear showed in the young man's eyes. He glanced away to the sunbaked cliffs, as if trying to shake it off. "Crazy stories . . ." he mumbled.

"About the mummified bodies," Painter coaxed, "about what was hidden there?"

A slow nod. "According to my grandfather, the bodies preserved in that cave were a clan of great shamans, a mysterious race of pale-skinned people who came to this land, bearing great gifts and powers. They were called the people of the *Tawtsee'untsaw Pootseev.*"

Kanosh translated. "People of the Morning Star." He turned to Painter. "Which rises each morning in the *east.*"

Jordan nodded. "Those old stories say the strangers did come from east of the Rockies."

Painter shared a look with Kanosh. The professor was clearly thinking these people came from much farther east than this.

His lost tribe of Israelites . . . the Mormon's Nephites.

"Once settled in these territories," Jordan continued, "the *Tawtsee'untsaw Pootseev* taught our people much, gathering shamans from tribes throughout the West. Word of their teachings spread far and wide, drawing more and more people to them, becoming one great clan themselves."

The Lamanites, Painter thought.

"The *Tawtsee'untsaw Pootseev* were greatly revered, but also feared for the power they possessed. As centuries passed, they kept mostly to themselves. Our own shamans began to fight with each other, seeking more knowledge, beginning to defy the warnings spoken by the strangers. Until one day, a Pueblo tribe to the south stole a powerful treasure from the *Tawtsee'untsaw Pootseev.* But the thieves did not know the power of what they had stolen and brought great doom upon themselves, destroying most of their own clan. In anger, the other tribes set upon the surviving members of the Pueblo clan and slaughtered every man, woman, and child, until they were no more."

"Genocide," Kanosh whispered.

Jordan bowed his head in acknowledgment. "This horrified the *Tawtsee'untsaw Pootseev.* They knew their body of knowledge was too powerful, too tempting to the tribes who were still warring. So they gathered their members throughout the West, hid their treasures in sacred places. Many were murdered as they sought to flee, leaving other clusters of survivors with little choice but to take their own lives to preserve their secrets."

Painter studied Kanosh out of the corner of his eyes. Was this the war described in the Book of Mormon between the Nephites and Lamanites?

"Only a handful of our more trusted elders were given knowledge of these burial caches, where it was said a great accounting of the *Tawtsee'untsaw Pootseev* was written in gold."

Kanosh took a deep breath, turning away, his eyes glassy, maybe from tears. Here was further confirmation of all he believed, about his people, about their place in history and in God's plan.

Still, Painter—long estranged from his own heritage—remained a skeptic. "Is there any proof of this story?"

Jordan took a moment to respond, studying his toes before looking up. "I don't know, but my grandfather says that if you want to know more about the *Tawtsee'untsaw Pootseev,* you should go to the place where their end began."

"What does that mean?" Kowalski asked sourly.

Jordan turned to him. "My grandfather knows where the thieves who stole the treasure met their doom. He also knows their name." He faced the others. "They were the Anasazi."

Painter could not help but let the shock show in his face. The Anasazi were a clan of the ancient pueblo people who lived mostly in the Four Corners area of the United States, known as much for their extensive cliff-dwelling homes as they were for their mysterious and sudden disappearance.

Kanosh stared significantly at Painter. "In the Navajo language, the name Anasazi means 'ancient enemy.'" Kanosh filled in more details. "The Anasazi vanished some time between 1000 and 1100 AD. But it's been hotly debated what triggered their disappearance. Various theories have been expounded: a great drought, bloody battles among tribes. But one of the newest theories from archaeologists at the University of Colorado has the tribe embroiled in a religious war, as violent as any battle between Christians and Muslims. It was said that some new religion drew them en masse to the south. Then shortly after that, the entire clan died out."

That theory certainly meshed with the ancient story told by Jordan's grandfather. Painter turned to the young man. "You said your grandfather knew where these Anasazi thieves met their doom. Where was it?"

"If you have a map of the Southwest, specifically Arizona, I can show you."

As a group, they all moved indoors. The inside of the pueblo was as dark as a cave after the morning's brightness. Kai moved around and flicked on several lamps. Painter drew out a map of the Four Corners region and spread it on the tabletop.

"Show me," Painter said.

Jordan studied the chart for a breath, cocking his head to the side. "It's about three hundred miles south of us," he said, and leaned closer. "Just outside Flagstaff. Ah, here it is."

He poked the map.

Painter read the name at his fingertip. "Sunset Crater National Park."

Well, that certainly makes sense . . .

Kowalski groused under his breath. "Looks like we're going from one volcano to another."

Painter began making arrangements in his head.

"I'm going with you," Kanosh said.

Painter prepared to argue. He wanted to leave the professor here with Kai, to keep them out of harm's way.

"My friends gave their blood, their lives," Kanosh pressed. "I'm going to see this through. And who knows what you'll find in Arizona? You may need my expertise."

Painter frowned, but he had no good cause to dismiss such help.

Kowalski came to the same conclusion. "Sounds good to me."

Kai stepped forward, ready to speak. Painter knew what she was going to say and held up his hand. "You'll stay with Iris and Alvin." He pointed to Jordan. "You, too."

They'd both be safer here, and he didn't want word to get out about where they were headed. Kai looked ready to fight about it, but a glance toward Jordan made her reconsider. Instead, she simply crossed her arms.

Painter thought the matter was settled, but Jordan stepped up. He pulled a folded piece of paper out of his pocket. He looked ready to pass it on, but held it half crumpled between his fingers.

"Before you go, my grandfather wanted me to give you this. But first, I must share one last thing. This is from me, not my grandfather."

"What's that?"

"The legends I just told you were sacred stories, going back centuries, passed from one elder to another. My grandfather only told *me* because he truly believes it's already too late."

Kowalski stirred. "What do you mean *too late*?"

"My grandfather believes that the spirit set free from that cave in the mountains will never be stopped—it will destroy the world."

Painter remembered Chin's description of the boil growing outward from the blast site, what he called a *nano-nest*, picturing microscopic nanomachines disassembling all matter it touched. The potential of it spreading indefinitely was terrifying.

"But it *was* stopped," Painter finally said. "The volcanic eruption bottled that genie back up."

Jordan stared him in the eye. "That was only the beginning. My grandfather says the spirit will sweep around the world from here, setting off more destruction until the world is a sandy ruin."

Painter went cold. The description was frighteningly similar to the physicists' theory that the neutrino blast in Utah had shot through the globe and lit the fuse on another cache of nano-material. He recalled Kat's warning about the impending explosion in Iceland.

Jordan stretched out his hand with the folded slip of paper. "My grandfather holds out little hope, but he wanted to share this. It is the mark of the *Tawtsee'untsaw Pootseev*. He says to let it guide you to where you need to go."

Painter took the piece of paper and opened it. What was written there made no sense, but it still caused him to go weak in his knees. He shook his head in disbelief. He recognized the pair of symbols smudged in charcoal on the paper, the sign of the *Tawtsee'untsaw Poot-seev*.

A crescent moon and a small star.

The same symbols were found at the center of the Guild's mark.

How could that be?

20

Thirty-two minutes . . .

Standing guard at the window, Gray tightened his fingers on his pistol. He had spoken to Kat a few minutes ago—not only couldn't she get his team any help, but she also shared disturbing news out of Japan. If those physicists were right, the island would blow shortly after 3:00 P.M. They had to be off this rock before then. There was only one problem—no, make that *eight* problems.

The skilled team of commandos had taken up secure positions across the front of the small lodge, keeping the place covered. A few minutes ago, the soldiers had begun to storm the place, but for some reason they suddenly retreated to the shelter of a group of basalt outcroppings.

"Why aren't they attacking?" Ollie asked. The old caretaker stood by the hearth with his shotgun in his hands. Harshly beaten, he'd rallied after Monk freed him, but it was clear that the waiting was wearing him down.

Seichan answered, but she didn't take her eyes off the window she guarded. "Like us, they must have heard the island is going to explode. They're just pinning us down here until they can make their escape."

Her words proved to be prophetic as the *whump-whump* of an approaching helicopter shook the panes of glass. A midsize transport helicopter swept over the lodge and out into the open meadow. The bird's tandem, four-blade rotors flattened the grasses as it hovered, its pilot searching for a safe place to land amid the broken rock.

We need to be on that chopper, Gray thought.

"Look!" Seichan called, and pointed. "Across the meadow, by the boulders. We've got more company."

Gray tore his eyes from the helicopter and spotted what had alarmed her. More soldiers fled out of the broken landscape, coming from the direction of the smoky signature that marked the recent TNT blast. In the lead ran a figure wearing civilian clothing: hiking boots, all-weather pants, and a heavy jacket, unzipped. The middle-aged man hugged a backpack to his ample belly. Behind him, two soldiers carried a stretcher between them, piled high with small stone boxes.

They must have successfully blasted their way into the treasure hold on the island. If Gray had any doubt, it was dashed when he spotted the glint of gold atop the pile of boxes. One of the soldiers waved frantically for the helicopter to land.

They definitely know the island's about to blow.

A scrape of a boot drew his attention around. Monk rushed up, breathless. "I checked the entire rear of the building. Looks clear."

"We'll have to move fast. They're evacuating."

Monk nodded. "I saw the chopper."

"Then let's do this."

After Gray made sure everyone knew what to do, Ollie and Monk took positions at the front windows while he and Seichan ran toward the back door to the lodge.

"Let's hope that old man knew what he was talking about," Seichan said.

Gray was betting their lives on it. The caretaker had been coming to the island for sixty years. If anyone knew its secrets, it had to be Ollie.

Together, he and Seichan burst out the door and into the sunlit meadow and sprinted low to the ground. The bulk of the lodge sheltered them from the view of the commandos. Gray headed toward a slight rise in the green field. Ollie had pointed it out, told him what to expect. Still, as he fled around the shallow hill, he came close to falling headlong into an open pit on the far side.

Seichan snagged his arm and pulled him to a stop at the edge. The rise in the ground was actually an old hardened bubble of lava, hollow on the inside. The far side opened into the source of that bulge: a lava tube. The mouth of the tunnel yawned amid a jumble of cracked basaltic rock, like so many broken teeth.

They shifted to where a pile of debris allowed them to climb down into the tube's throat. Gray flicked on a flashlight. The beam revealed a smooth-walled tunnel, barely wide enough for one person and no headroom.

"Follow me," Gray said, and set off at a fast clip.

According to Ollie, the tube ran under the lodge and down to a small cavern below the meadow. It was a crossroads of sorts. From there, another tunnel led back to the surface, opening on the far side of the meadow. The caretaker had hurriedly mapped it out. Afterward, Gray had memorized the route, but he also recalled the trawler captain's description of the island: *a hardened chunk of Swiss cheese, carved by wind and rain*. It would be easy to get lost in here—and they had no time for mistakes.

In under a minute, they reached a high-arching cavern. Boulders cluttered the floor. Pools of dank rainwater splashed underfoot, and the air smelled of mold and salt. Gray turned in a circle, sweeping out with his light. There were a half-dozen exits. Ollie had marked only *four* on his \ map.

With his heart thudding against his rib cage, Gray went back to the lava tube and did his best to circle along the wall, checking each opening. He'd been told to take the second passage along this side. The first opening he came to was a crack. He shone his light down it. It squeezed shut after only a couple yards. *Did that count? Or had Ollie skipped it because it wasn't a true tunnel?*

Gray hurried along. The old caretaker struck him as no-nonsense and practical. There was nothing superfluous about the sea-hardened man. He would stick only to the details that were important. Trusting that, Gray ignored the blind crack, bypassed the next tunnel, and headed to the one after that. This had to be the *second* passageway marked on Ollie's map.

It proved to be another lava tube, which was good, but it drilled deeper, heading *down*. That didn't seem right, but Gray could waste no more time. Taking a deep breath, he entered the tunnel. It was even tighter than the first one.

"Are you sure this is the right way?" Seichan said.

"We'll find out."

Gray hurried along and began to doubt his decision until the tube dipped and started to rise again, aiming back toward the surface. After another long minute, the tunnel brightened on its own. He flicked off his flashlight. The bell beat of twin rotors echoed down to them.

The opening appeared ahead, blindingly bright. A hard breeze blew down at them, stinging them with grit.

He turned and bent to Seichan's ear. "We must be close to the helicopter."

She nodded, freed her pistol, and waved him forward.

He rushed the rest of the way, but slowed the final steps, canvassing the opening. The tube dumped into a nest of broken stony pinnacles that looked like a giant game of pickup sticks. He crept out and crawled into cover. Behind him, Seichan rolled free and slipped into the shelter of a stony deadfall.

Gray assessed the situation at a glance.

Only ten yards away, the helicopter rested on its wheels in the meadow, rotors churning. It must have just landed. Two soldiers were pulling the side doors open. The other commandos clustered nearby, twenty in all.

The stretcher rested in the grass, its cargo still waiting to be shifted to the chopper's hold. Gray noted the gold shining on top. It came from a broken stone box, revealing a stack of metal tablets inside.

Same as the Utah cave.

Standing next to the stretcher, still clutching the pack to his chest with one arm, was the civilian he'd noted before. Gray got a better look at his face. Blond hair framed a pale complexion, with pouting lips and a scruff of patchy beard. It was the face of someone who led a soft life and found little he liked about it. As soon as the helicopter's door was fully open, the man rushed forward. Soldiers helped him inside.

Beyond the chopper, the lodge remained dark and quiet on the far side of the meadow. Monk waited for his signal. It would be hard to miss.

Gray aimed his SIG Sauer P226. The magazine held twelve .357 rounds. Same as Seichan's weapon. Each shot had to count. Seichan matched his pose, ready.

Gray aimed for the soldier guarding the helicopter. He couldn't risk any of the enemy gaining shelter inside the chopper's hold. He centered his shot and squeezed the trigger.

The crack of his pistol was loud, triggering an echo from Seichan's weapon. Gray's target dropped. Before the soldier could hit the ground, Gray shifted and blew the throat out of a second.

Confusion reigned for several breaths. The soldiers, jammed together and deafened by the helicopter's engines, struggled to ascertain who was shooting at them. One of the eight original commandos fired at the lodge, believing it to be the source of the attack.

A shotgun blast responded from the building, shattering out a window as Ollie took a potshot at the attackers.

Good job, Ollie . . .

All eyes turned in the lodge's direction.

A mistake.

With everyone looking the wrong way, Gray took out another two men in the back, while Seichan concentrated her fire on the eight commandos who had the lodge pinned down. Her accuracy was scary good. She emptied her clip, taking four men down at some distance.

As she ejected one magazine and slapped in another, Gray shifted his focus to the closest two soldiers. The pair had backed away from the lodge, coming close to their hiding spot, unaware of the danger. He took them both out, emptying his magazine into them while hurtling out of hiding, staying low.

They needed more firepower.

Reaching the bodies, he grabbed one of their automatic weapons, snatching it in midrun. Seichan shadowed him, firing her pistol. He swung the rifle up, thumbed it into full automatic, and fired from the hip. He strafed into the line of soldiers, taking several down and driving the rest away from the chopper and into the sheltering boulders.

Seichan gained the other rifle.

Together, they dove into the helicopter's hold.

The only occupant was the pudgy civilian. His hands were struggling at his waist, trying to free a holstered weapon, but Seichan slammed him hard with the butt of her rifle. He fell limply into his seat. She headed toward the pilots, determined to sway them to their cause at gunpoint.

Gray continued his barrage, fierce enough to allow Monk and Ollie to make a break from the lodge. They ran low while Gray covered them. Monk fired, too, offering further discouragement.

The two reached the chopper safely. Gray yanked them inside and tugged the cabin door closed. His ears rang from all the gunfire.

"Stay low!" he yelled at Monk and Ollie.

The reason for this command became clear as the helicopter was fired upon. Rounds pinged off the sides. But already the engines were howling up. Apparently Seichan had been persuasive enough—or the pilots already knew about the impending explosion of the island.

Gray checked his watch.

Four more minutes . . .

He had time to spare.

He was wrong.

A tremendous blast rocked the chopper. The ground bucked under the helicopter, knocking Gray to his hands and knees. Overhead, the engines screamed. The helicopter rose unsteadily, canted nose first, its liftoff bungled by the quake. The hatch crashed back open, improperly latched in his haste.

Beyond the door, clouds and smoke obscured half the island.

"Gray!" Monk hollered.

Gray twisted to see the civilian, his nose broken and bloody, diving for the open door, still clutching his pack. Gray rolled after him and snatched at the bag, catching a strap. Whatever was inside had to be important enough if the man was willing to die to keep it from him. But the guy would not let go. He had an arm hooked in the other strap as he plummeted out of the helicopter.

The man's weight, as he jarred to a stop, dangling by the pack, yanked Gray toward the open door. On his belly, half out the door, Gray refused to let go of the pack. The man whipped his body back and forth, trying to free himself and his precious prize.

Gray slid farther out the door—then a heavy weight fell across his legs, pinning him in place.

"I got you," Monk said.

The chopper rose higher, struggling for height. As they climbed, one section of the ancient volcanic cone broke away and slid heavily toward the sea. Deep fissures skittered across the remainder of the island. Men scurried in all directions, fleeing the destruction—but there was no escape.

Not even by air.

The helicopter shuddered and suddenly dropped several yards in a single second. Gray rose off the floor, then crashed back down. Monk struggled to keep him from falling out the door.

"We're losing pressure!" Seichan yelled from the cockpit.

Before Gray could respond to the new danger, he heard the blast of a pistol. A searing burn clipped the edge of his ear. He stared below. His nemesis was hanging by one arm, but he'd finally succeeded in freeing his weapon with the other. If the chopper hadn't dropped so suddenly, Gray would already be dead.

Not that he had a long life expectancy at the moment.

As the pilot sought to steady the helicopter, the stubborn civilian fixed his aim more carefully. At point-blank range, he wouldn't miss a second time.

The man smiled up at Gray, yelled something in French, and pulled the trigger. The blast was deafening—but it didn't come from a pistol. It came from a shotgun.

The next thing Gray knew, Ollie was straddling him, holding his smoking weapon.

Below, half the man's face was gone. Slowly, his slack arm fell free of the pack, and his body tumbled end over end toward the ruins of the island.

Monk pulled Gray and his hard-earned prize back inside.

Monk shook his head. "From now on, arms and legs inside the ride at all times."

Gray reached out and clasped Ollie's hand. "Thanks."

"Owed him." Ollie gingerly touched his broken nose. "No one punches me in the face and gets away with it."

Again the helicopter bumped violently and began a dizzying drop earthward. They all grabbed for handholds, waiting for the plunge to stop. It didn't. Gray stared out the open door. The island, cracking apart and crumbling, rose up toward them. Fires now glowed within the depths of the deepest fissures, smoldering with the promise of worse to come.

As they continued to fall, the chopper began a slow spin.

Seichan popped her head into the hold from the cockpit. "We've lost all pressure to the rear rotors!" she said, and added what all of them already knew: "We're going down!"

21

Kai stood on the porch in the shade. She crunched a roasted piñon nut between her teeth, savoring the salty, rich flavor. Iris had gathered the seeds from the native piñon pines growing here. She was still inside shaking her winnowing tray over an open fire, preparing more nuts to be ground into flour.

Iris tried to show her how it was done, how to keep from burning the nuts, but Kai knew the old Hopi woman was only trying to distract her. Instead, Kai stared at a thin pall of dust retreating across the badlands. Painter and the others had wasted no time, gathering gear and flying off in the rented SUV, even taking the dog.

But not her.

Earlier, she'd reined in her anger, knowing it would do her no good. Bitterness still burned like coal in her gut. She'd been here at the start of all of this mess. She deserved to see it through to the end. They kept saying that she had to bear the consequences of her actions like a woman, yet still treated her like a child.

She popped another nut in her mouth, grinding it between her teeth. She was used to being left behind. So why should today be any different? Why should she expect anything more from her uncle?

But deep down, she had.

"That guy's sort of intense."

Kai turned to find Jordan Appawora standing in the doorway. He'd changed out of his suit into cowboy boots, a faded blue T-shirt, and black jeans held up by a belt with a large silver buckle in the shape of a buffalo head.

"So Painter Crowe's your uncle?" he asked.

"Distantly." At the moment she was ready to sever their blood ties entirely.

Jordan stepped onto the porch. He held a cowboy hat in one hand and juggled a small fistful of steaming piñon nuts in the other, trying to cool them. He must have taken them straight from Iris's pan. He noted her attention, flipping one into his mouth.

"They're called *toovuts* in Paiute," he said as he chewed the kernel. "Do you want to know what they're called in Hopi?"

She shook her head.

"How about in Arapaho or Navajo?" he asked, now grinning. He came closer. "It seems our host is willing to share all she knows about piñon nuts. Did you know the pitch from piñon pine trees was used as chewing gum, or that it also acted as a balm on cuts and wounds? Seems the sticky stuff was both the Trident and Neosporin of the Old World."

She hid a grin, turning away.

"I had to get out of there," he whispered conspiratorially, "before she started teaching me the Hopi rain dance."

"She's only trying to help," Kai scolded, but could not hold back her grin.

"So what do we do now?" Jordan asked, donning his cowboy hat. "We could take a hike to Three Finger Canyon. Or Alvin's grandkids left their mountain bikes . . . we could take a ride to Black Dragon Wash."

She glanced to him, trying to ascertain his motives. His tanned face, with high cheekbones that made his dark eyes shine, seemed innocent and open. But she suspected there was more to the invitation than exercise and sightseeing. She'd caught him staring a bit too often her way. Even now, she felt a blush heating her cheeks and stepped toward the open doorway. She already had someone interested in her, someone important to her.

She pictured Chayton Shaw back with her friends at WAHYA. It would feel like a betrayal to go out with Jordan. She'd already compromised herself enough. She still stung from the e-mail she'd read earlier. She didn't intend to make things worse.

"I better stick close," she said, heading inside. "In case my uncle calls . . ."

It was a lame excuse, even to her own ears, but he didn't call her on it, which made it that much harder to turn her back on him and head inside. Still, she glanced over a shoulder, staring at Jordan as he stood silhouetted against the morning's brightness. She couldn't help but compare him to Chay, whose fierce activism was all too often blunted by peyote, mushrooms, or weed. Though she'd known Jordan for less than an hour, there was something purer and more honest about his tribal pride, the way he doted on and supported his grandfather, the way he listened patiently to Iris's teachings.

Seeming to sense her attention, he began to swing around. She hurried away, bumping into the table, almost knocking over a tray of cooling piñon nuts. She headed to the back room, needing some privacy.

She stood in the darkness and covered her burning cheeks with her palms. *What am I doing?*

Across the room, the closed laptop's idle button glowed like a green cat's eye in the dark. Painter had left the satellite hookup and one of his linked sat-phones, in case he needed to reach them. She was thankful for that.

Needing something to distract her, she crossed to the desk, sat down, and opened the laptop. She feared seeing a second note from John Hawkes, but she had to check. She called up her e-mail account, and after an interminable wait, saw she had no new mail. She reached to close the laptop, but her eyes drifted to the saved note from WAHYA's founder. Scrunching up her face in determination, she opened it again. She wanted to read it once more, maybe as some sort of punishment, maybe to see if it was as bad as she remembered.

As she read it again, she felt no despair as she had felt last time—instead, anger slowly built with each line. Already bitter from Painter's abandonment, she recognized that John Hawkes was trying to do the same. To shuck her off when there was the least bit of trouble.

After all I did . . . all I risked . . .

Before she could think otherwise, she hit the reply button. She didn't intend to send the response. She just needed to vent, to get it off her chest. She typed rapidly, unloading her fury through her fingertips. She wrote a long, rambling letter, declaring her innocence and explaining how she was actively clearing her name without any help from WAHYA. She underlined that last part. It felt good to do so. She expressed her disdain for the lack of loyalty and support shown to one of their own. She listed all of her accomplishments and contributions to the cause. She also let John Hawkes know how much WAHYA meant to her, how this betrayal and mistrust of her wounded her to the marrow of her bones.

By the time she typed those last words, tears were welling up in her eyes, blurring the screen. She knew they came from somewhere deep inside, from a wound that would not heal. She wanted to be loved for who she was—for the good, the bad, the noble, and the weak—and not to be tossed aside when her presence grew inconvenient. In the end, she recognized a truth about herself. She wanted to be loved like her father had loved her. She deserved that. She wanted to scream it at the world.

Instead, she stared at the screen, at the letter—and did the next best thing. She reached out, moved the cursor, and allowed her finger to hover. Painter said the Internet connection was vigorously encrypted.

What could be the danger?

Taking back a bit of control over her own life, she hit send.

9:18 A.M.
Salt Lake City, Utah

Rafe smiled as the in-box chimed with new mail. He checked his watch. It was hours earlier than he'd anticipated. Matters were moving forward splendidly. He straightened with a luxurious stretch, wearing a plush hotel robe and slippers, his hair still damp from a shower.

He glanced around the presidential suite, situated at the top of the Grand America Hotel at the heart of Salt Lake City. For the first time since arriving in the States, he almost felt at home, ensconced amid all the European appointments of the room: the handcrafted cherrywood Richelieu furniture, the Carrara marble in the spa bathroom, the seventeenth-century Flemish tapestries. From his perch atop the hotel, floor-to-ceiling windows looked out onto breathtaking views of the mountains and down to the meticulously tended parterre gardens far below.

A sniffling sob dampened his good mood.

He turned to the scrawny young man, stripped naked and taped to one of the Richelieu dining chairs. Duct tape sealed his mouth. Twin lines of snot ran from his nose. He gasped, struggling for air, eyes wide and glassy like a wounded fox.

But he wasn't a fox.

He was Rafe's hawk . . . a hawk he'd sent hunting.

The biographical data on Kai Quocheets had listed her affiliations, including her participation in WAHYA, the fierce young wolves fighting for Native American rights. It had taken less than an hour to determine where the organization's leader had squirreled himself away. He'd come to Salt Lake City to be close to the action in the mountains, ready for the exposure that came with such a tragedy. But apparently John Hawkes had other needs, too. Bern had collected him out of a strip club near the airport. Seems the Native American activist liked his women white and blond, with perky fake breasts.

Another whimper rose from the chair.

Rafe held up a finger. "Patience, Mr. Hawkes. We'll get back to you soon enough. You've been most cooperative. But first let's make sure your hunt was successful."

It had not taken much to convert John Hawkes to their cause. Two of his fingers still pointed toward the ceiling. Ashanda had snapped them back as easily as breaking small twigs. Rafe, with his brittle bones, knew that particular exquisite pain. Over the course of his life, he'd broken every one of his fingers and toes.

Not always by accident.

Eventually they won Mr. Hawkes's cooperation, gaining all the necessary insight and personal details about Kai to craft a letter intended to draw out Rafe's little escaped bird. And it had apparently worked.

Much faster than I expected . . .

In the e-mail sent out, he'd set a noon deadline for her to respond. She wasn't wasting any time. He didn't intend to either.

"Sir, we've succeeded in decrypting the e-mail's text," the team's computer asset informed him.

Rafe turned to the man. The technician went simply by the name TJ—but Rafe had never been curious enough to ask what those initials stood for. He was an American, emaciated, often hyped on stimulants so he could run code for days at a time. The expert stood before a bevy of mini–mainframe/servers, all interconnected by Cat 6 cables and hooked into a T2 broadband line.

Rafe didn't understand a tenth of it. All he cared about were results.

"The text will be coming up on your personal screen in a moment, sir. We're tracking IP addresses, triangulating sat-nodes, sifting server connections, and running a killer algorithm to untangle packet pathways."

"Just find where it was sent from."

"We're working on it."

Rafe rolled his eyes at the use of the word *we*. TJ was no more than a glorified assistant. The true digital magician sat in the center of the wired nest of equipment. Ashanda's long fingers danced over three keyboards, as swiftly and elegantly as any concert pianist's on a baby grand. In place of sheet music, her gaze swept through lines of flowing code. On another screen, server nodes and gateway protocols splintered into a tangled web that spread across a digital global map. Nothing could stand in her way. Firewalls toppled before her like dominoes.

Satisfied, Rafe crossed to his personal laptop and read the text message on the screen from Kai Quocheets. He tapped a finger against his lower lip as he read through the wash of teenage angst and hurt feelings. A small part of him felt a twinge of sympathy, drawn by her passion, by her raw exposure on the screen. He glanced over to John Hawkes, suddenly feeling like breaking a third finger on the man's hand. Clearly the leader sorely used his fellow members, taking advantage of their youth and exuberance. In the end, he let others suffer the consequences while he took all of the glory.

That was simply poor management practices.

TJ whistled, drawing back Rafe's attention. He leaned over Ashanda's shoulder. "I think she's got it!" he said, his voice rising in pitch. "She's crashing through the last doors!"

Rafe stepped over, nudging TJ to the side. If they were victorious, he wanted to savor the moment with Ashanda.

Standing behind her, he leaned to her ear. "Show me what you can do . . ."

She gave no sign of acknowledgment. She was lost in her own world, as surely as any artist in the heat of inspiration. This was her medium. It was said that when a person lost one sense, another would grow stronger. This was Ashanda's new sense, a digital extension of herself.

He ran a hand down one of her arms, feeling the old bumps of scarification under her skin. Such scarring was a ritualistic practice among the African tribe to which she had belonged. The bumps had been more prominent when she arrived at the château as a child. Now they could be felt only under the fingertips, like reading Braille.

"She's almost there!" TJ said, breathless.

Ashanda leaned ever so slightly closer to Rafe's cheek. He felt the warmth of her skin across the distance. No one truly understood their relationship. He couldn't put it into words himself, and that was certainly true for her as well. They'd been inseparable since childhood. She was his nanny, his nurse, his sister, his confidante. Throughout his life, she was the silent well into which he could cast his hopes, his fears, his desires. In turn, he offered her security, a life without want—but also love, sometimes even physical, though that was rare. He was impotent, a side effect of his brittle disease. It seemed that even that most intimate of *bones* was damaged.

He studied her hands as they flew between the keyboards. He remembered how in private moments she would occasionally bend his finger,
torturing him between agony and ecstasy until it finally snapped. It wasn't
masochism. Rather, there was a kind of purity in that pain that he found
freeing. It taught him not to fear his body's weakness but to embrace it, to
tap into a primal well of sensation that was unique to him.

She let out the softest sigh.

"She did it!" TJ whooped, lifting his arms high, like a soccer fan after
a goal.

Rafe leaned closer to her, allowing his cheek to touch hers. "Well
done," he whispered in her ear.

Not moving, he stared at the screen. The digital map had swelled, and
glowing green lines converged into a single locus situated in Utah. Rafe
noted the location and smiled at the serendipitous sight of his own name
on the screen.

"San *Rafael*," he said. Amusement lifted his spirits. "Oh, that's just too
perfect."

He turned to John Hawkes.

The man's eyes were wide upon him.

"Looks like we won't be needing our hunting hawk any longer," he
mumbled.

He crossed toward the naked man, who let out a loud, panicked
moan. Rafe believed he owed John Hawkes a small gift for his services—
in this case, a lesson in good management practices, something that the
man sorely lacked.

Rafe stepped behind him, hooked an arm around his thin throat. It
wasn't easy to snap a man's neck, nothing like in the movies. It took him
three tries. But it was a good lesson. Sometimes even a leader had to get his
hands dirty. It helped maintain morale.

He moved back, wiping a pebbling of well-earned sweat from his
brow.

"With that out of the way . . ." Rafe held forth an arm for Ashanda.
"Shall we move on, *mon chaton noir*?"

22

Gray braced himself behind the pilot, Seichan at his side. Her hand was clamped hard to his forearm, as much from a need to hold herself steady as it was from terror.

The helicopter plunged toward a fiery doom, spiraling down. Rotors screamed overhead, struggling to hold them aloft. Beyond the cockpit window, clouds of smoke billowed while hot particulate rattled against the sides of the plummeting craft like hail. The engine's air intakes sucked in the same debris, choking the motors further.

In the seat, the pilot fought the cyclic stick between his legs with one arm and flipped switches on the console with the other. He was one of the enemy, one of the mercenary commandos, but at the moment his fate was tied to theirs—and the outlook was not good.

"We're fucked!" the pilot yelled. "Nothing I can do!"

The island flew up toward them, a steaming, shattered chunk of rock. Fissures continued to tear apart the ancient volcanic cone. Fires raged within the deepest chasms. Seawater flooded into the island's interior and blasted upward in steaming geysers as icy water met molten rock.

It was hell on earth down there.

Their best hope, Gray determined, was out at sea, but the waters were frigid, capable of killing in minutes. He climbed into the empty copilot seat and pressed his face against the curve of the window. He searched the waters around the island. Sunlight reflected brightly off the waves, a sight that was far too cheery considering the circumstance. But the column of smoke and steam rising from the island cast a dark shadow to the south. It was within that shadow that he could discern a sliver of white riding the dark sea.

"There!" Gray exclaimed, and pointed down and to the right. "At your two o'clock! South of the island."

The pilot turned to him, his face deathly pale under his helmet. "What . . . ?"

"A boat." It had to be Captain Huld's fishing trawler. "Crash this bird as close to it as you can."

The pilot canted the helicopter on its side and searched below. "I see it. Don't know if I even have enough lift to clear the island, let alone get that far out to sea."

Still, the pilot knew they had no other choice. Adjusting the cyclic stick and collective pitch, he angled their plunge to the south. Even this small maneuver caused them to lose altitude. Hobbled with only one set of working rotors, the large craft dropped precipitously. The island filled the world below. Gray lost sight of the boat beyond the rocky cliffs.

"Not going to make it . . ." the pilot said, fighting stick and throttle.

An explosion of boiling water and steam blasted out of a crack ahead, shooting high into the sky. The craft crashed through it, blinding them all for a frightening breath. Then they were past it. The water blew clear of the glass, revealing a deadly plunge toward a scalloped curve of volcanic cone. It rose like a rocky wave ahead of them, blocking the way to the open water.

"Not enough power!" the pilot hollered above the strained wail of the rotors.

"Give it everything you can!" Gray hollered back.

The ground grew closer. Gray spotted the sprawled bodies of cattle in the open field, killed by either the extreme heat or toxic gases—or maybe simply from sheer fright.

Then suddenly the island began to fall away. The meadow receded beneath them.

We're climbing again.

The pilot saw it, too. "That's not me!" He pointed to the altimeter. "We're still falling!"

Gray shifted closer to the window and stared below. He realized his error. The helicopter wasn't climbing—*the ground was falling under them.*

As he watched, a chunk of cone broke away, split off by the boiling crack behind them. A quarter of the island slowly tipped and slid toward the sea, upending like a drunk falling off a bar stool.

Ahead, the wall of the volcanic rock lowered, tilting and dropping away, clearing a path to the open sea. But they weren't out of the woods.

"It'll be close!" the pilot said.

Below, boulders bounced and rolled across the meadow. One rock sailed past the cockpit window.

The pilot swore, bobbling the craft to avoid a collision.

Still, they continued to hurtle toward the lip of the cone. It was dropping away too slowly. The pilot groaned, fighting the stick with everything he had. Gray activated the copilot seat's controls. He didn't have any skill with this particular craft, but he could lend some muscle. He hauled on the collective. It fought him, felt like he was trying to crowbar the craft higher.

"No good!" the pilot bellowed. "Hold tight! We're going to cr—"

Then they hit.

The wheels and lower skids slammed into the rocky lip of the cone, tearing away beneath the craft with a screech of metal. The helicopter was tossed up on its nose. Through the windshield, Gray got a dizzying look at the dark sea below as the craft flipped clear of the crumbling island.

The helicopter flew farther out, toppling on its side, spinning the world into a kaleidoscope.

3:22 P.M.

Seichan caught glimpses of the dark sea as the helicopter spun wildly. She clutched a handle overhead, her legs pinned against a spar to hold her in place. Monk bellowed from the back, accompanied by a sharper cry from the old caretaker. Closer at hand, Gray was tossed from the co-pilot's seat and struck the windshield hard, cracking his head against the frame.

Beside him, strapped in place, the pilot continued to wrestle with his controls, trying every trick he knew to stabilize the craft, to slow their dive. With a final yank on the stick, the chopper's nose lifted slightly, slowing the spin.

Gray crashed crookedly back to his seat, kneeing the pilot in the helmet. Blood ran from Gray's scalp, drenching half his face.

The pilot pushed him away. "Clear out of here! Brace yourselves."

Seichan reached with her free arm, knotted a fist in the collar of Gray's jacket, and pulled him back with her. They tumbled together into the rear cabin. Monk fought to strap Ollie into a seat.

The side door slammed open and closed wildly, offering a juddering view of the island's ruins. The broken ridge of cone struck the water, welling up a massive wave and sending it seaward. Beyond it, smoke hid most of the landmass, rising from several chutes. At the heart of the darkness, a flaming fountain glowed, bubbling mostly near the surface, occasionally splashing higher.

But more frightening was the sea as it rushed upward.

With only seconds to spare, Seichan shouldered the dazed Gray into a wall covered in cargo netting. He understood enough to tangle his arms into the material. She moved to do the same, turning in time to see the giant wave cast off by the broken island rise underneath the helicopter, reaching up to meet the plummeting craft.

They hit the wave hard. Her body slammed to the floor. She heard metal scream—then nothing, as icy water swamped the cabin. The flood tossed her body like a rag doll. Her leg hit something sharp, tearing through her jeans, ripping a hot line of fire across her thigh. Then she was shoved violently into Gray, his head still in a pocket of air. He tried to grab her with one arm. She tried to snatch at the netting.

Both efforts failed.

The current tore her away as the helicopter rolled deeper, flushing her out the open door amid a rush of bubbles. She tumbled end over end, choking on seawater, trailing blood. Below, the broken helicopter sank into the dark depths amid a spreading cloud of oil. She saw no one else swim clear as the craft vanished into the blackness.

Gray . . .

But there was nothing she could do. Even if she could swim down, the helicopter was already too deep. No one could make it back to the surface before drowning.

Hopeless and despairing, she fought her heavy heart and twisted away. She craned up toward the wan sunlight. She had not realized how far she'd been pulled down herself. Desperate for air, unsure if she could make it, she kicked for the surface, the cold cutting through her like a flurry of knife blades.

Then something dark swept past overhead, blocking the sun: a black, sleek shadow. She froze, hovering in the icy depths. Other shadows appeared around her, circling, fins cutting through the waters. One swept close, rolling a large eye toward her as it passed. She read the intelligence in that gleam, the cunning, along with a raw hunger.

Orcas . . .

Drawn by her seeping blood.

Though the waters chilled her down to her bones, a prickling heat swept through her. She stared below, sensing the danger.

A black shape swept up out of the depths toward her, the mouth splitting wide, revealing a maw of sharp teeth.

She screamed, swallowing seawater, kicking frantically.

It was no use.

Teeth cut through her pant leg, into her flesh.

3:24 P.M.

Holding his breath, nearly out of air in the sinking helicopter, Gray yanked loose the cargo straps with numb, icy fingers. Pressure pounded his head, staking needles into his skull. He freed the two-foot rubber cube from its webbing and kicked free.

He bumped into Monk, who had liberated his own package. He hugged Ollie under one arm. The old man lolled loosely, unconscious, possibly drowned. Gray had checked on the pilot shortly after the crash. He was dead, still strapped in place, a large chunk of metal pierced through his throat.

No hope there.

With everything they needed, Monk and Gray kicked out of the open hatch and into the twilight waters. Sun and air were far overhead. They'd never make it to the surface on their own, especially not in time for any hope of resuscitating Ollie. But Gray owed the old man his life. He intended to return the favor.

Gray passed his rubber package to Monk. Air bubbled from his friend's lips as his prosthetic hand clamped hard to the rope handle dangling from the cube. He read the agony in Monk's eyes, imagined he looked the same. If the cold didn't kill them, the lack of air soon would.

Gray grasped Monk's belt with one arm, ready to hug Ollie between them. But first he reached and tugged the cord on the compressed air cartridge alongside the cube.

With one pull, the Rapid Deployment Craft inflated, swelling open overhead into a yellow life raft. Normally, RDCs were tossed out of aircraft to drowning sailors. Gray hoped that putting one to this new use would rescue them. The raft's buoyancy immediately began tugging them upward—at first slowly, then more and more rapidly.

In a matter of seconds, they were rocketing through the water.

Gray held tightly to Monk and Ollie as they flew toward the surface. The waters grew rapidly lighter around them. Gray relieved his screaming need for oxygen by letting air escape his chest, blowing out, tricking his lungs into thinking he was about to inhale.

He hoped it wasn't just a trick.

His vision narrowed from lack of oxygen, darkening his view, making it hard for him to tell how much farther they had to go.

Then, like a cork from a champagne bottle, they shot out of the water. The raft leaped free, clearing the waves, tossing them high. They all flew, crashing back to the sea. Gray managed to keep his grip on Ollie. Monk kept hold of the raft.

Gray sputtered, gasping, coughing out seawater. Monk towed the raft to his side, a tiny rescue lamp blinking brightly from its bow. They clambered out of the icy waters, limbs shaking, teeth chattering. Gray sprawled Ollie across the raft while Monk quickly checked him.

"Not breathing, but I got a weak pulse."

Monk rolled the man over and began pumping his chest. It was difficult on the floating, rubbery surface. Still, water flowed from Ollie's lips and nose. Once he was satisfied, Monk flipped him back over. The old man's skin looked a frightening grayish purple. But Monk's medical training would not let him give up. He began mouth-to-mouth.

Gray offered a silent prayer heavenward. He owed Ollie a debt. And it had already cost them too much to come to this damned island. Gray shrugged off the backpack he'd stolen from the civilian member of the commando team. He let it drop to the raft. He'd recovered it from the helicopter. He wasn't about to leave it behind. It was all they had to show for this mission.

But at what price?

He searched the waters around the raft. He pictured Seichan being ripped away from him, vanishing out of the cabin in a swirling tempest. He didn't hold out much hope. She couldn't survive more than a few minutes in these icy waters.

Where could she go?

Gray looked around, but thick smoke covered the seas south of the island, swallowing everything up. He could see no more than a handful of yards in any direction. The air reeked of burning brimstone and salt, but at least for the moment it was warm.

Overhead, the sun was a dull orange blur. Brighter by far was the nearby island. The ruins of Ellirey lay only a couple of hundred yards away. It was a dark shadow topped by a crown of fire. Flames splashed high into the air while ribbons of glowing lava flowed down its sides. Steam rimmed the broken shores, marking the spot where molten rock seeped into the icy waters.

All the while the world rumbled and roared.

They were still far too close to the island.

This became clear as a deafening *boom* sounded, accompanied by a fountain of fire bursting from the island's heart. Smoke swirled more fiercely while a cloud of fine hot ash began to rain out of the sky, sizzling into the water, stinging any exposed skin. Large rocks struck the water, unseen through the smoke, but heard as loud splashes.

A smaller cough drew Gray's attention.

Ollie heaved and coughed again. More water spilled from his lips and nose. Monk knelt back, looking relieved. He helped the old man sit up. The caretaker stared blearily around him.

His voice was hoarse. "I knew I'd always end up in *helviti*."

Monk clapped him on the shoulder. "You're not in hell yet, old man."

Ollie glanced around. "You sure?"

Flakes of ash began to fall more heavily, drifting like fiery snow, beginning to cover the water in a fine layer. A large blazing cinder struck one of the boat's pontoons. Before it could be brushed away, it melted through the polyurethane surface. Air hissed out, escaping rapidly, deflating that side.

"We need to get farther away from the island," Gray warned. "Out of this ash cloud. We'll have to paddle by hand."

"Or we can just hitch a ride," Monk said, pointing behind Gray.

The loud burst of an air horn split across the water.

Gray turned. The bow of a large boat pushed out of the smoke and headed their way, a ghostly but familiar apparition.

It was Captain Huld's fishing trawler.

The boat slid alongside them, expertly piloted by Huld's son.

The captain called from the open deck, wearing a wide grin. "What the *fjandanum* did you do to my island?"

Huld met them at the stern deck and helped them aboard. Ollie, still weak, had to be carried, slung between Monk and Gray.

"A bunch of drowned rats, the lot of you," Huld scolded. "Come. We've got blankets and dry clothes below."

"How did you find us?" Gray asked.

"Spotted that little blinkin' light of yours." He pointed to the emergency LED at the raft's bow. "Plus we couldn't leave the area till we found you. She wouldn't have it."

From the wheelhouse, a lithe form limped out, wrapped in a blanket, her left leg bandaged from calf to midthigh.

Seichan . . .

Gray came close to dropping Ollie in a sudden desire to rush forward.

Monk swore in surprise.

"Darnedest thing," Huld said. "That same pod of orcas we saw earlier has been hugging our sides since the fireworks began, like frightened kids hanging on to our skirts. Then suddenly the whole lot of 'em goes and sinks away. Thought they were abandoning us. Only half a minute later, they pop back up with your woman, nearly drowned, and nosed her over to the boat."

Gray knew that the term *killer* in killer whales was a misnomer. In the wild, no orca had ever attacked a human. In fact, just as it was with their close relative, the dolphin, there were reported cases of orcas protecting humans in the water.

It seemed the playful pod—fed and respected by Huld—had returned that affection today.

Seichan hobbled over to join them, looking more angry than relieved. "I could've made it to the surface on my own."

Huld shrugged. "They did not think so. And they know these waters better than you, my *stúlka*."

She scowled.

"I've got Ollie," Monk said, shifting the caretaker's weight. "I need to get him somewhere warm, do a more thorough exam. He swallowed a lot of seawater."

They all had, but Gray urged Monk to do as he'd suggested.

Huld went to help his son, but not before passing on some news. "Been listening to the shortwave. Word is this eruption's gone ahead and triggered some magma blowouts along the rift that splits the seabed here. Before all is through, we may have another island or two."

With those dire words, Huld left them alone on the deck.

Seichan stood with her arms crossed. She wouldn't look at Gray and stared out to sea. The boat trudged away from the blasted island, slowly drawing clear of the ash cloud.

"I thought you were dead," Seichan said. Her voice was a whisper. She shook her head. "But I . . . I couldn't give up."

He moved next to her. "I'm glad you didn't. You saved our lives by making Huld stay."

She looked at him, searching his face, seeing if he was being flippant. Whatever she found there made her turn swiftly away, but not before Gray noted a rare flicker of uncertainty in her eyes.

She wrapped her blanket more snugly around her. Neither of them spoke for several breaths.

"Have you searched the bag yet?" she asked.

He was momentarily confused until she glanced over to the backpack he'd abandoned on the deck.

"No," he said. "I haven't had a chance."

She lifted an eyebrow at him.

She was right. Now was as good a time as any.

Gray crossed to the bag, knelt next to it, and opened the main compartment. Seichan hovered over him.

He sifted through the sodden contents. There wasn't much: a couple of wet T-shirts, pens, a spiral notepad whose pages had become mush. But buried within the nest of shirts, perhaps meant to cushion it, was something sealed in a plastic Ziploc bag. Gray pulled it free.

"What is it?"

"Looks like an old book . . . maybe a journal." Gray unzipped the bag and slipped out the contents.

It was a small leather-bound volume, brittle with age. He flipped the book open carefully. A meticulous handwritten script filled the pages, along with drawings that had been done with an equally precise hand. The book definitely appeared to be a journal or diary.

He scanned the writing.

"French," he said.

He turned to the first page, where a set of initials was floridly etched.

A.F.

"A.F.," he read aloud, and stared up at Seichan.

They both knew those initials, the author of this journal.

Archard Fortescue.

23

"Shouldn't be much farther," Hank Kanosh said from the backseat.

Lost in thought, Painter stared out the window at the passing scenery of the high desert. The midday sun had beat the landscape into shades of crimson and gold, broken by patches of sagebrush and stands of prickly yucca trees.

Kowalski sped along Highway 89. They were headed northeast out of Flagstaff, having landed in Arizona only fifteen minutes ago after a short hop in a private charter from an airfield outside of Price, Utah. Their destination—Sunset Crater National Park—lay forty minutes from the city.

"We're looking for Fire Road 545," Hank said. The professor's dog sat at the other end of the SUV's bench seat, his nose glued to the glass after he'd spotted a wild hare bounding away from the highway. The dog was now on high alert. "The fire road's a thirty-five-mile loop off the highway that passes through the park and a slew of ancient Pueblo ruins. Nancy Tso will meet us at the visitors' center near the park's entrance."

Their contact, Nancy Tso, was a Navajo woman, but also a National Park Service ranger. Earlier, Hank had made a few discreet calls, channeling through his contacts, and discovered the names of those who knew the region the best. On the flight here, Painter had read up as well as he could about the area. They all had. Kat had sent reams of information from D.C., but Painter preferred firsthand knowledge. The plan was to interview the guide, to see what they could learn.

Still, Painter had a hard time focusing. He had heard from Kat about the events in Iceland, listened to radio reports as news coverage of the volcanic eruptions spread. The entire archipelago south of Iceland's main coast was steaming and quaking. In addition to the one on the island, two submarine volcanoes had begun to boil the seas, spewing lava along the seabed and building steadily higher.

A giant volcanic plume was headed for Europe. Airports were already grounding planes. Gray, though, had gotten out ahead of it. He was already in the air, winging his way back to Washington with the prize in hand: an old journal belonging to the French scientist Archard Fortescue.

But would it shed any light on their predicament?

"There's the exit," Hank said, leaning forward and pointing.

"I see it," Kowalski said sourly. "I'm not blind."

Hank slipped back into his seat. They were all getting testy from lack of sleep. Silence settled over the vehicle as they took the exit off the highway and drove onto a two-lane road. There was no mistaking their destination as they continued the last few miles.

Sunset Crater appeared ahead of them. The thousand-foot-tall cinder cone rose above islands of pine and aspen. The cratered mountain was the youngest and least eroded cinder cone of the San Francisco volcanic fields. Over six hundred volcanoes of different shapes and sizes spread outward from here, most of them dormant, but beneath this chunk of the Colorado Plateau, magma still simmered close to the surface.

As they drove, Painter imagined the earthquakes and lava bombs that must have shaken the region a thousand years ago. He pictured the storm of flaming cinders and swirling clouds of burning ash, setting fire to the world, turning day to night. In the end, the ash field covered eight hundred square miles.

As they drew closer, the singular feature of this cratered mountain—in fact, the reason it had earned its name—became apparent. In the sunlight, the crown of the cone glowed a ruddy crimson, streaked and pooled with splashes of brilliant yellow, purple, and emerald, as if the view of the crater were forever frozen at sunset. But Painter had read enough to know there was nothing magical about this effect. The coloring came from a violent spewing of red oxidized iron and sulfur scoria that had settled around the cone's summit during its last eruption.

From the backseat, Hank offered a less geological viewpoint. "I've been reading the Hopi legends about this place. This was a sacred mountain to the Indians of this region. They believed angry gods once destroyed an evil people here with fire and molten rock."

"That doesn't sound like a legend," Painter said. "It pretty much matches the story told by Jordan's grandfather—and for that matter, even the history of the place. The volcano erupted here around 1064 AD, about the same time that the Anasazi vanished."

"True. But what I find most interesting is that the same Hopi legend goes on to warn that the people who died here are *still* here, that they remain as spiritual guardians of the place. Which, of course, makes me wonder *what* still needs guarding here."

Painter stared at the red cone, pondering the same mystery. Jordan Appawora's grandfather had hinted that something lay hidden here, something that could shed light on the ancient people, the *Tawtsee'untsaw Pootseev*—Hank's mythical lost tribe of Israelites.

Kowalski pointed ahead as they passed through the gates of the national park. "Is that our lady?"

Painter sat straighter. A slim young woman climbed out of a white Jeep Cherokee equipped with a blue light bar on top. She wore a starched gray shirt with a badge affixed to it, along with green slacks, black boots, and a matching service belt, including a holstered sidearm. As she stepped clear of the vehicle, she pulled on a broad-brimmed campaign hat and crossed toward the passenger side of their vehicle once it came to a stop.

Kowalski let out a low whistle of appreciation.

"I don't think your girlfriend back in D.C. would approve of that," Painter warned.

"We got an agreement. I'm allowed to look, just not touch."

Painter should have scolded him for his behavior, but in the end he couldn't disagree with the man's assessment of the park ranger. Still, as

striking as the ranger was, she didn't hold a candle to Lisa. He had spoken
to his girlfriend an hour ago, assuring her that everything was okay. She
had hurried to Sigma command, joining Kat as this situation escalated.

As the park ranger reached their car, Painter rolled down his window.
She leaned toward his door. Her skin was a coppery mocha, her eyes a
dark caramel, framed by long black hair done up in a braid down her back.

"Ranger Tso?" he asked.

She checked the front and back seats. "You're the historians?" Her
voice was rife with skepticism as she eyed Painter and Kowalski.

It seemed her instincts were as refined as her looks. Then again, park
rangers had to wear a lot of hats, juggling duties that varied from overse-
ing national resources to thwarting illegal activities of every sort. They
were firemen, police officers, naturalists, and historical preservationists
all rolled up into one—and all too often, psychiatrists, too, as they did
their best to protect the resources from the visitors, the visitors from the
resources, and the visitors from one another.

She pointed to a neighboring lot. "Park over there. Then tell me what
this is all really about."

Kowalski obeyed. As he turned into the parking lot, he glanced to
Painter and mouthed the word *wow*.

Again, Painter couldn't disagree.

In short order, they were all marching down a trail, gravel grinding
underfoot. As it was midweek and midday, they had the path to themselves. They climbed toward the crater, passing through a sparse pine forest, along a route marked as LAVA FLOW TRAIL. Wildflowers sprouted in the
sunnier stretches, but most of the path was crumbling pumice and cinders
from an ancient flow. They passed a few spatter cones, known as *hornitos*
or "little ovens" in Spanish, marking where old bubbles of lava burst forth,
forming minivolcanoes. There were also strange eruptions from cracks—
called "squeeze-ups"—where sheets of rising lava hardened and curled
into massive flowerlike sculptures. But the main attraction was the cone
itself, climbing higher and higher before their eyes. Up close, the mineral
show was even more impressive as the lower slope's dark gray cinders rose

up into a spectacular display of brilliant hues, reflecting every bit of sunlight.

"This looped trail is only one mile long," their guide warned. "You have my attention for exactly that length of time."

Painter had been making tentative, vague inquiries, learning mundane tidbits that were getting them nowhere. He decided to cut to the quick.

"We're looking for lost treasure," he said.

That got her full attention. She drew to a stop, her hands settling to her hips. "Really?" she asked sarcastically.

"I know how that sounds," Painter said. "But we've been following the trail of a historical mystery that suggests something was hidden here long ago. Around the time of the eruption . . . maybe shortly thereafter."

Nancy wasn't buying it. "This park has been scoured and searched for decades. What you see is what you get. If there's something hidden here, it's long buried. The only things under our feet are some old icy lava tubes, most of them collapsed."

"Icy?" Kowalski asked, wiping his brow. He'd already soaked through his shirt as the day had grown hot, and the trail offered little shade.

"Water seeps through the porous volcanic rock into the tubes," Nancy explained. "Freezes during winter, but the natural insulation and lack of air circulation in the narrow tubes keeps the ice from melting. But just so you know, those tubes were mapped both on foot and by radar. There's nothing but *ice* down there." She began to turn away, ready to head back to the parking lot. "If you're done wasting my time . . ."

Hank raised a hand, stopping her, but his dog tugged him to the side of the trail. Nancy had insisted that the professor use a leash inside the park, and Kawtch was clearly not happy about it—especially now that they'd stopped. The dog sniffed the air, apparently still looking for that wild hare.

"We're pursuing an alternate hypothesis regarding the disappearance of the Anasazi," Hank said. "We have a lead that the volcanic eruption here might be the cause of—"

She sighed, fixing Hank with a hard stare. "Dr. Kanosh, I know your reputation, so I was willing to give you the benefit of the doubt, but I've heard every crackpot theory about the Anasazi. Climate change, war, plague, even alien abduction. Yes, there were Anasazi who lived here, both the Winslow Anasazi and the Kayenta Anasazi, but there were also Sinagua, Cohonina, and other tribes of the ancient Pueblo people. What's your point?"

Hank stood up to her disdain. As an Indian who practiced Mormonism, he was no doubt well accustomed to dealing with ridicule. "Yes, I know that, young lady." His voice took a professorial tone, practically browbeating the young woman. "I'm well versed in the history of our people. So don't dismiss what I'm saying as some peyote-fueled fantasy. The Anasazi did vanish from this region suddenly and swiftly. Their homes were never reoccupied, as if people feared moving into them. Something happened to that tribe—starting here and spreading outward—and we may be on the trail of an answer that could change history."

Painter let this little war play out. Nancy's face flushed—but he suspected it was more from shame than from anger. Painter had been raised enough of an Indian to know it was rude to talk harshly to an elder, even one from a different tribe or clan.

She finally shrugged. "I'm sorry. I don't see how I can help you. If you're looking for more information on the Anasazi, maybe you shouldn't be looking here but over at Wupatki."

"Wupatki?" Painter asked. "Where's that?"

"About eighteen miles north of here. It's a neighboring national park."

Hank elaborated. "Wupatki is an elaborate series of pueblo ruins and monuments, spread over thousands of acres. The main attraction is a three-story structure with more than a hundred rooms. The park is named after that place. *Wupatki* is the Hopi word for 'tall house.'"

Nancy added, "We Navajo still call it *Anaasazi Bikin*."

Hank translated, glancing significantly at Painter. "That means 'House of the Enemies.' Archaeologists believe it was one of the last Anasazi strongholds before they vanished out of the region."

Painter stared up at the brilliant cinder cone. According to the tale told by Jordan's grandfather, the birth of this volcano was the result of a theft by a clan of the Anasazi, a mishandling of a treasure not unlike what had recently happened up in the Utah Rockies. He eyed the massive cone. Had a great settlement once stood here? Had it been destroyed, buried under ash and lava? And what about the survivors? Had they been hunted down and slaughtered? Painter remembered Hank's one-word description.

Genocide.

Maybe they *were* looking in the wrong place.

Painter reached into his shirt pocket and removed the slip of paper that Jordan Appawora had given to him. The kid's grandfather had said it would guide them to where they needed to go. He unfolded it and showed the pair of symbols to the park ranger.

"These markings may be tied to what we came seeking. Have you ever seen them?"

She leaned over, doubt fixed on her face. But as she studied the sketch of a crescent moon and five-pointed star, her eyes got huge. She glanced up to him.

"Yes," she said. "I know these symbols. I know exactly where you can find them."

12:23 P.M.
San Rafael Swell

Kai raced after Jordan through Buckhorn Wash. He rode a black four-wheel all-terrain vehicle while she pursued him in a white one. She kept low, swerving right and left, looking for a break so she could pass him, eating too much of his dust. The screaming whine of the two engines echoed off the cliffs to either side as they sped along the bottom of the wash, following an old off-road trail.

The Swell's two thousand square miles of public land had little restrictions against ATV use. Over the years, enthusiasts had carved hundreds of miles of trails that crisscrossed the region. A part of Kai railed against such abuse of the land, especially as a Native American.

But she was also young, needing an escape.

After sending her e-mail to John Hawkes, she had repeatedly checked for a response. A half hour later, still with no answer, she could no longer sit by herself in a dark room. She had to get out, clear her head. She found Jordan still sitting on the porch. With a conspiratorial glint in his eye, he showed her what he had discovered in a shed behind one of the pueblos. Iris and Alvin had reluctantly handed over the keys to the ATVs, with firm instructions to stick to the flat dirt roads.

They had—for about twenty minutes, until both felt capable enough for more of a challenge.

Ahead of her, Jordan whooped as he wheeled around a sharp turn in the wash, skittering a bit in the loose talus. Coming out of the curve, he fishtailed his bike. Kai grinned madly, hunkered down, and hit her throttle. She shot past him as he foundered, close enough to give him the finger.

He laughed and hollered at her back. "This ain't over!"

She smiled and raced along the trail, bumping over smaller rocks, going airborne across a small dip. She landed on all four tires, jarring her teeth. Still, the grin never left her face.

At last the wash petered out, and the mountain trail joined the dirt road again. She braked, sliding to a stop.

A second later, Jordan joined her, expertly skidding sideways to come to rest beside her. That bit of fancy maneuvering made her wonder if he'd been coddling her during the race.

Still, when he tugged off his helmet and goggles, the pure joy and exhilaration that she saw in his eyes mirrored her own. With half his face pasted with road dust, he looked like a raccoon.

She imagined that she looked no better.

He reached to his water bottle and upended it over his head, washing the worst away, then took a long drink. She watched his Adam's apple bobbing up and down as he swallowed. With a shake of his hair, he smiled at her, making the hot day just that much warmer.

"How about two out of three?" he asked, nodding toward another trail.

She laughed and had to turn away a bit shyly.

Still, it felt so good.

"Maybe we should be heading back," she said, and pulled out her cell phone to check the time. "We've been out two hours."

She hadn't realized how long it had been. Time had passed swiftly as the pair raced through the Swell, stopping every now and again to check out some set of petroglyphs or to poke their heads in one of the old mines that pocked the canyons.

Jordan looked a little crestfallen but agreed. "I suppose you're right. If we're gone much longer, Iris and Alvin will be sending out a search party. Besides, I could use some lunch . . . that is, as long as it's not more of those roasted piñon nuts."

"*Toovuts,*" she reminded him.

He nodded appreciatively. "Well done, Ms. Quocheets. Going native Paiute on me, are you?" He bumped a fist against his chest. "Does a brave proud."

She pretended to swing her helmet at him.

He dodged back. "Okay, I surrender!" he said with a wolfish grin. "Back we go."

They took a more sedate pace for the return trip, sticking to the road, ambling along in no particular hurry, squeezing out every last moment together. At last they reached the circle of small pueblos. They sidled over to the shed, parked the vehicles, and climbed off.

As she took a step, her legs wobbled a bit, still vibrating from the ride. Jordan caught her arm, his fingers tightening much too hard. She turned, ready to shake him off, but his face had gone all tense.

He drew her back into the shadows of the shed.

"Something's not right here," he whispered, and pointed. "Look at all the fresh tire tracks."

Now that he'd pointed it out, she realized that the sandy dust was all cut up with multiple treads. But where were the vehicles? She suddenly was too aware of how silent it was, as if something were holding its breath.

"We need to get out of here . . ." he started.

But before they could take a step, they saw men in desert combat gear come sweeping out of the shadows behind the pueblos on the far side, spreading wide. Kai's heart climbed into her throat, choking her. She instantly knew that this assault was her fault, knew how the enemy had found her.

The e-mail . . .

Jordan tugged her around—only to find a monstrously tall blond figure, also dressed in khaki camouflage, standing before him. The man lashed out with a rifle, punching the butt into Jordan's face.

He dropped to his knees with a cry that sounded more surprised than pained.

"Jordan!"

The attacker turned and leveled his rifle at Kai's chest. His words were gruff, his manner frighteningly cold. "Come with me. Someone would like a word with you."

11:33 A.M.
Flagstaff, Arizona

Standing at the foot of the towering structure, Hank Kanosh appreciated its name. Wupatki. It certainly was a *tall house.*

The ruins of the ancient pueblo climbed three stories, constructed of flat slabs of red Moenkopi sandstone, quarried locally and mortared together. An amazing feat of engineering, it climbed high and spread outward into a hundred rooms. A part of the pueblo also included the remains of an old masonry ballpark and a large circular community room.

He imagined how all of this must have once looked. In his mind's eye, he put the thatched and beamed roof back in place. He rebuilt walls. He pictured corn, beans, and squash growing in the neighboring washes. He then populated the place with Indians from various tribes: Sinagua, Cohonina, and of course, the Anasazi. The different tribes were known to live in relative peace with one another.

Standing beside the ruins with Kawtch at his side, Hank stared at a view that had changed little from ancient times. Wupatki had been built on a small plateau overlooking a vast distance, revealing the breadth of the tabletop mesas that encompassed the high desert, the brilliant beauty of the Painted Desert to the east, and the snaking green path of the Little Colorado River.

It was a picturesque spot.

Still, a dark mood settled over him as he studied the dusty ruins. Why did these ancient people leave? Were they driven out, slaughtered? He pictured blood splashing the red walls, heard the screams of children and women. It was too much. He had to turn away.

Down at the foot of the ruins, Painter and his partner wandered near the community amphitheater. The group, led by Nancy Tso, had traveled the short distance from Sunset Crater National Park, but they were still waiting for the ranger to get permission for an overland hike. It was forbidden to stray from the public areas of the park here without guidance. The more remote ruins and monuments—close to three thousand of them—were considered too fragile, as was the desert's ecosystem, for sightseeing.

Once Nancy received permission, she would guide them herself to where she had seen the symbols Painter had shown her, the mark of the *Tawtsee'untsaw Pootseev,* the People of the Morning Star. Hank's blood pounded harder at the thought of them. Could they possibly be one of the lost tribes of Israel, as described in the Book of Mormon?

Impatient and done exploring, he hiked down to the others, drawing a sullen Kawtch along by his leash. He spotted Nancy Tso heading the same way from the visitors' center.

Reaching the group first, he found Kowalski amusing himself with one of the other unique features of the pueblo. He stood before what appeared to be a raised fire pit, newly constructed of mortared flagstone. But the square pit in the center was not meant to hold a fire.

The big man leaned over the opening. He had to hold on to the Stetson he'd bought for the hike to keep it from blowing off of his head. A stiff breeze blew up from below, coming out of the pit.

"It's cool," Kowalski sighed. "Like air-conditioning."

Painter stood by the information sign. "It's a blowhole."

Hank nodded. "It's the opening to a *breathing* cavern system. It's dependent on atmospheric pressure. When the day's hot as it is now, it exhales the cool air trapped below. In the winter, when it's cold, it inhales. It can get to blowing up to thirty miles per hour. Archaeologists believe this is one of the reasons the pueblo was established here. Blowholes, which were considered to be openings to the underworld, were held sacred by the ancient people, and as you mentioned, it doesn't hurt that it offers some natural air-conditioning in the summer."

Painter read from the posted sign. "Says here that back in 1962, excavations below found pottery, sandstone masonry, even petroglyphs down there."

Hank understood the interest he could see on Painter's face. On the drive here, Nancy Tso had told them *where* she'd seen the moon and star symbols drawn by Jordan's grandfather. They were part of some petroglyphs found deep in the desert, near one of the many unmarked pueblo ruins out there.

"It also says here," Painter continued, "that the *size, depth, and complexity* of the cavern system below have never been fully determined."

"That's not necessarily true," Nancy Tso said, interrupting. She crossed down the last of the path and joined them, noting their attention. "Newer studies that have been published within the last couple of years suggest the limestone cavern system under this plateau may be around seven billion cubic feet in size, stretching for miles underground."

Painter studied the blowhole. The opening was sealed with a locked grate. "So if someone wanted to hide something from prying eyes—"

Nancy sighed. "Don't start that again. I agreed to show you where I saw those symbols. That's all I'm going to do. Then you're all clearing out." She checked her watch. "Park closes at five o'clock. I plan on being out of here by then."

"So you got permission for us to explore?" Hank said.

She slapped some permit forms against her thigh. "It's a good two-hour hike."

Kowalski straightened and seated his Stetson more firmly on his head. "Why can't we just take that Cherokee of yours? It's got four-wheel-drive, doesn't it? We could be there in under ten minutes, shorter if I drive."

She looked aghast at the suggestion.

Painter did, too, but Hank suspected it was for a very different reason. Painter's partner had little regard for speed regulations—or common road courtesy, for that matter.

"Let's get some rules straight at the outset," Nancy said, and held up a finger. "First rule. LNT. *Leave no trace.* That means what you carry in you carry out. I've arranged for backpacks and water. It's all inventoried and will be checked when we return. Is that understood?"

They nodded. Kowalski leaned toward Painter and whispered. "She's even hotter when she's mad."

Luckily, Nancy didn't hear this—or at least she pretended not to. "Second, we tread carefully. That means no hiking poles. They've been proven to be too destructive to the fragile desert ecosystem. And last, no GPS units. The park service doesn't want the exact locations of the un-marked ruins mapped electronically. Are we clear?"

They all nodded. Kowalski only grinned.

"Then let's get moving."

"Where are we going?" Painter asked.

"To a remote pueblo ruin called Crack-in-the-Rock."

"Why's it called that?" Kowalski asked.

"You'll see."

She led them to the spot where their gear was stacked. Hank pulled on a backpack. It came equipped with a CamelBak water pouch and a supply of PowerBars and bananas.

Once everyone was ready, Nancy set off into the desert, moving at a hard pace, apparently determined to shave some minutes off her two-hour estimate. It certainly was no sightseeing trip. The group marched in a row, following behind her, passing through fields of sagebrush, Mormon tea, saltbush, and princess plume. Lizards skittered out of their way. Hares leaped in great bounds. At one point, Hank heard the coarse rattling complaint of a hidden diamondback and pulled Kawtch closer. His dog knew snakes, but Hank wasn't taking any chances.

They also passed some of the park's other monuments: tumbled piles of sandstone marking a small pueblo, a ring of stones from a prehistoric pit house, even the occasional Navajo hogan or sweathouse. But their destination—one of the towering mesas—lay much farther out, a hazy blip on the horizon.

To help with the passage of time and to distract himself from the burn of the sun, Hank walked beside Painter. "The moon and the star," he said. "I've been thinking about that symbol and the name for the tribe. *Tawtsee'untsaw Pootseev.*"

"The People of the Morning Star."

Hank nodded. "The morning star that shines so brightly in the eastern skies at dawn is really the planet Venus. But Venus is also called the evening star because it shines brilliantly at sunset in the *west*. Many ancient astrologers figured this connection out. That's why the crescent moon is often associated with the morning star." He swung his arm in a low arc from east to west. "The two horns of the moon represent the star's rise in both the east and the west, connecting them together."

"Okay, but what are you getting at?"

"This particular pairing of moon and star is an ancient symbol, one of the oldest in the world. It speaks to man's knowledge of his place in the universe. Some religious historians believe the Star of Bethlehem was in fact the morning star."

Painter shrugged. "The symbol's also found on the flags of most Islamic countries."

"True, but even Muslim scholars will tell you that the symbol has nothing to do with their faith. It was in fact co-opted from the Turks." Hank waved this all away. "But the symbol's reach goes much further back. One of the earliest attestations of this paired symbol goes back to the lands of ancient Israel. From the Moabites, who were relatives of the Israelites according to the Book of Genesis—but who also had ties to the Egyptians."

Painter held up a hand, stopping him from elaborating in more depth. "I get it. The symbol may further support your conjecture that these ancient people came from Israel."

"Well, yes, but—"

Painter pointed toward the horizon, toward the distant mesa. "If there are any answers, hopefully we'll find them out there."

12:46 P.M.
San Rafael Swell

What have I done?

Kai stood still, dull with shock, in the middle of the Humetewas' main room. Iris sat in a chair by the hearth, her tears bright in the firelight, but the old woman kept her face hard. Her fingers clenched the arms of her chair as she looked at her husband. Alvin was lying on his back across the pine table, stripped to his boxers. His thin chest rose up and down, much too rapidly. Blistered red welts marked his ribs. The reek of burned flesh filled the room.

A large-boned black woman stoked the fire. A second iron poker rested in the flames. Its tip was of the same shape as Alvin's blisters. The shadowy woman didn't even look up as Kai was dragged into the room.

Behind her, the giant blond soldier who'd captured them threw Jordan to the floor in the corner. With his wrists tied behind his back, he could not brace himself against his fall, but he twisted enough to hit the ground with his shoulder and skid up against the wall.

The other occupant of the room was seated at the head of the table. He stood up, pushing on a cane. Kai thought he was an older man—maybe it was the cane, or the ultraconservative suit, or the frailness that seemed to emanate from him. But as he thumped around the table, she saw that his face was smooth, unblemished, except for a dark stubble of beard, as artfully groomed as the sharp lines of his dark hair. He could be no older than his midthirties.

"Ah, there you are, Ms. Quocheets. My name is Rafael Saint Germaine." He glanced to his watch. "We expected you much sooner and had to start without you."

The man waved his cane over Alvin's body. The old man flinched, which tore the hole in Kai's heart even wider.

"We've been trying to ascertain the whereabouts of your uncle, but Alvin and Iris have been most uncooperative . . . despite the tender ministrations of my dear Ashanda."

The woman by the fire glanced up.

At the sight of her face, Kai's insides went slippery and cold. The woman, apart from her large size, looked ordinary enough, but as her eyes glinted in the firelight, Kai noticed that they were unfathomably empty, a mirror for whoever looked into them.

The crack of the cane on the floor drew her full attention. "Back to business." The man named Rafael waved for his torturer to remove the hot iron. "We still need an answer."

Kai stumbled forward to the table. "Don't!" she blurted out. It came out as a half sob. "They don't know where my uncle went!"

Rafael's eyebrows rose. "That's what the Humetewas have been claiming, but how can I believe them?"

"Please . . . my uncle never told them. He didn't want them to know. Only I know."

"Don't tell them," Iris said, hoarse with anger and grief.

The man named Rafael searched the beams overhead and sighed. "Such melodrama."

Kai ignored Iris and kept her focus on the man with the cane. "I'll tell you. I'll tell you everything." She found her voice again. "But not until you let the others go . . . all of them. Once they're safely gone, I'll tell you where my uncle went."

Rafael seemed to weigh this offer. "While I'm sure you're an honest and forthright person, Ms. Quocheets, I'm afraid I can't take that chance." He waved the black woman closer to Alvin. "Mouths have a tendency to be harder to pry open without good leverage. It's all a matter of basic physics, of action and reaction."

The poker lowered toward Alvin's cheek. Its iron tip glowed a smoldering red, smoking and softly hissing.

Rafael leaned both hands on his cane. "This particular scar will be much harder to hide. That is, of course, if he lives."

Kai had to stop this. There was only one option. In order to buy some time and keep them from torturing Alvin, she had to tell them the truth.

She opened her mouth, but Jordan spoke first.

"Keep me prisoner!" he called from the floor. "If you need Kai's cooperation, you can use *me* as leverage. But please let the Humetewas go."

Kai latched onto that chance. "He's right. Do that, and I'll talk."

"My dear, you'll talk whether we release Iris and Alvin or not."

"But it will take longer," Kai pressed. "Maybe too long."

She turned and matched gazes with Iris, trying to absorb the old woman's strength. If need be, Kai would resist for as long as possible, do her best to convince the interrogators that they would only waste precious time in torturing Alvin and Iris, that they could get what they needed much faster by letting the old couple go.

She turned back to Rafael and let that determination shine forth. He stared back at her. She dared not flinch.

After several long breaths, Rafael shrugged. "Well played and argued, Ms. Quocheets." He pointed his cane at the blond soldier. "Gather up the Humetewas, pile them onto one of those ATVs, and send them off into the canyons."

"I want to watch," Kai said. "To make sure they're safe."

"I wouldn't have it any other way."

In a matter of minutes, Iris and Alvin sat atop the white ATV. Alvin was too weak from his abuse to drive, so he rode behind his wife. Iris nodded to Kai, in that single gesture both thanking her and telling her to be careful.

Kai returned the nod, passing back the exact same message to Iris.

Thank you . . . and be careful.

Iris revved the throttle and took off. The pair trundled down a wash and quickly vanished around a turn in the canyon.

Kai remained standing outside the pueblo. She watched the trail of dust get farther and farther away, winding deep into the badlands.

Rafael stood on the porch in the shade. "I believe that should satisfy you."

Kai turned and let out a rattling sigh. She stared at the man and at the dark shadow of the woman who was hovering behind his shoulder. Any lie Kai told would be punished—and it would fall upon Jordan's shoulders to bear the brunt of that abuse. But if she cooperated, she knew her captors would keep them alive.

To be used as leverage with Painter.

As the bastard had said, it was only basic physics.

"My uncle flew to Flagstaff," she finally admitted. "They were heading to Sunset Crater National Park."

And she quickly told him why—just to be fully convincing.

As she finished, Rafael looked disconcerted. "Seems they know much more than I expected . . ." But he quickly shook it off. "No matter. We'll deal with it."

He leaned on his cane and turned to the open doorway. He spoke to the tall blond soldier. "Bern, radio your sniper. Tell him to take his shots and haul back to the helicopter."

Sniper?

Kai took two steps toward the porch.

Iris and Alvin.

Rafael turned to her. "I said I'd let them go," he explained. "I just didn't say how *far* I'd let them go."

Off in the distance, a sharp crack of a rifle echoed.

Soon followed by a second.

1:44 P.M.
Flagstaff, Arizona

Painter stared up at the top of the mesa. He sucked deeply from the tube connected to his CamelBak water bottle. After two blistering hours in the heat, he'd come to believe that they'd never reach this mesa, that it would continue to retreat from them forever, like some desert mirage.

But here they were.

"Now what?" Kowalski asked, fanning his face with his Stetson. He'd become a walking sweat stain.

"The pueblo's up top," Nancy said.

Kowalski groaned.

Painter craned his neck. He saw no way up.

"Over here," she directed, and headed around the base of the mesa to where a crumbling trail ran up its side.

As they followed her, Painter noted large swaths of rock art along the cliff faces: snakes, lizards, deer, sheep, fanciful human figures, and geometric designs of every shape and design. The petroglyphs appeared to be two types. The more common was formed as the darker "desert varnish" of the surface stone was chipped or scraped away to reveal the lighter stone beneath. Others were formed by drilling hundreds of tiny holes into the soft sandstone, outlining figures or sunlike spirals.

Painter followed behind Hank, noting the professor scanning the same cliffs, likely looking for the star and a moon of his lost Israelites.

At last, after climbing a good way up, they reached a broken chute in the cliff face, the eponymous *crack* in Crack-in-the-Rock pueblo. The opening was narrow, but the sandstone was worn smooth by rain and wind.

"It's a short climb up from here," Nancy promised.

She led the way, sliding into the chute and climbing up the boulder-strewn path. As the crack split its way to the top of the mesa, Kowalski cursed under his breath. He had to squeeze through sideways a few times to get past some old choke stones that partially blocked their way.

But they all finally made it topside, exiting from the crack into a room of the pueblo itself. They stepped clear and out onto the open mesa. The jumble of ruins here was not as impressive as those that they had seen back at Wupatki, but the view made up for it. It overlooked the Little Colorado River and offered vistas for hundreds of miles in all directions.

"One of the theories about this place," Nancy said, putting on her guide voice, "is that this was a defensive outpost. If you look at this shield wall along the edge of the mesa, there are small angled holes, perhaps for shooting arrows, but others have suggested this might have been an ancient observatory used by shamans, especially as some of the holes in the wall angle *up*."

But such theories were not why they'd made the long trek.

"What about the petroglyphs you mentioned?" Painter asked, staying on task. "Where are they?"

"Follow me. We don't normally take anyone this way. The path is dangerous, steep, full of slippery talus. A wrong step and you could go sliding to your death."

"Show us," Painter said, undaunted.

Nancy headed to a pile of rock where a wall had collapsed long ago. They had to climb over the rubble to reach what appeared to be another crack or chute. This one headed down. The footing was indeed treacherous. Rocks slid under Painter's boots. He had to pin his hands to either side of the crack to keep from losing his balance. It didn't help that Hank's dog danced between them with all the ease of a mountain goat, stopping to mark the occasional stone or bit of weedy brush.

"Kawtch!" Hank yelled. "I swear if you bump me again . . ."

Nancy had agreed to let Hank unleash his dog, but only for as long as they were on top of the mesa. Apparently everyone was regretting this decision now—except for Kawtch himself. He lifted his leg again, then vanished below.

This new chute was narrower and longer than the crack they had passed through earlier. Even if they moved with care, it took some time to traverse, but finally they reached the bottom. Rather than breaking through to the outside, the group ended up within a high-walled chasm, open to the sky overhead, but offering no way out.

Hank stared around, his mouth hanging open. "Amazing."

Painter had to agree. Great sprawling displays of petroglyphs covered the walls on both sides, every square inch of them. They were almost too dizzying to look at.

But their guide, having been here before, was more impatient than impressed.

"What you came to see is over here," Nancy said, and led them to a smooth section of the stone floor. "This is the other reason we don't let anyone down here. Can't have them walking all over this masterpiece."

Rather than scratching into the wall, the artist here had used a different canvas: the floor of the chasm.

Again it was a riotous panoply of prehistoric art—but in the center, wrapped around by one of the ubiquitous spirals, was a distinct crescent moon and five-pointed star. There was no mistaking it. The design was identical to the one drawn by Jordan's grandfather.

Painter lifted a foot, ready to cross the field of art. He looked to Nancy, who tentatively nodded.

"Just be careful."

Painter headed out. Hank followed with Kawtch, but Kowalski stayed with Nancy, making plain where his true interest lay. Reaching the piece of art, Painter knelt beside it. Hank assumed the same position on the far side of the display. They studied the work together.

Including the spiral wrapped around it, the singular piece of art had to be a full yard across. The ancient artist used both techniques that they had seen demonstrated elsewhere. The moon and star had been scraped out of the rock, but the spiral was composed of thousands of pinkie-sized drill holes.

Kawtch sniffed at the surface—at first curious, but then his hackles rose. He backed away, sneezing in apparent irritation.

Hank and Painter stared at each other. Painter leaned down first, putting his nose close to the art. Hank did the same.

"Do you smell anything?" Painter asked.

"No," he answered, but there was still an edge of excitement in his voice.

Then Painter felt it, too—the smallest brush against his cheek, like a feathery kiss. He sat back and held his palm over the petroglyph, over the small drill holes.

"You feel that, right?" Painter asked.

"A breeze," Hank said. "Coming up from below through the holes drilled in the spiral."

"There must be a blowhole under here. Same as at Wupatki."

Painter leaned over and gently brushed his hand across the surface of the art. Some of the fine rock dust billowed up as it passed over the drill holes, but that wasn't his goal. He was clearing it for another reason.

He ran his fingertips along the edges of the petroglyph, then reached to Hank's hand, urging the professor to do the same.

"Feel this," Painter said, and drew one of Hank's fingers along a seam that circled the piece of art.

Shock filled the professor's voice. "It's been mortared in place."

Painter nodded. "Someone sealed this blowhole with a slab of sandstone. Like a manhole cover over a sewer."

"But they left holes so the caverns below could still *breathe*."

Painter's eyes locked on Hank's. "We must get down there."

24

This day was never going to end.

In the shadow of the Washington Monument, Gray headed across the National Mall, casting a withering glare toward the sun. It seemed to refuse to set. Though the flight from Reykjavik had taken five hours, because of the time change, he'd landed back in D.C. only an hour after he'd left Iceland—and as much as he traveled, such changes still mucked up his inner clock.

Some of his irritation also came from the two hours he'd spent underground, beneath the Smithsonian Castle at Sigma command. He'd gone through a thorough debriefing, while chomping at the bit to discover the contents of Archard Fortescue's journal.

It had to be important, and he bore the proof of that. He touched his left ear gingerly. A liquid plastic bandage, barely visible, hardened the graze from the bullet he'd taken as he wrestled the backpack from the Guild agent on the island. But injuries he had received weren't the worst from that trip.

"Slow down!" Seichan called behind him.

She hobbled after him, limping on her right leg. Medics at Sigma had also tended to her lacerations, suturing up the deeper bite marks and pumping her full of antibiotics and a lighter dose of pain reliever, as evidenced by the slight glaze to her eyes. She'd been lucky the orcas had treated her as gently as they had, or she could have lost the leg.

Gray reduced his pace so she could catch up to him. "We could've caught that cab."

"Needed to stretch my legs. The more I keep moving, the faster I'll heal."

Gray wasn't so sure that was the case. He'd overheard one of the doctors warning Seichan to take it easy. But he noted the feral glint behind that medicated glaze. She hadn't liked being cooped up underground for two hours any better than he had. It was said sharks couldn't breathe unless they were constantly moving. He suspected the same was true of her.

Together, they crossed Madison Drive. Her left foot slipped as she stepped from the curb. He caught her around the waist to keep her from falling. She swore, balanced herself, and began to push off of him—but he pulled her back, took her hand, and placed it on his shoulder.

"Just hold on."

She started to lift her hand away, but he frowned at her. She sighed, and her fingers tightened on his shoulder. He kept his hand on the small of her back, under her open jacket, ready if she needed more help.

By the time they crossed the street and cut between the Natural History Museum and the National Gallery of Art, her grip was digging deep into his deltoids. He slid his hand around her waist, resting it under her rib cage to support her.

"Next time, the cab . . ." she gasped out, offering him a small grin as she limped along.

At the moment Gray was selfishly glad they had walked. She leaned heavily against him. He smelled the peach scent of her hair, mixed with something richer, almost spicy from her damp skin. And down deeper, he was enough of a primitive male to appreciate this rare moment of weakness, of her need for him.

Her pressed his hand harder against her, feeling the heat of her body through her blouse, but such intimacy did not last long.

"Thank God we're almost there," she said, leaning away but keeping one hand on his shoulder for balance.

The National Archives Building rose ahead of them. They were to meet the curator and his assistant down in the research room. Shortly after reaching Sigma, Gray had had a photocopy of the old journal's pages hand-delivered to them. The original was safely secured in a vault at Sigma. They weren't taking any chances with it.

Out on the street, Gray easily spotted the two agents assigned to watch the Archives. Another pair should be inside. They were keeping close track of even the photocopies.

As he helped Seichan with the steps, his phone jangled in his pocket. He reached in and pulled it out enough to check the caller ID. He'd left Monk with Kat. The pair was overseeing events in Iceland, trying to determine if they'd triggered another Laki eruption. But as was the case in Utah, the heat of the eruption likely killed the nano-nest out there, but would that exploding archipelago lead to another global catastrophe like the one Fortescue had witnessed?

As it turned out, the call was not from Monk, but from Gray's parents' home phone. He'd already talked to his mother after he'd landed in D.C., checking on his father after that bad night. As usual, his dad was fine the next morning, just his usual forgetful self.

He flipped it open and held the phone to his ear. "Mom?"

"No, it's your dad," he heard. "Can't you tell from the sound of my voice?"

Gray didn't bother to tell him he hadn't said anything until then. He let it go. "What do you need, Dad?"

"I was calling to tell you . . . because of . . ." There was a long confused pause.

"Dad?"

"Just wait, dammit . . ." His father shouted to the side. "Harriet, why was I calling Kenny?"

His mother's voice was faint. "What?"

"I mean *Gray*. Why was I calling Gray?"

Well, at least he got the name right.

He heard some jabbering in the background, his father's voice growing gruffer and angrier. He had to stop this before it escalated.

"Dad!" he shouted into the phone.

People looked in his direction.

"What?" his father groused at him.

He kept his voice calm and even. "Hey, why don't you just call me back? When you remember. That'll be fine."

"Okay, yeah, that sounds good. Just have a lot going on . . . 's got me all messed up."

"Don't worry about it, Dad."

"Okay, son."

Gray flipped the phone closed.

Seichan stared at him, silently asking if everything was okay. Her hand had shifted from his shoulder to his hip, as if helping to hold him upright.

He pocketed the phone. "Just family stuff."

Still, she stared a bit longer, as if trying to read him.

He pointed to the door. "Let's go find out what Fortescue thought was so important that he had to hide his journal in Iceland."

5:01 P.M.

Seichan lowered herself onto one of the conference chairs, leaning her weight on her good hip and kicking her right leg straight out. She tried her best not to moan with relief.

Gray remained standing. She studied him, remembering the strained look on his face, the glimmer of fear in his eyes as he spoke with his father. There was no evidence of it now. Where had he bottled it away? How long could he keep doing that?

Still, he was in his element now, and for that she was relieved—almost as much as she was about the weight off her leg. But both their burdens would not stay away for long.

"So what can you tell me about Fortescue's journal?" Gray asked.

Dr. Eric Heisman nodded vigorously as he paced the room. The space was even more of a shambles than before. Documents and books had trebled in number on the table. Someone had wheeled in another two microfiche readers from a neighboring research room. Other people in the building must be wondering what was going on in here, especially with the armed guard posted at the door. But considering all the valuable documents preserved in the Archives' expansive vaults and helium-enriched enclosures, maybe the sight of a guard wasn't that unusual.

Still, by now, Heisman looked more like a mad scientist than a museum curator. His shirt was rumpled, rolled to the elbows, and his white hair stuck up like a fright wig. But the impression came mostly from his eyes, red-rimmed and wired, shining with a fanatical zeal.

Again, though, the latter might have come from the pile of empty Starbucks coffee cups filling the room's lone trash bin.

How long had the man been up?

"Truly astounding stuff in here," Heisman said. "I don't know where to begin. Where did you find it?"

Gray shook his head. "I'm afraid that's classified, as is our conversation."

He waved the words away. "I know, I know . . . Sharyn and I signed all the necessary documents for this temporary clearance."

His assistant sat at the other end of the table. She hadn't said a word when they'd entered. Her dark eyes merely lifted long enough from the photocopied pages to nod at them. At some point, she had changed out of her clingy black dress and into a smart blouse and casual slacks.

Wary, Seichan kept half an eye on her. There was nothing the woman had done to warrant suspicion, beyond her stunning looks, with her smooth skin, petite features, and flatironed black hair. What was someone so beautiful doing as a mere assistant to a curator in a vault of dusty manuscripts? This woman could easily be walking down a runway in Milan.

Seichan also didn't like how Gray's eyes lingered on her whenever she shifted in her seat, to turn a page, to jot a note.

"Why don't you start at the beginning?" Gray suggested, trying to jump-start the discussion.

"Not a bad suggestion," Heisman said, and pointed Gray to a chair. "Sit. I'll tell you. It's a remarkable story. Fills in so many blanks."

Gray obeyed.

Heisman continued to pace, too agitated to sit. "This journal is a diary of events, beginning when Franklin first approached Archard."

Archard . . . ?

Seichan hid a smirk. Looked like the curator was now on a first-name basis with the Frenchman.

"It starts with the discovery of an Indian mound in Kentucky." Heisman turned to Sharyn for help.

She didn't even lift her head. *"The Barrow of the Serpent."*

"Yes, very dramatic. It was there that they discovered a golden map lining the inside of a mastodon skull, which was itself wrapped within a buffalo hide. It was the hidden Indian map that the dying shaman had told Jefferson about."

Heisman continued, gesturing as he spoke for emphasis when needed, which apparently was a lot. "But that wasn't the first time Jefferson and Franklin met with a Native American shaman. Chief Canasatego brought another shaman from a distant Western tribe to meet with Jefferson. It seems this old fellow had traveled a long way to meet with the new white leaders to these shores. The shaman told Jefferson a long story about previous *pale Indians* who once shared their lands, a people with great powers. It was said that they also came from the east, like the colonists. This, of course, drew great interest on the part of those two Founding Fathers. Likewise, a fair amount of skepticism."

Gray nodded. "No doubt."

"Eventually the shaman returned with proof. Making sure that what transpired was cloaked in great secrecy, he demonstrated evidence of a technology that baffled and astounded Franklin and Jefferson." Heisman turned to his assistant. "Sharyn . . . could you read that passage?"

"One moment." She shifted pages, found the right one, and read. *"'They came with a gold that would not melt, weapons of a steel that no Indian had ever wielded, but most important, with a silvery dry elixir a very pinch of which was a thousandfold more powerful than a mountain of black powder.'"*

Gray shared a look with Seichan. The immutable gold had to be the same metal as they had seen on the tablets. It was far denser and harder than ordinary gold. And the *silvery dry elixir* . . . could that be the source of the powerful explosions that had been witnessed in both Utah and Iceland?

Heisman continued, "Because the Iroquois Confederacy very much wanted to be part of the new nation, they were trying to broker a deal."

"For the Fourteenth Colony," Gray added.

"The Devil Colony, yes. The negotiations, though held in secret, were fairly well along. It would be a trade. The Iroquois Confederacy even staked out its territory." He turned, but this time Sharyn was ready.

"'They wished to possess a great land beyond the French territories, lands unexplored and unclaimed, wishing not to threaten the growing interest of the colonists to the east. The Iroquois would give up their old lands and their great secret knowledge in exchange for a permanent new home and a solid stake in this new nation. Additionally, it was ascertained through private meetings with Chief Canasatego that at the heart of the Indian colony was a lost city, the source of these miraculous materials. But of that place's location, they remained duly cryptic.'"

As his assistant read the translation, Heisman slid an open atlas across the table. It displayed an old map of the United States. He poked at a shaded section that spread northward from New Orleans in a V shape, covering most of what would later be the middle of the country. "Here are the lands bought from the French by Jefferson."

"The Louisiana Purchase," Gray said.

"From the journal entry, I think the proposed Fourteenth Colony desired by the Indians must lie somewhere west of the Purchase. But Archard never goes into any more detail on where exactly it was. There's only one tangential mention."

"What was it?" Seichan asked.

"After Archard unearthed that Indian map at the serpent mound, he determined the metal of the map was composed of the same strange gold. And on that map were marked two spots."

"*Iceland* was one of them," Gray muttered, plainly working the puzzle in his head.

"That's right. The second was far out to the west. Archard believed that the site marked in the Western territories might be the location of that lost city, the proposed *heart of the new colony*. But it was too far west—off in uncharted lands of that time—and the map apparently was not precise enough on the details, so Archard decided to investigate Iceland first, as that sea journey was well charted by sailors."

Gray leaned back. "I don't suppose the Frenchman thought to make a copy of that map to include with his journal?"

"No. According to Archard, Thomas Jefferson kept the map a great secret. He would not let anyone but his inner circle see it. No copies were to be made."

Seichan understood his caution. The president must have feared his unknown enemy and didn't realize how badly his government had already been infiltrated. *Mistrust and paranoia.* Yes, she could easily put herself in Jefferson's shoes.

"What became of the map?" Gray asked.

Heisman only had to turn to his assistant.

Sharyn read, "*Ever crafty, Jefferson devised a way to preserve the Indian map, to protect it, yet keep it forever out of the hands of the faceless enemy. He would use the very gold to hide it in plain view of all. None would suspect the treasure hidden at the heart of the Seal.*'"

Gray frowned. "What does that mean?"

Heisman shrugged. "He never elaborates. That's pretty much the first half of the journal. We're still working on translating the second half, starting with Archard's secret mission by sea to Iceland."

Gray's phone rang. "Sorry," he said, and checked who was calling.

Seichan again noted the flicker of worry shine brighter, always hidden just under the surface. He let out a small sigh of relief, though he was probably not even aware of it.

"It's Monk," he said quietly to her. "I'd better take this outside."

Gray excused himself, ducking out into the hall. Heisman used the break to consult with Sharyn as she finished working through the translation of the last half of the journal. The two bent and whispered over the photocopies.

"They should see this . . ." Heisman said, but the rest was lost in whispers.

Gray popped his head back into the room and motioned for Seichan to join him.

"More trouble?" she asked as she stepped out.

He pulled her over to a quiet, out-of-the-way corner. "Monk just heard from the Japanese physicists. During the Iceland explosion, another massive spike in neutrinos was generated from the island, ten times larger than the Utah spike. It's already subsiding, as is the volcanic activity throughout the archipelago. So we may be lucky in that regard. The consensus is that the extreme *heat* of Iceland's volcanic eruption killed the nano-nest out there, stopping any further spread."

Seichan heard no relief in his words. Something more was coming.

"But the latest news from Japan came in about five minutes ago. The physicists have picked up yet another site that's going hot. They think the Iceland explosion has destabilized a *third* cache of nano-material."

Seichan pictured a chain of explosions linked together.

First Utah . . . then Iceland . . . and now this third one.

Gray continued: "And according to the physicists' recordings, this new deposit must be massive. The wave of neutrinos being generated is so large and widespread that they're having difficulty pinning down its source. All they can tell us right now is that it's here in the States, somewhere out west."

"That's a lot of territory to cover."

Gray nodded. "The scientists are coordinating with other labs around the world, trying to get us more information."

"That's a problem," Seichan mumbled.

"Why?"

"We were ambushed in Iceland by Guild operatives. That means they're keyed into the same information stream as we are. Since we thwarted their efforts on that island, they're not going to sit idly by and let the same thing happen again. I know how these guys think, how they'll react. I worked long enough in that organization that I share their DNA."

"Then what's their next move?"

"They're going to shut down our access to any new information, dry it up so that only they have the critical intelligence from here on out." Seichan stared up at Gray, ensuring that he understood the gravity of her next words. "They'll go after our assets in Japan. To silence them."

June 1, 6:14 A.M.
Gifu Prefecture, Japan

Riku Tanaka hated to be touched, especially when he was agitated. Like now. He had donned a pair of cotton gloves and had inserted earplugs in order to tone down the commotion around him. He tapped a pencil on his desk as he stared at the real-time data flowing across his screen. Every fifth tap, he would flick the pencil and expertly flip it in his grip. It helped calm him.

Though it was early in the morning, his lab—normally so quiet, buried at the heart of Mount Ikeno—was bustling with activity. Jun Yoshida-*sama* had summoned additional support staff after the huge neutrino surge was picked up: four more physicists and two computer technicians. They were all gathered around Yoshida at a neighboring station, attempting to coordinate data from six different labs around the world. It was too much to take, so Riku had retreated to the lone console, away from the others, at the back of the lab, as far from them as possible.

While they worked on the larger puzzle, he concentrated on the smaller one. With his head cocked to the side (it helped him think better), he studied a global chart that was glowing on his screen. Various small icons dotted the map. Each represented a smaller neutrino spike.

"Not worth our time," Yoshida had declared when Riku had first presented the findings to him.

Riku thought otherwise. He knew Yoshida was wasting his energy, stirring and making so much noise. He would fail. The new surge detected out along the western half of the United States was beyond pinpointing. While it bore the same heartbeatlike pattern seen from Iceland, this surge was 123.4 times larger.

He enjoyed the sequential numbering of that magnitude.

1, 2, 3, 4.

The sequence was pure coincidence, but the beauty of it made him smile inside. There was a purity and exquisiteness in numbers that no one seemed to understand, except him.

He continued to stare at the map. He'd detected these anomalous readings after the first neutrino blast in Utah. While that blast had ignited something unstable in Iceland, it had also triggered these smaller surges, little flickers from spots around the globe. He'd recorded them again after Iceland went critical.

Not worth our time . . .

He pushed aside that nagging voice, staring at the small dots, looking for a pattern. One or two were out west, but the exact locations were obscured by the tsunami-like wave of neutrinos from out there, a flood that washed away all details. That was why Yoshida would fail.

"Riku?"

Someone touched his shoulder. He flinched away and turned to find Dr. Janice Cooper standing behind him.

"Sorry," Janice said—she preferred to be called Janice, though he still found such informality uncomfortable. She removed her arm from his shoulder.

He pinched his brow, trying to interpret the small muscle movements in her face, trying to connect an emotional content to them. The best he could come up with was that she was hungry, but that probably wasn't right. Due to his Asperger's syndrome, he was wrong too often in his assessments to trust them.

She slid a chair over, sat down, and placed a cup of green tea near his elbow. "I thought you might like this."

He nodded, but he didn't understand why she had to sit so close.

"Riku, we've been trying to figure out why this surge out west happened."

"The Iceland bombardment of neutrinos coursed through the planet and destabilized a third source."

"Yes, but why now? Why didn't this deposit destabilize earlier, following the Utah spike? Iceland went critical, but not this new deposit out west. The anomaly is troubling the other physicists."

Riku continued studying his screen. "Activation energy," he said, and glanced to her as if this should be obvious. And it *was* obvious.

She shook her head. Was she disagreeing or not understanding?

He sighed. "Some chemical reactions, like nuclear reactions, require a set amount of energy to get them started."

"Activation energy."

He frowned. Hadn't he just said that? But he continued: "Often the amount of energy is dependent on the volume or mass of the substrate. The deposit in Iceland must have been smaller. So the quantities of neutrinos from the Utah spike were sufficient to cause it to destabilize."

She nodded. "But the neutrino burst from Iceland was much *larger*. Enough to destabilize the deposit out west. To light that fatter fuse out there. If you're right, this would mean that the western deposit must be much *bigger*."

Again, hadn't he just made that clear?

"It should be 123.4 times larger." Just speaking the numbers helped calm him. "That is, of course, if there is an exact one-to-one correlation between neutrino generation and mass."

Her face went a bit paler as he gave this assessment.

Uncomfortable, he turned back to his screen, to his own puzzle, to the tiny flickers of neutrinos.

"What do you think those smaller emissions are?" Janice asked after a long moment of welcome silence.

Riku closed his eyes to think, enjoying the puzzle. He pictured the neutrinos flying out, igniting the fuses of the unstable deposits, but when they hit the smaller targets, all they did was *excite* them, triggering mini-bursts.

"They can't be the *same* as the unstable substance. The pattern is not consistent. I don't see any parallelism. Instead, I think these blip marks are a substance *related* to those deposits but not identical to them."

He leaned closer and reached to the screen but dared not touch it. "Here's one in Belgium. One or two again out in the Western United States—but they're obscured by the new burst. And an especially strong response from a location in the Eastern United States."

Janice shifted forward. "Kentucky . . ."

Before he could fathom why she had to lean so close, his world shattered. Sirens blared, red lamps flashed along the walls. The noise cut through his earplugs like knives. He slammed his palms over his ears. To the side, the others began to yell and gesture. Again he could divine no meaning from their faces.

What is happening?

On the far side of the room, the elevator doors opened. Figures in black gear burst forth, spreading wide. They had rifles in their grips. The head-splitting *rat-a-tat* of their weapons drove him to the floor—not to dodge the barrage of bullets, but to flee the noise.

Screams only made it worse.

From beneath his desk, he saw Yoshida fall and roll. A large chunk of his skull was missing. Blood was pouring from his head. Riku could not take his eyes off the spreading pool.

Then someone grabbed him. He fought, but it was Janice. She snatched a handful of his lab jacket and dragged him around his desk. She pointed her arm toward a side exit. It led to an open cavernous space, a former mine, but now home to the Super-Kamiokande detector.

He understood. They had to flee the lab. It was death to remain hiding here. As if to underscore this thought, he heard the *pop-pop* of rifle fire. The invaders were killing everyone.

Staying low, hidden by the row of desks, he followed Janice as she headed to the side exit. She burst through, and he dove out at her heels. She slammed the door behind him and searched around.

Gunfire echoed from the tunnel ahead. It was the old mine shaft that led to the surface. Besides the new elevator, it was the only way into or out of the facility. The assassins had both exits covered and were converging here.

"This way!" Janice reached back and tugged his arm.

Together, they fled in the only direction they could, running down another tunnel. But Riku knew it led to a dead end. The gunmen would be on top of them in a matter of moments. Thirty meters farther along, the tunnel emptied into a cavern.

He could see the domed roof stretching far above him. It was draped in polyethylene Mineguard, to block radon seeping from the rock. Beneath his feet was the Super-Kamiokande detector itself, a massive stainless-steel tank filled with fifty thousand tons of ultrapure water and lined by thirteen thousand photomultiplier tubes.

"C'mon," Janice said.

They dashed together around the electronics hut. The cavernous space was littered with equipment and gear, with forklifts and hand trucks. Overhead, bright yellow scaffolding held up cranes, all to service the Super-Kamiokande detector.

A harsh shout in Arabic rebounded behind them, echoing off the walls. The assassins were sweeping toward them.

Riku searched around. There was nowhere to hide that wouldn't be discovered in seconds.

Janice continued to draw him along with her. She stopped at a rack of diving gear—then he understood.

And balked.

"It's the only way," she urged in a hard whisper.

She pushed a heavy air tank, already equipped with a regulator, into his arms. He had no choice but to hug it. She turned the valve on top, and air hissed from the mouthpiece. She grabbed another tank and rushed to a hatch in the floor. It opened into the top of the giant water-filled vault below. Divers used the hatch to service the Super-Kamiokande detector's main tank, mostly to repair broken photomultiplier tubes.

Janice fumbled the regulator's mouthpiece between his lips. He wanted to spit it out—it tasted bad—but he bit down on the silicon. She pointed to the dark hole.

"Go!"

With a great tremble of fear, he stepped over the opening and jumped feetfirst into the cold water. The weight of the tank pulled him quickly toward the distant bottom. He craned up and saw Janice splash overhead, pulling the hatch closed behind her.

Complete and utter darkness swamped him.

Riku continued his blind plunge, screaming out air bubbles as his feet crashed into the bottom. He crouched on the floor, hugging his air tank, shivering—for now in fear, but the cold would soon make it worse.

Then arms found him and encircled him. He felt a cheek press against his, so very warm. Janice was holding him in the dark.

For the first time in his life, a touch felt good.

May 31, 5:32 P.M.
Washington, D.C.

"It took Archard a full month to sail to Iceland," Dr. Heisman was saying. "The seas were especially rough."

Gray sat at the table beside Seichan as the curator set about summarizing the contents of the back half of Fortescue's journal. Sharyn had finished the translation while Gray had been raising the alarm concerning a possible attack in Japan.

His knee bounced up and down. He needed to hear this tale, but he also wanted to be at Sigma command, to find out if the Japanese physicists were okay.

He glanced to Seichan.

Is she just being overly paranoid?

He didn't think so. He trusted her judgment, especially when it came to the Guild. He had promptly called in the warning to Kat, who had alerted Japanese authorities of the potential threat. They were all still waiting to hear back.

"On that long trip," Heisman continued, "Archard spent many days writing at length concerning his theories about the *pale Indians,* the mythical people who gave the Iroquois' ancestors these powerful tokens. He'd collated the stories he had heard from many tribes, hearing often of white men or white-skinned Indians. He collected rumors from the colonists who claimed to have found evidence of previous settlements, homesteads of non-Indians, as evidenced by the sophisticated building techniques. But mostly Archard seemed fixated on a possible Jewish origin to these people."

"Jewish?" Gray shifted taller in his seat. "Why?"

"Because Archard describes some writing found on the gold Indian map. He thought it looked like Hebrew but different."

Sharyn shared the passage from the journal. *"'The scratches on the map are clearly those of some unknown scribe. Could they have been written by one of the pale Indians? I have consulted the most learned rabbinical experts, who all agree that there appears to be some commonality with the ancient Jewish writing, yet as one, they say it is not in fact Hebrew, though perhaps related to that language. It is a confounding mystery.'"*

As she read, Heisman grew more excited, nodding his head. "It *is* a mystery. While Sharyn was finishing her translation and you were busy contacting your people about Japan, I received word on something that was troubling me about that early sketch of the Great Seal, the one with the fourteen arrows."

Heisman reached to a stack of papers and pulled it free. "Look beneath the Seal itself. There is some faint writing, almost like notations."

Gray had noticed the marks before but hadn't placed any significance on them. "What about them?"

"Well, I consulted an ancient-language expert. The writing is an odd form of Hebrew, just like Archard mentioned. The curve of letters beneath

the Seal spelled out the word *Manasseh,* which is the name of one of the
ten lost tribes of Israel."

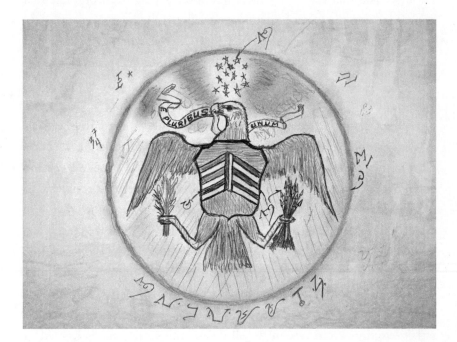

Gray's attention sharpened. Hours earlier, Painter had passed on information speculating that these ancient people, the *Tawtsee'untsaw Pootseev,* could possibly be descendants of a lost tribe of Israel. Painter had
also referenced the Book of Mormon, whose scripture contended that an
exiled tribe of Israelites had come to early America—*specifically the clan of
Manasseh.*

Heisman continued: "In fact, the Founding Fathers seemed a bit
obsessed with the lost tribes of Israel. When the committee to draft the
original Great Seal first got together, Benjamin Franklin expressed a wish
for the design to include a scene out of the Book of Exodus, when the
Israelites went into exile. Thomas Jefferson suggested a depiction of the
children of Israel in the wilderness."

Gray studied the sketch of the Seal. *Had the Founding Fathers known about this lost tribe reaching these shores? Did they somehow learn that the "pale Indians" described by the Iroquois were in fact exiled Israelites?*

It seemed that way. They must have been trying to incorporate that knowledge into the Great Seal, to memorialize the tribe.

Heisman's next words suggested that Gray was right. "What I find odd is that the tribes of Israel were all represented by different *pairs* of symbols. In the case of the Manasseh clan, it was an *olive branch* and a *bundle of arrows.*" Heisman glanced up to Gray. "Why would the Founding Fathers plant the symbols of the Manasseh tribe in the Great Seal?"

Gray suspected that he knew the answer to this question, but he had a more immediate concern. He waved Heisman onward. "That's all well and good, but let's continue to the place where Fortescue reached Iceland . . ."

Heisman looked disappointed, but he slid the draft of the Great Seal aside. "All right. Like I said, it took Archard about a month to reach Iceland, but eventually he grew confident that he'd found the right island, as marked on the map. But once there, he had no luck in finding anything. After twenty-two days of searching, he began to despair. Then his luck changed. One of his searchers dropped an apple while investigating a rather lengthy cavern system. It fell down a chute no one had noted. A lamp lowered down that hole revealed a glint of gold near the bottom."

"They found the spot," Seichan said.

"He goes into great length describing the deep cavern. How stone boxes held hundreds of gold plates inscribed with the same proto-Hebrew writing. He also found solid gold jars filled with the oft-mentioned *silvery dry elixir.* He was quite excited and drew many pictures."

From the tick in the curator's voice, it was clear that he was also excited. Heisman slid one of the pages over to Gray and Seichan. The curator tapped the picture in the center. "Those are the golden containers for the elixir."

Gray stiffened at the sight. The drawing showed tall urns topped by various sculpted heads: that of a jackal, a hawk, a baboon, and a hooded man.

"Those look like Egyptian canopic jars," he said.

"Yes. Archard thought so, too. Or at least he recognized that they were of Egyptian origin. He postulated that perhaps the pale Indians were in fact refugees from the Holy Lands, some secret sect of magi who had roots in both the Jewish faith and Egyptian traditions. But such speculations came to an abrupt end. After this point in the journal, his writing becomes very sloppy and hurried; it's clear that he was in a state of panic."

"Why?"

At a cue from her boss, Sharyn began to read. "*I have heard word that a ship approaches Iceland. That the Enemy has discovered our investigation and closes upon us. They must never find this cache of lost treasures. My men and I will do our best to lure them away, to keep them from this island. Pray that I am successful. We will strike for the coast, to the cold mainland, and draw them after us. I will take a small sampling of the treasure in the hopes that I can still reach the shores of America. But I leave this journal as a testament, in case I fail.'*"

Heisman crossed his arms. "That's how the journal ends, with Archard fleeing his enemy. But I think we can piece together what happened after that."

"The Laki eruption," Gray said.

"The site of that volcano is not far from the coastline. Archard must have made it some distance, but then catastrophe struck."

Gray had witnessed such an event himself. He pictured the explosion, followed by the violent volcanic eruption.

Heisman sighed. "After that, we know from Jefferson's letter that our Frenchman went into deep seclusion, regretting the actions he had taken, actions that led to the death of more than six million people."

"Until he was summoned twenty years later by Jefferson to undertake a new mission. To join Lewis and Clark on their sojourn west." Gray let the pieces fall together in his head. "According to the date on the map you showed us earlier, Jefferson concluded the Louisiana Purchase in 1803. That very year, Jefferson commissioned his friend Captain Meriwether Lewis to put together a team to explore those former French territories and the lands west of there."

Gray's head buzzed with the certainty of his assessment. "Fortescue went with them. He was sent to find that spot on the Indian map, to find what Fortescue himself believed was *the heart of the new colony,* that lost city."

Seichan kept pace with him. "And he must have found it. He vanished out of history, and Lewis was murdered."

Gray turned to Heisman. "Do you have a map that marks the trail that Lewis and Clark took?"

"Of course. Just one moment." He and his assistant combed through their stacks and quickly found the right book. "Here it is."

Gray stared down at the page. He ran a finger along the trail, starting at Camp Wood in St. Charles, Missouri, and ending at Fort Clatsop on the coast of the Pacific Ocean.

"Somewhere along this route—or close to it—has to be the location of the lost Fourteenth Colony."

But where?

His phone rang again. He'd left his cell on the tabletop; a glance at it showed Sigma's emergency number.

Seichan saw it, too.

"I'll be right back," he said, and headed again to the door. Seichan dogged his heels and joined him in the hall.

He flipped open the phone. "Monk?"

"It's Kat, Gray. Monk's on his way over to meet you with a car."

"What's wrong? What's the news from Japan?"

"Bad. An assault team killed nearly everyone at the facility."

He swore silently. They'd been too slow.

Kat continued: "But two key personnel survived. Japanese authorities fished them out of the neutron detector's water tank. Rather clever place to hide. They were whisked into PSIA custody at our request."

PSIA was the acronym for the Japanese intelligence agency. Calling in the latter was a wise precaution. If no one knew about the survivors, Sigma command had a chance to get a step up on the Guild. Kat knew it, too.

"I've been on the phone with one of them," Kat said. "An American postgraduate student. She reports that before the attack, the Japanese physicists had been making no headway on discovering the source of the latest neutrino surge. But she related something odd, something that was noted by the other physicist who survived. He was concerned about some spotty neutrino bursts he'd detected. I didn't give this detail much thought until she told me *where* those readings originated."

"Where?"

"Maybe one or two sites out west, but he couldn't pinpoint the locations due to the background rush of neutrinos from the larger spike. Of the two he *was* able to identify, one was in Belgium."

She let this piece of news hang. It took Gray only a breath to recognize its significance. He remembered Captain Huld's description of the hunters who'd come to Ellirey Island before Gray and his team. He'd said they were from Belgium. Monk must have made the same connection. It could be a coincidence, but Gray wasn't buying it.

He told Kat as much. "The assault team in Iceland was from Belgium. That's got to be significant. But what about that other spot the physicist noted? Where is it?"

"It's in Kentucky."

Kentucky?

Kat went on: "Monk's on his way over to pick you up. I want you to check out the location. You're wheels-up in fifteen minutes. We must take full advantage of this intel while we still can."

Gray sensed some hesitancy on her part. "What does Director Crowe think about all of this?"

"He doesn't. I've not been able to raise him since we got this news. He was heading deep into the desert. I'll keep trying to reach him while you're en route. But we can't wait. If things change, I'll let you know. I'm also in contact with the president's chief of staff."

That startled him. "Why involve President Gant?"

"Where you're going, you'll need a presidential order to get inside. It will take Gant's signature to open those doors."

"What doors? Where are we going?"

The answer left him dumbstruck. After a few more details, Kat signed off. Gray closed his phone to find Seichan staring at him.

"Where are they sending us now?" she asked.

He slowly shook his head, trying to make sense of what he'd just heard, and told her.

"Fort Knox."

PART III

GOLD RUSH

25

"What you're doing violates both state and federal law," Nancy Tso said.

Painter ignored her threat as he used a dagger to dig out the last of the mortar that sealed the slab of sandstone over the blowhole.

Nancy Tso stood, fists on her hips, at the edge of the field of petroglyphs carved into the chasm floor. Kowalski guarded her, holding the ranger's pistol in his hand. Earlier, he'd relieved the woman of her sidearm before she knew what was happening.

"I'm sorry, Nancy," Hank Kanosh said. "We're trying to be as careful as we can."

Proving this, Hank picked out a broken chunk of mortar from the spiral artwork on the slab, flicked it clear, and gently brushed fine sand from the moon-and-star symbol in the center.

Kawtch sniffed after the tossed bit of mortar, as if this were a game.

Painter continued to scrape and dig, sweating under the sun, his exposed neck burning. After another five minutes, the plate began to vibrate under his palm.

Hank felt it, too. "You must've gotten it loose. The air blowing up from below is starting to rock the slab."

Painter agreed. He worked around the edges, on his knees, and searched until he found a decent-sized gap where he could wedge the knife blade under the rock's lip. The block's edges angled inward, like a rubber stopper. He pushed down on the dagger's hilt and pried the stone up slightly. It was about four inches thick, too heavy for Hank to lift on his own.

He lowered it and waved to Kowalski. "Give me a hand with this."

"What about her?" Kowalski thumbed toward the park ranger.

Painter sat back on his heels. He needed the woman's cooperation, which meant he needed to be honest with her, to let her know the gravity of the situation. "Ranger Tso, I'm sure you've heard about the volcanic eruptions up in Utah and over in Iceland."

The angry creases around Nancy's eyes and the hard set to her mouth did not relax. She just glared at him.

"What we're searching for here is related to both of those disasters. Many people have died, and many more will die, too, unless we get answers. Answers that may lie below."

She shook her head, scoffing. "What are you talking about?"

Hank answered, "The Anasazi. We happen to have evidence that the volcanic activity today is directly related to the destruction that gave rise to the Sunset Crater and the annihilation of the Anasazi in the area. I can't go into much further detail, except that the symbols we showed you—the moon and star carved into the slab's petroglyph—are clues to that tragedy."

"If we're going to save lives," Painter pressed, "we have to keep moving."

She stared from Painter to Hank and back again. Finally, she sighed, the deep creases fading—somewhat. "I'll give you both a little latitude. For now. But be careful." She held out her hand toward Kowalski. "Can I have my weapon back?"

Painter studied her, reading her body language, trying to judge if this was a ruse to regain her pistol. She seemed sincere, but ultimately they couldn't keep watching their backs.

"Do it," he instructed Kowalski.

Kowalski looked like he was going to refuse, but he finally flipped the gun around and offered the grip to the ranger. She took the weapon, held it for a long moment as they all waited, then promptly holstered it.

She waved Kowalski forward. "C'mon. I'll help you."

With Painter prying the stone up, it took all three to grip the exposed edge and pull the stone cork out of its hole. Balancing the slab up on its edge, Kowalski rolled it to the chasm wall and leaned it there.

"Satisfied?" he asked Nancy, brushing his hands on his pants.

She refused to respond and turned to the hole. Painter fished out a flashlight from his pack and pointed it down. The beam illuminated a wide shaft, angled steeply as it dropped away.

"They're steps," she said, awed.

Steps was a generous term. Carved into the rock were distinct footholds, not much larger than would hold a toe or heel. Still, it was better than nothing. They wouldn't need ropes.

Kowalski joined them, leaning over the opening. "Phew." He waved a hand in front of his face. "Stinks."

Hank nodded. "Sulfur. And warm. Unusual for a blowhole."

Must be some geothermal activity below . . .

A disconcerting thought, but they had no choice except to continue.

He turned to Nancy. "Would you mind waiting here? If we're not out within two hours, radio for help."

She nodded.

"But please give us those two hours," he stressed, fearing that as soon as they were gone, she'd call her friends at the park service.

"I gave you my word," she said. "I'll keep it."

With his tail tucked between his legs, Kawtch backed away from the hole. The smell and strangeness must have spooked the dog. Painter couldn't blame him.

Hank held out his dog leash toward the ranger. "Could you keep an eye on Kawtch, too, while you wait?"

"I don't think I have much choice. He's not going down there. Probably the smartest of all of us."

With matters settled, Painter made a quick call to Sigma command, letting Kat and Lisa know the situation here. Once this was done, he ducked and climbed down into the passageway, careful to plant the heel of his boot into each carved hold. He didn't want to go sliding down to oblivion. He led the way, pointing his flashlight. Kowalski manned the rear with another light.

The tunnel continued down a long way. After several minutes, the hole to the surface shrank to a tiny sunlit dot far behind them. Ahead, the way grew hotter, the air more foul. Painter's eyes and nostrils burned, an unpleasant sensation that was only exacerbated by the steady wind blowing in his face. He didn't know how much farther they could go before they'd have to turn back.

"We must be deep beneath the mesa," Hank estimated. "At least a hundred feet. Feel the walls. The rock has changed from sandstone to the limestone that underlies most of the Colorado Plateau here."

Painter had noted the change, too. *How far down does this go?*

Kowalski must have wondered the same. He sucked loudly on the tube to his water pouch, then spat it out and swore. "If we come across a guy with hooves, carrying a pitchfork, we haul ass out of here, right?"

"Or even sooner than that," Hank said, coughing on the bad air.

Still, Painter trudged onward, until a steady hissing and gentle roaring reached his ears. The beam of his light revealed an end to the tunnel.

Finally.

"Something up ahead," he warned.

He continued more cautiously, crossing the last few yards, and pushed out into a cavity that was both wondrous and terrifying in its beauty. He moved out of the way so that the others could join him.

Kowalski swore as he stepped out.

Hank covered his mouth, offering up a small, "Dear God . . ."

The tunnel emptied into a large cavern, tall enough to house a five-story apartment building. Overhead, the roof was perfectly domed, as if the chamber had been formed out of a bubble in the limestone. Only this bubble had cracked long ago.

To the left, a wide fracture high up the wall allowed a river to gush forth, pouring down into the cavern in a turgid fall—but it was not a river of *water*. From the crack, black mud boiled and flowed, popping and spewing a sulfurous steam, as it ran thickly downward. It pooled into a great lake that filled half of the cavern, fed additionally from a dozen trickles weeping out of smaller fissures in the wall. The pool then emptied into a gorge that split the cavern. Down that chasm, a river of seething mud, bubbling and roiling, swept past, until it vanished down a dark gullet on the far side.

"Amazing," Hank said. "An underground river of mud. This must be one of the geothermal arteries flowing all the way through the Colorado Plateau from the San Francisco range of volcanic peaks."

But they weren't the first ones to discover this giant artery.

An arched bridge, built of long, narrow slabs of sandstone, all mortared together, spanned the steaming gorge. The pattern and design were readily identifiable as the handiwork of the ancient Pueblo Indians.

"How did anyone build that down here?" Kowalski asked.

Hank answered, "The old tribes of this region were phenomenal engineers, capable of constructing extensive and complex homes halfway up sheer cliffs. This bridge would be easy for them to make. Still, they must have hand-carried each of those thin slabs down here."

The professor's eyes went glassy—either from the sting in the air or from imagining such an engineering feat. Hank moved forward. A jumble of broken rock littered the cavern floor, but some ancient hand had cleared a path to the bridge long ago.

Painter followed, knowing the professor's goal. A similar path threaded from the far side of the span to a tunnel opening in the opposite wall. It seemed that their journey through this subterranean world wasn't over yet.

As they approached the bridge, the heat spiked to a blistering degree. The air grew nearly impossible to breathe as its sulfur content swelled. The only reason they'd made it this far was that the continuing breeze sweeping through the cavern flushed the worst of the toxins up the shaft behind them.

"Do you think it's safe to cross?" Kowalski asked, hanging back with Hank, who looked equally uneasy.

"This bridge has stood here for centuries," Painter said, "but I'll go first. Alone. If it looks okay, I'll have you follow one at a time."

"Be careful," Hank said.

Painter intended to be. He stepped to the edge of the bridge. He had a good view down into the chasm. Mud bubbled and spat, splattering the limestone walls to either side of the gorge. It would be instant death to fall down there.

With little choice, he placed one foot on the span, then the other. He stood for a breath. Seemed solid enough, so he took another step then another. He was now over the gorge's edge. Hearing sandstone grating slightly, settling a bit under his weight, he waited, swallowing his fear. Sweat trickled in streams down his back. His eyes watered and itched.

"Are you okay?" Kowalski called.

Painter lifted an arm, acknowledging that he was fine, but he feared calling out. This was foolish, of course. He continued onward, step by step, until finally he reached the far side and happily leaped to solid ground.

Relieved, he leaned down, resting his hands on his knees.

"Should we follow?" Hank yelled.

Painter merely lifted an arm and waved them over.

In short order, they all crossed and made it safely to the far side. After a moment to collect themselves, they headed toward the dark tunnel, leaving the muddy caldera behind them.

Once they reached the mouth of the passageway, they were rewarded with a cold breath blowing out of the tunnel. The air had a mineral tang, but it was a welcome respite from the sulfurous burn of the cavern.

Kowalski held a hand to the breeze. "Where's this coming from?"

"Only one way to find out." Painter led the way again.

Hank offered a more detailed answer as they headed down. "The cavern system must extend much farther underground. For a cave to breathe like this, it takes a great volume of cold air below." He pointed behind him. "That hot cavern is drawing the chilled air upward, and the breeze continues from there to the surface, flushing that heat upward and out."

Painter remembered the volume estimate of the cavern system beneath Wupatki's blowhole. *Seven billion cubic feet.* He sensed that this was bigger. But how far down would they have to go?

The tunnel continued deeper, turning steeper in some spots, almost flat in others. But it never turned upward. The way also grew steadily colder. After another ten minutes of hiking, a pearly sheen of ice began to coat the walls, reflecting the beam of Painter's flashlight. He remembered Nancy's story of the icy lava tubes that lay beneath the cone of the Sunset Crater. The same phenomenon was happening here.

Soon, even their footing became more treacherous. Kowalski took a hard fall and cursed loudly. The breeze blew stronger, the icy chill burning Painter's cheeks as readily as the sulfuric heat had some minutes ago.

"Is it just me," Kowalski asked as he picked himself up, "or is anyone else thinking of the phrase *when hell freezes over?*"

Painter ignored him as his light revealed the end of the tunnel at last. He hurried forward, half skating on the slick surface. He slid into another cavern and stopped once again at the entrance, stunned by what he saw before him.

Kowalski whistled sharply.

Hank gaped in awe. "We've found them."

Painter knew what he meant.

They'd found the Anasazi.

4:14 P.M.

"It's almost like watching a video game, *n'est-ce pas?*" Rafael asked.

He sat in the rear cabin of a surveillance helicopter—one of two aircraft borrowed at some expense from a private militia group who spent time patrolling the Mexican border for "narco-terrorists." With heavily tinted bulletproof windows and engines idling, the two helicopters sat in the desert about a mile from the mesa.

The rear cabin of Rafe's craft was equipped with two captain's chairs that swiveled easily between a bench seat on one side and an entire wall of equipment, including digital recorders, DVD players, a bank of three LCD monitors, all of it tied into microwave receivers and cameras bristling on the outside.

On the center LCD monitor, a jangling view revealed a team climbing up a crack in the mesa's side, aiming for the ruins on top. The feed came from Bern's helmet-mounted camera, allowing Rafe to once again monitor the assault.

He turned his chair to face Kai Quocheets, who sat on the bench seat beside one of Bern's teammates. She stared sullenly back at him with her arms crossed in front of her. Clearly still furious about his betrayal, she hadn't said a word since they'd left the pueblos after the shooting of the two elderly Hopi natives. He felt a bit bad about that. He admitted to himself now that it had been a feckless act on his part, one beneath him, but he'd been sore from the ride to the pueblos and already in a foul temper over how the old woman had resisted his interrogation. He now truly believed the elderly pair knew nothing.

A waste.

And if the young woman hadn't been so obstinate, he might have thrown her a bone, but instead he let her sulk.

So be it.

He turned around and faced the monitors. Bern's team had reached the mesa's top and circled to where the satellite feed had last spotted Painter Crowe's team vanishing down another chute on the far side. The resolution had not been good enough to reveal anything more.

It hadn't been hard to track the director of Sigma to this location. A few calls, a few interviews, and it was over, especially after Painter's group posted trail permits with the National Park Service office. No names had been mentioned—but then again, how many three-man teams of hikers were headed into the deep desert *with a dog*? Descriptions were matched, and through the Saint Germaine family's contacts in the scientific community, Rafe was able to gain access to a geophysical satellite and monitor the desert around the Crack-in-the-Rock pueblo.

After that, they had flown in from the unpopulated north side of the park. Once within a mile of the mesa, Bern's team had off-loaded and headed out across the desert on foot.

Rafe leaned closer to the screen.

"Where is that *chiant* uncle of yours now?" he whispered to the monitor.

He watched Bern climb with the effortless grace of a true athlete, moving from stone to stone, carrying a heavy pack with a rifle ready at his shoulder. Rafe found his left hand rubbing his thigh in envy. He forced his fingers to curl into a fist. The best he could hope for in life was to live vicariously through others. As he was doing now. If he stared hard enough, blocked out other stimuli, he could *be* Bern for short periods of time.

His second-in-command slipped to the front of his team, assuming the point position. Bern was not one to let a subordinate take a risk he himself wasn't willing to face. He edged over a pile of crumbling bricks, part of an ancient wall, and reached a hidden chute. Before he entered, a hand rose into view. Bern gave silent signals. Rafe interpreted them, repeating the hand signals on his knee.

Move quiet. On my mark. Go.

From the corner of his eye, he caught Kai's reflection in one of the dark monitors as she shifted forward, trying to get a better look. She might act the disinterested, estranged niece, but Rafe noted how her breathing quickened whenever she overheard him talking about her uncle.

Or whenever he mentioned their other captive.

The boy—Jordan Appawora—was in the other helicopter, parked twenty yards away, a bit of insurance for Kai's continued cooperation.

On the screen, Rafe could see Bern sliding carefully down the chute, ready for any contingency. He imagined the burning sensation of the sun on his face, the tightness in his chest as he restricted his breathing, the tension in his back and arms as he handled the heavy rifle.

Bern reached a turn in the chute and took a split-second peek into a blind chasm. That's all the time that was required. There was an advantage to having a partner sitting on your shoulder. Rafe brought up the image again and froze it on his screen to study it more closely.

The chasm's rock walls were wildly decorated with petroglyphs, but he found only a *single* living figure standing in the tight space. A woman, likely the park ranger who acted as a guide for Painter Crowe's team. She stood with her back to the camera, holding a leash, staring down a hole in the ground.

Ah, so that's where you went . . .

Rafe sighed. "You're not going to make this easy, are you, *mon ami?*"

He lifted the radio to his lips. "Bern, looks like we must do this the hard way. We'll have to make it personal in order to draw our quarry out."

Rafe caught Kai's reflection again as he gave the order.

"Take down the guard. We're coming in."

On the screen, Bern popped around the corner with his weapon raised.

The ranger must have heard something and started to turn. Bern's rifle jerked silently on the screen, and the woman crumpled to the ground.

Kai gasped behind him.

Rafe reached to the other captain's chair and found Ashanda's hand. She had been sitting silently, a dark statue, almost forgotten, but never far from his heart. He gave her fingers a squeeze.

"I'm going to need your help."

4:20 P.M.

From the edge of the cavern, Hank stared at the frozen tomb of the Anasazi, preserved for centuries deep underground. He struggled to understand what he was seeing.

It can't be . . .

Thick blue ice coated the walls, flooded the floors, and formed massive icicles that dripped like stalactites from the arched roof. Across the way, embedded half into the ice, stood a village frozen in time. The tumbled blocks of ancient pueblo homes climbed four stories high, stacked into a ragged pile, all draped and barred by more flows of ice. It was Wupatki reborn, only larger. But the residents here hadn't fared any better. Blackened, mummified bodies sprawled frozen in the ice, looking as if they'd been washed from their homes. Clay pots and wooden ladders lay cracked and buried, mostly to one side of the cavern, along with tangles of blankets and woven baskets preserved in frost.

"There must have been a flash flood through here," Painter said, pointing to the other tunnels that ran into and out of the cavern. "Drowned everyone, then froze over again."

Hank shook his head. "First, their people died in fire . . . then by ice."

"Maybe they were cursed," Kowalski said with unusual somberness.

Maybe they were.

"Are you sure they're Anasazi?" Painter asked.

"From what I can tell from the clothing, along with the architecture of the buildings and the unique black-on-white markings on the pottery, these poor people were some clan of the Anasazi."

Hank stepped forward to bear witness. "These must have been the last survivors, those who escaped both the volcanic eruption and the slaughter. They must have fled Wupatki, tried to start a new home here, hidden away underground, the entrance protected by the small citadel above."

"But who sealed the entrance?" Painter asked. "Why did they mark it with the moon-and-star symbol of the *Tawtsee'untsaw Pootseev*?"

"Maybe a neighboring tribe who was helping to hide this last bastion of the clan. They sealed it with a gravestone, engraving it with the mark of those who they believed brought such punishment down upon these people. A warning to others against trespass."

Painter checked his watch. "Speaking of which, we should explore what we can, then head back up."

Hank heard the disappointment in his voice. He must have been hoping to discover more than just an icy graveyard. They spread out, careful where they stepped. Hank was not ready to examine any of the bodies. He took out his own flashlight and set about searching the lowest levels of the pueblo.

He had to crack through fangs of icicles that blocked the door to squeeze inside. He found another body, that of a child, which had been washed into a corner like so much refuse. A tiny clawed hand stuck out of the ice, as if asking to be rescued.

"I'm sorry . . ." he whispered, and pushed on to a room farther back.

Frost and ice covered everything, reflecting the beam of his flashlight with a certain macabre beauty. But beneath that bright sheen lay only death.

As he searched deeper, he had a vague destination in mind, the true heart of the pueblo, a place to pay his respects. Ducking through a doorway, he stepped into an atrium-like space in the center of the tumble of rooms. Terraces led up, festooned in runnels of ice. He imagined children playing there, calling to one another, mothers scolding, kneading bread.

But he had to look only farther up to dash such musings. Massive ice stalactites pointed menacingly down at him from the roof. He pictured them fracturing and falling, spearing him clean through, punishing him for his intrusion into this haunted space.

But the dead gods of these people had other plans for this trespasser.

His gaze focused upward, Hank missed seeing the hole until it was too late. His right leg dropped into it. He screamed in surprise as he crashed through the manhole-sized opening. He scrabbled for the sides, losing his flashlight, but it was no help. Like a skater falling through thin ice, he could find no grip.

He dropped, plunging feetfirst, expecting to die.

But he fell only about the length of his body—then his boots hit solid ice. He stared down. The only thing that saved him from a broken neck, or at least a broken leg, was that the chamber he'd fallen into was half filled with ice. He reached down and picked up his flashlight, then stared up at the hole.

Painter called to him. "Hank!"

"I'm okay!" he shouted back. "But I need some help! I fell down a hole!"

As he waited for rescue, he swept his light around the chamber. The room was circular, lined by mortared bricks. He slowly realized he'd fallen into the exact place that he'd been hoping to find.

Some god, he was sure, was laughing with dark amusement.

He searched around. Small niches marked the wall, about at the level of the flooded ice. Normally the alcoves would be halfway up the chamber's sides. A glint drew his attention to the largest niche, reflecting his light.

No . . . how could this be?

Shadows danced across the ice floor. He swung his light up and saw Painter and Kowalski peering down at him.

"Are you hurt?" Painter asked, out of breath, clearly concerned.

"No, but you might want to hop down here yourself. I'm not sure I should be touching this."

Painter frowned, but Hank waved, urging him down.

"Okay," Painter conceded, and turned to his partner. "Kowalski, go secure a rope and toss it down to us."

After the big man left, Painter twisted around and dropped smoothly into the ice-flooded chamber. "So what did you find, Doc?"

Hank waved to encompass the chamber. "This is a *kiva,* a spiritual center of an Anasazi settlement. Basically their church." He pointed his beam up. "They built them in wells like this. That hole we both dropped through is called a *sipapa;* to the Anasazi it represented the mythical place where their people first emerged into the world."

"Okay, why the religious lesson?"

"So you'd understand what they worshipped here, or at least preserved as some sort of token to the gods." He swung his light to the large alcove. "I think this object may be what the thieves stole from the *Tawtsee'untsaw Pootseev*—what led to the Anasazi's doom."

5:06 P.M.

Painter stepped closer to the alcove, adding the shine of his own flashlight to the professor's. Not that the object needed any better illumination. It shone brightly, without a speck of tarnish, just a thin coating of ice.

Amazing . . .

Within the niche stood a gold jar, about a foot and a half tall, topped by the sculpted head of a wolf. The tiny bust was perfectly detailed, from the tipped-up ears to the furry scruff of mane. Even the eyes looked ready to blink.

Moving his light down, he recognized a familiar writing inscribed across the front of the jar in precise and even rows.

"It's the same writing found on the gold tablets," Painter said.

Hank nodded. "That must be proof that this totem once belonged to the *Tawtsee'untsaw Pootseev,* don't you think? That the Anasazi stole it from their cache."

"Maybe," Painter mumbled. "But what about the container itself? Am I wrong, or does it look like one those vases used by ancient Egyptians to hold the organs of their dead?"

"Canopic jars," Hank said.

"Exactly. Only this one has a wolf's head."

"The Egyptians adorned their bottles with animals from their native lands. If whoever forged this jar did so in North America, then a wolf makes sense. Wolves have always been powerful totems here."

"But doesn't that ruin your theory about the *Tawtsee'untsaw Pootseev?* Aren't they supposed to be the lost tribe of Israel from the Book of Mormon?"

"No, it doesn't dash my theory." Excitement rose in the professor's voice. "If anything, it supports it."

"How so?"

Hank pressed his hands to his lips, trying to control his elation. He looked ready to fall to his knees. "According to our scriptures, the gold plates that John Smith translated to compose the Book of Mormon were written in a language described as *reformed Egyptian.* To quote Mormon chapter nine, verse thirty-two. *'And now, behold, we have written this record according to our knowledge, in the characters which are called among us the reformed Egyptian, being handed down and altered by us, according to our manner of speech.'*"

Hank turned to face Painter. "But no one's ever actually *seen* that writing," he stressed, "because the original golden plates vanished after John Smith translated them. They were said to have been returned to the angel Moroni. All we know about this writing is that it was supposed to be a derivation of Hebrew, a variant that evolved since the time the tribe left the Holy Lands."

"Then why call it Egyptian at all? *Reformed* or otherwise."

"I believe the answers are here." Hank pointed. "We know the tribes of Israel had complicated ties to Egypt, a mixing of ancestries. As I told you before, the earliest representation of the moon-and-star symbol goes back to the ancient Moabites, who shared bloodlines with both the Israelites and the Egyptians of the time. So when the lost tribe came to America, they must have had a heritage with a foot in each world. Here is that very proof, a pure blending of Egyptian culture and ancient Hebrew. It must be preserved."

Painter reached for the jar. "On that we can agree."

"Careful," Hank said.

The base of the vessel was lodged a couple of inches into the ice, but that was not what worried the professor. They'd all seen what happened when someone mishandled artifacts left behind by the *Tawtsee'untsaw Pootseev.*

"I think it should be okay," Painter said. "It's been frozen for centuries."

Painter remembered Ronald Chin's contention that the explosive compound needed *warmth* to keep it stable, or extreme heat to destroy it. It only destabilized when it got *cold.* Still, he held his breath as he reached toward the wolf's-head lid. He lifted it free, cracking through a thin scrim of ice, then shone his flashlight down inside.

He let out the breath he'd been holding. "Just as I thought. It's empty."

He passed the cap to Hank, then set about breaking the jar loose from the ice. With a few sharp tugs, it came free.

"It's heavy," he said as he replaced the cap. "I wager this gold is the same nano-dense material as the plates. The ancients must've used the metal to insulate their unstable compound."

"Why do you think that?"

"The denser the metal, the better it retains heat. It might take longer to warm, but once this gold heats up, it would retain its warmth for a longer span of time. Such insulation would act like an insurance policy in case there were any sudden variations in temperature. It would also allow them additional time to get the substance from one heat source to another."

Hank shook his head at such ingenuity. "So the gold helped these ancient people stabilize their compound."

"I think this jar might have been one of their *unused* containers. But considering what happened at Sunset Crater, the Anasazi must have also stolen one that was *full*." Painter turned the jar over in his hands. "And look at this. On the opposite side of the jar."

Hank moved closer, standing shoulder to shoulder with him.

Inscribed on the back was a detailed drawing of a landscape: a winding creek, a steep mountain fringed by trees, and in the middle of it all, something that looked like a small erupting volcano.

"What do you make of it?" Painter asked.

"I don't know."

Before they could ponder it further, a rope fell heavily, coming close to knocking the jar out of Painter's hands.

"Careful, Kowalski!" he called up.

"Sorry."

Painter stepped under the opening and lifted the jar with both arms. "Come take this!"

Kowalski gladly took the prize and held it at arm's length, letting out an appreciative whistle. "At least we found some treasure! Makes my bruised ass feel less sore."

With a bit of effort, Painter and Hank climbed out of the *kiva,* and they all worked their way free of the frozen pueblo. Once out in the open cavern, Painter packed the gold jar, accepting the burden for the return trip, wrapping it next to the plates Kai had stolen. His pack had to weigh something like sixty or seventy pounds. He did not look forward to the long climb back to the sun, but there was no choice.

"We should head up before Nancy calls in the cavalry."

As he turned to the tunnel, a dark shape came flying out the opening and shot past his legs, almost knocking him off his feet. Hank stumbled back in fear—then suddenly recognized a familiar friend.

"Kawtch?" the old man blurted out, surprised.

The dog hugged the professor's legs, circling and circling, whining deep in his throat. The leash still hung from his collar, tangling up Hank's feet. He dropped to a knee to calm his dog.

"Must've run away from Nancy," Hank said.

"I think it's worse than that." Painter pointed his flashlight down at the ice. A dark crimson streak skittered across the surface, left behind by the dragging leash.

Blood.

26

Hurry up and wait . . .

Monk kept forgetting that this was the motto of the military. He hated cooling his jets—in this case, literally. The three of them sat in the cabin of a Learjet 55 outside a private terminal at the Louisville Airport. It was an older model, but it got them here to Kentucky in one piece, and he appreciated these aged birds with a little air under their tails. He stared out the window, looking down the length of the white wings, searching the dark tarmac.

The trio was waiting for a military team from the U.S. Army Garrison over at Fort Knox to arrive and escort them to the Bullion Depository. They'd been here for over ten minutes. His knee began to bounce. He'd hated leaving Kat over at Sigma. She was starting to have cramps, which, with her being eight months along, set him on edge. She claimed it was just back spasms from sitting for long stretches, but he was nervous enough to interpret every bit of indigestion as a potential miscarriage or impending labor pains.

Kat had practically pushed him out the door for this trip, but not before a long embrace. He had kept one palm resting on her belly—as proud *father,* as loving *husband,* even as *army medic,* making sure she was doing well. He knew how frightened she'd been during the debriefing following the events in Iceland, though she kept her game face on the whole time.

But he knew better.

And now this evening hop to Kentucky. He wanted to get this over with and be back at her side ASAP. He loved missions, hated downtime, but with a baby due any day, he just wanted to be at her side, rubbing her feet.

Yes, he was *that* much of a man.

Monk pressed his forehead against the glass. "Where are they?"

"They'll be here," Gray said.

Monk fell back into his seat, glaring at Gray, needing someone to blame. The bird's-eye maple interior of the jet was configured with four leather seats: two facing forward, two toward the tail. He sat directly across from Gray, while Seichan sat next to his partner, her bad leg propped up on the opposite chair.

"Do we even know what we're looking for here?" Monk asked, not expecting an answer, just seeking to distract himself.

Gray continued to stare out the window. "Maybe I do."

Monk's knee stopped bobbing. Even Seichan looked over at Gray. Before the wheels had lifted off in D.C., the basic plan had been simply *to pop in and take a look around Fort Knox*. Not exactly the most brilliant strategy, but no one knew the mysterious source behind these radiating neutrinos. The anomalous readings picked up by the Japanese physicist might be significant, or they might not. The three of them were on a fishing expedition and had left home without their poles.

"What's your idea?" Monk asked.

Gray picked up a folder tucked into the side of his seat cushion. He'd been reading through all the intelligence reports concerning this mission. If anyone could pick through miscellaneous details and come up with a pattern, it was Gray. Sometimes Monk wished his own mind worked that way, but maybe it was better it didn't. He knew the burden often placed on his friend's shoulders. He was more than happy to play the support role. Somebody had to haul out the garbage and make sure the dog got fed.

"I read over the physicist's assessment again," Gray said, and glanced up. "Did you know he has Asperger's syndrome?"

Monk shrugged and shook his head.

"Guy's a genius, likely a superb intuitive, too. He believed the small neutrino bursts he detected—here, out west, and in Europe—came from something closely related to, but different from, the compound that destabilized and exploded both in Utah and Iceland. He posited that the new substance might be a closely related isotope or maybe even a by-product of the explosive material's manufacture. Either way, he's convinced they're connected somehow."

"So what are you getting at?" Seichan asked, suppressing a yawn with a fist.

"Hear me out. The other ancient nanotech artifacts found inside that Indian cave were the strange steel daggers and those gold tablets." Gray stared hard at Monk. "Painter has a couple of those gold plates with him out *west*."

"Where the other readings were recorded," Monk said, catching on.

"They also picked up a reading in Belgium, where the Guild team that we tangled with in Iceland originated. I'm guessing the Guild has one of those plates. Look at how hotly they went after Painter's niece. Maybe their plate is secured in Belgium."

Seichan lowered her injured leg and sat straighter. "And now all of us are heading to a *gold* depository."

Monk thought he understood. "You think there might be some of those gold tablets hidden at Fort Knox."

"No," Gray corrected him, and tapped the file on the seat. "I've been doing research on the history of Fort Knox and the early United States Mints. Did you know Thomas Jefferson helped found the very first mint, located in Philadelphia? He even had a set of silver coins minted with his face that were sent with the Lewis and Clark expedition. But he also had *gold* coins minted."

Monk tried to follow Gray's train of thought, but it left him at the station.

"The Philadelphia Mint's first director was a man named David Rittenhouse. Like Benjamin Franklin and Jefferson, the guy was a Renaissance man: clockmaker, inventor, mathematician, and politician. He was also a member of the American Philosophical Society."

Monk recognized that name. "Like that Frenchman. Wasn't Fortescue part of that group, too?"

Gray nodded. "In fact, Rittenhouse was great friends with Jefferson, like all the significant players involved in this affair. He was surely in Jefferson's inner circle, a trusted companion."

"Okay . . ." Monk said hesitantly.

"According to Fortescue's journal, the Indian map was hidden by Jefferson." Gray quoted from the diary by heart. "*Ever crafty, Jefferson devised a way to preserve the Indian map, to protect it, yet keep it forever out of the hands of the faceless enemy. He would use the very gold to hide it in plain view of all. None would suspect the treasure hidden at the heart of the Seal.*'"

Seichan got it before Monk. "You think Jefferson had Rittenhouse help him hide the map at the mint," she said. "To *hide it in plain view*."

"I do. Then in 1937, the Philadelphia Mint was emptied, and its gold transported to Fort Knox by boxcar. There are reports from that time about the discovery of old bullion caches found deep in the Philadelphia Mint, gold going back to the colonial era. That gold was also moved to Fort Knox."

"Which means the map might've been moved, too," Monk said. "But how can we be sure? Wouldn't someone have noted a map made out of gold, especially one stuck on chunks of mastodon bone?"

"I don't know," Gray said. "We'll have to go look ourselves. But one last item. Fortescue described that Indian map as being made out of the same *gold that would not melt,* the same material as the inscribed tablets."

Monk understood. "So if the tablets are emitting neutrinos, so would the map."

Gray nodded.

Monk leaned back, selfishly appreciating how his friend's unique mind worked. With such insight, they might all just get back to D.C. before midnight.

A squeal of brakes drew his attention back around. A large sand-colored Humvee pulled to a stop alongside the jet.

Monk pushed up. "Looks like our ride's finally here."

8:37 P.M.

Could the map truly be hidden at Fort Knox?

Nagged by worries, Gray sat in the rear seat of the Humvee, staring out as the massive vehicle roared down the Dixie Highway and swung sharply to take the Bullion Depository exit. The armored beast also carried their escorts: four combat brigade soldiers from the U.S. Army Garrison at Fort Knox. When they reached the base's main gates, passes and identification were shown and a guard waved them through. From there, the vehicle forged on through the warm evening, heading toward the country's most guarded structure: the Fort Knox Bullion Depository.

Gray spotted the fortress ahead, lit up in the night like a granite prison, rising from a cleared field and ringed by fences. Sentry boxes guarded the gates, while four guard turrets rose from each corner of the depository, like stubby towers on a castle. He knew that once they were inside, there would be additional layers of countermeasures defending the premises against attack: alarms, cameras, armed guards, and more esoteric technology, like biometric analyzers, facial-recognition software, even seismic sensors. And that only accounted for the defenses that were generally known. The remaining defenses were classified. It was rumored that the facility could be flooded at a moment's notice—whether by water, as was done at the Bank of France, or even by toxic gases.

Of course, reaching the ring of fortress gates meant first penetrating the hundred-thousand-acre military base surrounding the depository—a daunting task, considering the base's numerous helicopter gunships, armored tanks, artillery, and its thirty thousand soldiers.

Gray stared down at his lap.

Entry was a difficult task unless you had the golden ticket.

The presidential order, folded and resting on his knee, bore a wax seal, both official and archaic at the same time. Freshly emblazoned across the front was the signature of President James T. Gant. The depository did not offer tours, visitors were forbidden, and only two U.S. presidents had ever set foot inside. The only way to enter the Bullion Depository was by presidential order. Gray knew that these papers had already been forwarded to the facility's officer in charge. They were to meet the man at the main entrance.

Gray fingered the seal, wondering what would happen if he broke it before the officer in charge verified the paperwork. It would be a foolish act. It had taken all of Sigma's resources to wrangle this document on such short notice. But then again, President Gant owed Sigma for saving his ass in the Ukraine, so his chief of staff took Kat's call.

The presidential orders were specific, covering the three visitors for tonight only. He glanced across the seat to Seichan and Monk. According to the paperwork, they were allowed a single supervised tour of the vault, in order to search for a threat to U.S. national security and remove it from the premises. That was the full breadth of their authority. To step beyond it would be deemed a hostile act.

The Humvee made the turn onto Gold Vault Road. Even with their orders in hand, additional clearances had to be made at a fenced gate flanked by sentry towers. Eventually they made it through and drove down a long road to the front entrance of the fortress.

"Honey, we're home," Monk mumbled under his breath.

Gray's friend reattached his prosthetic hand to its wrist cuff and flexed his fingers. On the thirty-mile drive to the depository, Monk had spent his time running a fast diagnostic on his new hand, clearly still anxious and needing to keep busy. Even after years of wearing the device, he still found it unnerving to see the detached prosthetic move all on its own, like some disembodied appendage from a horror movie. A wireless transmitter built into Monk's wrist cuff could independently control the motors and actuators of the prosthesis, along with accessing the hand's other unique features. Luckily, the guards up front missed that little freak show in the backseat.

At last, the Humvee pulled to a stop. A tall man in a navy-blue suit stepped out of the doorway and approached the vehicle.

He had to be the officer in charge. He was younger than Gray had expected, early thirties, with a blond crew cut and a swagger to his step that had Texas written all over it. He shook Gray's hand in a firm but un-threatening grip.

"Mitchell Waldorf," the man said with a slight drawl. "Welcome to the Depository. It's not often we have visitors. Especially at this hour."

A gleam of amusement sparkled in his gray-green eyes.

Gray made introductions and proffered their presidential orders. The man barely glanced at them and led them promptly toward the entrance, leaving their military escort outside. As they pushed through the doors into a marble lobby, Waldorf passed their orders to a uniformed man standing inside. There was nothing welcoming about the hulking black man's countenance. Without a word, he retreated with their orders through a door marked CAPTAIN OF THE GUARD. Gray suspected their papers would undergo a thorough inspection and verification process. Kat had built up an ironclad cover story and supplied them with false IDs and badges—as agents of the National Security Agency. Hopefully, their paperwork would clear.

In the meantime, they had to undergo their own inspection.

"Latest security protocol," Waldorf explained. "Just added two months ago. Whole body scanners. Have to be thorough nowadays."

Stepping into the machine, Gray endured the millimeter-wave scan of his physique as a seated technician wearing a U.S. Mint police uniform studied the small screen. Other mint officers backed him up, but the facility looked lightly manned at this hour. Then again, most of the security measures were electronic in nature and hidden out of sight.

Once the scan finished, the technician waved Gray into the main lobby space. As he waited for the others, he stared at a display of a giant set of weight scales positioned against the back wall. They rose twelve feet high, supporting four-foot-wide pans. A bit farther down the hall rose the massive steel doors to the bullion vault itself. Above it rested the seal of the Department of the Treasury, made out of gold.

"You can't bring that in here," the technician said behind him.

Gray turned, expecting Seichan to be causing a ruckus at the security post. Had she forgotten about some dagger hidden on her body? It turned out, though, that the true source of the technician's consternation was Monk.

His friend still stood within the cage of the machine and held up his prosthetic hand. "This is attached to me," he complained.

"Sorry. If the scanner can't penetrate it and clear it, it stays out here. You can wait back by the door or leave your prosthesis with us."

"That's our policy," a gruff voice said behind Gray.

He turned to find that the captain of the guard had returned.

By now, Monk's cheeks had gone scarlet. "Fine." He worked the magnetic connections attaching his hand to the surgically implanted wrist cuff and tossed the prosthesis to another technician, who deposited it in a plastic bin. Monk passed the scan the second time and stalked over to join them all.

"I'll have you know," he said, "that such a policy is not even vaguely ADA compliant."

The captain of the guard ignored this and introduced himself. "I'm Captain Lyndell. I'll be accompanying you while you're here. The officer in charge will answer any of your questions, but before we open the vault, I have a query for you: What *exactly* is the scope of the national security threat you're investigating?"

"I'm afraid we can't divulge that, sir," Gray said.

The man didn't like that answer.

Gray understood his frustration. He wouldn't be any happier if this were his facility. "To be honest, the threat is likely minor, and we may have a challenge even identifying it. Any help you or Officer Waldorf can offer would be appreciated."

This appeal to cooperation seemed to mollify the man.

Somewhat.

"Then let's get this done."

Lyndell crossed to the vault door and dialed in a long combination. Two more people waited to do the same. No single person ever had the complete combination to the lock. After the first two finished, the captain of the guard entered one last additional sequence.

A red light flashed to green above the dial, and the massive steel-plate door began to swing open on its own, all twenty tons of it. It took a full minute to part wide enough for the group to walk through.

"If you'll follow me," Waldorf said as he led the way inside. He clearly would be acting as their tour guide.

Lyndell prepared to follow behind, ready to keep a close watch on them.

"At the present," Waldorf said, "we're storing around a hundred and fifty million ounces of gold here. That's enough to forge a twenty-foot cube of solid gold. Of course, that's not a very convenient method to keep it. That's why we have the depository. It's two stories high. Each floor is subdivided into smaller compartments. We'll be entering the first floor, but there's a basement level, too."

Waldorf stepped to the side to allow them to enter and turned to Gray. "That means you've got a lot of ground to cover. If there's any way to narrow that search, now's the time to reveal it. Otherwise, we'll be in here for a long time."

Gray passed through the thick steel door and into a corridor that was broken into smaller vaults. Stacks of gold bars glinted inside them, piled from floor to ceiling. The sheer volume was daunting.

He pulled his eyes away and addressed Waldorf. "I guess the first question to ask is whether anything unusual is stored here, something besides gold."

"What? Like vials of nerve gas, narcotics, biological agents? I've heard it all. Even heard we had the body of Jimmy Hoffa and the Roswell aliens in here. Now, in the past, the depository *has* stored some items of priceless historical value. During World War Two, we preserved the original copy of the Declaration of Independence and Constitution down here, along with the Magna Carta from England and the crown jewels from several European nations. But for decades, nothing's really changed here. In fact, no gold has been moved into or out of the depository for many years."

"Then tell me about the gold itself?" Gray asked. "I see lots of gold bars, but what about gold in other forms?"

"Well, sure. We keep individual gold coins and coin gold bars—made by melting coins together. Beyond the standard mint bars, we also have a mix of older bricks, plates, blocks, you name it."

"Old gold bullion?" Monk asked, zeroing on target.

"Yes, sir. We've got bullion from every era of American history."

Gray nodded. "That's what we'd like to see. Specifically anything taken from the Philadelphia Mint that dates back to the colonial era."

Waldorf's easy demeanor hardened slightly. "Why would that be of interest to national security?"

"We're not sure," Gray said, which was basically true. "But we might as well start there."

"Okay, you're in charge of this hunting expedition. We'll have to go down to the basement, where much of the gold hasn't been moved since it was first hauled to Kentucky by railroad car."

Waldorf headed to a set of stairs and led them down to the section of the vault that lay belowground. Gray again wondered if it was true that this place had been engineered to flood if there was a security breach. He pictured the vault filling with water and imagined drowning amid all of this wealth.

"This way," their guide said, and strode purposefully along the corridor.

The vaults down here weren't as neatly stacked as above, mostly because of the lack of uniformity in the size of the bars.

Waldorf waved ahead. "This whole section originally came from Philadelphia. We've got gold stored here that came from the very first stampings out of that mint. That's kept in the compartment at the end. Follow me."

When they reached their destination, Lyndell used a key to unlock the barred gate to the ten-foot-square space. It looked haphazardly packed— but it was also unfortunately *full*. One section of the room contained irregular rectangular blocks that looked like small anvils, another had stacks of square rods, a third had flat plates about the size of small lunch trays.

Gray stared with dismay, picturing waves of subatomic particles washing out of the space. If this was the right vault, how were they to find the needle in this golden haystack?

Never one to shirk from hard labor, Monk squeezed into the room and began to search around. His friend was more a man of action than deep introspection—and sometimes that temperament paid off.

"Hey, come look at this." Monk pointed to one of the wide plates on a shorter stack. "It's stamped with the Great Seal."

Gray joined Monk, shoulder to shoulder. Crudely stamped into the center of the flat gold block was an outstretched bald eagle, clutching an olive branch and arrows.

"Remember what Fortescue wrote about the Seal," Monk said.

Gray knew it well: *None would suspect the treasure hidden at the heart of the Seal.*

"Maybe he meant the Great Seal," Monk added.

Gray studied the topmost plate. It was roughly fourteen inches by ten and about an inch thick. While there was no precise description of the old Indian map's dimensions, it had been found lining a mastodon's cranium. That meant it had to be fairly big—like these flat blocks.

He studied the room. *There have to be over a hundred of these plates.* Which one could it be? Did one of these plates—buried and hidden among the others—depict a crude map on its surface? There was only one way to find out. He would follow Monk's example. It was time to simply use brute force.

Gray waved at the stacks. "Let's start taking them out."

9:10 P.M.

Seichan stood to the side as Gray and Monk labored, carrying each gold block out of the small compartment and stacking them outside. Her bad leg precluded her from helping. But even healthy, she'd have struggled to lift one. Each weighed over seventy pounds.

She didn't know how Monk managed the effort with only one hand.

By now, the two men had stripped out of their jackets and rolled up their sleeves. Their forearms bulged as they hauled the blocks out, one by one. Gray examined both surfaces, plainly looking for some evidence of a map. He'd also asked the two mint supervisors to let them do this alone. Cooperating, Waldorf and Lyndell had backed away a couple of compartments, talking in low whispers, but keeping a close eye on Gray and Monk's efforts.

The captain of the guard looked darkly dubious.

And rightfully so.

They were halfway through the stacks with no success.

Gray came out with another plate. Seichan noted that his lips had gone bloodless and thin as he settled the plate to the pile. It wasn't from the strain, but from frustration. He dropped to one knee to examine both sides, teetering the plate up on its edge. Sweat streaked his brow.

She limped next to him. "I'll search this side, you take the other."

"Thanks." He eyed her over the top of the upended block. "Are we on a wild-goose chase here?"

"Your assessment sounded solid to me." Seichan ran her fingertips over the gold surface, feeling for any evidence of a faint map. "All we can do is keep looking."

"Anything on your side?"

"No."

He manhandled the plate and settled it atop the others. He lowered his voice. "Something's been nagging me. If Jefferson embedded the old map onto one of these plates, why didn't someone see it? Comment on it?"

"Maybe the map wasn't minted *onto* the plate, but *into* it."

"What do you mean?"

"According to that French guy, the map was made of that nano-gold, a much denser gold that wouldn't melt at normal temperatures. So to preserve and hide the map, why not pour *regular* gold over it, cover it completely? There's no risk. If the map was needed later, you could always melt the ordinary gold off of it, since the nano-gold would require a much higher temperature before it softened."

Gray raised a palm to his damp forehead. "You're right. I should have thought of that."

"You can't think of everything."

And you can't take care of everyone.

She had noted him checking his phone regularly during the trip. The sun had set in D.C., and she knew he was worried about his father's mental state.

"It was right there in Fortescue's journal," Gray said, kicking himself. *"'The treasure's hidden at the* heart *of the Seal.'"*

Monk called from the vault. "Better look at this."

Gray and Seichan joined him inside the compartment, but it was cramped.

Supported by his one palm, Monk leaned over the next plate on the stack. He shifted back. "Look at this one's seal."

Seichan stared over Gray's shoulder, feeling the dampness of his back through his thin shirt. She didn't understand what had Monk all worked up, but noticed that the muscles across Gray's shoulders tightened to hard rocks.

"That's got to be the one," Gray said.

"But there's no map on it," Monk argued. "I checked both sides."

"You didn't check *inside* it . . ." Gray said, glancing back to Seichan, his lips almost touching her cheek.

She tilted away to speak. "What are you two getting at? What's so important about this block?"

Gray drew her forward, pulling her against him. He took her fingers and had her feel the sheaf of arrows clutched by the eagle. "There are *fourteen* of them."

She turned to him. She remembered the crude sketch of an early rendition of the Great Seal, done when Jefferson and his allies were contemplating the creation of an Indian colony. It also had fourteen arrows.

"This has to be it," Gray stressed.

"But how can we be sure?" Monk asked. "Shouldn't we look through the rest of the stacks?"

Gray shook his head. "There's a way we can double-check. If this plate is hiding a map at its *heart,* we should be able to tell by merely comparing its weight against one of the others in this series. The map—if it's inside—is made of a denser material, so the plate holding it will weigh slightly more."

"What about those giant weight scales we saw coming in?" Seichan said.

"Probably too crude, but we can ask Waldorf to help. With all of this gold around here, they must have a precise scale for measurement."

Gray lifted the plate himself, guarding the prize. Monk and Seichan worked together to haul a second one, something to use for comparison. They hobbled over to Waldorf and Lyndell.

Gray explained what they needed but offered no reason as to why, which clearly irritated the captain of the guard.

Lyndell stepped between Monk and Seichan. He relieved them of their burden, lifting the plate as if it were made of wood. "Let's go. There's a weights and measures office in the hall outside the vault. The sooner we get this done, the sooner you're all out of here."

Following him, they paraded back up to the first floor and out the vault doors. They'd taken only a few steps into the hall when a cordon of armed U.S. soldiers accosted them, pointing rifles at their group.

"What's the meaning of this?" Lyndell asked.

One of the mint officers stepped forward and held out a slip of paper to the captain of the guard. His other hand pointed at Seichan. "Sir, we've just received word. That woman's a known terrorist, wanted by the CIA and several other foreign governments."

Seichan went cold all over. Her cover had been blown. It made no sense. Her credentials had been perfect. She eyed the security station in the lobby. According to Waldorf, the whole body scan had been newly installed. Could it have triggered some alert, sending out a three-dimensional facsimile of her face and physique that matched a database somewhere, prompting this alarm? No matter the cause, the end result was the same.

All eyes—and weapons—swung to point at her.

The officer continued, "We were ordered to take her and anyone with her into immediate custody. To shoot if they resisted."

Lyndell turned on them, his face flashing with vindication. "I knew there was something wrong about you all." He pointed to the gold plate in

Gray's arms. "Officer, return all the gold to the vault immediately. Seal it up tight."

Seichan turned to Gray, silently apologizing.

Waldorf swung toward Gray, ready to take the treasure away. He removed a pistol from a shoulder holster under his suit jacket, looking disappointed in them. As he stepped forward, he lifted the weapon quickly to the back of Lyndell's skull and fired.

The blast made them all jump and duck.

Lyndell's plate crashed to the floor, cracking the marble tile.

It was only the beginning. On Waldorf's signal, four soldiers at the back of the cordon—the same four who had transported them from the airport—opened fire on the other mint officers. Bodies dropped. It was over in seconds.

A cold-blooded slaughter.

"You bastards," Gray said.

Monk slid over to check Lyndell for a pulse. He lowered his hand and eyed the dead mint officers with equal dismay.

"Grab that gold plate," Waldorf ordered the soldiers. "Move the prisoners into your vehicle. Take them to the rendezvous point." He then pointed to his own leg. "Do it."

One of the soldiers adjusted his rifle and fired, clipping the man in the thigh. Waldorf twisted and fell with the impact, letting out nothing more than a loud *oof.*

Seichan understood. They were making it look like Gray's group had attacked the others and fled. Even the delay at the airport now made sense. She imagined the original escort team was dead in some ditch, replaced by these impostors. She stared over at Waldorf. She knew that the Guild had agents in all manner of secure facilities. How long had it taken Waldorf to snake his way into this position of power? Had the Guild been using the facility as their own personal bank?

Or were their doings more diabolical than that? Had the Guild always suspected something important was hidden at Fort Knox? They just couldn't find it—until Sigma sniffed out the information for them.

We were used, she realized.

The Guild must have taken full advantage of the emergency to employ Gray's unique talents and puzzle-solving abilities to do their work for them.

And now the enemy was preparing to run off with the prize.

Unarmed, she and the others could offer no resistance as one of the soldiers grabbed the plate from Gray. Three others kept their weapons pointed, ready to fire if there was any sign of a threat.

The soldiers marched them toward the entrance.

Seichan was under no delusions. She had betrayed the Guild.

Now they would exact their revenge.

27

Kai clung to the rope with both hands as the sled under her was lowered from the hovering helicopter. Dust billowed up from below; winds from the roaring rotors whipped all around. She stared down as the top of the mesa rose up toward her, a dizzying view made worse by desert thermal gusts buffeting the sling.

"We're almost there," Jordan said.

He shared the aluminum swing with her. Both his eyes were blackened from the gun butt to his face, but he seemed oblivious to the pain. He kept one hand on the rope, too, but he had his other arm around her shoulders. She had never been a fan of heights—and was even less so now.

But at last, soldiers on the ground caught their sled and roughly unloaded them. Kai stood on shaky legs, glad to find Jordan's arm still around her. At gunpoint, they were led to the chute she'd seen on the video screen earlier. It was a steep descent, but they had no choice.

Reaching the bottom of the chasm revealed a transformed space. A score of soldiers bustled about. Equipment and crates, several broken open, littered the space. Somewhere a drill was grinding into stone. She couldn't figure out what was happening. In the middle of the chaos, she spotted a familiar figure.

Rafael Saint Germaine leaned on his cane, standing over a hole in the ground. She was pushed toward him from behind. He noted her approach.

"Ah, there you two are. Looks like we're all in attendance now."

A shape emerged from the hole, thick with black body armor and wearing a bulky helmet. Still, even without seeing his face, Kai knew it was the blond giant named Bern. When he did look up, she saw that his face was streaming with sweat, which dripped from his eyelashes and off his nose.

"Sir," he said to Rafael, "we've got the ambush site locked down. We just need the bait."

His gray-green eyes flicked toward Kai.

"*Très bien,* Bern. Then we're ready. We'll take them both down. No reason not to play all of our cards."

Kai turned to Jordan. He had been staring to the side—toward a shape half covered in a tarp, booted legs sticking out. She again pictured the rifle shot that had taken out the park ranger and began to shake. Jordan turned, noting the focus of her attention, and stepped to block her view. He put his other arm around her and held her.

Impatient, Bern reached to rip them apart, but Jordan knocked his arm aside. Surprisingly, he was successful.

"We can move on our own," Jordan said coldly, and helped Kai along.

They both knew where they were headed.

Down that black hole.

But what fate awaited them below?

6:22 P.M.

Alone, Painter climbed up the remaining length of the passageway toward the cavern that contained the boiling mud fountain. He'd left Hank down below at the Anasazi tomb. Kowalski had Painter's pistol in hand and had taken up position behind an ice-encrusted rock fall a few yards behind him.

Painter's mind ran through various scenarios, doing his best to anticipate every eventuality, to think a dozen steps ahead of his opponent. He advanced unarmed. What was the use of a weapon? He and the others didn't have enough firepower to lay down a barrage and storm their way out of this hole without getting killed. Instead, he needed to be smart.

He reached the end of the tunnel and stepped into the sulfurous, sweltering cavern. Again a mix of awe and gut-wrenching terror struck him as he viewed the surge of bubbling and roiling mud that flowed down the wall and across the cavern. The heat seemed worse than before, but maybe that was because of the chill of the tomb below.

Steeling himself for what was to come, he stepped out of the tunnel and into the open. Beyond the bridge, a spread of lamps revealed a tight knot of soldiers gathered on the far side. They weren't trying to hide themselves. The enemy must have guessed that the fleeing dog had alerted their quarry.

Figures rose out of the rubble of dark boulders to either side of him, with rifles mounted at their shoulders. Painter held up his arms, palms open, showing he had no weapon, and continued forward. All he had on his person was his backpack with his flashlight secured to it. He hadn't wanted anything in his hands to be mistaken for a weapon.

One of the soldiers attempted to enter the black tunnel behind him, to go after the others. The *pop* of a pistol discouraged him.

"I have a man at a bottleneck down the passageway!" Painter called out without turning. "He's got plenty of ammunition and can pick you off one at a time. Stay back. I know what you want! We can settle this quickly!"

Painter continued forward, step by step, heading toward the bridge.

Across the way, a thin man broke from the knot of soldiers and moved toward the bridge, too.

One of the mercenaries accompanied the man forward. Painter recognized the commando who'd shot Professor Denton back at the university lab. He pictured the blood on the dog leash. It was smeared on his pants where he'd wiped his hands. That was another death he knew he could lay at that soldier's feet.

I'm sorry, Nancy . . . I should never have involved you.

Darkness narrowed his vision as he studied the helmeted giant.

But now is not the time for revenge.

That was clear enough. The commando was dragging a young man behind him, all trussed up and gagged. It was Jordan Appawora. Painter was not overly surprised to see the young man here. He'd already worked out in his head that someone had to tip off the Guild team to his location in Arizona. That left few choices.

Outnumbered, he had to get their attention and gain some control.

"I'm not going for a weapon," Painter called out, and slowly reached to the open side pouch in his pack. With one hand, he carefully extracted the two gold tablets and held them aloft. "I believe this is what you came after, yes?"

From across the bridge, the thin man eyed Painter suspiciously, clearly struggling to figure out what angle was being played here. After a long breath, he simply relaxed with a shrug, perhaps deciding he still had the upper hand.

"Monsieur Crowe, my name is Rafael Saint Germaine." His accent was French, cultivated, with just a touch of a Provençal lilt, placing his origins somewhere in the south of France. He pointed a cane. His arm shook with a very fine tremor, which continued down the length of the cane. The palsy was unusual for someone so young, likely something he'd been born with, made worse by the climb down here and the heat. "I believe I will take those from you."

"Of course," Painter said. "But you can have them freely. As a sign of good faith."

Still, a soldier stalked up from behind and tore them from his grip.

The Frenchman motioned for the soldier to hurry over, but his focus never left Painter. Despite the air of frailty about the man, a dark cunning shone from his eyes. Painter dared not underestimate him. A hunted animal was most dangerous when it was wounded, and this man had been wounded since birth. Yet, despite that, he'd survived amid a group that tolerated no weakness—and not only survived, but *thrived.*

Rafael examined the plates. "Such generosity is most confusing. If

I may be blunt, I expected more resistance. What is to stop me from killing you right now?"

Weapons were cocked behind him.

Painter took another step forward, stopping at the edge of the bridge. He wanted to make sure this man understood.

"Because," he said, "that was a sign of my cooperation. Because what we found down below makes the worth of those two plates pale in comparison."

The man cocked his head, turning his full attention to Painter.

Good.

"May I?" Painter asked, reaching to the open pouch on the other side of his pack.

"Be my guest."

Reaching inside, Painter removed the sculpted top of the gold jar they'd found. He held up the wolf's-head totem.

The man went weak at the knees at the sight of it, barely catching himself with the cane, slipping into French in surprise. *"Non, ce n'est pas possible . . ."*

"From that reaction, you must know what we found."

"Oui. Yes." The man struggled to collect himself, raw desire shining in his face.

"At the moment another of my companions is far below. If I don't return, he is ready to cast the gold bottle into another boiling mud pit, where the sludgy current will carry it away forever."

The man trembled, frustrated, but his eyes also danced with the challenge. "Fair enough. What are your terms?"

"Your men will pull back from this side of the bridge. I want the boy as a sign of your goodwill. Then I will go below and fetch the jar. After that, we will make our final trade."

"For what?"

"You know very well what I want." Painter let some of the fierceness he'd been suppressing leak out. "I want my niece."

6:28 P.M.

Très intéressant . . .

It seemed these negotiations had suddenly become far more challenging and exciting. Breathless, Rafe stared at the sculpted gold lid. He
indeed knew what it represented. Such bottles had the potential to be
the Holy Grail of nanotechnology, a key to a lost science of alchemy that
promised a vast new field of industry and a source of incalculable wealth.
But more than that, it would allow his family to buy their way further up
the hierarchy, to rise perhaps as high as the one surviving True Bloodline.

And it would be the brittle-boned son who brought home that glory
for the Saint Germaine lineage. Nothing must stop this from happening.

Rafe turned to Bern. "Do as he says. Pull your men back. Free the boy
and send him over the bridge."

His second-in-command looked ready to argue, but knew better. The
prisoner's hands were cut free, the gag ripped away.

"Go," Bern ordered, giving him a push.

The youth fled across the bridge, skirting around the soldiers who
were returning from the other side. Once he reached Painter, the pair
bowed their heads for a time, then the young man nodded and headed
toward the far tunnel.

That left just one last demand.

Rafe held up his arm. Another soldier hauled Kai Quocheets forward.
Gagged, she struggled with her bound wrists. Her eyes grew large when
she spotted Painter.

At the same time her uncle rushed forward, ready to help her. He
stumbled several steps out onto the bridge, allowing his guard to drop.
Half blind with an avuncular need to defend his niece, Painter threw off
his backpack, letting it dangle from his wrist . . . and only then did Rafe
realize his own mistake.

Oh no . . .

6:30 P.M.

Painter read the understanding in the Frenchman's eyes. It took all of his strength to pull his attention away from Kai. He had seen the deep bruising on Jordan's face. It had set his blood to pounding in his ears.

Had they hurt Kai as well?

Such questions would have to wait.

Instead, he stopped on the bridge. He'd taken only a few steps, but that put him out over the chasm, yet still well enough away from the hostile party on the other side. He kept his arm out. The heavy pack dangled from his fingertips over the gorge. The steam burned his exposed skin while bathing his arm in yellowish clouds of toxins. The river below hissed and gurgled.

"You already have the gold jar with you," Rafael said, his voice a mix of dismay and respect. "You've had it all along."

Painter reached out over the chasm and unzipped the pack's main compartment. He let the gold shine out. "Shoot me, and it drops into the river below. If you want this treasure, you'll let my niece go. Send her across the bridge. Once she's safely in the tunnel behind me, I'll throw the bag to you."

"And what guarantee do I have that you'll do as you say?"

"You have my word."

Painter refused to break eye contact with Rafael, not to intimidate but to make his intention clear. He was being honest. There was no subterfuge, no clever plan. He had to risk everything to get Kai to safety. Kowalski had a good spot from which to defend them. Rafael would likely flee with his prize, rather than try to dig the others out of that hole. Kai would have a chance to live.

But that didn't mean Rafael wouldn't order his men to shoot Painter after he tossed the package. Anticipating this, he would do his best to retreat to the shelter of the boulders and work his way back to the tunnel himself.

It wasn't a great plan, but it was all he had.

Rafael kept staring back at him, doing his best to read his enemy. Finally, he nodded his head. "I believe you, Monsieur Crowe. You are right. We can end this like civilized men." He gave Painter a slight bow. "Until we meet again."

The Frenchman turned and motioned for his men to free Kai. They undid her hands. Painter watched. Still gagged, she had a wild-eyed stare—but she was not looking at him.

She was looking behind him.

Because of the bubbling of the muddy river, he hadn't heard the approach until it was too late. As he turned, he felt a telltale tremble in the sandstone trusses of the span as someone's feet pounded onto the bridge. He got a glimpse of a tall dark shape hurtling toward him. A shoulder hit him low in the rib cage, lifted him off his feet, and slammed him to the stone bridge, knocking the wind from his lungs. Strong fingers ripped the backpack from his grasp. Then the figure flew past him.

He twisted around to see a woman sprint to the far side and reach Rafael. As promised, the Frenchman had pulled back his *men*. Painter should have been more specific.

The tall black woman—a veritable Amazon—handed Rafael the bag. "*Merci,* Ashanda."

Painter knelt on the stone span, defeated.

Rifles pointed back at him, but instead of ordering him shot, Rafael waved his men to retreat. He matched gazes with Painter. "You'd best be off that bridge, *mon ami.*"

With a nod to the side, one of his soldiers raised a transmitter and twisted a dial on it. A resounding blast sounded from under the span. The far side of the bridge exploded in a blast of sandstone and mortar. Deafened, blinded, Painter fell back and rolled off the bridge's end and onto solid rock.

He raised himself up on his hands and knees to see Rafael and his group retreating for the surface on the far side. The remaining span of the bridge crumbled apart and crashed with mighty, muddy splashes into the river below, churning up more sulfur and heat.

As Rafael reached the tunnel, he held Kai by the shoulder. He took off her gag and called to him. "So she can say good-bye!"

Kai had to be held up by the tall commando. Her voice was a wail of fear and grief that ripped into his belly. "Uncle Crowe . . . I'm sorry . . ."

Then she was hauled up the tunnel. Still on his knees, he listened to her sobbing cries fade away.

Footfalls sounded behind him. Kowalski came running up with Jordan. "What happened to the bridge?"

"They'd mined it," Painter said hollowly.

"Kai?" Jordan asked, his face aghast.

Painter shook his head.

"What are we going to do?" Kowalski asked. "We can't make it across that."

Painter slowly collected himself, gained his feet, and stepped to the edge of the steaming gorge. They had to get across. It was Kai's only chance. With no further use for her, Rafael would soon kill her. Painter had to stay alive, so she could live, too. Still, despair washed over him. Even if they made it out, what did he have to bargain with to win her back? Rafael had the gold tablets *and* the canopic jar. He stared down at his empty hands.

Then the ground shook, and an echoing blast reached them. A wash of dust and smoke belched out of the far tunnel, accompanied by the distant grumble of rock.

"Seems the bastards mined more than just the bridge," Kowalski said.

Painter pictured the chasm cliffs above crashing down, sealing them in. As the dust settled, the air grew strangely still. The sting of sulfur worsened, and the heat rose rapidly. With the opening of the blowhole above now blocked, any circulation of air stopped down here.

Jordan covered his nose and mouth. "What are we going to do?"

As if in answer, a thunderous detonation cracked through the enclosed space. But it was no explosion.

Painter turned as the fissure high up the wall broke wider, splintering outward. The concussion of the charges above must have traveled deep into the earth, to this bubble in the limestone, weakening its already fractured structure.

The flow of boiling mud surged through the widening gap. Boulders began to break off the wall and fall crashing into the pool below. Mud splashed high, raining down.

As Painter and the others retreated from the hail of muddy gobbets, more and more of the wall broke away, falling apart in pieces like a crumbling dam. The sludge fall became a torrent, gushing forth, flooding the river and overflowing the banks of the bubbling pool.

At last, Painter had an answer for Jordan's question.

What are we going to do?

He pointed to the tunnel as a wall of mud rolled toward them.

"Run!"

28

The plan had failed . . .

Gray folded his hands atop his head. Seichan and Monk did the same as rifles pointed at their backs. Soldiers forced them at gunpoint past the bodies of the mint officers, the marble slick with their blood.

Waldorf limped behind them, nursing his wounded leg, leaving bloody footprints. "Take them out the gates," he instructed the man carrying the plate of gold. "I'm heading to my office. I'll sound the alarm in five minutes. You want to be out of here by then."

"Yes, sir."

As they passed through the security station in the lobby, Gray spotted the Humvee idling outside, its tailpipe smoking as the night grew cooler. They had only one chance.

One of the soldiers dashed ahead to the door, moving sideways, still keeping an eye on them. Now was as good a time as any. Gray glanced to Monk, who already knew what to do. His friend gave the smallest nod, a sign that Gray understood. Atop his head, Monk's fingers blindly tapped a code onto his wrist cuff, preparing to transmit a wireless signal.

"Eyes closed, hands over ears," Gray whispered to Seichan.

She looked momentarily confused, then her gaze shifted to the plastic tray holding Monk's disembodied prosthetic hand.

"Now," Gray said breathlessly.

Monk tapped the go signal, activating a small flash-bang charge built into his prosthesis, one of its unique new weapons system upgrades. Gray slipped his hands over his ears and squeezed his eyes closed. It wasn't much protection. As the hand exploded, the *flash* of the charge outlined his fingers against his eyelids, and the *bang* stabbed into his head.

Men screamed as they went temporarily blind and disoriented.

Rifles fired wildly.

Gray had only seconds before their sight returned. He twisted around and hauled the gold plate out of the arms of the team leader. He continued his turn, dropping and pivoting on his toes, swinging back full around and heaving the heavy plate into the legs of the same soldier. Bones shattered. The man's scream turned high-pitched.

At the same time Seichan had grabbed a gunman's rifle out of his dazed grip, expertly flipped it around, and fired point-blank into his chest. His body flew back into another soldier. Seichan continued firing, taking down that other man, too.

Monk had lunged low toward the door, out of firing range. He threw a meaty fist up, square into the guard's nose, crunching deeply. His target fell limply against the door and slid down. Monk retrieved the man's weapon.

Seichan continued to fire, strafing deeper into the lobby.

Gray spotted her target.

Waldorf limped and fell through his office door, slamming it shut behind him. Seichan continued to fire, but the rounds pelted into steel. The door must be reinforced like the rest of the fortress.

"Damn," she said.

Seconds later, an alarm Klaxon rang out, echoing throughout the building. Waldorf must have hit a panic button in his office. Monk stood beside the exit as a blast shield began to trundle down from above, preparing to seal the place up.

"Time to go!" he called out, and held the door open.

Gray and Seichan sprinted toward him. Even with her bad leg, Seichan reached the exit first and dove out. Slower, encumbered by the heavy gold plate, Gray had to duck to get under the lowering blast shield.

Monk followed, gasping. Sirens rang throughout the base, spreading the alarm. "I thought breaking *into* Fort Knox was hard," he said. "Breaking *out* may be even harder!"

"Into the Humvee!" Gray ordered.

They ran for the idling truck. Gray hopped behind the wheel. Monk took the passenger side. Seichan leaped into the backseat. All three doors slammed at the same time.

Gray shifted into gear and wheeled the Humvee around, gunning the massive engine and barreling up speed along the entry road. In the rearview mirror, he spotted Seichan sidling over to a window and cracking a side panel so she could poke her rifle out.

"We don't shoot!" Gray said. "These are U.S. soldiers just doing their job."

"Oh, this just gets easier and easier," Monk complained.

They had one hope.

Gray had already noted their ride had been outfitted with an "up-armor" kit for combat use, which included reinforced doors, bullet-resistant glass, side and rear plating, and a ballistic windshield capable of withstanding explosive ordnance. It was not an unusual vehicle to find here, since Fort Knox was home to the U.S. Army Center for Armored Warfare. It was a proving ground for tanks, artillery, and all manner of armored beasts.

To avoid killing anyone, they needed to ram their way to freedom. For the moment they had the advantage of surprise—and confusion. It wasn't like someone broke into or out of Fort Knox on a regular basis.

Gray aimed for the gates, which had already closed. Sentries milled about, plainly unsure if this was a false alarm or merely a training exercise. The Humvee charging at them cleared up that confusion.

Rifles were raised. Rounds cracked against the windshield.

From the sentry tower, someone fired a rocket-propelled grenade, but in his haste, the shot went wide, blasting through the fencing to the side.

"Hang on!" Gray called.

He didn't slow, trusting the soldiers to leap out of the way in time.

They did.

The Humvee's armored grille hit the gates and bulled through with a screech of torn fencing. Then they were flying down Gold Vault Road. Rifle fire peppered the rear of the truck.

"They'll have birds in the air in less than five minutes," Monk said. *Birds* being Apache helicopter gunships. "It should take them longer to mobilize a more significant armored threat. But we could get hit by—"

A sharp whistling cut through the engine's roar.

"—mortars," Monk finished.

The rocket shot past their hood and exploded in the neighboring field, casting up a fountain of grass, dirt, and rock. Smoke billowed across the road.

Gray roared through it and quickly reached the end of the road. But instead of turning onto Bullion Boulevard, he drove straight across the street, bounced across a ditch, and crashed through another fence, clipping a sign that read THORNE PARK. He trundled overland across a field dotted by woods. The Humvee's wide tires trenched deep tracks. He headed south through the park, aiming for the Dixie Highway that ran alongside the base.

Another rocket exploded into an oak tree, shattering it into flaming splinters. The Humvee smashed through the remains with a great wash of fire and smoke, blinding them all.

Then they were past it.

"That one was closer," Monk said.

"You think?" Seichan asked sarcastically.

"They may not even be trying to hit us, only slow us down." Gray yanked the wheel and sent the vehicle into a slightly new trajectory, trying to make them a harder target if he was wrong.

"I see lights rising from the airfield," Seichan warned.

"Maybe that's why they're trying to delay us," Monk realized aloud. "They're sending out the gunships."

Gray sped faster. They needed to get clear of this base and into civilian territory before serious firepower was employed. If they could escape from this place, the military would be confined to tracking them from the air, utilizing civilian police forces on the ground.

A line of lights appeared through the trees, moving slowly, car headlamps marking the Dixie Highway. They were almost there. He floored the accelerator.

"Here come the helicopters!" Seichan called out.

The Humvee rocketed toward the highway, churning mud and weeds. Then they hit the slope of the highway embankment, shooting up over the gravel and concrete apron. Gray looked for a break in the stream of car lights, found it, and skidded the massive vehicle around on its side, fishtailing into traffic.

Horns bleated in protest. Tires squealed, smoking rubber on asphalt.

A small SUV bumped their rear.

Gray did not slow. He gunned the engine and set off down the highway in a wild, careening course, blaring his horn to help clear the way. The small town of Radcliff appeared as a sea of lights ahead. He raced toward it, barreling at twice the speed limit as the highway became a road at the city's edge.

"We got company!" Seichan yelled.

A brilliant light speared the darkness behind them, reflecting from the truck's mirrors. It was the spotlight from a helicopter sweeping down the highway toward them.

"Take the next turn!" Monk yelled.

Gray trusted him and swung around the corner onto a narrow street, not bothering to slow. Seichan slid across the backseat.

Fourplexes and taller apartment buildings lined both sides of the avenue, likely off-base housing for military personnel. The tight row of buildings offered them a temporary reprieve, blocking them from the helicopter's view.

But that wouldn't last long.

"There!" Monk said, and pointed. "I saw the sign from the road."

Up ahead, a neon advertisement slowly turned atop a tall pole.

That would do.

It was another necessity around off-base housing.

Gray swung into the parking lot of an all-night automated car wash. Individual enclosed bays with coin-operated hoses and vacuums lined one side. He swung into one of the bays, pulling fully under the enclosure, hiding them from sight by air.

"Bail out," Gray ordered.

He grabbed the gold plate. Monk and Seichan snatched up their rifles and some extra ammunition they'd found inside the Humvee. They heard the *whump-whump* of searching helicopters and stared skyward. Three helicopters patrolled the town, sweeping the streets with their searchlights. Gray and the others had to be out of here before roadblocks locked the place down.

There was another patron of the car wash who was also watching the air show.

Monk crossed to him, a tattooed and pierced kid in a dirty T-shirt with a Harley emblem and ragged jeans.

Monk pointed his rifle.

Wide-eyed, the kid stared from the weapon to Monk's face and said, "Shit." He pointed to an older, rust-pocked Pontiac Firebird and backed away, sliding a bit in the suds. "Listen, man. Keys are in the car."

Monk pointed to the Humvee. "So are ours. Feel free to take it."

The kid did not seem so inclined. He was no fool. He had taken stock of the situation.

Gray hurried to the Firebird, threw the priceless plate in the trunk, and got behind the wheel. Keys hung from the ignition, along with a silver skull-shaped fob. He hoped that wasn't a bad omen.

The others piled in, with Seichan taking the front passenger seat this time. Monk clambered into the back. A minute later, they were crossing out of the city limits. Gray had them yank the batteries from their cell phones, to keep anyone from tracking them. He couldn't take any chances, not with the treasure that was sitting in the trunk.

Before pulling his battery, he noted an unopened voice mail from his parents' home number. He didn't have time to deal with it at the moment.

He also didn't want to risk drawing undue attention to himself and the others by calling his parents. Besides, he had supplied his mother with a list of emergency numbers. That should hold them for a while.

Eventually Gray knew that the three of them would have to buy disposable phones, something that couldn't be connected to them, in order to reach Sigma and determine the best course of action from this point. But for now they had to keep moving, keep under the radar.

With all their electronic tails severed, Gray headed due south, using a map he purchased with cash from a gas station. He edged his speed up along the back roads, avoiding major thoroughfares, eking out as much power as the old V-8 engine could muster. The only trail he left behind was oily smoke rising from his tailpipe, coming from a bad cylinder head.

At least he hoped that was the only trail.

As he drove, the tiny silver skull kept knocking against the steering wheel column, as if trying to warn him.

But of what?

29

It'll be okay . . .

Down on one knee, Hank Kanosh patted Kawtch's flanks, trying to calm the dog. The explosions a moment ago had set them both to trembling. That and the cold chill of the icy tomb. With only the one flashlight, he sat in a solitary pool of light. The dark tomb loomed over his shoulder as he stared at the tunnel opening.

What is happening up there?

He should never have agreed to stay down here.

Kawtch burst up from his haunches to his paws, hackles bristling. A low growl of warning emanated from his throat. Then Hank heard it, too. Muffled voices, faint and growing louder, echoed out of the tunnel.

Who is coming? Friend or foe?

Then the scraping of boots sounded—and a small shape slid on his backside out of the icy passageway. The limber form bounded to his feet. Kawtch barked a greeting while Hank backed a wary step until his mind made sense of the newcomer, recognizing him.

"Jordan?"

"Get back!" the young man said. He ran up, grabbed Hank by the arm, and hauled him away from the tunnel.

"What's going—?"

Painter and Kowalski fell out of the opening next.

They split in opposite directions, diving away.

Then an impossible sight.

From the mouth of the passageway, a massive black worm extruded into the cavern, shooting all the way to the ice-encrusted ruins. The tubular shape quickly grew misshapen, melting, sighing out with a sulfurous steam. A large bubble burst, spattering out hotter, molten material from the interior.

Mud.

More of the thickening goop poured out of the tunnel, piling and worming into the space, building higher and higher, continually burbling outward in surges and belches of half-molten mud.

Painter joined Hank and Jordan while Kowalski skirted around the cooling edge.

"The enemy sealed us in," Painter explained, gasping a bit, holding his side. He waved them all farther back. "The explosion cracked through the cavern wall, unleashing a lake of flaming mud."

Jordan rubbed his arms against the cold chill.

"We have to keep moving." Painter eyed the mountain building behind them. "The cold down here is the only thing that saved us. It's cooling the mud, turning it to sludge, forming a semiplug in the tunnel. But we can't count on it holding. The lake building above will eventually melt its way down here, or the mounting pressure will blast the plug out. Either way, we don't want to be here when that happens."

Hank agreed. He stared at the Anasazi tomb. The dead souls here would finally get a proper interment, buried in more than just ice.

Jordan asked an important question. He tried to sound as brave as the others, but a squeak to his voice betrayed his terror. "Where can we go?"

"This must be a huge cavern system," Painter said. "So for now we keep moving."

Making the necessity for this abundantly clear, at that moment a great gout of fresh mud burst out of the tunnel, swamping across the cavern, steaming, bubbling with gas—before cooling. As they backed away, more and more hot mud flowed into the cavern, flooding in faster.

Painter pointed to one of the tunnels—the largest—that exited the cave. "Go!"

They fled at a reckless clip. Painter took the lead with a flashlight; Kowalski kept behind them with another. The tunnel ran deeper underground, still treacherously icy. Hank pictured the ancient flood that had drowned the Anasazi's hidden settlement, imagining it draining away down this very tunnel, eventually turning to ice.

Jordan ran a hand along the low ceiling. "I think we're in an old lava tube. This could keep going down and down forever."

"That's not good," Painter said. "We need to find a way *up*. The mud will continue to drain deeper. We have to get clear of its path."

"And we'd better find that way fast!" Kowalski called from the back.

Hank looked over his shoulder, but Kowalski flashed his beam down. It took a breath for Hank to note the water trickling underfoot now, pouring down from above. Kawtch's paws splashed in the thin stream. The mud must have reached this tunnel's mouth, melting the ice above and sending it flowing after them.

Painter set a faster pace.

After another ten minutes—which seemed more like an hour—they finally reached the tube's end.

"Oh no," Hank moaned, stepping next to Painter.

The tunnel ended high up a cliff wall. Painter pointed his light over the edge. They couldn't even see the bottom of the precipitous drop, but a gurgling rush of water was echoing upward. Directly ahead, across an eight-foot gap, stood the opposite cliff. The lava tube continued on that far side. It was like some mighty god had taken a giant cleaver and split this section of the earth, cutting the tunnel in half.

"It's a slip fault," Painter said. "We'll have to jump. It's not that far. With a running start, we should be able to dive into that other tunnel."

"Are you mad?" Hank asked.

"It looks worse than it is."

Kowalski sided with Hank. "Bullshit. My eyesight's not that bad."

"I can do it," Jordan said, and waved everyone back. "I'll go first."

"Jordan . . ." Hank cautioned.

"It's not like we have any choice," the young man reminded him.

No one could argue with that.

They backed up the tunnel and gave him enough room for a running start.

"Careful," Hank said, patting Jordan on the shoulder.

He gave them a thumbs-up—then ran low, splashing in the growing stream, and leaped headlong across the gap. Like a young muscular arrow, he shot straight through the air and dove cleanly into the far opening, sliding on his belly across the icy bottom of the next tube. He vanished for a bit—then popped back.

"It's really not that bad," he said, panting, wearing a huge smile.

Easy for him to say . . .

"I'll go next," Painter said. "Once I'm there, Kowalski, you throw me the dog."

Kowalski looked at Kawtch; the dog looked at the big man.

Neither looked happy about that idea.

After a bit of maneuvering, Painter ran and made the leap as smoothly as Jordan.

Kowalski then picked up Kawtch, slinging him between his legs. The dog wiggled until Hank got him to calm down with a pat and whispered reassurances.

"Sheesh, Doc. What are you feeding this guy?"

"Just be careful," Hank said, holding a hand to his throat.

Kowalski stepped to the edge of the drop-off, bent deep at the waist—then heaved upward. Kawtch yelped in surprise, legs splaying out like a flying squirrel. Painter leaned out and caught the dog cleanly. They both fell back into the tunnel amid a rout of barking protest.

Hank choked out his relief—until Kowalski turned to him.

"That means you're next."

He swallowed and shook his head. "I don't know if I can."

"It's that or I throw you across like your dog. Your pick, Doc."

Hank couldn't decide which was worse.

Painter called from the other side. "I'll be here if you need me."

"Okay, let's do this," Hank said, forcing as much bravado into those words as he could.

He backed up the tunnel alongside Kowalski.

"I can push you . . . give you a running start," the large man offered.

Before he could answer, a low sighing gasp made them both turn. Kowalski pointed his flashlight up the lava tube. The beam ended at a wall of mud about twenty feet away. It had crept up on them silently, like some skilled assassin, oozing down the tube. As they watched, the sludge wall melted open and hot mud began to run out of its center, extending its reach.

"Now or never, Doc."

A low rumble alerted them to trouble.

The flowing mud suddenly exploded toward them. Hot sludge pelted their bodies, burning skin, stinking of sulfur. Bubbling mud followed in its wake, pouring down at them.

"Run!" Kowalski said.

Hank took off, Kowalski at his heels.

Crouched over, Hank ran as fast as he could, but as he reached the end, the water-slick ice betrayed him. His legs went out from under him and he toppled crookedly over the edge.

"Got you, Doc!" A beefy arm scooped him around the waist—then carried him in a hurdling tackle across the dark chasm.

Hank wanted to close his eyes, but that scared him more.

They failed to hit the tunnel as smoothly as the other two. Kowalski clipped his shoulder, sending them tumbling in a tangle of limbs down the throat of the icy tunnel. They crashed into Painter, who could not get out of the way in time.

But eventually they came to a halt. After a bit of figuring whose limbs belonged to whom, they gained their feet. Jordan had returned to the tunnel's mouth, staring across the gap.

Hank joined him, bruised in odd places.

A new mud waterfall had been born. From the far tube, they could see sludge gushing in a flowing, sulfurous stream. As Hank watched, he caught a flash of a blackened leg poke out of the flow. It was one of the Anasazi bodies, washed from its icy tomb.

The corpse, now buried in mud, vanished below.

Hank said a silent prayer for the lost soul, for all of them—then turned back.

Kowalski expressed what all of them were thinking. "Now what?"

7:28 P.M.

They all sorely needed the rest break.

"We'll stop here," Painter said, and sank to his butt, exhausted.

After escaping the mud, he had led them to the end of the lava tube. It had dumped them into a growing maze of tunnels, chutes, rock falls, and blind alleys. For the past half hour, Painter kept trying to climb upward, hoping for the best, but each time, they were eventually driven back deeper.

Needing to collect himself and think, he called for a stop in this small cavern. He searched around. Tunnels branched off in three different directions.

Where now?

Painter stared at his mud-coated companions. Hank let the others take turns sipping from his CamelBak water pouch. Kowalski had already drained his, and Painter had lost his pack to that Amazon woman. They kept hearing water but could never find its location. Dehydration, more than anything, threatened them. If the chill didn't kill them, the lack of water would.

How long could they keep this up?

Hank looked one step away from collapsing as he sat next to his dog. Kowalski fared little better. He sweated like a racehorse, losing pints of water every few minutes. Even Jordan looked hollow-eyed and lost.

Painter knew that what was weighing them all down, making every step harder, was the futility of their situation. He felt doubly crushed. If he closed his eyes, he could still see Kai's face as she was dragged away, hear her sobbing cries.

Was she even still alive?

That worry plagued another. Jordan had voiced similar questions as they hiked, never straying far from that same fear. The two had apparently grown close.

Jordan leaned his head back against the wall, too tired to move. Painter studied him, suddenly recognizing how truly *young* he was. Jordan had held up as well as any man, but he was still barely out of boyhood.

As Painter stared, he noted the youth's small cowlick—really just a few hairs sticking up—bend ever so slightly, quivering. Jordan scratched his head, perhaps feeling it, too.

It took Painter a few extra moments to realize the truth.

That's the answer . . .

He sprang up, shedding his exhaustion like so much dead skin. "There's a breeze blowing through here," he said. "It's faint, but it's here."

Kowalski opened one eye. "So?"

"This is a *breathing* cavern system. And it's still *breathing.*"

Hank's eyes widened, the dullness fading. He lifted a damp hand, trying to feel that faint breath.

Painter explained. "Just because *one* blowhole got plugged, that doesn't mean they *all* did. By following the direction of this breeze, it should lead us to a way out."

Kowalski slapped a palm on his thigh and stood. "Then what are we waiting for? Once we're out of here, I'm looking for the nearest watering hole. And for once in my damned life, I really mean *water.*"

With renewed hope, they set off.

But not before Kowalski made an addendum to that last statement. "Of course, just to be clear, that doesn't mean I would turn down a cold beer if someone offered."

The hike from this point on was no less strenuous or frustrating than what came before, but hope now buoyed their spirits, kept them moving forward. They tested each crossroads with a small match from Hank's backpack, watching the direction of the smoke. The breeze grew stronger and stronger over the next two hours, which only encouraged them to move faster.

"We must be near the surface," Hank said, and sucked on the blue plastic tube to his CamelBak. From the forlorn gurgle as he sucked, he was empty.

They needed to find the way out.

Painter checked his watch.

9:45 P.M.

After another hour, it still seemed they were no closer to the surface. Out of water, down to one flashlight with working batteries, they were running out of time.

Hank heard a strange *popping-crackle* sounding underfoot. A rock had shattered under his boot. He pointed his light down. Bits of black-and-white pottery skittered across the limestone.

It wasn't a rock, but a pot.

He bent down and picked up a shard. "This is Anasazi handiwork."

Painter focused his beam up the rocky chute they'd been climbing along the past ten minutes. He spotted more bowls and clay vessels resting on shelves of rock.

"Look at this," Jordan said behind him. "Cave art."

Hank moved down to the youth's side. Painter had missed seeing the clue when he passed by it a moment ago, exhaustion making him sloppy.

"Petroglyphs," Hank said, and stared up the chute. "Painter, could you turn off your flashlight?"

Painter sensed that the professor was onto something and flicked off his lamp.

Total darkness closed over them.

No, not *total* darkness.

Painter stared up. Faint light glowed up there, barely more than a grayness against the black backdrop.

"I think I know where we are," Hank said out of the darkness.

Painter turned his light back on.

Hank's eyes were huge as he waved Painter forward. "It shouldn't be much farther."

Painter believed him. Their pace became hurried, especially as crude steps appeared, carved into the rock. They led up to a square of moon-light overhead, crosshatched by a steel grate. Painter had seen that grate before—but from the other side.

"This is the blowhole at Wupatki," he mumbled. He remembered the park ranger's estimation of the cavern system beneath it.

Seven billion cubic feet . . . stretching for miles.

That had proven to be true—and might even be an underestimation.

Hank could not restrain his excitement. "This must be how the sur-viving Anasazi escaped the massacre here. They fled down here, crossed underground through this cavern system, and set up a new home beneath the other blowhole. There they lived until the flood wiped them out."

With one mystery solved, Painter faced another.

He reached up and rattled the grill. "It's padlocked."

"No worries." Kowalski pushed forward and raised his pistol. "I got the key."

30

"They're still hunting you," Kat said, her voice sounding tinny through the cheap disposable phone. "They will be all night."

Gray sat in the passenger seat of a nondescript white Ford van—the more *nondescript* the better, it seemed, according to Kat's report. They'd ditched the muscle car hours ago in a wooded park outside of Bowling Green and hot-wired their new vehicle from a used-car lot. The van shouldn't be missed until the dealership opened in the morning.

Still, they kept moving, knowing that the dragnet for the escaped Fort Knox terrorists would be ever widening. To stay ahead of it, they traveled back roads, avoiding main thoroughfares, threading their way south until they reached Nashville.

"You've got everyone looking for you," Kat continued. "FBI, military intelligence, civilian law enforcement. It's still a clusterfuck out here in D.C., especially with all of this coming down in the middle of the night. Now that the terrorist flag has been raised, everyone's scrambling."

As Monk drove slowly through a suburban industrial park on the outskirts of Nashville, Gray glanced to the backseat. Seichan sat with her arms crossed, staring at the dark mix of warehouses, supply stores, and mechanic shops. Because of her past crimes, she was not officially a member of Sigma. She could never be. Her recruitment as an asset and spy was known only by a small handful of people within their organization, all well trusted. To the rest of the world's intelligence agencies, she remained a wanted terrorist, a deadly assassin for hire.

"How did that alert at Fort Knox get raised in the first place?" Gray asked. "All of our identification was solid. What tipped them off? We were scanned and photographed at the depository. Did Seichan's picture get flagged by some database?"

"I'm still working on that," Kat replied. "But I can tell you the alert wasn't generated from Fort Knox. It came from an outside source, but I can't trace it. At least not right now. It's too early. Everyone is still covering his or her ass at this point. I imagine files are being shredded all over D.C."

"So we were set up. It was an ambush from the start." He could guess who orchestrated it all, picturing the officer in charge at Fort Knox. "Any further news on Waldorf?"

Gray had spoken to Kat an hour ago after purchasing the disposable cell phone. The conversation had been brief as she tried to quell a hundred fires while blowing chaff to keep Sigma's involvement a secret and misdirecting the nation's various intelligence and security agencies to keep Gray and his teammates from getting caught.

"No," she said. "I've made numerous inquires, but Waldorf vanished shortly after the base alert got raised. But he must be hunting for you as desperately as everyone else."

"Why do you say that?"

"It was one of the reasons I was calling you back. To warn you. The Learjet that you took from D.C. was blown up in midair about fifteen minutes ago, shortly after taking off from the Louisville Airport. A blast took out the tail section. Estimates are that it was a bomb tied to an altimeter timer. The plane reached a certain height and the ordnance blew."

Gray remembered the young pilot. A hot coal of anger settled deep in his belly. "Waldorf was gunning for us. But he must have known we wouldn't be on that plane."

He squeezed a fist on his knee as he realized what this meant. The bombing was an act of pure vengeance, a murderous tantrum after Waldorf had been thwarted.

"I thought you should know," Kat warned. "It's another reason you must keep moving."

"Understood." He heard her sigh loudly, sensing more was to come. "What?"

"I heard from Dr. Janice Cooper again."

It took Gray a moment to place that name—then he remembered. "She was working with that Japanese physicist."

"They're both still under guard, but her partner who survived the massacre has been continuing to consult with other labs. At our request, he's been studying the massive neutrino surges rising from the West."

"Has he been able to pin down the location?"

"No, but he has been able to extrapolate the magnitude of the coming explosion. He says it may be over a hundred times larger than the one in Iceland."

Gray pictured Ellirey Island crumbling to fiery ruin.

A hundred times larger than that?

The level of destruction would be massive, the scale unimaginable.

Kat continued, "Which brings me to the real reason I called. The Japanese physicist has worked up a rough estimate for *when* it might blow. Like he did with Iceland."

"When?" Gray asked, tensing his abdomen, anticipating the punch.

"In about five hours."

A sinking despair settled through him. What could they do in five hours? Even if they weren't being hunted, they'd have a hard time even flying to the West Coast in time to accomplish anything. But Sigma already had other operatives out there.

"Any word from Director Crowe?"

Her voice grew strained. "No. He had gone down into a cavern system under some ruins, but local rangers reported an explosion there, burying much of it in rubble. I have Lisa monitoring teams combing the desert where he'd last been seen. She's a wreck. Nothing's turned up. And I've spoken to Ronald Chin at least a dozen times. He's heard nothing from Painter either."

Gray hoped the director was okay, but they still needed someone out west who could address the trouble that was escalating in that region. "Did you tell Chin about the geological timer ticking down?"

"I did, but without a location, what can he do? That's why I need you to find a way to free that old Indian map from the gold plate. If there's some clue as to where this cache of unstable nanotech is hidden, we need to know it now."

"I'll do what I can, but I'll need some foundry where I can heat up this gold plate. See if I can't melt away the ordinary gold and expose the map at its heart."

"I anticipated that."

Of course she did.

"I have the name of a small goldsmith shop near you. I'll give you the address. The owner will meet you there in fifteen minutes."

She passed on the location. It was only a few blocks away, in the same industrial park they were driving through. Leave it to Kat to have every variable covered.

But there remained one last *variable.*

"Can I have a word with Monk?" she asked, sounding stern.

"Hang on." He held out the phone to his friend. "Looks like you're in trouble."

Monk kept hold of the steering wheel with the stump of his wrist and took the phone. He cradled it between his shoulder and chin and regained his grip on the wheel.

"Hey, babe," he said.

Kat's voice whispered from the phone, but the words were too faint to make out.

"No, I didn't lose another hand," Monk said, tightening his fingers on the steering wheel. "I just lost my prosthesis. Big difference, hon."

Gray imagined Kat scolding her husband in an operatic duet that has been going on between husbands and wives for ages, that eternal mix of exasperation and love.

A slow smile spread across Monk's face. He whispered back words that were mundane and ordinary—but in fact were as loving as the lyrics of any aria. "Uh-huh . . . okay . . . yeah, I'll do that . . ."

In an effort to give them privacy, Gray turned to study the dark streets, but his eyes caught on the rearview mirror. He saw Seichan staring at the back of Monk's head, her face soft and lost, not knowing anyone was watching.

But she was still a hunter.

As she sensed his attention, her gaze flicked and trapped him in the mirror's reflection. Her face went hard again as she turned away.

Monk's voice suddenly grew sharper. "*What?* Just now?"

Gray drew his focus back up front.

Monk lifted his chin to address the car. "Kat's just heard. Lisa's on the phone with him now. Painter's been found."

31

May 31, 11:32 P.M.
Flagstaff, Arizona

Less than five hours until the next explosion?

After speaking with Lisa, Painter had been fully debriefed by Kat. He checked his watch. That would put the time just at sunrise out here. But the big question remained: *Where exactly would it blow?*

Kat continued: "I have Gray working to narrow the search radius. Our only hope is that he truly has found the old Indian map and can pinpoint the location of that lost city."

Ever since clawing his way to freedom, Painter had felt as if his hands were tied. He and the others had escaped the caverns below Wupatki about an hour ago. Members of a search party, bivouacked at the site of the ruins, had been surprised when Painter's group appeared out of nowhere, asking for water and food. They'd been promptly evacuated to a ranger station, where Painter set about discovering what had been going on during his absence.

Apparently a lot.

But one question remained foremost in his mind. He asked it again: "Kat, has there been any news about Kai?"

"No." Her next words were spoken carefully. "We're combing all the counties in Arizona and Utah. No law enforcement agencies have reported the discovery of a dead body matching your niece's description."

He steeled his voice, keeping control, knowing it would serve no one to do otherwise. "Jordan Appawora said the commando team had helicopters. They could have traveled farther."

"I'll extend the search."

"What about spreading the word—through clandestine channels and local media—that I survived?"

"Already done. I sent a breaking news ticker out through all the major wires. About the rescue, including photos of your group. If Rafael Saint Germaine or any of his crew turn on a television, radio, or check the news online, they'll know."

"Good."

His niece's best chance for survival—if she was still alive—was to get that Frenchman's attention. After that, Rafael would keep her safe, if only to use her as a bargaining chip again. Now all Painter had to do was figure out what *chip* he had that would set her free.

Over the next ten minutes, Kat went over additional notes: about Fort Knox, the ongoing manhunt for Gray and company, and the status of the neutrino reports.

Once he was caught up, he signed off.

"Sir," a voice said behind him. He turned to find Jordan standing in the doorway. The others had sacked out in a bunk room at the back of the ranger station. Jordan looked like he'd not slept a wink. "Any word?"

"Nothing yet." Noting the grim look on the boy's face, he added, "And that's *good* news. Until we hear otherwise, we assume she's alive, right?"

Jordan gave a sullen nod. "Okay, but when I was crashed back there in the dark, I got to thinking. They took everything from me when I was captured. That included my cell phone. What if they still have it? What if we tried calling my number?"

Painter felt the cords binding his wrists loosen slightly at that thought. *Could they still have the kid's phone?* It was worth investigating. Besides, he hated sitting here doing nothing.

Jordan continued to argue his case, not realizing he'd already won it. "Maybe someone will answer my phone and we could threaten them, scare them enough to let Kai go."

For that matter, we could also track the phone, Painter thought, running through various possibilities. *Or turn it into a remote bug by activating its microphone.*

Of course, all of this was a long shot. The Frenchman was no fool. He would've dumped that phone by now. Painter tapped a finger atop the table. Then again, Rafael thought they were all dead. Maybe his men hadn't purged everything yet.

Still, Painter knew it would take time to track that phone, especially out here in the remote desert—*time* that Kai might not have.

Painter had to buy her an extension. "What's your cell number?"

Jordan gave it to him.

Painter memorized it and asked a ranger for a landline and a bit of privacy. Once alone in a back office, he dialed the number. It rang and rang as he prayed for someone to pick it up.

Finally, the line clicked open. A thickly accented voice spoke slowly, unconcerned. "Ah, Monsieur Crowe, I see we're not quite done with each other yet."

June 1, 12:41 A.M.
Salt Lake City, Utah

Rafael lounged once again in the presidential suite atop the Grand America Hotel in downtown Salt Lake City. He had been woken up half an hour ago and shown footage of muddy figures standing over a grated hole.

Painter Crowe lived.

Remarquable.

Shocked, he had stood there in his bathrobe for a full minute, unable to respond. Emotions had warred in his breast at the sight: rage, awe, and yes, a trickle of fear—not for the man, but for the fickleness of fortune.

In the photo, Painter had been staring straight into the camera.

Rafe read the challenge in that steely gaze. He knew the director of Sigma had orchestrated this media blitz. This was a message sent personally to Rafael.

I am alive. I want my niece.

As Rafe held the phone to his ear, ignoring the bundle of cables and wires dangling from the gutted mobile device, he stared over at the closed door. It seemed that fortune was smiling as warmly on the niece as it had smiled on the uncle. He had wanted to interrogate Kai more fully before dispatching her. She had been inside the Utah cavern, saw the mummies and the treasure. He wanted every detail of that trespass. Potentially she also knew more about Sigma, its operatives, and other tidbits gleaned from her short time with her uncle.

But such interviews were too taxing after the long day.

Morning would be soon enough, so he let her live to see one more sunrise.

And now he was glad he'd shown such generous restraint.

"Do not bother tracking this call," Rafe warned his adversary. "I employ a crack team of encryption experts. We're bouncing this signal all around the world."

"I wouldn't think of it. You were clearly expecting this call, so I can only assume you had countermeasures in place."

Exactement.

After seeing the photo earlier, Rafe had known Painter would discover some way to reach out to him. He was somewhat surprised it had taken this long. Ashanda—along with assistance from TJ—had worked their technological magic on the device, ensuring no one could track the phone or trace the signal.

"I've called to restart our negotiations," Painter said. "To continue where we left off."

"Fair enough."

"First, I want some guarantee Kai is still alive."

"No, I don't believe I'll give you that." Rafe enjoyed the long pause, knowing how it must torture the man. "Not until I understand what you're bringing to the table."

The pause stretched, stoking suspicion.

Are you preparing to bluff?

Truly, in the end, what could the man offer of interest?

Rafe stared at the gold jar resting atop the dining table. He had studied it at length, drinking in every bit of it, trapping it forever in his mind's eye. Even now, he rotated the jar in his head, tracing a finger over each inscribed letter of the lost language and feeling anew the detailed landscape that was etched across its golden surface.

This treasure promised far more than wealth. It could guarantee eternal glory, for him, for his family. What more could he want?

Painter told him. "In exchange for Kai's safe return, I will reveal the location of the Fourteenth Colony."

Rafe slowly smiled, shocked yet again.

The man never ceased to amaze.

Remarquable.

12:44 A.M.

"Uncle Crowe, you're alive!"

Painter sagged in his seat upon hearing her voice, wanting to express the same sentiments himself.

She was alive!

Instead, he kept his questions practical, knowing he'd have little time. "Kai, are you okay? Have they hurt you?"

"No," she answered, stretching that single word to encompass so much more.

Painter knew the trauma she must be undergoing: the deaths, the bloodshed, the terror of the unknown. But he also heard the bravery in that one utterance. She had the blood of warriors in her.

"I'm going to come get you. I promise."

"I know." Her response held both tears and hope. "I know you will."

The phone was taken from her. Rafael returned to the line.

"So we have a deal, *n'est-ce pas?*"

"I will call you with a time and location for the exchange."

"And I will want proof of what you claim, Monsieur Crowe."

"You'll have it. As long as she is safe and unharmed."

"So be it. *Au revoir.*"

As the line cut off, Painter continued to hold the phone, fingers clamped tightly to it, as if trying to keep his connection to Kai. He felt light-headed with relief.

A voice rose behind him. "So is Kai still alive?"

He swung around in the chair. Jordan's bruised face was raw with worry. Focused on the call, Painter had not heard the boy creep into the office. Either the youth was remarkably light-footed, a trait well known to his Ute clan . . . or Painter was simply too exhausted to pay his usual attention.

Maybe it was a combination of both.

Painter faced the young man, knowing he had to be truthful. Jordan had earned it. "They've not harmed her," he said. "But she's still in danger."

Jordan stepped forward. "So then you'll tell them what they want to know . . . to get them to let her go?"

While this was a question, Painter heard the note of demand in it, too. "I will try."

That's the best he could offer. He'd been bluffing with Rafael over the phone, buying time for Kai. But how much leeway had he bought her? How long could he keep stringing the Frenchman along?

In truth, Painter had no idea of the location of the lost Fourteenth Colony. Only one person had a chance of gaining that knowledge—and he was on the run, being hunted by every law enforcement and intelligence agency in the country.

The fear had returned to Jordan's face.

Painter stood, crossed over, and placed a reassuring hand on his shoulder. "It's okay to worry, but don't lose heart. I have one of my best men on the case."

Jordan nodded, took a deep breath, and let it out slowly.

Painter looked down at the telephone handset still in his grip. Rafael would be expecting another call in an hour. Painter needed some answers by then. He turned to the dark office window, staring across the breadth of the country.

Gray, don't let me down.

32

Standing beside Seichan, Gray leaned his face closer to the oven window. Heat bathed his face. Inside the chamber, the golden plate rested atop a ceramic grate, canted at an angle, showing the Great Seal with the fourteen arrows.

Rows of blue flames waved along the bottom of the oven, slowly raising the temperature inside. Above the door, the readout from the digital thermometer steadily climbed higher, crossing above six hundred degrees Celsius.

"Shouldn't be much longer," the shop owner said.

The goldsmith was Russian, around fifty, with salt-and-pepper hair. He stood no taller than five feet but had a linebacker's build with a bit of a paunch hanging over his belt. He scratched at a gold chain tucked under his T-shirt. The name of his business was GoldXChange, located amid a jumble of industrial complexes on the outskirts of Nashville. He bought old gold for cash, but also melted clients' rings, coins, necklaces, and other jewelry into ingots.

He'd also had some trouble with the IRS. Kat had pressured the man to cooperate, threatened him with imprisonment if he did not keep silent about tonight's enterprise.

The owner was plainly nervous, sweating through his shirt.

"Gold melts around a thousand degrees Celsius," the Russian said. "See how the metal is already glowing."

Inside the oven, the ruddy surface of the plate had burned to a sun-bright sheen. As he watched, a single, shimmering droplet appeared atop the stamped U.S. Seal, where the gold formed the image of the eagle's feathers. It rolled down the slanted slope to drip into a ceramic pan beneath the grate. Soon more blazing teardrops began to weep and flow in rivulets, slowly erasing the details of the Seal. The crisp, sharp edges of the plate grew soft, melting away in a river of gold.

"That should be hot enough," Gray told the shop owner. "Hold the temperature right there."

Gray did not want to risk damaging the map if it was buried inside. The denser nano-gold had a higher melting point than the rest of the plate, but that didn't mean it wouldn't soften if it got too hot. They dared not melt away the details of the map.

Once the temperature was set, Gray pointed the Russian to the door. "You'll need to leave now. Go join my partner outside."

The goldsmith did not hesitate. With a nod, he backed away, turned, and quickly strode to the exit. Monk was outside watching the street. They did not want to be ambushed again.

Gray waited for the man to leave before returning his attention to the oven, in which molten gold was flowing like liquid sunshine. Slowly the plate eroded before their eyes, shedding more and more of its mass.

"Look along the top," Seichan said, reaching out to grip his wrist.

"I see it."

A dark ragged ridge appeared, protruding from the leading edge of the plate, a shadow against the brilliance of the molten gold. Over the next few minutes, more and more of the blazing metal poured away, revealing a greater expanse of the hidden object. That new metal smoldered also—but less brilliantly, a ruddy rosiness against the yellowish gold.

"It's the map," Seichan whispered.

This became clear as the remaining gold drained away, flowing across the rosy metal surface, exposing another long-held secret.

This hidden bit of cartography wasn't a *flat* engraving.

"It's a *topographical* map," Gray said, awed by the artistry.

Tiny, sculpted mountain ranges appeared, along with deep-cut river valleys and pockets that marked lakes. The melting gold revealed a darkly glowing scale model of the upper half of the North American continent.

As Gray watched, one of the last molten droplets slid like a sailing ship down a large river valley splitting the middle of the continent.

That has to be the Mississippi.

He continued to identify other landmarks: a chain of depressions that marked the Great Lakes, a small crack that could only be the Grand Canyon, a raised spine of mountains that mapped the Appalachians. Even the coastlines looked uncannily accurate. Then, to the northeast of the continent, out in the ocean, rose a peaked series of islands around a larger mainland.

Iceland.

Soon only the map remained on the ceramic grate. Its edges were rough, misshapen, slightly curled up at the corners. A fine, straight crease split the middle, the two halves fitting perfectly together. Gray pictured the map lining the cranial cavity of a mastodon's skull. Jefferson's people must have burned away the ancient bone to preserve the map.

"Is that writing?" Seichan asked.

"Where?"

"Along the map's margins."

Gray leaned closer to the oven, the radiating heat burning his face. Seichan's eyes were sharper than his. Faint lines of script did indeed run along the map, to the west of the continent, like notations of a cartographer.

Pinching his eyes, he studied it. "Looks like the same writing we saw in Fortescue's journal, the ancient lettering he copied from one of those gold plates." He turned to Seichan. "Grab some paper from the office here. You've got better eyes than me. I want that all copied down."

Seichan obeyed without asking questions. She knew the challenge that was facing him and was happy to leave him to it.

Gray returned his attention to the tiny sculpted map of Iceland. To the south of the mainland, smaller peaks marked the Westman archipelago. Atop one of the islands, a tiny dark crystal shard—*possibly a black diamond*—had been embedded deep into the metal. It glinted in the dance of fire going on in the oven.

Ellirey Island.

He moved his attention to the west, to another diamond shining against the rosy metal. This shard was much larger than the one set in Iceland, perhaps indicating the relative size of the western deposit. It was a disturbing reminder of the danger brewing out there.

Gray frowned at the map, struggling to get his bearings. The lack of state lines and city names made it difficult to judge with great accuracy where this marker pointed, only that it lay somewhere in the chain of Rocky Mountains, well to the north but still within what would eventually become the United States.

Given the lack of clarity, it was no wonder that Fortescue had decided to go to Iceland first.

Seichan returned with pen and paper and began copying the notations found on the map's borders.

As she worked, Gray followed the spine of the Rockies farther south. There, he found what he was looking for, the barest sliver of crystal, easy to miss unless you were looking for it.

That must be the Utah site.

Compared to the chunk of diamond to the north, it was nothing. So minuscule, in fact, that Jefferson and Fortescue had either overlooked it or hadn't even thought it worth mentioning. Gray stared between the three crystals, growing more certain that their different sizes reflected the relative importance of the various sites—and also the relative danger each posed.

He checked his watch, all too aware of the clock ticking down.

Seichan finished her work and pointed her pen at the largest diamond. "Any idea where that is?"

"I think I might know," he said, putting the pieces together in his head. It all made dreadful and terrifying sense. But he had to be sure before sharing his theory. "I need to check a map of the Western United States."

Seichan pointed to the oven. "In the meantime, what do we do about *that* map?"

Gray showed her. He reached and dialed up the digital thermostat on the oven. He kept turning, watching the temperature setting climb above three thousand degrees Celsius, three times the melting point of ordinary gold. The blue acetylene flames shot higher inside the oven, dancing more vigorously.

Seichan stared at him, one eyebrow raised.

"We can't risk the map falling into Waldorf's hands," he explained.

"So you're going to destroy it?"

"I'm going to try. The map's metal is denser, so it's not going to melt at the low temperatures of ordinary gold. But there must be some temperature at which it *does* melt."

To make sure this happened, Gray continued to twist the oven's thermostat dial until the temperature setting changed from digital numbers to just three letters: *MAX.*

Hopefully that should do it.

Gray kept vigil with Seichan as the oven's temperature rose higher and higher. Soon the radiating heat drove them back another few steps. Inside the chamber, the map's rosy glow became a blinding brilliance, shining like a minisun.

Maybe it won't melt . . . not even at these temperatures.

In another minute, Gray had to shield his eyes against the glare.

"Do you feel that?" Seichan asked.

"Feel what?" he began—then he felt it.

A prickling across his skin, a fine vibration, as if all the molecules in the room had grown excited. A second later, the heavy oven began to quake against the concrete floor.

Gray grabbed Seichan's elbow and pushed her toward the door. "Run!"

He fled behind her. He pictured the tightly packed atoms in the nano-gold, squeezed abnormally close together, trapping massive amounts of potential energy in that strained state, like a rubber band stretched tautly.

He glanced behind him. If that rubber band were suddenly cut, if all that potential energy were released at once by overheating the metal . . .

It wasn't going to melt.

It was going to—

The explosion blew him into Seichan and rolled them both through the shop door and out into the night. Shattered glass and splintered wood rained down around them. The scorched door of the oven flew past and crashed through the windshield of the shop owner's Chevy Suburban, parked just outside.

Gray scrambled up, hooking an arm around Seichan's waist and drawing her up with him. He pictured the shop's rows of pressurized gas tanks. The next explosion knocked them back to the ground with a scorching blast of heat. A massive fireball blew out the remaining shop windows behind them and rolled high into the sky.

They regained their feet, each helping the other up.

Across a small parking lot that fronted the business, Monk stared back at them. He stood beside the stunned Russian next to their stolen white van. As they ran up, the goldsmith fell to his knees.

"What have you done to my shop?" the man demanded.

"You'll be reimbursed," Gray said, waving the man aside and the others toward the vehicle. "As long as you stay silent."

They all piled into the van, with Monk behind the wheel.

"Hang on," Monk warned.

He shifted into reverse, pounded the gas pedal, and sent the vehicle flying in reverse, tires squealing across the parking lot. Bouncing over a curb, they hit the surface street teeth-jarringly hard—then Monk yanked back into forward gear so fast that they risked whiplash.

Gray understood the need for speed. They all did. They had to be long gone from the area before any emergency response teams arrived. He stared back at the burning complex. Flames continued to lap around it and smoke roiled high into the night sky, like a signal flare. Their trail, which had grown cool, was suddenly hot again. He couldn't trust the Russian to remain silent. Word would spread—likely reaching Waldorf.

"What happened back there?" Monk finally asked.

Gray told him.

"So, at least, you found the Indian map," Monk commented. "But what about the location of the Fourteenth Colony? Do you know where it is?"

Gray nodded, his head still ringing. "I have an idea."

"Where?"

"In the very worst place it could be."

33

Painter leaned on a table in the main lodge of the ranger station. "If Gray's right, how much trouble are we in?"

Across a swath of topographical maps and reports from the U.S. Geological Survey, Ronald Chin shook his head.

"I'd say a shitload."

The normally reserved geologist's slip into profanity spoke volumes. Chin had arrived thirty minutes ago, along with a member of the National Guard—Major Ashley Ryan. The pair had already been en route from Utah to Arizona, intending to help with the search for Painter's lost group. After landing in Flagstaff and learning of their rescue, they had joined Painter's team here at the station, which had become a makeshift situation room.

"Could you be any more specific?" Painter asked, and stared down at a splayed open map of Montana and Wyoming. It was here that Gray believed the lost city of the ancients was hidden, the final resting place of the *Tawtsee'untsaw Pootseev,* where they stored their greatest treasures and where a doomsday clock was ticking downward, one neutrino at a time.

He studied the boundaries of the national park outlined on the map.

Yellowstone.

The first of the nation's parks, and the granddaddy of all geothermal areas on this continent. If the *Tawtsee'untsaw Pootseev* had wanted a warm and permanent home to preserve and protect their fragile treasure, this would be the place, with its ten thousand hot springs, two hundred geysers, and countless other steaming vents, bubbling fumaroles, and mud volcanoes. In fact, half the geysers in the entire world were located within this park.

But it was also a lot of park to search.

Over two million acres.

Before deciding to concentrate their efforts fully on that one location, Painter wanted to be sure. Off in one of the back offices, Hank Kanosh was mobilizing his Native American resources, struggling to substantiate Gray's claim. At this point, it was still a theory. Even Gray admitted that his estimation of the location was a best guess and that a large margin of error remained. In the meantime, his team would seek further corroboration by investigating the historical angle.

While all that was being done, Painter wanted some idea of what to expect. For this, he needed the expertise of a geologist.

Chin stepped around the table, dragging a topographical map of the national park along its surface. It showed a ring of mountains sheltering a vast plateau, the true geothermal heart of Yellowstone. The steaming valley stretched four thousand square kilometers, large enough to hold all of Los Angeles—but it was no ordinary valley. It was a caldera, the cratered top of a supervolcano that simmered beneath the park.

"This is the problem," Chin said, tapping the center of the crater, where a vast lake pooled. "The Yellowstone caldera marks a geological hot spot, a continual upwelling of hot, molten mantle rock from the earth's core. It feeds into a massive magma chamber only four to five miles beneath the surface. From data collected by the Yellowstone Volcano Observatory, we also know that there are pockets of magma much closer to the surface, seeping into the crust, driving all the hydrothermal activity in the area. With all the rainfall locally, the heat drives a massive and ancient hydraulic system, the world's largest steam engine. That force alone has triggered massive hydrothermal explosions in the valley. Yellowstone Lake itself was formed from one of those blasts, when rain and springwater filled the crater that resulted."

Chin's finger came to rest on that lake. His eyes rose to Painter's face.

"But deeper underground, the pressure keeps slowly mounting as the molten mantle rock rises, building up inside that colossal magma chamber."

"Until it eventually explodes."

"Which Yellowstone has done *three* times over the past two million years. The first explosion tore a hole in the crust the size of Rhode Island. The last eruption left most of the continent covered in ash. These blowouts occur on a regular basis, as steady as the blasts from Old Faithful geyser. They occur once every six hundred thousand years."

"When was the last one?" Painter asked.

"Six hundred *and forty thousand* years ago." The geologist looked significantly at Painter. "So we're overdue. It's not a matter of *if* that supervolcano will erupt, it's a matter of *when*. The eruption is inevitable, and geological evidence indicates that it will be soon."

"What evidence?"

Chin reached and pulled up a sheaf of U.S. Geological Survey studies and seismographic reports from the volcano observatory. He shook the pages in his hand. "We've been collecting data going back to 1923. The land around here has been steadily rising as pressure builds below, but starting in 2004, that bulging of the land has surged to three times the annual average, the highest ever recorded. The bottom of one end of Yellowstone Lake, which overlies the caldera, has risen enough to spill water out of the other end, killing trees. Other sections of forest are dying because their roots are being cooked by the subterranean heat. Hot springs along trails have begun to boil, severely injuring some tourists, requiring some paths to be shut down. Elsewhere, new vents have been opening deeper in the parks, observed by passing airplanes, spewing steam and gouts of toxic vapors that have killed bison on the spot."

Chin slapped his papers down on the table. "This is a powder keg waiting to explode."

"And someone just lit the match," Painter said.

He pictured the massive waves of neutrinos flowing from somewhere inside that park, counting down to an inevitable explosion, one a hundredfold larger than the one that had occurred in Iceland.

"What can we expect if we fail to stop this?" Painter said. "What happens if the caldera does erupt?"

"Cataclysm." Chin stared at the spread of reports and data sheets. "First, it would be the loudest explosion heard by mankind in over seventy thousand years. Within minutes, a hundred thousand people would be buried by ash, incinerated by superheated pyroclastic flows, or killed by the explosive force alone. Magma would spew twenty-five miles into the air. The chamber would release a volume of lava large enough, if spread over the entire United States, to cover the country to the depth of five inches. But most of that flow would be confined to the Western states, wiping out the entire Northwest. For the rest of the country—and the world—*ash* would be the real killer. Estimates say it would cover two-thirds of the country in at least a meter of ash, rendering the land sterile and uninhabitable. But worst of all, the ash blown into the atmosphere would dim the sun and drop the earth's temperature by twenty degrees, triggering a *volcanic winter* that could last decades, if not centuries."

Painter imagined the worldwide starvation, the chaos, the death. He remembered Gray's description of the Laki eruption in Iceland shortly after the founding of America. That small-by-comparison volcanic event killed six million people.

He stared at Chin's ashen face. "You're talking about an extinction-level event, aren't you?"

"It's happened before. Only seventy thousand years ago. A super-volcano erupted in Sumatra. The volcanic winter that followed in its wake wiped out most of the human population, dropping our numbers down to only a few thousand breeding pairs worldwide. The human species survived that eruption by the breadth of a hair." Chin fixed Painter with a dead stare. "We won't be so lucky this time."

12:28 A.M.

Seated in the back office, Hank listened to Chin's dire prediction.

His hands rested on the computer keyboard, but his eyes had gone blind to the screen. He imagined all of civilization wiped out. He remembered the Ute elder's apocalyptic prophecy concerning that cave up in the Utah mountains, how the Great Spirit would rise up and destroy the world if anyone dared trespass.

It was now coming true.

A shadow stretched over his long, knobby fingers. A warm hand, unlined by age, squeezed his own.

"It's okay, Professor," Jordan said. The youth was seated beside him, where he'd been collating pages from a laser printer. "Maybe Yellowstone isn't even the right place."

"It is."

Hank could not shake his despair, made worse by his memories of Maggie and all of the others who had died.

All this death.

He grew suddenly resentful of his companion's youth, of his unflagging optimism and his steadfast belief in his own immortality. He glanced up at Jordan—but what he found in the young man's face told a different story. The black eyes, the bruised features, the fear expressed in every muscle—it was not a lack of maturity that engendered such hope in the young man. It was simply who Jordan was.

Hank took a deep shuddering breath, casting back the shrouds of the dead. He was still alive. So was this resolute young man. A tail thumped under the table.

You, too, Kawtch.

Hank returned Jordan's support, momentarily sharing that warm squeeze, before his focus returned to the situation at hand. He still hadn't changed his opinion concerning the final resting place of the *Tawtsee'untsaw Pootseev.* Painter's colleague out east had read that golden map correctly.

At least, Hank believed so.

"What did you find?" Jordan asked.

"I've been reading through reams of Native American lore concerning Yellowstone, attempting to discern possible correlations among the various myths and legends that would support the existence of a lost city hidden in that valley. It's been frustrating. Native Americans have been living in this region for over ten thousand years. The Cheyenne, Kiowa, Shoshone, Blackfeet, and more recently, the Crows. But so little is spoken among all these tribes about this unique valley. It's a resounding and loud silence, suspiciously so."

"Maybe they didn't know about it."

"No, they had names for it. The Crows called it *land of burning ground* or sometimes the *land of vapors.* The Blackfeet described it as *many smokes.* The Flatheads used the phrase *smoke from the ground.* Can't be more accurate than that, can you? Those early tribes definitely knew about this place."

"Then maybe they didn't talk about it because they were scared."

"That was the view that was held for the longest time. That Indians believed the hissing and roaring of the geysers were the voices of evil spirits. It's still bandied about in some circles, but it's pure hogwash. The newest anthropological studies have revealed that not to be the case. The early Indians had no fear of this steaming land. Instead, that false story got told and retold, mostly by early white settlers, perhaps to make their savage neighbors appear foolish and dull of mind . . . or maybe to help justify the taking of their lands. If the pioneers could claim that Indians were too scared to enter Yellowstone, then the entire territory was up for grabs."

"Then what is the true story?"

Hank pointed to the screen. "The evidence confounded the scholars of the time. This is what historian Hiram Chittenden wrote about it back in 1895. *'It is a singular fact that in Yellowstone National Park, no knowledge of the country seems to have been derived from the Indians . . . Their deep silence concerning it is therefore no less remarkable than mysterious.'"*

"Doesn't sound like they were scared," Jordan said. "More like they were hiding something."

Hank touched his nose—*dead on, my boy*—then pointed to the screen. "Look at this. I found this passage in a recent study; it's an excerpt from an old journal of one of the earliest settlers, John Hamilcar Hollister. I could find nothing like this anywhere else, but it speaks volumes on that deep Indian silence."

Jordan leaned closer.

Hank read the words quietly again alongside him.

There are but few Indian legends which refer to this purposely unknown land. Of these I have found but one, and that is this— that no white man should ever be told of this inferno, lest he should enter that region and form a league with the devils, and by their aid come forth and destroy all Indians.

Jordan sat back, stunned. "So they *were* hiding something."

"Something our ancestors didn't want to have fall into the wrong hands, fearing it would be used against them."

"That lost city must be there."

But where?

Hank checked his watch, fighting against a return of the paralyzing despair that had gripped him moments before. He would follow Jordan's example. He would not give up hope. He caught the young man staring out the window toward the lights of Flagstaff in the distance. But Hank knew his mind was much farther away, with a worry that had nothing to do with volcanoes and lost cities.

This time it was Hank who reached over and gave Jordan's hand a squeeze of reassurance. "We'll get her back."

1:38 A.M.
Salt Lake City, Utah

It had been almost an hour since Kai had spoken to Uncle Crowe. She sat in a dining room chair, unbound, but there was nothing she could do, except chew at her thumbnail.

The suite of rooms bustled with activity. Commandos had shed combat gear for civilian clothing that looked ill-suited to such hardened mercenaries. They set about packing, storing gear, breaking down weapons. They were readying to move out.

Even the computer equipment had been racked up inside a tall, wheeled cargo case, modified out of a Louis Vuitton steamer trunk. From the stack, several lines of cable trailed back to Jordan's gutted cell phone.

Rafael paced around the container, waiting for Kai's uncle's call.

She lowered her hand to her lap, clasping her palms between her legs, just as anxious as the man who kept her prisoner, balancing on a razor of terror.

Before Painter's call, convinced he was dead, she had been locked in one of the bedrooms of the suite. At the time she knew these people were going to kill her. She didn't care. Drained to a hollow shell of herself, she had simply sat on the bed's edge. She was still aware of feeling fear, coiled around the base of her spine, but it was nothing compared to the feeling of desolation that gripped her. She had seen too much blood, too much death. Her own life held little meaning. She considered breaking the mirror in the bathroom and using a shard of glass to spill her own blood, as if by so doing she could wrest back some modicum of control.

But even that had felt too much like fighting.

She simply didn't have the strength.

Then the call had come. Her uncle was alive, so were the professor and Jordan, and even that walking refrigerator called Kowalski. She'd seen their picture on Rafael's computer screen, some frozen image from a broadcast of the group's rescue.

After the call, jubilation filled those hollow spaces inside her, shining a warm light into that dark vacuum. Her uncle's last words stayed with her.

I'm going to come get you. I promise.

He'd said he would not abandon her—and she believed him, which is what ignited the keening terror inside her now. She suddenly wanted to live, and in allowing herself to feel that desire, she realized that once again she had everything to lose.

But there was no escape.

She glanced over to her sole companion at the dining room table. It was the muscular African woman named Ashanda. Kai had initially been terrified of the woman, but then, at the time, the woman had been heating irons in the fire, carrying out a torture upon Rafael's orders. But over time, that fear mellowed into something that resembled discomfort mixed with a kind of curiosity.

Who was she?

The woman was so unlike the others, clearly not a soldier, though she fought for Rafael. Kai pictured Ashanda rising from the shadows of the mud-heated cavern, running with a lithe speed that defied her size. Kai had also seen Ashanda working at the computer as she herself talked to Painter, the woman's dark fingers racing over a keyboard. It was clear that she was more than a technician.

In the bright light of the room, Kai noted vague scars thickening the woman's skin, forming rows of small dots that made stripes along her arms, looking almost like the skin of a crocodile. Her face was similarly scarred but in a more decorative pattern, one that accentuated her dark eyes and swept in wings to her temples. Her hair was done in tight, dark braids that spread from the crown of her head and draped gracefully to her forehead and shoulders.

Kai watched the woman staring at Rafael. Before she had seen only emptiness in those eyes, but this was no longer true. Deep within those dark mirrors, Kai knew, stirred a well of sadness. Ashanda sat so very still, as if afraid of being seen, yet at the same time, wanting more. There was devotion in that gaze, too, along with weariness. She sat like a dog waiting for a touch from its master, knowing that a mere touch was all she was ever going to get.

The reverie ended with the chiming ring of a phone.

Kai swung around.

At last.

1:44 A.M.

Rafael appreciated punctuality. The director of Sigma had placed his follow-up call precisely at the time he had promised. It was not the call itself, but what the man offered when he spoke, that dismayed the Frenchman, coming as it did so unexpectedly.

"A truce?" Rafe asked. "Between us? How does that serve me?"

Painter's voice remained urgent. "As promised, I'll tell you where the Fourteenth Colony is located. But it will do you no good. The cache is set to explode in approximately four and a half hours."

"Then, Monsieur Crowe, if you wish your niece to live, you'd best make this exchange as quickly as possible."

"Listen to me, Rafael. I'll tell you the location *now*. The Fourteenth Colony is hidden somewhere in Yellowstone National Park. I'm sure that such a resting place makes sense to you, does it not?"

Rafe fought to understand such a drastic turn of events.

Is this a ruse? To what end?

Painter did not let up, speaking rapidly. "Give me an e-mail address. I'll send you all the relevant data. But in a few short hours, that cache is going to go critical, triggering a blast over a hundredfold stronger than the one in Iceland. But you know that's not the true danger. That explosion will release a mass of nanobots. They'll start disassembling any matter they encounter and keep spreading and growing larger. The nano-nest will eat its way down until it reaches the magma chamber under Yellowstone, where it will ignite the supervolcano buried beneath that park. The resulting cataclysm will be the equivalent of a mile-wide asteroid slamming into the earth. It means the end of most life, certainly all *human* life."

Rafe found himself breathing harder. *Could he be telling the truth?*

"I doubt that such destruction will serve even your aims," Painter continued. "Or those of anyone you work with, for that matter. We either team up, share our knowledge, in order to stop this from happening, or it's the end of everything."

"I . . . I will need time to think about this." Rafe hated to hear the stammer in his own voice.

"Don't take long," Painter warned. "Again I will send you all of our data—whatever you want. But Yellowstone is spread over two million acres, and this creates a huge challenge to us. We must still discover and pinpoint the lost city's exact location, and we must do it while the clock keeps ticking downward."

Rafe checked his wristwatch. If the director was telling the truth, they had until 6:15 A.M. to find the lost city and neutralize the material that was hidden there.

"Send me what you have," Rafe said, and gave him an e-mail address.

"You have my number." Painter signed off.

Rafael lowered the phone, hanging his head in thought.

Do I believe you, Monsieur Crowe? Could you be telling the truth?

Rafe lifted his head enough to glance toward Kai Quocheets.

The director had never asked once about his niece. That, more than anything, spoke to his honesty. What did it matter if he negotiated for one life when the lives of all of mankind were at risk?

The phone rang again, making Rafe jump. He stared down at the mobile device in his hand, wired to the encrypting software. But that wasn't the source of the ringing. He turned to the dining room buffet, where his personal laptop and cell phone rested. He watched his phone vibrate and heard it ring again.

Leaning more heavily on his cane than he usually did, he stepped over and retrieved the device. His personal phone was meant only for direct communication with his family, along with a few of his associates at the research facilities back in the French Alps. But the caller ID simply listed the caller's name as blocked. That made no sense. His phone didn't accept blocked calls.

He was ready to dismiss the matter and not respond, but the phone was already in his hand and he needed something to distract himself with while he awaited the data from Painter Crowe.

Irritated, Rafe lifted the device to his ear. "Who is this?"

The voice was American, soft-spoken, nondescript, perhaps a hint of a Southern accent, but too faint for Rafe to tell anything more than that. The man told him his name.

Rafe's cane slipped from his hand and clattered to the marble floor. He reached back to the buffet to catch himself. He noted Ashanda rising, ready to come to his aid. He sternly shook his head at her.

The caller spoke calmly, distinctly, with no threat in his voice, only certainty. "We've heard the news. You'll cooperate with Sigma to the fullest extent. What is to come must be stopped for all our sakes. We have full confidence in your abilities."

"Je vous en prie," he said breathlessly, cringing to note that he'd slipped into French inadvertently.

"Once you've accomplished your goal, anyone outside your party who has knowledge of what is discovered must be destroyed. But be warned. Director Crowe has been underestimated in the past."

Rafe's gaze flicked to Kai. "I may have a way of neutralizing any threat he poses, but I will still be careful."

"With such brittle bones, I'm sure that is a trait you've honed well."

While this might be taken as a vague insult, the gentle amusement—even in such trying times—made it clear that the speaker's intent was nothing but good-natured.

"Adieu," the man said in French, equally accommodating. "I have matters I must address out east here."

The phone clicked off.

Rafe turned promptly to TJ, who was packing the last of the computer gear. "Raise Painter Crowe for me." To Bern, he said, "Have the men ready to leave in fifteen minutes."

"Where are we headed?" Bern asked. He wasn't prying; it was just a need-to-know inquiry to better prepare his team.

"To Yellowstone."

TJ interrupted. "Connection's ringing, sir."

Rafe took the phone, ready to make the deal.

He knew better than to disobey. The honor of the moment warmed through him, hardening his resolve, if not his bones. He was the first in his family to ever speak to a member of the True Bloodline.

34

It would soon be getting lighter.

Gray wasn't sure if this was a positive development. They'd barely made it out of Nashville, having to take surface streets and back roads, sticking to the speed limits. Monk had done the driving while Gray coordinated matters with Painter Crowe.

With one goal accomplished, the director had assigned him another: to attempt to narrow down the location of the Fourteenth Colony settlement by following the historical trail. They'd dogged Archard Fortescue's path to Iceland and back. Now they had to see if they could track the Frenchman's subsequent footsteps.

That meant they weren't the only ones who were getting no sleep.

"Calling this early is becoming a habit, Mr. Pierce," Eric Heisman said over the phone, but rather than irritated, he sounded excited.

Kat had arranged the call, passing it through the Sigma switchboard to scramble the connection.

"I've got you on speaker," Gray said. He needed everyone's input. Now was not the time to miss a critical insight or overlook an important detail. Gray wanted everybody's fingerprints all over this case.

Seichan sat up from the backseat, listening in.

Monk was driving slowly down Shelbyville Highway south of the city. At this hour, it was deserted, which allowed him to focus all of his attention on the call. Kat also listened in on the other end, from Sigma command.

Heisman filled them in where he'd left off in his scholarly investigations. "Sharyn and I pulled everything we could on the Lewis and Clark expedition and its relationship to Yellowstone. I also consulted with Professor Henry Kanosh just a few minutes ago. He saved me much time and effort by researching the Native American side of the equation."

Gray urged the man along, sensing the press of time. Kat had already informed him that Painter, along with a French team of Guild operatives, was already en route to Yellowstone, where the two groups would jointly work on the puzzle from ground zero. Not a good situation from any perspective. Gray was determined to help from afar in any way he could.

"And you found no evidence that Lewis and Clark's team ever entered Yellowstone?" Gray asked.

"No. But I find it odd, almost beyond comprehension, that they missed it. The expedition crossed to within only *forty* miles of the park. According to Professor Kanosh, the Native American tribes had been secretive about the geothermal valley, but the expedition had bushels of trinkets and coins to ply Indians for any information about unique natural features: plants, animals, geology. Someone would have eventually tipped their hand and talked about such an unusual valley."

"So you think they did find it?" Seichan asked from the backseat.

"If they did, they erased their tracks very well. So far the only evidence we do have to support such a claim is weak at best. We know all records of Archard Fortescue came to a halt after he left with the expedition led by Meriwether Lewis. We know Lewis was murdered a few years after returning. But that's a far cry from saying either of them found that lost Indian city, that heart of the Fourteenth Colony."

"Then let's work this backward," Gray suggested, turning the puzzle around in his head. "Let's start with the death of Meriwether Lewis. Let's assume the expedition *did* discover the truth and that Lewis's murder was somehow connected to the discovery. Can you tell us again about the manner of his death?"

"Well, he was struck down in October of 1809, at a wayside inn called Grinder's Stand in Tennessee, not far from Nashville."

Gray glanced to the others.

Nashville?

Monk mumbled, "Oh yeah, looks like we're still dogging after those guys. First to Iceland and now Tennessee."

Heisman didn't hear him and continued: "Again, there's no solid explanation for Lewis's death. Despite the double gunshot wounds—one to the gut, one to the head—his death was deemed a suicide. It remained the belief for centuries, until just recently. It's now widely accepted that Lewis was indeed murdered, whether as part of a robbery or an outright assassination or both."

"What details do we know about the night he died?" Gray asked.

"There are numerous accounts, but the best comes from Mrs. Grinder herself, the innkeeper's wife, who was there alone that night. She reported gunshots, sounds of a struggle, and heard Lewis call out for help, but she was too scared to check on him until daybreak. She eventually found him dying in his room, barely hanging on to life, sprawled atop his buffalo-skin robe, which was soaked in his blood. It is said his last words were mysterious. *'I have done the business.'* As if he'd thwarted his murderers in some manner at the end."

Gray felt his pulse quicken with the telling, knowing this had to be important. But there was something else Heisman had mentioned . . .

The curator wasn't done. "But rumors are many about Lewis's last days, about who might have killed him. The best evidence points to Brigadier General James Wilkinson, a known conspirator of the traitor Aaron Burr. Some believe the general orchestrated the murder. Those same stories hint that Lewis was still acting as Jefferson's spy, that he had with him something vital that he wanted to bring to D.C."

Gray pictured one of the gold plates. Was Grinder's Stand the place where the Guild originally got hold of their own plate? He recalled how he imagined Lewis as a colonial version of a Sigma operative: *spy, soldier, scientist.* Was Wilkinson one of the great enemies mentioned by Jefferson and Franklin, a predecessor to the modern Guild? Did he murder Lewis to gain possession of that tablet?

Gray felt history repeating itself.

Is that same battle still going on two centuries later?

Still, he sensed he was missing a key element to the story, something that snagged in his mind, but slipped through without catching.

Seichan beat him to it. "You mentioned that Lewis bled out on top of a buffalo-skin robe."

"That's right."

Gray glanced at her appreciatively, but Seichan merely shrugged. "Dr. Heisman," he asked, "didn't Fortescue's journal mention that the mastodon's skull was wrapped in a *buffalo skin?*"

"Let me check." Heisman whistled slowly, the sound accompanied by a shuffling of pages. "Ah, here it is. It's mentioned simply as *'a painted buffalo hide.'*"

"Whatever happened to it?" Seichan asked.

"It doesn't say."

Gray followed up with his own question. "Is there any record of Jefferson ever owning a *painted* buffalo skin?"

"Now that you mention it, yes. In fact, the president amassed a huge private collection of Indian artifacts that he kept in his home at Monticello. A highly decorated skin was one of his showcase items. It was said he received the hide from Lewis, who sent it back from the trail during the expedition. It was said to be stunning and very old. But upon his death, most of Jefferson's collection, including that spectacular hide, vanished."

Odd . . .

Gray ruminated for a time. Could the buffalo hide in all these stories be the same one? Had Lewis taken it with him in order to help him find that lost city? Did it take both the map *and* the hide to solve the puzzle of the Fourteenth Colony? Afterward, did Lewis send the hide back to Jefferson as some token of his success?

Gray knew he had nothing solid to go on: there were too many suppositions, too many holes. For example, why was the skin again in Lewis's possession at the time of his death? Was its presence the reason he spoke those cryptic words in the final moments of his life—*I have done the busi-*

ness? Had he lost the gold tablet to Wilkinson or some other thief, but retained the more important buffalo hide?

A new player in the game spoke. "Dr. Heisman," Kat asked over the phone, "can you tell us anything about what happened to Lewis's body?"

"Nothing special. A tragedy considering he was such a national hero. But because his death was deemed a suicide, he was buried on the spot, on the grounds of that same inn. There in Tennessee."

"And can we assume he was interred with all of his possessions?" Kat asked.

"That was usually done. Sometimes the authorities would send any money found on the bodies or something of sentimental value to their surviving heirs."

"But not likely a blood-soaked buffalo hide," Gray added.

Monk stirred, taking his eyes off the road. "You think he might still be buried with it?"

"There's only one way to find out," Gray said. "We have to dig up the body of Meriwether Lewis."

PART IV

WOLF AND EAGLE

35

The helicopter lowered toward the steaming geothermal heart of Yellowstone. Night still claimed the primitive landscape of bubbling pools, white-gray cones, and fog-enshrouded rivers and creeks that spanned the upper geyser basin. Farther out, dark meadows and black stands of lodgepole pines stretched toward the distant plateaus and mountains.

But man had carved his own mark into this national treasure, this contrasting mix of quiet natural beauty and hellish geological activity. In the predawn darkness, lines of streetlights and trails of headlamps mapped the few roads winding through the park. The evacuation Painter had ordered was under way, turning the park at its peak season into a massive traffic jam. The flashing blue lamps of park service vehicles dotted the thoroughfares, as rangers did their best to empty the park.

He checked his watch.

Two hours left.

Not everyone would get clear in time, but he had to try. He had started the evacuation two hours ago as he left Flagstaff and raced north in a private jet to the small airport in western Montana, a few miles from the western entrance to the park. The helicopter ferried him the rest of the way to the rendezvous point.

A parking lot rose up below them. Two other helicopters already rested below in neighboring lots. It looked like Rafael's team had beaten him to the place, but they had a head start, flying directly out of Salt Lake

City. The two teams were to meet inside the Old Faithful Inn, a colossal landmark of the park, built in the early 1900s. The seven-story rustic hotel, with its steep roofs and heavy beams, was the largest log structure in the world, built from locally harvested pine and quarried stone.

It had been built here as the perfect vantage point from which to view its namesake.

As the skids of the helicopter touched down, the geyser lived up to its reputation. A vast flume of steam and boiling water jetted nearly two hundred feet into the air from the most famous of the valley's geysers. Old Faithful's eruptions occurred roughly every ninety minutes.

Painter prayed that the valley would still be around for the next scheduled show.

Beyond the geyser, the dark Firehole River wound across the upper basin, lined by more geysers, each with crazy names—Beehive, Spasmodic, Castle, Slurper, Little Squirt, Giantess, and many more—along with numerous vents, pools, and steaming springs.

The helicopter door cracked open, releasing Painter's party into this blasted, wondrous world. But they weren't here for sightseeing.

"Stinks," Kowalski commented—but Painter didn't know if he was referring to the air's sulfurous taint or their dire situation. His partner stared sourly around, tugging his long duster more firmly over his shoulders.

Hank climbed out next, followed by his dog, who ran ahead to mark a lamppost. Jordan helped the professor out. Painter had tried to get the young man to remain behind at Flagstaff, but the kid offered a good argument.

If you fail, I die anyway. I'd rather go down fighting.

But Painter also knew what it was that drew Jordan north. The young man's eyes stared toward the massive hotel. He wasn't appreciating the architecture, but trying to spot any sign of Kai. Painter was anxious, too. The fate of the entire world was too large a notion to take to heart, too bulky a concept to fully grasp.

Instead, it came down to those you loved.

Jordan's fear was simple to read, concern for the safety of a single terrified girl squeezed the young man's heart into his throat. Likewise, Painter prayed he'd get to see Lisa again. Their last conversation on the phone had been necessarily brief, given that the fate of the world was hanging in the balance. Lisa had been strong, but he heard the tears behind her words.

"Let's go," Painter said, waving forward the last members of their group.

Ronald Chin followed, along with Major Ashley Ryan. Three other National Guard soldiers accompanied them, carrying large trunks. Ryan had collected the additional manpower at the Montana airport, teammates up from Utah, while Painter had ordered the trunks of equipment flown in.

According to the parley Painter had with Rafael prior to leaving Flagstaff, each team was restricted to the same number of members. Painter didn't want this to become a pissing contest. They had work to do—and it had to be done fast, with a minimum of drama.

Reaching the hotel's front entrance, Painter pushed through a huge set of plank doors, painted a fire-engine red and strapped and studded in black iron. As he stepped inside, the sight took his breath away. It was like entering a lamp-lit cavern made of logs. The sheer volume of the open four-story space drew his eyes upward. Balconies and staircases climbed toward the roof, all railed by twisted, contorted pine logs, stripped of their bark, glowing golden in the light. In the middle, dominating by sheer mass, rose a towering stone fireplace. It was the central pillar and hearth of the lobby.

The cavernous space seemed especially large because it was empty. Like the park, the hotel had been evacuated, except for a skeleton crew who'd volunteered to remain behind and protect this treasured place. It was a futile gesture. No one could protect anything against what was coming—they could only try to stop it.

To that end, upon spotting Rafael's party, Painter crossed toward them. They had taken up residence amid a collection of Mission chairs, rockers, and coffee tables. A larger trestle table from the neighboring lobby restaurant had been carried over and turned into a makeshift computer lab. Miniservers, LCD screens, and other digital equipment were being rapidly assembled, overseen by a scrawny, nervous-eyed technician and a familiar-looking dark woman.

From that woman's shadow, another familiar figure appeared.

"Uncle Crowe . . ." Kai stepped into view.

Jordan ran forward. "Kai!"

Her face brightened upon seeing him. She moved to greet him as he hurried toward her, raising one of her arms to hug him. But suddenly she was snagged to a stop by the larger woman's grip on her wrist. A jangle of steel links drew Painter's eye, correcting his assumption. The African wasn't holding Kai—the two were handcuffed together.

Jordan drew to a stop, also noting the situation.

"What's the meaning of this?" Painter asked, stepping forward.

"Merely insurance, Monsieur Crowe." Rafael rose from one of the chairs, needing his cane to help him up. Small wrinkles of pain etched the corner of his eyes. Apparently the ride here had taxed his frail body.

"What do you mean, insurance? We had a deal."

"Indeed. I am a man of my word. The agreement was that I'd safely return your niece once you revealed the location of the lost city."

"Which I did."

"Which you did *not*." Rafael lifted his arm to encompass more than just this hotel. "Where is this lost city, then?"

Painter realized that the Frenchman was right. He stared into Kai's forlorn and scared eyes. Her hand had found Jordan's during his exchange with Rafe. He also noted the thickness of the cuff's bracelet around Kai's other wrist. A tiny red light was blinking.

Rafael noticed his attention. "An unfortunate necessity. The handcuffs are powered, creating a closed circuit, connecting the two bracelets. Break that circuit, and a small, but powerful charge will explode with enough force to take off your niece's arm and likely a good portion of her torso."

Kai looked aghast at Rafael. Apparently her captor had not revealed this extra bit of security to her.

"I thought this best," Rafael explained. "Now you will not be distracted by the thoughts of wresting your niece from me. We can both concentrate on what must be done. In the meantime, she is perfectly safe until we complete our transaction."

The tension in the room seemed to thicken the air between the two forces. Backing up Rafael, his Aryan bodyguard rested his palm atop his holstered sidearm. Five mercenaries flanked their leader.

They were at an impasse—and time was running out.

Painter had said he didn't want drama, and here he was adding to it. He needed to end this.

Painter gave Kai a firm look of assurance. He would get her through this—somehow. He turned back to Rafael. "Did you bring the gold wolf's-head jar?"

"Of course." Rafe hobbled around. "Bern, bring that valise to the table."

The soldier obeyed, stalking across to a medium-size case on the floor. He hauled it atop a coffee table and opened its lid. The golden canopic jar lay nestled in protective black foam. The two gold tablets, stolen by Kai out of the Utah cave, were also inside.

Hank noted the tablets, too, and moved closer, but Bern extracted the jar and snapped the lid closed. The soldier crossed and placed the artifact on the table next to the computer workstation.

Again Painter was struck by its beauty, from the perfectly sculpted head of a timber wolf to the handsomely etched mountain landscape. But he did not have time to appreciate such artistry. Instead, he studied it as if it were a piece to a puzzle.

Without turning, he pointed his arm back. "Kowalski, go unpack our gear."

Rafael stepped beside Painter, his movement accompanied by a waft of spicy cologne. He leaned on his cane with both hands. "Do you truly think this will help us narrow down our search of these two million acres?"

"It must. The satellite passes of the park are of little use."

En route to Yellowstone, Painter had pulled every string he could, raising the alarm all the way up to the Oval Office. With President Gant's signature, along with approval of the Joint Chiefs of Staff, Painter had commandeered every available satellite in orbit. The entire park had been scanned across every spectrum: ground-penetrating radar, geomagnetic potentials, thermal gradients . . . anything that might offer a clue as to where a lost city might be buried.

He'd come up with nothing.

"Problem is," Painter said, "this terrain is riddled with caverns, caves, vents, lava tubes, and hot springs. Pick almost any spot in the park and there seems to be some cavity or pocket underground. The city could still be anywhere."

"And the physicists?" Rafael asked.

"We've got every expert in subatomic particles trying to calibrate and pinpoint the source of the massive neutrino flow from this region. But the volume of production is so prodigious that they could narrow the scope only to a two-hundred-mile radius."

"Useless," Rafael commented.

Painter agreed. He had one hope. It rested on the table. The landscape on the canopic jar. Some ancient artist had taken a great deal of time to etch it so meticulously upon the bottle.

The foreground of the landscape showed the confluence of two creeks, flowing into the distance down a forested valley. In the background rose towering clifflike mountains, fringed by lodgepole pines, so detailed that each needle had been carefully scratched in place. And in the middle, rising between the creeks, rose a tall cone, slightly steaming, like a small smoldering volcano. Around it stood smaller anthill-like cones.

So realistic were the details that it seemed impossible to believe them to depict anything other than a real place. The steaming geothermal structures in the center certainly suggested that such a spot might be found within this park. Painter pictured the artist sitting in a field, meticulously working the metal to preserve an image of this place. If it was important enough to etch onto this canopic jar, it must represent a site sacred to the *Tawtsee'untsaw Pootseev*. Perhaps it was a view from their new refuge here in Yellowstone.

That's what Painter hoped.

By now, Kowalski had unpacked the cases Painter had ordered him to bring here. He set the disassembled pieces of the digital laser scanner on the table, next to all of the other computer equipment.

Painter glanced from Rafael to the scrawny computer tech. "Do you have all the satellite uplinks and parameters set on your end?"

"We do."

"Can your guy help me assemble and get it cabled in properly?"

Instead of addressing the tech, Rafael turned to the tall African woman. "Ashanda, perhaps you should oversee TJ's handiwork. We don't want to risk any mistakes." He drew Painter aside. "Let them do their magic."

Even with the use of only one hand and without speaking a single word, Ashanda orchestrated the assembly of the laser device, along with its calibration and integration into the workstation. Even Kai helped run some of the cabling, plainly needing to do something—though every jangle of the handcuffs drew a scared glance from her.

Within a few minutes, a window opened on one of the monitors, ready to accept data. The window ledger read LASER TECHNIQUES COMPANY, LLC. It was a company out of Bellevue, Washington, that worked with NASA, developing patented tools to detect erosion, pitting, scuffing, or cracking in metallic surfaces, covering a gamut of uses that included space-shuttle thrusters, military hardware, nuclear steam generator tubes, and underwater pipelines. The laser device could pick up and photograph minute changes in metal that the eye could easily miss.

Painter needed that precision now.

Ashanda turned and silently announced the completion of her work with a small bow of her head.

Is she mute? Painter wondered absently. But he could give the question no more attention than that. At the moment he had a more important puzzle to solve.

"Guess that's my cue," he said.

He stepped back to the table and switched on the laser mapping system. A bluish holographic cone glowed from the scanner's emitter. Painter positioned it until a set of crosshairs were fixed to the center of the golden landscape. Once this was done, he activated the scan.

Dark azure lines flowed up and down across the golden surface, then back and forth, absorbing every detail off the jar, from the tiniest wisp of steam to a minuscule pinecone hanging off the branch of a tree in the background.

On the computer monitor, the image formed—at first a static flat image, then, as the scan finished, it rendered out into an extrapolated 3-D view. A square slice of landscape, topographically accurate, spun slowly on the screen.

"Amazing," Rafael said.

"Let's see if it helps us." Painter moved to the computer keyboard, opened a data stream to a NASA technician in Houston, and sent the large file. Once it was received, the team in Houston would set about using the satellite data collected over the past hour and compare the real-world terrain of Yellowstone to this holographic image. With a bit of luck, they'd find a match.

"This may take a few minutes," Painter said.

Rafael stared at the golden jar and muttered. "Let's hope not too many minutes."

4:34 A.M.

Hank crouched beside the table, opposite from Painter and the Frenchman. He kept his gaze fixed on the canopic jar, feeling possessive about it, as he'd been the one who found the artifact down in the Anasazi's *kiva*. He imagined one of the *Tawtsee'untsaw Pootseev* devoutly inscribing this sacred object. Painter was right. It had to be important and could point them to the location of the lost city.

Hank also felt that the landscape was a significant clue. In fact, it nagged at him. There was something vaguely familiar about the picture, especially that small volcano in the center; he felt as if he'd seen it somewhere before, yet he'd never visited Yellowstone.

So how could that be? What am I forgetting?

Racking his memory, he finally gave up and turned his attention to the other mystery on the gold jar.

Leaning down, Hank studied the writing etched onto its opposite side, wondering again if he was gazing upon the letters of the language that the Book of Mormon described as *reformed Egyptian*. His linguist colleague back at BYU who had helped identify the writing on the gold plates had an equally fanciful name for this script: *the alphabet of the Magi.*

Hank studied the writing and considered the scribe who had etched the letters onto the jar ages ago. Were the *Tawtsee'untsaw Pootseev* some kind of scholarly sect, masters of a lost technology who had fled the Holy Lands centuries before Christ's birth? Did these fleeing Israelites—*these Nephites*—come to North America to preserve and protect their knowledge, some mix of Jewish mysticism and Egyptian science?

Oh, if only I could talk to one of them . . .

But maybe one of them was speaking to him now, through these flowing lines of proto-Hebrew. Still, Hank knew he would need help to understand the message he was receiving.

He straightened and interrupted Painter, who was in conversation with the Frenchman. It seemed as if the enemies had become colleagues. Still, Hank noted the nervous edge to Painter's mien, the quickness with which his fingers formed themselves into fists, the angry pinch to his eyes, the clipped manner of his speech. He imagined it was taking all of the man's control to keep from ripping Rafael's head from his shoulders. Hank also saw the raw wound in Painter's eyes, born of guilt and pain, whenever he looked in Kai's direction.

It was made worse by the waiting and tension.

Hank offered him something to do. "Painter, could we use your tool to take a photo of the writing on this side of the jar? I can send it to my colleague, the expert in ancient languages and linguistics. When I spoke to him last, he believed he might be able to help us translate it. Not the entire message, mind you. He thought he might be able to pick out a few words here and there, those bits that still bear some relation to modern Hebrew."

"At this point, I'll take any help I can. Even a single word could be the final key to solving this puzzle."

Hank was hanging back while Painter and the French team worked to get a copy uploaded to BYU when he accidentally bumped into the carrying case that had been used to transport the canopic jar.

Hmm . . .

Painter suddenly called out, drawing everyone's attention.

"NASA just sent word. We got a hit!"

36

The sun had come up by the time they were able to off-load the backhoe from the flatbed. Gray trundled the earthmover across the empty parking lot of the Meriwether Lewis State Park. The recreation area lay about eighty miles south of Nashville along the Natchez Trace Parkway. At this hour, the park was still closed, and the gravesite they sought was well off the road, surrounded by thick forest.

If they moved quickly enough, they shouldn't be disturbed.

Earlier, Kat had cleared the way for this little bit of grave robbing by arranging permits for a bogus sewer repair job to cover their actions, along with renting the backhoe from a local heavy-equipment dealer in the nearby town of Hohenwald.

Monk and Seichan, both suited up in blue utility jumpers and carrying shovels, led the way from the parking lot.

Gray followed, working the two brakes to control his turns and peering over the top of the loading bucket. He'd driven tractors and backhoes as a kid back in Texas. He was rusty, but it was coming back to him.

Entering the main grounds, they passed several commemorative and informational signs, as well as a restoration of the original Grinder's Stand, where Lewis died. The log structure stood to one side of the park. The grave marker lay ahead, across a swath of lawn. It was a simple monument with a stacked stone base holding up a broken plinth of limestone, symbolic of a life that was cut short.

Gray headed across the lawn toward it, going slowly.

Once they got close enough, Monk circled his arm in the air. "Turn her!"

Gray obeyed, swinging the backhoe fully around, to bring the rear boom and bucket to bear. He shifted into neutral and set the brake. Once the machine was ready, he swiveled his seat to face the stubby controls to the rear digging arm and lowered the stabilizer legs to either side.

But before digging, he had to do a little clearing.

With a cringe against the violation he was about to commit and a silent apology to the dead pioneer, Gray lifted the boom and extended the arm, using the bucket like a ram against the top of the pillar. Hydraulics whined and slowly the broken plinth toppled over, ripping out of its stacked-stone base. It crashed, penetrating deep into the lawn on the far side.

Once that was done, it took another fifteen minutes to remove the base: scooping stone and mortar and dumping it to the side. After this, Gray pointed the bucket's teeth to the ground and began to dig in earnest, one scoopful at a time.

Monk and Seichan helped guide his actions, checking after each bucket load, jumping in and searching around with their spades. Finally, a sharp whistle drew Gray's attention. Monk straightened from the hole and pointed down.

"Time to wake up the dead!"

Monk and Gray cleared the rest of the way with the shovels. Monk had a bit of difficulty with only one hand, but he'd learned long ago to manage most tasks through the artful use of his stump.

Seichan watched from the lip of the open grave.

According to information supplied to them by Eric Heisman, Gray's team was not the first to violate Lewis's resting place. A monument committee had dug up Lewis's body back in 1847, to confirm that it was indeed the famous pioneer in this grave before allowing the construction of the broken-pillar grave marker. The committee's report to the state legislature also stated their firm belief that Lewis met his end through murder, not suicide, declaring he'd *"died at the hands of an assassin."*

The coffin was probably dated back to that time.

A worry nagged at Gray. Had the committee, he wondered, committed any further violation, such as emptying anything they found here?

They were about to find out.

Inside the grave, Gray set the edge of his spade and broke the rusted locks from the wood coffin. With Monk's help, he got the lid raised. Skeletal remains rested in the tattered remnants of an old suit. Dried bits of flesh still clung in flaking patches.

Monk fell back a step and pointed a thumb up. "I think I'm going to go join Seichan."

"Go ahead," Gray said, releasing him from duty.

They were done here.

Folded neatly over the body's skeletal legs was the hide of a buffalo. It looked to be in poor shape, the fur of the pelt ragged, almost bald, but the leather itself appeared intact.

Gray bent closer to examine it as the crack of a rifle suddenly split the bright morning quiet. Monk came falling back into the grave, sprawling atop the bones.

Gray reached to his side, and his fingers came back bloody.

Seichan leaped down to join them as more shots blasted into the edge of the grave. "Where are our rifles?" she asked.

"Still in the backhoe's cab," Gray said.

It was a foolish oversight.

Monk groaned. "Looks like we dug our own graves."

37

Half an hour after getting word from NASA, Painter stood within the landscape pictured on the canopic jar. While he was being airlifted here, dawn had broken across Yellowstone, though the sun had yet to fully rise. The soft glow of a new day cast a magical quality on the small valley.

According to the ranger they'd spoken with, this was one of the most remote areas of the park. Fewer than twenty-five people had ever set foot in this small geothermal basin. To use the ranger's words, "More people have been to the summit of Everest than have made it to Fairyland Basin."

Despite the whimsical name, the reason for the lack of visitors was plain to see. The basin lay seventeen miles away from the nearest trailhead, and treacherous cliffs rose fifteen hundred feet all around. Only the most foolhardy dared risk coming here.

Luckily they had helicopters.

The chopper lifted off behind him after the search party had been unloaded.

Ducking against the beat of the rotor wash, Painter yelled to be heard. "We have a little over one hour, people! We need to find that lost city!"

Other helicopters circled overhead, carrying insulated blast boxes that were normally used to explode suspicious packages. The plan was to find the cache of unstable compound. If they couldn't neutralize it here, the nano-material would be transported hot, out of the valley, and dumped clear of the caldera. That was the primary goal, to protect the super-volcano.

After that, they would address whatever destructive and denaturing force was released by that blast. Kat had the Japanese physicist working up various scenarios, not ruling out a nuclear option if necessary.

But this was a bridge they'd cross later.

First, they had to find the tomb of the *Tawtsee'untsaw Pootseev*—and it would not be easy. Painter gaped at the towering cliffs, the dark stands of dark lodgepole pines, and the green meadows that rolled outward from the confluence of two silver creeks.

It was a beautiful spot, but it might not be the *right* spot. That ancient artist may have etched this valley in gold for no other reason than that it appealed to him. It might have had nothing to do with that lost city.

Someone disagreed with him.

"This is the place!" Professor Kanosh stood several yards away, holding a hand to his forehead. "Why didn't I remember this before?"

Painter headed over to him. Hank stood amid the geothermal structures that gave this valley its fanciful name. *Fairyland* came from the chalk-gray geothermal structures rising up between the shores of those two streams. They were geyserite cones, according to Chin, formed by the aggregation of mineral deposits left by small geysers. There had to be over forty of them spread over an area half a football field in size. Some were as squat as knee-high toadstools; others towered ten feet tall, reminding Painter of giant African termite hills. Most had long gone dormant, but a handful continued to puff with steam or run with boiling water. According to the ranger, many of the larger cones had specific names: Magic Mushroom, Phallic Cone, Pitcher's Mound . . .

It was the last of these before which Hank was standing. Steam rose from the top of the largest cone, a minivolcano amid its more stalklike neighbors. Water ran down its sides and flowed in rivulets across the chalk-stone ground.

Painter headed toward the professor as Kawtch splashed in the shallows of the neighboring creek. Jordan stood at Hank's side, though his gaze shifted often to Kai. Rafael's party gathered in a clutch on the far side of the geothermal field's expanse.

Sweeping his cane high, Rafael ordered Bern and his men to begin a systematic search, concentrating on the cliffs. *Smart.* If there were an entrance to a subterranean city, it would most likely be found there.

"Major Ryan," Painter called out. "Take your men and check the cliffs on this side of the valley. Chin, you're with me. I want your assessment about this steaming hot spot here."

Kowalski followed them, eyeballing the French team across the way with suspicion. "I trust that guy as much as I trust a snake in a boot."

Painter thought this was a fair assessment, but for now, they had to work together.

"Hank, what did you find?" he asked as he reached the professor's side.

The professor pointed to the rippled sides of the Pitcher's Mound cone. Its name clearly derived from the fat fingerlike projections along the rim, making it look like an open pitcher's mitt.

"Look at this," Hank said, crouching down and pointing. "Over the centuries, the slow aggregation of minerals must have remodeled this cone somewhat, but the resemblance is still uncanny. Study the silhouette."

"Resemblance to what?"

"To one of the most revered Jewish landmarks, from out of the Book of Exodus, the mountain Moses came down bearing the Ten Commandments."

"Are you talking about Mount Sinai?" Painter asked. He bent at the waist and stared at the hill, trying to picture it as a miniature model of that famous mountain.

I guess so, he thought, but he remained unsure. It was like staring at clouds and seeing what you wanted to see. To Painter, the big cone appeared as much like Mount Sinai as those other bent-backed gray towers looked like gnomes.

Kowalski shook his head, plainly not buying it either. He searched around at the field of stalklike gray rocks. "They all look like penises to me."

"What difference does it make," Painter asked, "whether it looks like Mount Sinai or not?"

"Because if the *Tawtsee'untsaw Pootseev* were descendants of a lost tribe of Israel, then the discovery of a cone shaped like Sinai would be a providential sign to them. This valley would be important, sacred enough to make it their secret home."

"I hope you're right," Painter said.

Chin had another opinion. He knelt atop the thick field of dried minerals and rocks called sinter, from which most of the cones arose. "Well, from a geologist's standpoint, this is the *worst* place for them to choose."

"Why is that?" Painter asked. "Besides the fact we're standing on top of a supervolcano?"

"That's deeper underground." The geologist patted the surface of sinter. "Feel this."

Painter reached down and pressed his palm against the chalky stone.

"What are you doing?" Rafael asked, joining them, along with Ashanda and Kai.

"It's vibrating," Painter said.

Chin explained. "This geothermal zone sits atop a plugged-up hydrothermal vent, known as a hydrothermal boil, a hot teapot that continually cycles the water seeping through the porous rock, then back up again as steam. The vibration is from the pressure underground, the pulse of the steam engine beneath us."

Before anyone could comment on this, Hank's phone rang. He checked the number and lifted his face. "It's my colleague from BYU, the one helping us decipher the lost language."

"Answer it," Painter urged, hoping the man had some good news.

Hank stepped away, pressed the phone to one ear, and placed a palm over the other. As the professor conversed, Painter watched his face go from hope to dismay to confusion. He finally snapped his phone closed and returned to them. He seemed momentarily unable to speak.

"Professor?" Painter urged.

"My colleague deciphered some bits of the writing on the wolf-totem jar. He found a smattering of words and phrases that spoke of death and destruction. Nothing more."

"So basically a warning label," Painter said.

Kowalski frowned. "Why didn't they just slap it with a skull and crossbones to begin with? It would've saved everyone a bunch of trouble."

"I think maybe they did," Hank said. "The early *Tawtsee'untsaw Pootseev* stored their elixir in containers that were meant to hold the organs of the dead. Egyptian canopic jars, modified for their purpose. But once they integrated here, they chose another totem of my early ancestors, the bones of animals long extinct. Perhaps it was to caution against tampering with this compound lest it destroy the human race, a symbolic warning against our own extinction."

Painter read some hesitancy in the professor's eyes, as if he wanted to say more. He noted the slightest glance in Rafael's direction. But the Frenchman had survived long in an organization that did not reward a lack of attention to detail.

"What aren't you telling us, *monsieur le professeur*?" Rafael asked.

Painter gave Hank a small nod. They were all long past secrets, at least most secrets. "Tell him."

Hank looked dismayed. "My friend was also able to translate the passage your colleague sent to you. The writing found on the margins of the gold map."

Rafael turned to Painter. "Why is this the first I've heard of this? You explained how the mark on the map revealed Yellowstone, but not this clue?"

"Because it was meaningless information until now."

"It may still be," Hank added. "My colleague could translate only a small section. It reads *'where the wolf and eagle stare.'*"

"What does that mean?" Rafael asked.

Hank shrugged and shook his head.

Another dead end.

Painter checked his watch and stared across the valley. Gray had sent them this clue. According to Kat, he was searching for another, something to do with a buffalo hide. Hopefully they'd all have more luck with that one.

But with the way their luck was running . . .

38

This will have to do . . .

Gray lifted his shovel, the only weapon he had at hand.

"Going primitive on their asses?" Monk asked with a wince, pushing up enough to lean on the wall of the freshly uncovered grave. He looked down to the spreading pool of blood through his blue coveralls. "Bullet went through and through. But I won't be getting my cleaning deposit back on these clothes."

"Can you walk?" Gray asked.

"Hobble, sure. Run, no way."

"Then you stay here."

"I wasn't really planning on going anywhere."

Seichan lowered herself from where she was watching a team move in from the parking lot. "I counted eight to ten. They've moved behind the cabin across the lawn for cover."

"Must think we have weapons," Gray said. "Or they'd have swarmed us by now."

"What's the plan?" Seichan asked.

Both she and Monk looked to him.

"We keep them thinking we have guns—at least long enough for us to get to our rifles. The backhoe is only a few yards away. Its bulk will offer some cover if we can reach it. But we'll be vulnerable climbing out of this hole."

Gray handed Monk his shovel, then twisted around and grabbed the other. "We need some sound effects. Our attackers are edgy, wary, moving in cautiously. So let's spook them some more. Crack the shovels together . . . loudly and rapidly."

Monk got it. "Make them think we're firing at them."

"It'll only work for a couple of seconds. Hopefully long enough for us to reach the backhoe's cab and our rifles."

"Got it."

"Then on my mark."

Gray crouched beside Seichan. Her eyes shone in the shadows of the grave. Her pulse beat at her throat as she stared up at the edge, ready to pounce.

"Go!"

With one shovel propped against the side of the grave, Monk banged the other spade against it with all of his might. The noise was so loud and sudden, it *did* sound like gunfire. Gray leaped to the lip, shoved hard with his arms against the edge, and rolled cleanly out of the grave and to his feet. He sprinted low for the cover of the backhoe.

Seichan kept next to him.

Reaching the momentary safety under the boom arm at the back of the earthmover, Gray checked on her. Her face was flushed, her lips slightly parted. She lifted an eyebrow toward him.

Good enough . . .

Without needing to say a word to each other, they split to opposite sides of the backhoe. Shots were fired at them, but they went wild, hitting the dirt yards away. The assailants were momentarily confused as Monk continued to bang his shovels.

Gray ducked into the cab. He'd left the backhoe idling when he went to check the grave. He slid into the seat, popped the parking brake, and raised the hydraulic stabilizers to free the earthmover.

Seichan grabbed both rifles, leaving the driving to him. She pointed, and he understood. This was not a vehicle to attempt to flee in. Besides, they couldn't leave Monk behind.

Gray raised the large front loader, using it as a shield across the windshield. He'd be driving blind, but at the moment he wasn't worried about sideswiping a car. He trundled out into the lawn. Rounds banged into the loader. He slowly angled toward the rear of the log home while Seichan leaned low out the door and fired under the raised bucket, keeping the men pinned down behind the cabin.

Once they reached the shadow of the cabin, Seichan rolled out.

That was the easy part.

7:07 A.M.

Monk sat in the grave, holding his shovel.

After he'd heard the *real* rifle fire, it was clear that his job here was done. He used the spade as a crutch to help him gain his feet. He wanted to see what was happening. With some effort, he stood up and peeked his head out of the grave—only to have it almost sheered off by a set of giant metal teeth.

Gray had returned with the backhoe, coming in low and fast with the front loader. The noise of the ongoing firefight had covered his approach.

Monk fell back as the scoop dug into the opposite wall of the grave, caving in a good section.

"Climb up!" Gray hollered.

Understanding dawned.

Monk hauled over, climbing through the dirt, and shoulder-rolled into the front loader. Hydraulics whined and raised the arm high while Gray twisted the hoe around. Monk slid inside the bucket, keeping hidden as shots were fired, pinging against the front loader.

Something bumped his shoulder.

He reached over and found an assault rifle.

And it's not even my birthday.

7:08 P.M.

After tossing the rifle into the bucket for Monk, Seichan had fled away from the backhoe and toward the cabin, keeping the stout log home between her and her assailants. But she couldn't count on such protection for long. The team would eventually come at her from both sides, outflanking her.

That must not happen.

Besides, she had to keep the commando team's attention on her while Gray freed Monk. So she sprinted toward the window on this side of the cabin. She raised her rifle and fired three rounds at the panes, striking the glass in a perfect triangle pattern. With the glass weakened, she leaped up, kicked out with her boot, and hurdled through the window. The rest of her body followed. She landed smoothly inside, sliding and skating atop the broken glass, keeping on her feet.

She raised her rifle while still moving.

She had burst into the cabin's main room and had a clear view to the window on the far side. A soldier stared at her, momentarily frozen. She fired—*pop, pop, pop*—and down he went.

She dove to the side, seeking the shelter of a cast-iron stove.

A rifle barrel shoved through the broken window and blindly strafed inside. Seichan ignored it, merely waited, centering her aim. A head poked into view, checking for damage. She fired only once this time. A body tumbled past the window.

With her back to the wall and the stove for shelter, she readied to make a stand. Hopefully she'd bought Gray the time he needed.

Then a grenade flew into the room and bounced across the floor.

It looked like she'd overstayed her welcome.

7:09 A.M.

Bent to peer under the raised front bucket, Gray rode past the cabin as an explosion blew out its windows and tore the door off its hinges. Smoke rolled out. He fumbled with his gears in surprise and worry.

Seichan . . .

Silence fell over the battlefield for a heartbeat—then the noise resumed. Two men popped around the cabin's corner. Monk strafed from his advantage atop his steel castle tower, balancing the front of his rifle between two teeth of the front loader. A third assailant threw a grenade from where the commandos were hiding, lobbing it over the roof toward the backhoe.

But they didn't know that Monk was an expert sharpshooter—or how pissed he was about getting tagged in the gut. Monk swiveled his weapon and pinged the grenade as if he were shooting skeet. It fell back behind the cabin. Another explosion blew back there, casting up dirt and smoke. A helmet rolled into view. It wasn't empty. Screams followed.

Then gunfire.

It sounded like a brief firefight—a one-sided firefight.

After a moment, through the smoke, a figure appeared.

Seichan, covered in blood and with her clothes still smoldering, crossed into view. She must have dived out a back window as the grenade inside the cabin blew. She pointed toward the parking lot. She wasn't indicating that it was time to go. A single figure remained, standing next to a Humvee.

Mitchell Waldorf.

The traitor turned toward the vehicle, but Monk was one step ahead of him. From his perch, he took out the truck's tires and drove Waldorf back from the vehicle. If they could capture him alive—a Guild operative buried deep in the government—he could prove to be invaluable, a resource capable of exposing much about the workings of the organization.

Waldorf must have realized the same thing.

He lifted a pistol to his chin.

Gray swore, goosed the backhoe for more speed. Seichan ran toward him. Waldorf smiled and shouted at them cryptically: "This isn't over!"

The single pistol shot rang brightly.

The top of the man's head erupted in a blast of skull and brain matter. The body slumped to the pavement.

Certainly looks over to me.

Still, the sight of the man's last smile stayed with Gray. A cold fear settled in his gut. What did the bastard mean?

7:19 A.M.

Ten minutes later, Gray and the others were speeding down the Natchez Trace Parkway in the second Humvee they'd stolen that day. They'd taken one of the assault team's vehicles, figuring they'd be less likely to be bothered that way. Plus, they needed the extra room.

Monk lay sprawled across the backseat, stripped to the waist, his belly bandaged in a pressure wrap from an emergency medical kit Gray had found in the back of the Army vehicle. Apparently the assault team had been expecting some injuries. He'd also found a morphine stick and jabbed Monk in the thigh with it.

His friend's eyes already had a happy glaze around their edges.

Seichan, with her cuts and lacerations taped, manned the wheel, leaving Gray to examine the buffalo hide. He'd fetched it from the grave before leaving. The leather was brittle, but he was able to unfold it, revealing an image of a riotous battle dyed into the skin, showing Indians in the midst of waging a great war. Thousands of arrows flew, each delicately but indelibly tattooed into the skin. Elsewhere, pueblos tumbled from cliffs. Faces, feathered and painted, screamed.

Gray remembered Kat's report from Painter, about the destruction of the Anasazi following the theft of sacred totems from the *Tawtsee'untsaw Pootseev*. Was that slaughter—that genocide—being memorialized on this buffalo skin?

This raised a larger question.

Gray had the buffalo hide open to the middle, spread over his lap. A large section was missing. He felt the surface with his fingers. It was much rougher.

"Lewis scraped this part of the artwork off the hide," Gray said.

"Why?" Seichan asked.

"He's written something here in the blank space."

He stared down at the meticulous lines of script, flowing in a large swatch down the middle. While everyone was tending his or her wounds, he had sponged off the old blood that still covered most of the hide. The iron in the hemoglobin had stained the skin, but the words he found there were still legible.

"Only it makes no sense," he said. "It's just a jumble of letters. Either it's a code, or Lewis really had gone mad."

Seichan glanced down at the hide, then back to the road. "Didn't Heisman say Lewis and Jefferson communicated in code? That they exchanged messages in their own private cipher."

"That's true."

Gray pictured Lewis dying over that long night, waiting for Mrs. Grinder to find him. He had plenty of time to write this last message to the world, but what did it contain? Did it name his killer? Was it his last will and testament?

Gray's fingers again rubbed the tough hide, where it had been crudely abraded. What did Lewis erase here? Along the edges, bits of what looked like a map remained: a corner of a river coursing down a mountain, some pass through another range, a piece of a lake. Was this a more detailed map of the terrain around the lost city of the *Tawtsee'untsaw Pootseev*? Did the gold map point to the general position, while this dyed rendition offered a more precise location? Is that how Fortescue was able to find it out west—that is, if he did in fact find it?

Gray put the bits together in his head. "I think the traitor, General Wilkinson, killed Lewis for the gold tablet in his possession, but he never knew about the significance of the buffalo hide. After his assassination, Lewis didn't want it to fall into the wrong hands, so he scraped it clean and left this last cryptic message to the world. He used his own blood and body to hide it."

"Why hide it?"

"Perhaps to keep his murderer from knowing he'd been named. Maybe he hoped the hide would reach Jefferson with his other possessions, and if not, he'd at least leave a final testament to the future. We may never know. All we know is that there's *no* map here to help Painter."

Gray's disposable phone rang. He picked it up. "Kat?"

"How's Monk doing?" she asked, trying to sound strong but cracking at the edges.

"Sleeping like a baby," he assured her.

Gray had already called her as they set off down the road, updating their situation. He'd given her a quick debriefing about the map.

"I have a jet waiting for you at a private airfield near Columbia," she said.

"Good. We should be there in a few minutes. But what about Seichan? Isn't everyone and their brother hunting her?"

"With what's going on in Yellowstone, no one is concerned with the three of you any longer, especially as I've passed on an intelligence briefing implicating Waldorf, explaining how the situation at Fort Knox was an inside job orchestrated by him, and how he'd fabricated his story of terrorists to cover his own actions. That should buy you all enough clearance to get back home."

"We'll be there as quickly as we can." Gray had one other concern. "Have you figured out how Waldorf managed to set up that ambush? How he knew we'd be digging up Lewis's body? As far as I know, only you and Eric Heisman knew about it. Possibly also the curator's assistant, Sharyn."

"As far as I can tell, they're both clear. And to be honest, with everything that's happening so fast, some bit of intel may have reached the wrong ears. And you know the Guild has ears everywhere." Kat sighed. "What about you? Did you make any further progress with the buffalo hide?"

"No. Nothing that can help Painter. I'm afraid he's on his own from here."

39

Kai moved through the forest of otherworldly cones with her shadow chained to her. Ashanda followed so quietly behind, even the handcuffs were silent. Despite the bomb on Kai's wrist, the woman's presence was reassuring in some odd way.

Maybe it's some sort of Stockholm-syndrome kind of thing, Kai thought.

But she sensed that it was more than that. She knew the woman did Rafael's bidding, but there was no enmity in her. In many ways, the woman was as much a prisoner as Kai herself. Weren't they both wearing handcuffs? Plus Kai had to admit that there was a kind of simplicity and beauty in Ashanda's quietness, and in the soft sound of her humming that Kai occasionally overheard—filled always with that sadness under the surface.

Still, Kai could never shed the weight of the bomb on her wrist. It grew heavier with each step, a constant reminder of the danger she was in.

Seeking diversion, she wandered the forest with Ashanda. The world had less than an hour of life remaining to it now. The soldiers from both sides had begun to drift back, empty-handed, after searching their sections of the cliffs.

The words of Hank Kanosh stayed with her, a puzzle to distract.

Where the wolf and eagle stare.

Walking through the forest with these words in her mind, she finally saw it, from the right angle, with the sun just rising. She froze so fast that

Ashanda bumped into her, a rare lapse in the African woman's sharp reflexes.

"Professor Kanosh! Uncle Crowe!"

The two men lifted their heads from where they were bowed.

"Come here!" Kai waved her arm, pulling up short, forgetting for the moment that her limb was handcuffed, but her urgency drew the men, along with Rafael.

"What is it?" Hank asked.

She pointed to the six-foot geyserite cone in front of her. It rose like a pillar. "Look at the top, how it's broken into two sharp points . . . *like ears!* . . . and below it, that thick knob of rock sticking out . . . doesn't that look like a dog's *muzzle?*"

"She's right," Hank said, and stepped closer. "The wolf and eagle are common Indian totems. And these natural pillars are like *stone* totem poles. Feel this."

Uncle Crowe reached his hand up. "They've been carved," he said, awed.

Hank ran a finger down the pillar. "But over time, new accretions of minerals have coated the surface, blurring the imagery."

Rafael spun, leaning on his cane. "We must find that eagle."

Over the next ten minutes, both teams scoured the stone forest. But none of the pillars looked birdlike in any way. The flurry of searching died down to head-scratching and plodding feet.

"We're wasting time," Rafael said. "Maybe we should just search in the direction of the wolf, *non?*"

By now, Kai had made a roundabout hike through the geothermal cones and ended up where she started. She stepped in front of the wolf pillar, putting her back to it, and gazed outward across the valley. The wolf had a long stare. It stretched clear across the longest axis of the basin, eventually striking a distant cliff.

She pointed toward it. "Did anyone search—"

Jordan cried out, gasping in surprise. "Over here!"

She turned, along with everyone else. Jordan stood before an ordinary column of bumpy rock. It looked nothing like an eagle. But he bent down into the meadow grasses and picked up a fluted chunk of rock. He fitted it to the pillar's side, from which it must have broken off. Once the piece was in place, a slight fluting on the other side paired up with it, forming a pair of wings.

Jordan motioned up. "That crest of flowstone near the top, pointed down, could be a beak." He pantomimed by lowering his chin to his chest and looking down his nose.

"It's the second totem pole!" Hank said.

Jordan stared across at Kai, smiling broadly, silently communicating a message: *We both found one.*

Kai returned to her post in front of the wolf and waved for Jordan to do the same. Once in position, she began to walk in the direction of the wolf's stare. Jordan followed the eagle's gaze. Step by step, they continued out across the field, slowly approaching each other, attempting to determine the spot where the stares of the two totems met.

Everyone followed.

Forty yards out, Kai reached out her free arm and took Jordan's hand, the two of them coming together at last. They stood before another cone. Standing four feet high and about three feet wide, it was squat and unremarkable looking, resembling nothing so much as a fat mushroom cap.

"I don't understand," Rafael said.

The Asian geologist came forward and examined the structure from all sides. "Looks like any of the others." He placed his palms atop it and stayed in this position for several breaths. "But it's not vibrating. Even the dormant ones have a palpable tremor to them."

"What does that mean?" Kai said.

He pronounced his judgment. "This is fake."

5:38 A.M.

Full sunrise brightened the day, but not their moods.

"Why don't we just blow it up?" Kowalski asked.

"It may come to that, but let's give Hank and Chin at least a minute to finish their examination."

Still, Painter had to consider Kowalski's option. They had roughly forty minutes until the valley exploded.

"Just in case," Painter asked, "do you have any C4 with you?"

He had asked Kowalski to secure some of the explosive for the flight here, in case they needed to blow their way into a tunnel or passage. But the man had come here with no satchel or pack.

"I have a little," Kowalski admitted. He stepped back and flared out both sides of his ankle-length duster, revealing a vest covered in cubes of C4.

"You call that a little?"

Kowalski glanced down. "Yeah. Should I have brought more?"

Over by the mushroom rock, Hank and Chin stood up together.

Hank gave their assessment. "We think it's meant to act like a plug, perhaps symbolic of an infant's umbilical cord. Either way, we need four strong men to hook their arms around that lip—which I believe is the very reason it's there—and lift straight up."

Kowalski volunteered, as did Major Ryan, Bern, and Chin.

Bending at the knee, the men circled the stone and linked arms.

"The rock is porous," Chin said. "Hopefully we can lift it free."

On a count of three, they all heaved up. From the strain on their faces, the geologist's assessment was proving questionable. But then a grating metallic sound groaned from the earth. The stone plug rose in the men's arms. With the stopper finally loosened, the men easily lifted the stone and sidestepped out of the way to set it down.

Painter moved forward with Hank and Rafael.

"Is that gold?" Jordan asked behind them.

If it was, they'd definitely found the right place.

Painter studied the bottom of the stone stopper. Gold coated the lower foot of the mushroom-shaped rock and rimmed the pit's edges.

"The precious metal must be to keep the plug from corroding into place permanently," Chin said.

Hank studied the hole. "This reminds me of the opening to a *kiva*. The entrance to the underworld."

Kowalski glared down that hole. "Look how well that turned out for us last time."

5:45 A.M.

Hank followed Painter down into the pit. The initial drop was only four feet, but the tunnel below sloped steeply from there, aiming back toward the heart of the geothermal basin and its strange cones. The air was hot but dry, smelling strongly of sulfur.

Painter led the way with a flashlight while a small parade of other people trailed behind him. Chin and Kowalski followed Hank. Behind them came Rafael, assisted by two of Bern's men and Ashanda, who by force brought Kai along. Everyone else stayed topside.

Jordan agreed to stay on top of the pit to watch Kawtch—though doing so brought an ominous chill as he remembered Nancy Tso and the fate of the dog's last caretaker.

The remaining armed military men on the surface stayed divided, grouping on opposite sides of the opening.

The tunnel sank steadily deeper, growing ever hotter. Hank touched one of the walls with his palm. It didn't burn, but the rock was definitely hot, reminding him of the hellfires burning below—both literally and figuratively.

Was this how the world ended?

After another minute, Hank thought he might have to turn back, his lungs on fire. How much deeper must they go? It felt like they were a quarter mile underground, but most likely only half that.

"We're here," Painter said at last.

The tunnel squeezed into a final choke point. Here the walls pinched close together, requiring them to sidle through sideways for the last couple of feet.

Painter went first.

Hank followed—then heard Painter gasp loudly as he broke free, sounding both amazed and horrified. Once he was through, Painter stepped rigidly to the side.

Hank pushed after him, stepping out and moving clear for the others. Still, his feet stumbled in shock. He had to reach to the wall behind him to keep himself steady. His other hand rose to cover his mouth.

"*Mon Dieu!*" Rafael wheezed out.

Kowalski swore.

As the rest of the party entered, the glow of more and more flashlights illuminated the vast chamber, pushing back the darkness.

Mummified bodies, thousands of them, covered the floor of a vast cavern, rising at least seven stories high. The desiccated figures seemed to have arranged themselves in rows, radiating out from a massive temple in the center like spokes on a wheel.

Hank struggled to keep his attention focused on the poor souls who ended their lives here. Like those they had seen in Utah, they all seemed garbed in Native American attire: feathers, bones, loose skirts, leather moccasins, and breechcloths. Their hair was worn long, often braided and decorated, but Hank witnessed shades of every color, certainly plenty of raven-haired men and women, but also blond, chestnut, even fiery red.

The *Tawtsee'untsaw Pootseev*.

Again dagger blades, mostly steel but several made of bone, littered the floor or were clutched in bony grips.

So much death.

All to keep a secret, to protect a world against a lost alchemy.

Staring up now, Hank understood the potential source of that science. A temple rose before him, built of native slabs of rock mortared together. It climbed six stories high, seeming to stretch toward the ceiling and filling the center of the massive chamber.

He knew what this place was.

Or rather what it had been modeled after.

Even the facade's dimensions seemed to be correct.

Twenty cubits wide, thirty-five cubits tall.

Right out of the Bible.

But it wasn't the dimensions that made him certain. It was the temple in its entirety. Stone steps led up to a porch, the entrance framed by two mighty pillars—the famous Boaz and Jachin—only rather than brass, these two columns were made of gold, as was the massive bowl standing before the temple.

The golden chalice rose nine feet tall and twice that wide, resting on the backs of twelve oxen. The original was named the Brazen Sea, or Molten Sea. It was a fitting name for this copy. The bowl sat in the middle of a steaming hot spring that rose from the floor and fed into the basin. Water spilled over its top to return to the pool before spilling over the top again in an endless cycle.

"What is that place?" Kai asked. "Looks like Pueblo construction but the shape's all wrong."

Hank shook his head. "The shape's perfect."

Painter looked aghast at the place.

How can you deny the truth now? Hank wondered.

"Is that what I think it is?" Painter asked, clearly recognizing it, too. "Or at least a Pueblo version of it?"

Hank nodded, exultant. "It's Solomon's Temple."

40

Major Ashley Ryan didn't like babysitting.

"Just stay out of our way," Ryan warned the Ute kid. He pointed to a boulder at the edge of a stand of pines. "Sit there. And make sure that dog doesn't lift his leg on my pack."

Jordan scowled, but obeyed.

The National Guard and the Indians in Utah did not get along—or, at least, not as far as this National Guardsman was concerned. Ryan still remembered the ruckus that had gone down before the explosion in the mountains. If the Indians just knew their place like everyone else did, they'd all get along fine.

Ryan stared across the field to where Bern and his mercenaries had staked a claim thirty yards from the hole. The blond giant had three men; so did Ryan. Even odds if you didn't count the kid and dog.

And Ryan didn't.

Bern stared his way, his hands on his hips, eyeballing the competition just as studiously. Then the big Aryan glanced toward the sky. A moment later, Ryan heard it, too.

Another chopper.

The constant bell beat of their rotors had already set his head to pounding, his eyeteeth to aching. A trio of choppers was circling above, ready with blast boxes. The pilots had already placed four insulated crates on the ground, preparing for fast handoffs and quick bunny hops out of the park.

Ryan checked his watch. *Twenty minutes.* That did not leave a lot of margin for error. As he listened, the sound of a second helicopter joined the first. He stared up as the first appeared, sweeping low over the ridge and diving down.

What the hell? Has something happened?

Then, from the back of the transport helo, heavy lines suddenly came coiling down, followed just as quickly by men. They wore the same black scare-gear as Bern's mercenaries.

Fuck.

Ryan swung and ducked, moving instinctively. He heard the crack of the pistol at the same time as a round buzzed over his head. Down on one arm, like a linebacker, he stared back at Bern. The blond man held his pistol pointed.

The gun blasted again.

One of Ryan's men flew off his feet and skidded on his back in the dirt.

He had a hole where his eye used to be.

Ryan bolted for the boulders where he'd sent the boy. His instinct was to protect the civilian. But he also had two men under his watch.

"Get to cover! Now!"

They had to find a castle to defend. The nest of boulders would do until he could figure out something better. Rounds blasted into the dirt around him. Ahead, Jordan had already ducked into hiding behind the rocks.

His two men—Marshall and Boydson—flanked Ryan, running low.

All three hit the boulders and dove down.

Ryan freed his rifle and found a crevice between two rocks to use as a roost. He stared as eight men vacated the first chopper. Moments later, the second dipped down like a deadly hummingbird and unloaded the same number.

That made it twenty to three.

Those were not good odds.

5:51 A.M.

Rafael checked his watch.

Bern should be securing the surface by now.

He tried to listen for the spatter of gunfire, but they were too far underground to hear. Plus, the large gold fountain they'd passed on the way to the temple was burbling and splashing over the bowl's lip, accompanied by gaseous popping sounds.

Rafe hurried past, holding his breath, followed by Ashanda and the girl. His two bodyguards kept several steps ahead, creating a shield between him and the others.

Sigma's geologist glanced back to the bubbling gold bath. "They've tapped into the geothermal currents running through here. This whole place must be resting at the edge of that steam engine driving the basin's natural hydraulics."

But eventually even the geologist was drawn forward, staring at the giant temple. It seemed to grow taller the closer they got, supported by gold pillars adorned with sculpted sheaves of wheat and stalks of corn, all wrapped with flowering vines.

Could this truly be a model of Solomon's Temple? Rafe wondered.

A part of him thrilled at that thought, but a much larger part sensed the danger pressing down upon them all.

The professor spoke as they climbed the stairs up to the front porch of the ancient structure. "Solomon's Temple—often called the First Temple of Jerusalem—was the first religious structure to be built atop Mount Zion. Rabbinic scholars say it lasted for four centuries until its destruction in the sixth century BCE. It stood during the time that the Assyrians scattered the ten tribes of Israel to the winds."

The old man waved an arm toward the structure before them. "This was their place of worship. But it was also a citadel of knowledge and science. King Solomon was said in many stories to wield magical, otherworldly powers. But what is one man's magic is another man's science."

Kanosh led them forward in space, while in his mind he went back in time. "Perhaps these *Tawtsee'untsaw Pootseev* were once magi in service to Solomon, bringing together Jewish mystical practices and Egyptian science. Until they were scattered by the invading Assyrians. After they arrived in the New World, they did their best to preserve the memory of that great temple to religion and science, borrowing the techniques of the ancient Pueblo people to construct it."

Reaching the porch, Professor Kanosh hurried forward toward the open doors.

"The first chamber should be the *Hekhal* or Holy Place," Hank said.

They all pushed across a vestibule into the first chamber. It was empty, its walls lined by pine logs, fashioned elaborately with animal totems: bear, elk, wolf, sheep, eagle.

"In Solomon's Temple, this chamber was decorated with carvings of cherubim, flowers, and palm trees. But these ancient builders clearly absorbed the physical characteristics of their new home into their design."

"But it's empty," Painter said, and checked his watch.

"I know." Kanosh pointed to another set of stairs that led up to a doorway partitioned by gold chains. "If we're looking for the temple's most sacred objects, they'll be there. A room called *Kodesh Hakodashim,* the Holy of Holies, the inner sanctum of Solomon's Temple. It is in here that Solomon kept the Ark of the Covenant."

Painter led the way, buffeted forward by the pressure of time. The others chased him up the steps. One of Rafe's guards offered Rafe an arm to help him follow. He did not refuse it.

He heard gasps ahead and hobbled faster, striking the stone floor hard with his cane, angry at his disability. Ashanda stepped forward with her young charge and held the chain curtain open for him. He ducked through on his own, releasing the guard's arm.

He stumbled into a room that left him trembling in awe. Gold covered every surface, floor to ceiling. Massive plates—three stories high—made up the walls, like gargantuan versions of those smaller gold tablets. And like those miniatures, writing covered the walls here in their entirety, millions of lines, flowing all around.

Hank had fallen to his knees between two fifteen-foot-tall sculptures of bald eagles, upright, side by side, wings outstretched to touch the walls on either side and tip to tip in the middle. "In Solomon's Temple, these were giant cherubim, winged angels."

Even Painter had halted his headlong rush forward to gawk. "They look like the eagles on the Great Seal. Did someone show Jefferson a drawing of this space?"

Hank just shook his head, too moved to speak anymore.

Rafe felt a similar stirring—how could he not?—but he knew his duty. "Record all of this," he ordered one of his men, sweeping his cane to encompass the walls. "This must not be lost."

"But where are the caches of nanotech?" Painter asked.

"That is a puzzle I will leave to you, Monsieur Crowe."

That cache was going to blow anyway, so Rafe saw no need to chase down that trail. The true treasure was here: the accumulated knowledge of the ancients. He ran a palm along the wall, casting his eyes from roof to ceiling, trying to preserve it all with his unique eidetic memory, to bank it away into his organic hard drive. He moved step by step around the room, lost in the rivers of ancient script. Here must be their history, their ancient sciences, their lost art, all recorded in gold.

He must possess it.

It could be his family's entry to the True Bloodline.

A shout rose to the side, but he did not turn.

It was Sigma's geologist. "Director, there's a door back here—and a body."

5:55 A.M.

Deafened by the continuous firefight, Major Ashley Ryan did not hear the small team flanking his nest of boulders. Pinned down, he and his two men did their best to hold their castle—picking off targets when they could, driving back raids and attempts to swarm them.

Bern's commandos had control of the valley floor, holding the entrance to the tunnel below. Ryan could not even reach his men's packs and extra ammo.

Then a sharp barking drew his attention back and to the left.

The alarm saved his life—all of their lives.

Ryan flicked a gaze in that direction. Spotted a shadowy trio of commandos slip low out of the dark tree line and race low toward his team's flank.

The dog leaped atop the boulder and bayed a challenge.

Ryan rolled, freeing his rifle from the boulder roost. He used the distraction caused by the dog to pop the lead assassin in the face with two rounds. The man went down. The other two commandos fired. The dog yelped, one foreleg shattering under him. The dog toppled off the boulder and hit the grass.

Motherf—

Ryan raised himself higher, exposing himself, and squeezed the trigger hard, strafing in automatic mode. By now, his two men had entered the fray, swinging around and firing. A brief barrage and the two commandos crumpled outside the castle of boulders. Their walls had not been breached, but it had been close. And they all had a problem.

"I'm out," Boydson said, discharging a smoking magazine from his rifle.

Marshall checked his weapon and shook his head. "One more volley then I'm spent."

Ryan knew he wasn't in any better shape.

Bern bellowed in German across the field, his voice rife with bloodlust. He must know their quarry had been beaten down, that they were running low on options and ammo. Ryan shifted forward again and peered out.

The enemy force—still fifteen strong—was readying for a final charge. Bern was going to lead it, standing exposed fifty yards away, fearless in his body armor and confident in his firepower.

A big arm pointed toward Ryan's position.

Ryan settled his cheek to his rifle.

Here we go.

9:56 P.M.
Tokyo, Japan

Riku Tanaka sat in front of the computer deep within the labyrinthine structure of the euphemistically named Public Security Intelligence Agency, Japan's premiere espionage organization. Riku could not even say what floor he was on—*likely underground, from the annoying hum of the air-conditioning*—or even what building.

He did not care.

His hand rested in the palm of Janice Cooper.

Since their rescue out of the frigid depths of the Super-Kamiokande detector's tank, he'd seldom been out of physical contact with her. Her presence helped him maintain his balance in the world, like an anchor securing a ship in questionable seas, while his psyche rebuilt itself.

They waited for the latest data from the various subatomic particle labs to collate through his refined software program. With the point of critical mass approaching, unknown variables were falling away, allowing a more exact estimate of the time when the explosion would occur.

Finally, the calculations were complete.

The answer glowed on the screen.

Riku's hand flexed, squeezing hard.

Janice returned his hold, needing an anchor now as much as he did.

"We're doomed."

5:56 A.M.
Yellowstone National Park

Painter crouched beside the body on the ground.

The man lay on his back atop a bison hide, hands folded to his chest.

The Native American garb on the man's mummified remains was brighter than the bodies outside. A pearlescent ring of white eagle feathers circled his bare, thin neck. A long braid of gray hair still had bits of dried flowers, where someone had placed them with great and loving care. A richly beaded cape—acting as a burial shawl—wrapped his bony shoulders.

This man had not committed suicide. Someone had interred him here in the Holy of Holies, a great honor.

Painter could guess why.

Two objects were placed under his shrunken, pale hands.

Under one, a white wooden cane, topped with a silver knob imprinted with a French fleur-de-lis symbol.

Under the other, a birch-paper journal bound in hide.

It was the body of Archard Fortescue.

Painter didn't need to read the journal to know that the man must have stayed here after the Lewis and Clark party left, intending to be the guardian and protector of this great secret. He must have gone native while he lived with the Indians, been accepted by them—and from the care with which his body had been laid, well loved.

Painter turned away. "Rest well, my friend. Your long vigil is over."

Chin stood by an open door at the back of the room. His words were awash with terror. "Director, you need to see this."

Painter crossed to Chin, who pointed his flashlight out the back door of the Holy of Holies. Hank and Kowalski joined them.

Beyond the threshold, steps led down to an expansive room that stretched far back and wrapped to either side of the inner sanctum.

"This is the temple's treasure room," Hank said.

Painter gaped, unable to speak.

Instead, it was Kowalski who summarized their situation the most succinctly.

"We're fucked."

5:57 A.M.

With his cheek against his rifle's stock, Major Ashley Ryan peered through his scope. Fifty yards away, Bern swept his arm down, his face bright with the flush of the final kill. Across the valley, commandos rose from hiding, preparing to charge the castle.

"Major?" Marshall asked.

Ryan had no consoling words for the kid. Or for Boydson, who sat slumped with his back to the boulders, clutching a dagger in his hand, his last weapon. His two men were barely into their twenties. Boydson had a new baby boy. Marshall had plans to propose to his girlfriend the following week, had even picked out the ring.

Ryan kept his focus forward.

He intended to take out as many of the enemy as possible, to make them pay in blood for each of his men's lives.

He studied Bern through his scope, needing him to be closer. He did not have ammunition to waste. Each round from here on had to count.

I want you.

Ryan, though, would not get the honor of this kill.

As he peered, Bern's hands suddenly clutched his throat. Blood spouted thickly from his mouth. An arrow had pierced through his neck. The big man fell to his knees as a savage whooping and hollering rose all around the valley. It echoed eerily off the canyon walls, causing Ryan's hair to practically stand on end.

A crashing behind him made Ryan roll himself around. He swung up his weapon, coming close to shooting Jordan in the chest. The young man bounded briskly up to the major. Ryan thought the kid had been buried farther back in the nest of boulders—where he'd been ordered to remain.

But Jordan was winded, his clothes damp and torn in places. Clearly Ryan's instructions had been ignored.

Jordan skidded next to him as the screams grew louder, setting Ryan's teeth on edge.

"I've got movement out in the woods!" Marshall yelled. "Shadows all around. Every direction!"

"Sorry that took so long," Jordan said. "We didn't want to be spotted until we had the valley completely encircled."

The young man shifted up and stared beyond the boulders.

As the major's gaze turned in the same direction, he noted that the kid seemed to be purposefully avoiding eye contact. Across the valley floor, the remaining members of Bern's team, leaderless now as the giant lay flat on his face in the grass, milled about in the valley. Some ducked back into cover.

But there was no cover any longer.

A sharper cry pierced the valley, and a volley of arrows swept out of the forest and dropped from every direction, hailing down atop the commandos' positions. Screams of shock and bloody pain now joined the war cries echoing off the wall.

Rifles fired at shadows.

Return fire followed from the forest.

Commandos fell one by one. Ryan could now make out shadows as the hidden hunters moved in. They wore no recognizable uniform. He spotted some military outfits, but most of the men simply wore jeans, boots, and T-shirts—though a few had on nothing but breechclouts and moccasins.

But they all had one thing in common.

They were Native Americans.

With the war clearly won, but not wanting to take any chances, Ryan waved to his men. "Get to our packs, haul them over here."

In case things went sour again, he wanted ammunition.

Jordan sank back down, breathless, and explained. "Before flying here, Painter had Hank and me roust up men we trusted fully from our tribes, from others. He arranged transports and helicopters. Once Painter knew where in Yellowstone we were going, he had our forces dropped into place before everyone got here. He didn't trust that the French guy wouldn't pull something like this."

Damned right, there . . .

"Our guys kept hidden way back in the valley. They came close to being spotted a few times, but we know how to move through the woods unseen when we want to. Once the fighting started, I went out to report on force levels and positions to coordinate the attack."

Ryan stared at Jordan with new eyes. *Who was this kid?* But he was still pissed.

"Why didn't Crowe tell me? Why didn't he involve the Guard to begin with?"

Jordan shook his head. "Seems there was some concern about in-filtration. I don't really know. Some problems out east with traitors in the government. Painter wanted to go old school here, sticking to his blood."

Ryan sighed. *Maybe that was for the best.*

Jordan searched around the castle. "Where's Kawtch?"

Ryan realized he hadn't seen the mutt since he'd gotten shot. He felt a flicker of guilt for his disrespectful lack of concern. The dog had saved his life.

Jordan spotted the small body in the weeds, not moving.

The kid rushed over. "Oh, Kawtch."

Before Ryan could offer sympathy or apology, Boydson came running up, threw down his pack, and held out the radio. "It's for you. Washington has been trying to raise you."

Washington?

The major lifted his radio. "Major Ryan here."

"Sir, this is Captain Kat Bryant." Ryan could feel the urgency in her voice pouring steel into his spine. Something was wrong. "Do you have access to Painter Crowe?"

Ryan looked over to the hole. With no radio contact through solid rock, someone would have to go down there. "I can reach him, but it might take a few minutes."

"We don't have a few minutes. I need you to get word to Painter im-mediately. Tell him the physicists have revised their timetable based on cleaner data. The cache will explode at six-oh-four, not six-fifteen. Is that understood?"

Ryan checked his watch. "That's in four minutes!" He lowered the radio and pointed at Jordan. Ryan needed to send someone Painter would trust without hesitation. "Kid, how fast can you run?"

6:00 A.M.

Painter pointed his flashlight into the treasure vault behind the Holy of Holies.

Hundreds of stone plinths supported golden skulls of every shape and size: fanged cats, ivory-tusked mastodons, domed cave bears, even what looked like the massive skull of an allosaurus or some other saurian beast. Amid them also stood scores of canopic jars, some etched with ancient Egyptian motifs, possibly originals carried over from their ancient home. But there were clearly others that had been modeled on local animals: wolves again, but also birds of every beak, mountain lion and other cats, grizzly bears, even a curled rattlesnake.

"We'll never be able to move all this in time," Chin said. "We have only fifteen minutes."

Kowalski nodded. "Time for Plan B, boss." He looked over at Painter. "You do have a Plan B, right?"

Painter headed back into the main temple. "We can try to move as much as we can. Maybe lessen the chance it'll ignite Yellowstone's caldera."

Kowalski followed, pitching other ideas like hardballs. "How about we come down here with blowtorches? Doesn't heat kill this stuff?"

"Take too long," Chin said. "And I don't think a flame's even hot enough."

"Then how about we drop a bunker buster up top."

Painter fielded that one. "We're too deep."

"What about the nuclear option?"

"Last resort," Painter said. "And we might end up causing what we're trying to prevent."

Kowalski tossed his arms high. "There's got to be something we can do."

As they entered the Holy of Holies chamber, a thin figure burst through the gold chain curtain. He skidded to a stop, gaping momentarily at all the gold.

Kai stepped toward him. "Jordan . . . ?"

He held up a hand, panting to catch his breath. "Washington called . . . timetable got shortened . . . stuff is gonna blow at six-oh-four."

Painter didn't have to check his watch. His internal clock had been counting down all on its own. *Two minutes.* All eyes stared at him for some solution, some insight.

They were out of options—except for one.

He pointed to the door. "Run!"

41

Two minutes . . .

Kai raced with the others through the massive temple. Jordan stuck to her side, which helped keep her on her feet. A part of her simply wanted to crash to her knees and give up. But Jordan would glance her way, silently urging her to stay with him—and she did.

Plus she had another massive incentive.

Ashanda was running alongside her like a juggernaut. If Kai fell, she was sure the woman wouldn't even slow; she'd simply drag her along. Past Ashanda's shoulder, Rafael was being carried between his two soldiers, hanging from their shoulders.

The group reached the exit to the temple.

Kai's uncle and the team geologist led the way, bounding down steps two at a time. Despite their speed, they were deep into a discussion. The geologist pointed to the boiling fountain. Uncle Crowe shook his head.

Behind them all came Kowalski. His large form was not meant for sprinting. He wheezed in the hot air, his face glowing and running with sweat.

"We'll never make it to the surface," Kai mumbled as she and Ashanda hurried down the steps.

Jordan refused to give in to despair. "The mouth of the tunnel is pinched. If we get past that squeeze point, we should be okay."

Kai didn't know if such an assessment was based on anything more than hope, but she took it to heart. *Just get to the tunnel.*

With a goal set, she felt better, ran faster.

A cry sounded behind her. Ashanda skidded to a stop. Kai wasn't as fast and got pulled off her feet by the handcuffs linking them together. Jordan braked and came back to them.

Behind them, Rafael and his two guards tumbled down the stone steps, landing in a tangled heap.

Ashanda headed back to them. Kai had no choice but to follow.

The soldiers disentangled themselves. One limped away a couple of steps, wincing on a twisted ankle. The other simply bounded to his feet, looked around in wild-eyed panic, and fled toward the distant tunnel.

The other guard watched him, seemed to reconsider his own options, and with a hopping, painful bounce to his step, chased after his comrade.

Jordan called to them: "What're you doing? Help us!"

Uncle Crowe and the geologist stopped as the guards ran past.

Kowalski waved Painter and Chin on. "Go! I got this guy!"

He bent to pick Rafael off the ground. The Frenchman screamed as Kowalski lifted him. Both of the man's legs were canting at odd angles. Broken. Startled, Kowalski almost dropped him again, not expecting such injuries from a simple tumble.

But Rafael hung on with one arm. *"Merci,"* he said, his brow pebbling with pained sweat. One hand palmed his ribs on that side, probably broken, too. He pointed his other arm, his eyes catching apologetically on Ashanda. Like Kai, he knew she wouldn't leave him.

"Go," he said, both to Kowalski and Ashanda.

They set off again.

Uncle Crowe and the geologist slowed enough not to leave the others totally behind. Kai's group gave chase, but that small delay may have doomed them all.

Less than a minute left.

"Run ahead!" Kai urged Jordan.

"No, I'll stay with you."

She feared for him. "Go, or we'll all get bottlenecked at that squeeze. Get there and get through. I'll be there. I promise."

Jordan wanted to stay, but he read the determination in Kai's eyes. "You'd better be!" he called back as he took off.

Kai looked over her shoulder. Kowalski was falling farther and farther behind, burdened by Rafael—who gasped and cried out every few steps, though he was clearly biting his tongue to keep from doing so.

Ashanda noted this, too.

The big woman finally fell back, taking Kai with her.

Oh no.

Ashanda scooped Rafael away from Kowalski and nodded to him to go.

He hesitated, but Kai waved him away with her free arm. They continued, moving faster. Kowalski led now, but Ashanda kept pace with him, even while carrying Rafael.

Uncle Crowe was waiting at the mouth of the tunnel. He wheeled his arm for them to hurry. "Twelve seconds!"

Kowalski eked out a bit more speed from his heavy legs and reached the tunnel.

"Get inside! Go as far down the tunnel as possible!"

Uncle Crowe rushed forward to Kai and the others. Trying to get them moving faster, he took Rafael and swung him bodily around like a rag doll. A bone snapped with an audible *crack*. A small cry escaped from the man, but nothing more.

"Seven seconds!"

Uncle Crowe pushed Rafael through the crack as if he were stuffing garbage down a chute. He then turned to Kai.

"Go!" she screamed, and rattled her cuff. "You're in the way! We have to go through together!"

He understood and flew into the tunnel. She doubted he even touched the walls.

"Five!" he called back.

Suddenly Kai was lifted off her feet, picked up by the shoulders, as Ashanda charged the choke point.

"Four!"

Kai twisted sideways as the woman shoved her through the crack. Rock scraped her back, her cheek.

"Three!"

She fell to her knees in the tunnel, wrenching her shoulder.

Rafael lay crumpled next to her. He held his arm out to her.

"Two!"

Ashanda pushed her large form into the crack—and stopped.

Rafael stared up at her, some understanding filling his eyes. "Don't, *mon chaton noir.*"

Kai didn't understand.

"One!"

Ashanda smiled softly as the world exploded behind her.

6:04 A.M.

Painter dove forward and shielded Kai with his body. The blast sounded like the end of the world, accompanied by the burst of a supernova from within the far cavern. Brightness blazed into the tunnel, piercing through the small gaps like a flurry of sodium lasers around the form of the woman who was jammed into the crack.

He pictured the volume of nanotech erupting, tearing a hole in the universe and collapsing the tunnel. But he also remembered the first explosion in the Utah mountains, how the concussive force of the blast was minor, killing only the anthropologist and none of the nearby witnesses.

That wasn't the true danger.

He rolled off Kai as the detonation echoed away and the blazing light dimmed back to darkness, leaving only traces burned into his retina. He blinked away the glare.

Kai sat up from where she'd been pinned down. "Ashanda . . ."

The woman hung limply in the crack, but she still breathed.

"Help her, please . . ." Rafael begged.

Painter stepped past Kai, who still remained tethered to the woman.

Reaching up, careful of where he touched, he drew her out of the crack and let her weight pull her to the floor. He leaned her against the wall next to Rafael.

Moving back, he stared past the crack into the far chamber. Chin had returned and pointed his flashlight. It was unable to penetrate that darkness. A black fog seemed to fill the space: rock dust, smoke, and something Painter feared should never be in this world. The nano-nest. As some of it settled, he noted a deeper shadow back there, the mass of the ancient temple. But rather than growing clearer as the fog continued to dissipate, the dark shadow faded, dissolving away, as if it were an illusion.

A groan drew him back to the tunnel.

Ashanda's eyes fluttered open, her head lolled back, as she struggled to regain consciousness.

"She was trying to protect us," Kai said.

Painter suspected that her altruism was meant more for Rafael than for anyone else—but maybe not. Either way, they'd all benefited.

"She did protect us," he agreed.

Even now, he watched the woman's clothing on the side closest to the blast begin to lose color and drift down in flakes of fine ash. The dark skin beneath grew speckled as if it had been sprinkled with fine chalk—then those dots grew bigger, spreading, beginning to weep blood.

She was contaminated, whether by Chin's nanobots or some other corrosive process. Using her own body like a shield, she had blocked the rain of particulate corruption from reaching them.

But the tunnel would not be safe for long.

The choke point at the end had begun to crumble, the rock turning to sand and sifting away.

"It's happening much faster than in Utah," Chin said. "A nano-nest of this size will likely grow exponentially from here."

Painter pointed up the tunnel. "Grab Kowalski. You know what you have to do."

"Yes, sir." Still, Chin's eyes looked longingly at the sight of the process as it began to spread, eating its way through all matter, his expression at once fascinated and horrified. Then he shoved around and headed up, collecting the others and herding them ahead of him.

Only Jordan refused to comply. He slipped under the geologist's arm and came back down. "Are you okay?" he asked Kai.

She lifted her tethered arm.

Painter returned his attention to Rafael. "Give us the code for the handcuffs."

But the Frenchman's gaze remained fixed on his woman. She had regained a dazed, weak consciousness, her head leaning crookedly against the wall, staring back at him. Her breathing was shallow and rapid from pain. Blood flowed down her contaminated side, which was missing skin now, showing muscle.

"What have you done, Ashanda?" he murmured.

"Rafael, we need the code for the handcuffs."

The bastard seemed deaf to Painter's pleas, but Ashanda lifted her good arm a trembling fraction of an inch and let it drop, her desire clear.

Painter remained silent, knowing he could offer no better argument.

So he waited, watching the world slowly dissolve around him.

6:07 A.M.

Shattered on the stone floor, Rafael gazed into Ashanda's eyes. She had sacrificed all for him. All of his life, he'd fought to prove himself, to others, to his family, even to himself—to rise above a shame that was no fault of his own. But in those dark eyes, such effort was never necessary. She saw him, watching in her silences, always there, always so strong.

In this moment he finally truly saw her.

The knowledge shattered him worse than any fall could have done.

"What have I done to you?" he whispered to her in French.

He reached to her cheek.

"Be careful," Painter said, sounding far away.

Rafael was beyond such concerns. He knew his injuries were severe, that he was growing cold and slipping into shock. He tasted blood on his tongue with each breath, coming from a ripped lung and fractured ribs. Both legs had multiple breaks, likely his hip, too.

He was done for, but he would last long enough.

For her.

He brushed his knuckles along her cheekbone, down the line of her jaw, touching the hollow of her throat.

Her eyes closed ever so slightly.

Her lips shifted into a ghost of a smile.

Oh, my love . . .

He pulled her gently into his arms, felt the hot blood along her back, the tremble of agony. She tried to push him away, ever protecting him.

No, let me be the stronger one . . . just this one time.

Whether hearing his plea or simply too weak, Ashanda collapsed with a sigh against him. Her head rested on his shoulder, her eyes looking up at him with a joy he'd never seen before. He cursed himself for denying such simple happiness to her—and to himself.

A voice nagged in his ear.

To be done with it, he spoke five numbers, the code to the handcuffs.

A shuffling followed. He heard two young voices, hopeful and intense and full of such raw affection. Then they took that brightness and fled away.

Once alone, he leaned down and gently kissed those lips. He felt them quiver under his. He held her this way for an eternity, feeling each breath against his cheeks . . . growing slower, slower . . . then at last nothing.

He felt the same corruption now eating into him, through the palm that held her, the shoulder that supported her, even the lips that kissed her. But it was a wonderful pain. It came from her, and he would have it no other way.

So he held her to him.

A voice intruded. He turned to find Painter still there at his side. He thought the man had left. What had seemed an eternity must have been only minutes.

"What do you want, Monsieur Crowe?" he whispered coarsely, feeling parts of himself drifting away.

"Who are you?" Painter asked, crouched a few feet away like some vulture.

Rafael leaned his head back and closed his eyes, knowing what the man truly wanted. Though his body was spent, his mind remained sharp.

"I know who you seek, but they are not me. Nor my family." He opened his eyes to stare at Painter. It hurt to talk, but he knew he must. "What you seek has no name. Not formally."

"Then what do you know about them?"

"I know your oldest families here in America have roots that trace back to the *Mayflower*. That is nothing, mere hiccups in the march of history. Off in Europe, families have unbroken roots that go back two, three, four times as far. But there is a handful—a chosen few—whose heritage goes back *much* further. Some claim to be able to trace their lineage to the time before Christ, but who knows? I do know that they've been gathering wealth, power, knowledge, while manipulating history, hiding behind shifting faces, always changing. They are the *secret* within all secret societies."

This seemed to raise an amused croak inside him—painful as it was to emit.

"Others have named these bloodlines *les familles de l'étoile,* the star families. I hear they once numbered more, but now there is but *one*, the True Bloodline. To stay strong, they seek to rebuild from younger families, like my own, families of the upper echelon."

"Echelon?"

"A ranking system among the younger families who seek to join the Bloodline. *First* tier is designated by a single mark: the star and moon of the oldest *mystère*. The *second* adds the Freemasons' square and compass. Another *énigmatique* order, *non*? And for our service in America, the Saint Germaine clan was granted entry to the *third* level. We were chosen— *I was chosen*—because of our knowledge of nanotechnology. An honor." He coughed thickly, tasting blood. "Come see."

Rafael turned his head and weakly lifted his hand to part the fall of hair that hid his mark. The third symbol had been added just days ago, inked in crimson around the older two, to mark his new elevation.

He heard Painter gasp, knowing what the man saw. In the center of the tattoo, the star and moon . . . encircling it, the square and compass . . . and around them both . . .

"The shield of the Knights Templar," Painter whispered. "Another secret order."

"And there are more, or so I've heard." Rafael let his arm drop heavily. "As I said, we are the secret within *all* secret societies. This third mark brings my family one step closer to joining the True Bloodline on that highest pedestal. Or at least it would have." Again a painful chuckle croaked forth. "Failure is severely punished."

Painter remained quiet for a long breath, then spoke. "But to what end? What is the goal of all of this?"

"Ah, even I do not know everything. Some things you'll need to discover on your own. I'll tell you no more because I know no more."

He closed his eyes and turned his face away.

After a time, Painter rose and headed back up the tunnel.

Once alone, Rafael Saint Germaine leaned down and gave one last kiss to his love, holding it until he felt those lips dissolve away—taking him with them.

42

Painter burst out of the darkness into light.

He didn't know what to think of Rafael's claims: grand delusions, lies, madness, or truth. All he knew was that the danger below had to be stopped.

While talking to the Frenchman, Painter had stared out into the cavern. Nothing remained. No bodies, no temple. As rock turned to sand and sand to dust, what he saw there offended him at a fundamental level, frightened him to the core of his being. Steps away, there had swirled a storm of pure entropy, where order became chaos, where solidity had no meaning.

The nano-nest had to be destroyed.

In the short time he'd been down below, the Fairyland Basin had changed into a bustle of frantic activity. Helicopters dotted the valley floor, ferrying everyone clear. They had one last chance to stop the growing cancer below from eating its way down into the depths of the volcanic caldera. And that hope hinged on striking while the nano-nest was still relatively small and confined.

Painter strode across the valley toward where Chin and Kowalski were working. It looked like they were ready.

As he passed one of the helicopters, he spotted Kai and Jordan seated next to Hank. Kai turned and waved, but Jordan's attention was on her alone. The professor leaned down and accepted a blanket-wrapped package from Major Ryan. Hank gingerly settled the dog to his lap, so as not to jar the broken leg. Ryan had insisted that Kawtch receive attention from the field medic before his own wounds were treated.

As Painter headed away, the chopper lifted off behind him, roaring skyward and kicking up a whirlwind. He joined Chin and Kowalski.

"Are you ready?" Painter asked.

"Just about done here." Kowalski sat cross-legged on the ground. Coiled at his feet was a spool of detonation cord threaded through cubes of C4. "It's just like stringing popcorn."

"Remind me not to come over to your house for Christmas."

He shrugged. "Christmas is okay. It's Fourth of July that scares most people away."

Painter could only imagine.

Kowalski plus fireworks. Not a good combination.

Chin stood beside the ten-foot geyserite cone called the Pitcher's Mound. He had topographical maps spread out on the chalky fields of sinter, along with scans of the basin that had been done with ground-penetrating radar.

"This cone's the best spot," Chin said. "GPR scans show this is the closest access point to the plug blocking the geothermal vent below. Release that and the superheated cauldron suppressed deep in the earth will come roaring up like a sleeping dragon."

The idea had been Painter's, but the execution was all Chin and Kowalski. The geologist had earlier described how two forces had shaped Yellowstone: the volcanic eruptions from deep underground and the shallower hydrothermal explosions. While they needed intense *heat* to kill the cancer below, a volcanic eruption was not an option, definitely not here. So the next best thing was to attempt a hydrothermal explosion.

Painter proposed triggering a shallow, superhot blast to fry the nano-nest before it had a chance to drill its way down to the volcanic magma chamber six miles underground. While there was some threat of the hydrothermal explosion disturbing that magma chamber, too, it was less risky than doing nothing and letting that nano-nest eat its way down unchecked.

But how do you trigger a hydrothermal blast?

"Okay, let's do this." Kowalski stood, hauled up his bulky spool of C4, and crossed to Chin.

The geologist had tilted ladders against the minivolcano's steep sides. The two of them climbed to the top, where steam was rising from a small opening, just large enough for a shaped charge of C4 to slip through. Lying on their bellies on the ladders, the two men fed the spooled C4—one cube at a time, a hundred cubes in all—down the mouth of the cone, sending the chain deep underground, dropping it as close to the rock blocking the hydrothermal vent as possible. Chin had calculated the amount of explosive they needed to shatter the rock.

Kowalski doubled it.

For once, Painter agreed with Kowalski.

Go all in . . . or go home.

"That'll do it," Chin said from atop the Pitcher's Mound.

The two men slid down their ladders.

Kowalski rubbed his palms together in happy anticipation. "Let's see if this C4 colonic works."

Painter glanced his way. It actually wasn't a bad description for blasting that blockage free. The trio hurried to the last helicopter, which was still waiting in the basin. Engines hot, its rotors already spinning. They climbed aboard, buckled in place, and took off.

The helicopter pilot spared no fuel.

The valley shrank rapidly below.

"That's good!" Painter radioed over his headset.

With the chopper slowly circling, Painter gave Kowalski a thumbs-up. He already had the transmitter in hand. With a fierce grin, Kowalski pushed the button.

From this height and with the charges buried underground, the explosion sounded like distant thunder.

Painter stared below. The Pitcher's Mound was still intact. The only change was a bit more steam rising from its cone.

"That sucked," Kowalski said. "I was expecting—"

The entire basin detonated below them. It cracked like a dropped plate and blasted upward in bus-sized chunks that cleared twice the height of the canyon walls and came crashing down, stripping forested hills. At the same time steaming water rocketed upward, forming a geyser twenty yards wide and shooting a thousand feet into the air.

"Now that's what I call a colonic!" Kowalski said.

The helicopter banked away, its pilot fearful of getting caught in the maelstrom of rock, water, and steam.

Chin watched. "That much heat should definitely have destroyed the nano-nest."

Still, another question remained: *Did the huge blast trigger the very thing they feared?* Everyone held their breath as the helicopter circled, rising ever higher. The geyser continued to churn, but its fountain slowly began to recede. There was no evidence of magma rising or lava erupting.

After another minute, Chin let out a loud puff. "Looks like we're okay."

The helicopter spun farther out, heading away.

As they turned, Painter got a bird's-eye view of the entire Yellowstone caldera. All across the basin, water was shooting high into the air, spiraling with steam.

"My God, it's every geyser," Chin said, amazed. "Every geyser's erupting!"

As the helicopter raced across the dazzling display, Painter stared out in wonder at the dance of waters, the twinkle of steamy rainbows, suddenly deeply struck by the wonder of this world, this gift to mankind in all its resplendent natural beauty.

With his face pressed to the window, Kowalski looked equally impressed. "Next time, we should use *more* C4."

43

Gray took a cab straight from the airport to the National Archives. He'd taken a short nap on the flight from Columbia, Tennessee, after discovering all had gone well out in Yellowstone. He felt worlds better. Painter would be spending another day or two out there to make sure everything was okay and to make sure his niece was settled into her classes at Brigham Young University.

Back at the airport, he'd wanted to go with Monk to the hospital, to make sure they took good care of him after his gunshot wound, but Kat had called him as they were landing. Dr. Heisman, she said, had been able to decipher Meriwether Lewis's coded message and wanted to share it right away. Kat offered to send someone else to the museum, but considering all the trouble and bloodshed involved in obtaining the buffalo hide and its message, Gray wanted to be the first to hear what it said.

He owed it to Monk.

He owed it to Meriwether Lewis.

So he said good-bye to Monk at the airport. His friend had been in good spirits. And for good reason. The private jet they'd flown had been stocked with an amazing selection of single-malt scotches. Kat would take Gray's place at the hospital. And probably just as well. She would keep Monk from hassling his nurses too severely.

The cab slowed to the curb in front of the Archives. Seichan stretched next to him in the backseat.

"Here already," she mumbled drowsily.

Gray caught the cabdriver staring at her in the rearview mirror as he paid the fare. He couldn't blame the guy. She'd changed out of her blue coveralls and back into her leather jacket, her black jeans, and a gray T-shirt.

They climbed out of the cab, and both hobbled a bit up the steps. Their bruises, scrapes, and injuries had stiffened up. Seichan leaned on Gray's shoulder without having to be asked. His hand found her hip without her really needing the added support.

They reached the doors to find Heisman already waiting for them.

"There you both are," he said by way of greeting. "Come. I have everything in the conference room. You didn't bring the buffalo hide here by any chance? I would love to see it with my own eyes, rather than that photo you e-mailed."

"I'm sure that can be arranged," Gray said.

They entered the same conference room they had been in before to find it all cleaned up again. Only a few books dotted the table. Apparently, deciphering a centuries-old message required merely a couple of spare hours and the same number of books.

As they settled into the room, Gray asked, "How did you solve it so fast?"

"What? Meriwether's final words? It wasn't hard. The code that Meriwether used with Jefferson is well known. I'm sure they probably used more involved ones occasionally, but for most correspondence, they used a simple cipher. And considering that Meriwether was writing this as he lay dying, I suspect he went with the cipher he knew best."

Gray pictured the man, shot twice—once in the gut, once in the head—struggling to leave this last message.

Heisman pushed and sent his chair rolling down the length of the table so he could grab a book. "I can show you. It's a code based on the Vigenère cipher. It was used in Europe at the time and was considered unbreakable. The key to it is a secret password known only to the parties involved. Jefferson and Lewis always used the word *artichokes*."

"Artichokes?"

"That's right. The code itself involves a twenty-eight-column alphanumeric table to—"

Gray's cell phone chimed with incoming voice mail. *Saved by the bell.* "Excuse me for a moment."

He stood up, stepped toward the door, but pointed back to Seichan. "Dr. Heisman, why don't you explain all about the cipher to my colleague? I'll be right back."

"I'd be happy to."

Seichan just glared at him and rolled her eyes in exasperation as he left.

Out in the hall, the smile on Gray's face faded as he read the number of voice mails on his phone. He'd been using the disposable for the past day and forgot to put his battery back into his personal phone until he hit ground again in D.C. Still, apparently it took over forty-five minutes to route and load the calls after he'd powered up.

He stared at the screen.

Maybe this is one of the reasons why it took so long.

He had received twenty-two messages over the past twelve hours, all from the same number. He kicked himself for not calling earlier. He remembered he'd gotten his mother's first voice mail as they were fleeing Fort Knox. He'd had no time to listen to it then—and it had slipped his mind during all the commotion.

He started from the beginning, already feeling that familiar tension at the base of his spine. He held the phone to his ear.

"Gray, it's your mother." She started every phone call that way. *Like I don't know your voice, Mom.* "It's ten-thirty, and I wanted to let you know your father's having a bad night. You don't have to come over, but I thought you should know."

Uh-oh.

Rather than listening to all the messages, he hit redial. Might as well hear how things had gone from the horse's mouth. The phone rang and rang and then went to voice mail.

That tension in his back squeezed his spine a little tighter. Wanting to know what happened, he listened through the rest of the messages.

"Gray, it's your mother again. It's getting bad, so I'm going to call that number for the home-health-care worker you left in case of an emergency."

Very good, Mom . . .

The next few messages grew increasingly more distraught. The home-health-care worker thought his father was having a bad enough episode to warrant a hospital visit.

"Gray, they want to keep your father for a couple days. Run another MRI . . . is that right, Luis?" In the background, he heard a faint, "That's right, Harriet." Then his mother again. "Anyway, everything's fine. I didn't mean to worry you."

But there were another five calls after that. He continued on, discovering that his mother was growing confused herself about tests, insurance, paperwork.

"Why aren't you returning my calls? Are you out of town . . . maybe you're out of town. I can't remember if you told me. Maybe I'd better water your plants anyway. You always forget."

The last message had been left only an hour ago. Gray was still in the air at the time. "Gray, I've got a hair appointment near your town house. Are you still out of town? I'm going to water your plants on the way to my appointment. I think I have your house key here. I told you I had a hair appointment, right? It's at one o'clock. Maybe if you're home, we can do lunch."

Okay, Mom . . .

He checked his watch. He should be able to finish here at the Archives and meet her at his house by noon.

Taking a deep breath, he headed back into the conference room.

Seichan must have read something in his face. "Are you okay?"

He shook his cell phone. "Family stuff. I'll get to it after this."

She offered him a sympathetic smile. "Welcome home."

"Yeah, right."

He returned his attention to Dr. Heisman. "So what did Meriwether have to say that was so important?"

"It was a strange letter, very full of paranoia."

"Well, he'd just been shot . . . twice," Gray said. "That would make anyone a little paranoid."

"True. But I wanted you to know about what he wrote at the end. I think it bears on the matters from yesterday, specifically about the great enemy that was plaguing the Founding Fathers."

"What does it say about them?" Gray asked, his interest pricking.

Heisman read from a text that was covered with lots of notes and jottings. *"They've found me on the road, those who serve the Enemy. I leave this message, covered in my own blood, as fair warning to those who come after. With great effort, we few have cast most of the fearsome Enemy from our shores, through purges of our great armies and noble houses.'"*

Gray interrupted: "Didn't you tell us something about that? How Meriwether acted as Jefferson's spy to discover who was disloyal in the armed forces?"

"That's true, but it seems they weren't entirely successful in flushing them all out." Heisman continued to read. *"Yet one family persists, rooted deeply in the South, too stubborn for us to pull out, like a weed. Lest in doing so we risk uprooting our young nation and tearing it apart. It is an old family with ties to slavers & rich beyond measure. Even here I dare not write that name down & alert the family of our knowledge. But a record will be left for those that follow, if you know where to look. Jefferson will leave their name in paint. You can find it thusly: In the turning of the bull, find the five who don't belong. Let their given names be ordered & revealed by the letters G, C, R, J, T and their numbers 1, 2, 4, 4, 1.'"*

"What does that last part mean?" Seichan asked.

"I have no idea," the curator answered. "It is not uncommon to bury a code within a code, especially concerning something that so clearly frightened them."

Gray's cell phone rang in his pocket. Concerned that it was his mother, he checked the number and was relieved to see it was only Kat. She must be reporting on Monk's condition.

"Kat, it's Gray." As he said those words, he realized how much he sounded like his mother: *Gray, it's your mother.*

Kat's voice came with a worried, yet relieved edge. "Good. You're okay."

"I'm still at the Archives. What's wrong?"

Her voice grew calmer, but it was clear that she was still shaken. "I came home to change clothes before heading to the hospital. Luckily I've had plenty of intelligence training. I saw the door had been tampered with. I discovered a bomb, a booby trap. Looks like the same design as the ordnance that took down your jet yesterday, the work of Mitchell Waldorf."

Gray pictured the bastard blowing the top of his head off and his final words: *This isn't over.*

His breath turned to ice in his chest.

Kat continued: "The bomb squad is here, and I'm sending them over to your—"

"Kat!" he cut her off. "My mother was heading to my town house. Today. She has my key."

"Go," Kat said, without pausing. "I'm out the door already with the bomb team. I'll alert local forces en route."

He snapped his phone closed and simply ran for the door. Seichan bolted out of her chair and followed.

She must have gleaned enough from listening to his end of the conversation to know what was happening. They fled together out the door to the street. He searched for a cab. She ran out into the street, where the midday traffic had stalled. She headed straight for a stranded motorcyclist and whipped out her black SIG Sauer. She pointed it at his head.

"Off."

The young man leaped and fell away.

She caught the bike one-handed before it dropped and turned to Gray. "You fit to ride?"

Until he knew otherwise, he was wired and focused.

He leaped into the seat.

She climbed behind him, wrapped her arms around him, and said in his ear, "Break any rules you need to."

He gunned the motorcycle and did just that.

The flight through the city was a blur, wind whipping, leaping curbs, dodging pedestrians. As he made the turn onto Sixteenth Street, he saw a thin column of smoke in the air. Piney Branch Road lay in that direction. He choked the throttle and raced down the rest of the way.

Emergency vehicles were already there, lights blazing, sirens going.

He braked hard, skidding sideways, and leaped off the bike. An ambulance sat crooked in the road, half up on the curb.

He ran toward it.

Monk came hurtling around the blind corner, still in his hospital gown.

He must have stolen the ambulance and used the sirens to beat Gray here from Georgetown University Hospital.

Gray came running up and saw the answer to his unposed question in Monk's face. His friend held up an arm, stopping him, but didn't say a word, just one tiny shake of his head.

Gray crashed to his knees in the middle of the road.

"No . . ."

44

"Where are my girls?" Monk called out into the apartment.

"Your girls are still *asleep*," Kat replied from the couch, "and if you wake them, you're staying up with them all night like I did."

She was resting on a maternity pillow, her back still aching from the delivery three days ago. She'd been two weeks early, but all had gone well with the birth of their second child, a baby girl. Monk was now surrounded by women here in the apartment, which was okay by him. He had enough testosterone for the whole family and was certainly around enough testosterone at work.

He plopped down on the couch next to Kat and placed the white takeout bag between them. "Feldman's bagels and cream cheese."

She placed a hand on her belly. "I'm so fat."

"You just had an eight-pound three-ounce baby girl. No wonder she demanded to come out early. No room in there."

Kat made a noncommittal sound at the back of her throat.

He lifted the bag out of the way, slid closer, and put his arm around his wife. She leaned into him, resting her head on his shoulder.

"You're beautiful," he said, and kissed her hair—then, after a long moment, added, "but you sort of stink."

She punched him in the shoulder.

"How about I warm up the shower—for the *both* of us?"

She mumbled into his chest. "That would be nice."

He began to scoot up, but she pulled him back down.

"Just stay here. I like this."

"Well, you're going to get a lot more of *this*. Me, sitting around the house."

She looked up. "What did Painter say?"

"He understood, accepted my resignation letter, but he wanted me to think about it while I'm out on family leave."

She settled against him, again making that noncommittal sound.

They'd had long conversations about his resigning from Sigma. He had a wife and two children who needed him. After getting shot, having a bomb placed in their home, and seeing the devastation that had been wrought upon Gray's family, he figured it was time. He already had offers from various biotech companies in D.C.

The couple remained locked in each other's arms, simply enjoying each other's warmth. He refused to put *this* at risk any longer.

Finally, Kat swung around, and with a bit of effort, put her feet in his lap. "Since you're no longer working . . ."

He took her feet and began to rub them, one-handed. His new prosthesis wouldn't be ready for another four days, but apparently one hand was enough.

She leaned back, stretching, and made a sound that was definitely not noncommittal. "I could get used to *this,* too."

But such bliss could not last.

The small wail rose from the next room, starting low and rising quickly to an earsplitting pitch. How could so much sound come out of such a little package?

"She's definitely got your lungs," Kat said, and raised herself up on an elbow. "Sounds like she's hungry."

"I'll get her." Monk rolled to his feet.

So much for that hot shower.

He crossed to their bedroom and found the new joy of his life, red-faced, with eyes squinted tightly closed. He scooped her up and out of the crib, lifting her to his shoulder.

She quieted—slightly—as he gently bounced her.

She'd been born the day of the funeral for Gray's mother. Kat had gone into labor during the memorial service. He knew how hard that day was for Gray, how much guilt he bore for his mother's death. Monk had no words that could comfort that bone-deep grief, but Gray was strong.

Monk had seen a glimmer of that strength, and the eventual recovery it promised, later, when Gray came to visit Kat at the hospital, to see the baby. Monk had never told his friend what he and Kat had both decided. The revelation brought a sad, but genuine smile to Gray's lips.

Monk lifted his girl around to stare her in the face. "Are you hungry, Harriet?"

8:04 A.M.

Gray sat in the bedside hospital chair, his face in his hands.

His father was snoring softly, stretched out under a thin sheet and blanket. He looked like a frail shadow of his formerly robust self. Gray had arranged for a private room here at the memory-care unit, to allow his father some measure of privacy in which to grieve. His mother had brought his father to the hospital a week ago.

He'd not left.

The MRI revealed that he'd suffered a very small stroke, but he was recovering well. It was more an incidental finding than anything. The real reason for the sudden worsening of his dementia—the hallucinations, the nighttime panic attacks, the sundowner's syndrome—had mostly to do with a dosage imbalance in his medication. His father had been accidentally overmedicating himself and became toxic and dehydrated, which led to the stroke. The doctors were currently correcting his meds and seemed to think that in another week he would be doing well enough to be moved to an assisted-living facility.

That would be the next battle.

After his mother's funeral, Gray had to decide what to do about his parents' house. His brother, Kenny, had flown in from California for the funeral and was talking to a lawyer and some real-estate people today. There remained some friction between the two brothers over a range of issues, and a lot of guilt, resentment, and blame. Kenny didn't know the exact details of his mother's death, only that it had been collateral damage in an act of revenge against Gray.

A voice rose behind him, speaking softly. "We'll be serving breakfast soon. Can I bring you a tray?"

Gray turned. "No, but thanks, Mary."

Mary Benning was an RN on the floor. She was a charming woman with a brownish-gray bobbed hairstyle and blue scrubs. Her own mother suffered from Lewy body dementia, so she understood what Gray and his father were going through. Gray appreciated such personal experience. It allowed them to shorthand their conversations.

"How did he do last night?" Gray asked.

Mary stepped more fully into the room. "Good. The new lower dose of Sinemet seems to be keeping him much calmer at night."

"Did you bring Cutie or Shiner with you today?"

She smiled. "Both."

They were Mary's two rehabilitation assistants, two dachshunds. Alzheimer patients showed a great response to interaction with animals. Gray never thought such a thing would work with his father, but he had come to the facility last Sunday to find Shiner sleeping in bed with his father as he watched a football game.

Still, even that day had been hard.

They all were.

He turned back to his father as Mary left.

Gray tried to come each morning, to be at his side when his father woke up. That was always the worst time. Twice now, he'd found his father had no memory of his wife's death. The neurologists believed it would take time for things to fully settle.

So Gray had to explain about the tragic loss over and over again. His father had always been quick to anger—the Alzheimer's made things worse. Three times, Gray had to face that wrath, the tears, the accusations. Gray took it all without protest; perhaps a part of him even wanted it.

A shuffling behind him drew his attention back to the door.

Mary poked her head in. "Are you okay with a visitor?"

Seichan stepped into view, looking uncomfortable, ready to bolt. She was wearing a pair of blue jeans and a thin blouse, carrying her motorcycle jacket over her arm.

Gray waved her inside and asked Mary to close the door.

Seichan crossed over, dragging another chair, and sat down next to him. "Knew I'd catch you here. I wanted to go over what I found out— then I'm riding up to New York. Something I want to follow up on. Thought maybe you'd want to come."

"What did you find out?"

"Heisman and that assistant of his—"

"Sharyn."

"Both clean. They weren't involved at all in the bombing. Waldorf seems to have orchestrated it all himself, using personal connections. I doubt he even got authorization from his Guild superiors. I think he acted alone, tried to murder both you and Monk in a cowardly act of vengeance. From the fact that the bombs were set hours before he killed himself, I think they were planted as backup, in case he failed to eliminate you in Tennessee."

Gray remembered the bastard's last words.

This isn't over.

His and Seichan's voices must have stirred Gray's father, who raised an arm, stretched. He opened his eyes and slowly focused, blinking a few times, then cleared his throat. It took him an extra moment to get his bearings, looking around the room, eyeing Seichan up and down, lingering there a bit, in fact.

"Seichan, isn't it?" he asked hoarsely.

"That's right." She stood up, ready to leave.

It always surprised Gray what his father remembered and what he didn't. Bleary eyes turned to Gray. "Where's your mother?"

Gray took a deep breath, facing the confusion and anxiety in his father's face. The small bubble of hope inside his chest popped and deflated.

"Dad . . . Mom's—"

Rather than leaving, Seichan leaned between Gray and his father. She squeezed the old man's hand. "She'll be by later. She needed some time to rest, to get her hair done."

His father nodded and leaned back into his bed, the anxiety draining from his face. "Good. She's always doing too much, that woman."

Seichan patted his hand, turned to Gray and nodded toward the door. Then she straightened, said her good-byes, and drew Gray out of the room with her.

"Where's breakfast?" his father called after them.

"It's coming," Gray said as he left, letting the door close behind him.

Outside, Seichan moved him into a quiet side hall.

"What are you doing?" Gray said, anger rising, gesturing halfheartedly toward his father's room.

"Saving you, saving him," she said, and pushed him against the wall. "You're just punishing yourself, torturing him. He deserves better than that—and so do you, Gray. I've been reading up on situations like this. He'll work through it in his own time. Quit forcing him to remember."

Gray opened his mouth to argue.

"Don't you see, Gray. *He knows.* It's in there, buried where it doesn't hurt as much right now. He's working through it."

Gray pictured the anxiety in his father's face. It had been there every morning. Even the relief he'd shown a moment ago hadn't completely erased it. Buried deep in those eyes, a trickle of fear remained.

He rubbed his face with his palm, scratching stubble, unsure.

Seichan pulled his arm down. "Sometimes delusions are a good thing, a *necessary* thing."

He swallowed hard, trying to accept these words. He was enough of his father to want to fight, to dismiss what wasn't solid and graspable with a callused hand. Just then his phone chirped in his pocket, allowing him a moment to collect himself.

He pulled it free, his fingers trembling with everything inside him. He fumbled the phone open and saw he had a text message. The caller ID read BLOCKED. But the message made clear who had sent it.

IT WAS NOT OUR INTENTION

Those few words were like a bomb dropped in his gut. The trembling inside him grew worse. He slipped down the wall, the world narrowing. All the conflict inside him flared for a breath, then collapsed like a dying star into a burning, dense ember. He went cold and hollow everywhere else.

Seichan followed him down, grasping his cheeks in both of her hot palms, holding him and staring into his face, inches away. She had read the message, too.

Her words gave voice to what was inside him. "I will help you. I will do whatever it takes to hunt them down."

He stared into the emerald of her eyes, flecked with gold. Her palms burned on his cheeks. Their heat spread into those cold empty places inside him. He reached to her face and pulled her closer, narrowing the distance between them until their lips touched.

He kissed her, needing her.

She resisted at first, her lips tense, hard, unsure.

Then they slowly softened, releasing, parting.

Each of them needed the other.

But was this real—or just a necessary delusion for the moment?

In the end, Gray didn't care.

It was real enough for now.

11:45 A.M.
San Rafael Swell

It felt good to be back . . . to shake off the ghosts that haunted her.

Kai Quocheets stood on the pueblo's porch as the sun hammered the canyon and badlands of San Rafael Swell. Dust devils danced up through the gulches and ravines. She smelled the scent of juniper and hot sand as she stared out across its expanse of buttes, stone reefs, and fluted canyon walls, striated in shades of gold and crimson.

Even after only a week, it was beginning to feel like home again.

She'd be spending her summer at the pueblos, earning college credits from Brigham Young University. She was taking a Native American studies class on the ancient Pueblo peoples. It involved recording petroglyphs, helping with the restoration of old ruins, and learning the old Hopi customs.

Like discovering how to roast piñon nuts.

"Who burned my best tray?" a voice shouted from inside.

Kai cringed, knowing she had to face the consequences of her crime like a woman. She'd been doing that a lot lately. Two days ago, she'd been officially pardoned for any wrongdoing involving the events in Utah. It seemed that her role in saving the world had evened her karmic balance with the Justice Department. Plus, having the likes of Uncle Crowe and Hank Kanosh as character witnesses never hurt.

But this was one crime she could not escape so easily.

Kai turned to the screen door and entered the deeper shadows of the main room. Iris Humetewa wore oven mitts and held up a scorched tray.

"You have to wait for the coals to burn off."

"I know, but Kawtch was chewing at his stitches, and by the time I caught him and got his cone put in place . . ."

She sighed, done with excuses.

Kawtch had lifted his head upon hearing his name, wearing a plastic funnel around his neck. They'd had to amputate his front leg. The rifle shot had left little bone and not much nerve, but he was recovering well.

They all were.

Alvin Humetewa's burns were mostly just deep red splotches against his tanned ruddy skin. The pair of old Hopi Indians had survived their encounter with Rafael Saint Germaine through sheer stubbornness and their wily knowledge of the local terrain.

The Hopi tribe had a saying: *Never try to hunt an Indian loose on his own land.* It was a harsh lesson for the early pioneers to learn—and one Rafael Saint Germaine had never known about.

Iris had suspected that the Frenchman's soldiers might come after them. So when she took off with her husband on the ATV, she aimed for the closest sandy bowl and kicked up a cloudy dust storm to hide their flight. Then once she heard the potshots, she rode into an old mine tunnel and trusted Rafael would not stick around long enough to find her and Alvin. She knew he was anxious to go after Kai's uncle Crowe. Even if he had left men behind, she could cover her tracks and reach help, if necessary.

It seemed there was much Kai could learn from that old Hopi woman.

"I'm sorry, Auntie Iris," she said. "I'll polish the tray and make up for it by cooking the next two nights."

Iris nodded, satisfied, and gave her a wink, expressing forgiveness and love in such a small movement.

The growl of engines drew both their attentions to the front door.

"Looks like the boys are back from their joyriding," Iris said.

The two headed out to the porch to greet them. A pair of dust-caked figures climbed from ATVs that looked more like fossilized stone than fiberglass.

Jordan peeled off his helmet and wiped his face with a gingham handkerchief. Kai felt her heart stutter as the beam of his smile reached her and grew even wider.

Beside him, his companion popped off his helmet, red-faced and grinning. "I could get used to this," Ash said.

Major Ashley Ryan and Jordan had become close friends after the events in Yellowstone. It seemed that the National Guardsman had developed a newfound respect for Native Americans.

Jordan reached over and patted the man's chest, hard, knocking dust off his T-shirt. It read I LOVE INJUNS, and it depicted a cartoon V8 engine wearing a feathered headdress.

"Tacky and offensive," Jordan said. "Both at the same time. That's going to get our asses kicked out here one of these days."

"Kid, that news just made this my *favorite* shirt."

With his chest puffed out proudly, Ash climbed up to the porch.

Jordan smiled over at Kai. "Oh, by the way, I think I beat your best time on the Deadman's Gulch run."

Iris nudged Kai with her elbow. "Are you going to take that?"

Hell, no . . .

Kai slipped the helmet out from under Ash's arm and leaped off the porch, her hair flying. "Let's go see about that!"

2:17 P.M.
Salt Lake City

From one temple to another . . .

Professor Henry Kanosh, a member of the Northwestern Band of Shoshone, was the first Mormon Indian to stand at the threshold of this temple's *Kodesh Hakodashim,* the Holy of the Holies' chamber at the heart of the Mormon temple in Salt Lake City.

Starting at dawn, he'd prepared himself: fasting and praying. He now stood in a vestibule of polished rock, before a door few men knew about. Pounded of raw silver, the portal rose fifteen feet high and eight wide, split down the middle.

In Hank's hands, he held the one gift he had to offer, the key to the temple's inner sanctum.

Ahead, the doors parted, and a single figure stepped out.

Hank knelt, bowing his head.

Soft footsteps approached, unhurried, calm.

Once they stopped before him, Hank raised his arms and offered up his gift. The gold plate was taken from his grasp, slipped from his fingers, and gone.

He had recovered the plate at the Old Faithful Inn. While everyone had been distracted by NASA's call, announcing that they had found a match to the landscape depicted on the canopic jar, Henry had been standing next to the Frenchman's case. He dared not take *both* plates, as Rafael would then have noted the theft much sooner. So setting aside greed, he satisfied himself with slipping *one* free and pocketing it in the back of his pants.

The gold plate belonged with the church. After seeing the re-creation of Solomon's Temple, he knew that for sure.

Footsteps retreated, again unhurried and calm.

Hank risked a glance up as the doors started to sweep closed.

Brilliant light flowed out from that inner sanctum. He caught a slivered glimpse inside. A large white stone altar. Beyond it, gold shone forth, coming from shelves that seemed to stretch forever.

Were they Joseph Smith's original tablets?

A tingling washed over his skin, awe prickling the small hairs over his body. Then the doors shut—and the world seemed a far darker and more ordinary place.

Hank stood, turned, and walked away.

Carrying some of that golden brilliance with him.

5:45 P.M.
Washington, D.C.

Alone, Painter headed across the National Mall, needing some fresh air, but also to follow up on a growing concern.

Everything was quieting down on the global level—at least, geologically speaking. Iceland had stopped erupting, doubling the landmass of Ellirey Island and birthing a small new atoll. Yellowstone remained quiet after a few swarms of quakes following the hydrothermal explosion. To be safe, Ronald Chin was still out there with a team of volcanologists, monitoring seismic activity. Dr. Riku Tanaka, out in Japan, had reported no new neutrino activity.

Still, while they had avoided triggering an apocalypse, the supervolcano still remained—and as Chin had warned, it was still overdue to erupt on its own. A frightening thought.

But there was nothing to be done about that today.

In the end, Yellowstone had a new crater lake, but all signs pointed to nothing worse brewing deeper underground for the moment. Kowalski petitioned to have the lake named after himself: *Kowalski Krater Lake.*

For some reason, the petition got squashed.

Painter attempted to investigate the remaining Saint Germaine clan in France, but within twenty-four hours of Rafael's death, fourteen of its most influential members were found murdered. No one else in the family seemed to have any knowledge about the Guild. It seemed the True Bloodline had set about to erase its connection to that family.

Even the site in Belgium where they'd picked up the other neutrino trace in Europe revealed only a firebombed and gutted mansion, one leased by a corporation that proved to be a shell, a false identity that evaporated upon inspection. The Guild clearly wanted to destroy any remaining evidence—fingerprints, papers, DNA—from that place.

So that trail also came to a dead end.

Leaving only one path open.

Painter reached his goal at the east end of the mall—the U.S. Capitol—and set about climbing the steps.

Though the building was open to the public only for another fifteen minutes, the place was a noisy jumble of life: kids ran up and down the stairs; tourists posed for photos; protesters shouted, carrying placards. He enjoyed such exuberance and chaos after being cooped up in his offices below the Smithsonian Castle.

Here was American life in all its glory, warts and all, and he'd have it no other way. It was more representative of democracy than all the stately parliamentary rules and political games going on under that neoclassical dome.

So he enjoyed his walk, despite the stifling humidity of the day.

He had plans to have dinner with Lisa later, but for now he needed to clear his mind. He had to see the painting for himself first, before committing to any course of action. Besides, he did not even know where to start. He had told no one of his discovery, not even his inner circle at Sigma.

It was not that he didn't trust that circle, but they had enough burdens at the moment. Monk had his new baby girl, Harriet. The man had proffered his resignation early that morning. Painter had agreed to keep it on file but convinced him to take family leave and use the time to reconsider. Hopefully, the life of crying children, diaper changes, and a long stretch of downtime would change Monk's mind, but Painter doubted it. Monk was a family man at heart. And a week ago, they'd all seen the consequences of his trying to live a double life.

Then there was Gray. He'd sunk into a dark pit of despair, but what would arise out of it: a stronger man or a broken one?

Only time would tell.

So Painter kept quiet for all their sakes. Even coming here was not without risk, but he had to chance it.

Reaching the top of the steps, he crossed under the dome and into the Capitol Rotunda. The huge vaulted space echoed with voices. He sought the second-floor gallery, where giant twelve-by-eighteen-foot canvases cir-cled the dome's walls. He found what he was looking for easily enough on the south side. It was the most famous painting up here: *Declaration of Independence* by John Turnbull.

He stood before it, sensing the waft of history that blew through this space. He stared at the brushstrokes done by a painter's hand centuries ago. But other *hands* had also been involved in this piece, just as influen-tial. He pictured Jefferson guiding Turnbull, preparing this masterpiece.

Painter gazed up, studying every inch of it, connecting to that past.

The massive canvas depicted the presentation of the Declaration of Independence to Congress. Within this one painting, John Turnbull at-tempted to include a portrait of everyone who signed the Declaration, a memorial to that pivotal event. But Turnbull couldn't manage to fit every-one into it. Yet, oddly enough, he did manage to get *five* people painted in there who had never signed the final draft.

So why include them?

Historians had always wondered.

In his research, Painter read how John Turnbull had offered some obfuscating answers, but none satisfactory—and it was indeed Thomas Jefferson, master of ciphers and codes, who oversaw the completion of this masterwork.

So was there another reason?

At least Meriwether Lewis believed so.

The words deciphered from the buffalo hide ran through Painter's head as he stared at the strokes of oil on the canvas: *Jefferson will leave their name in paint. You can find it thusly: In the turning of the bull, find the five who don't belong. Let their given names be ordered & revealed by the letters* G, C, R, J, T *and their numbers 1, 2, 4, 4, 1.*

It wasn't a hard cipher to decode.

Turning of the bull referred, of course, to Turnbull, who had been commissioned to do many public paintings in early America.

Find the five who don't belong indicated the five nonsigners depicted on the canvas:

John Dickinson
Robert Livingston
George Clinton
Thomas Willing
Charles Thomson

The last of that list, Thomson, *did* sign an early draft, but he was *not* invited to inscribe the famous version with its fifty-six signers.

The next bit of the passage—*Let their given names be ordered & revealed by the letters* G, C, R, J, T—simply meant taking their first names and putting them in the order of those five letters listed.

George
Charles
Robert
John
Thomas

Then all that needed to be done was to select the corresponding letter in each name that matched the number: *1, 2, 4, 4, 1.*

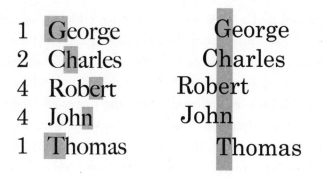

1	George	George
2	Charles	Charles
4	Robert	Robert
4	John	John
1	Thomas	Thomas

The name of Meriwether Lewis's enemy, the traitorous and secretive family who had confounded the early Founding Fathers, was *Ghent*.

It seemed meaningless at first—until Painter pondered it more, especially in light of the conversation he had had with Rafael Saint Germaine. The Frenchman had mentioned that the Guild was really a group of ancient families who had been accumulating wealth, power, and knowledge over centuries—possibly millennia—until in modern times only one family remained. His story closely matched Lewis's tale of the purging of America, in which one family turned out to be rooted too deeply to remove, *with ties to slavers & rich beyond measure.*

Were these two stories speaking of the *same* family?

Ghent.

Again, Painter might not have attributed much to this code breaking, except for one nagging coincidence. Ghent was a city in *Belgium*. That country had kept popping up of late: the team who attacked Gray in Iceland had come from there, as had that smaller burst of neutrinos similar to those at Fort Knox.

So Painter had kept on digging. Ghent was a common surname for people from that city. Someone was *John of Ghent* or *Paul of Ghent*. But in more modern times you became simply *John Ghent* or *Paul Ghent*. And sometimes just the anglicized pronunciation was used, as it was easier to spell phonetically.

And that's where Painter found the truth—or so he believed.

Not that he could do anything about it.

He stepped farther back from the painting, taking in its entirety. He studied the figures of Jefferson and Franklin, picturing them standing before this same painting, faced with the same challenge and threat. His own hands were tied as surely as the Founding Fathers' had been.

During Painter's research concerning the suspected family, he had discovered that they indeed had roots going back to Ghent, had even used that name before extending their reach to America. They'd been in the colonies at the beginning, entrenched in the slave trade to such an extent that any attempt to remove that single family by force could have ripped the new union apart.

They were the weed in the garden that could not be pulled.

And they still were today.

As America grew, so did this family, rooting and entwining into multiple industries, corporations, and yes, even in the halls of government. They were a thread woven throughout the fabric of this country.

So was it any wonder that Sigma could make no headway against them?

Rafael had said this ancient group of families—*the secret in secret societies*—went by many names, whispers that were only shadows: the Guild, Echelon, *familles de l'étoile,* the star families. But Painter knew the true name of the enemy—then and now—anglicized for the American tongue.

They were the Kennedys of the South.

But no longer were they called *Ghent.*

Now they were called *Gant.*

As in President James T. Gant.

AUTHOR'S NOTE TO READERS: TRUTH OR FICTION

While I'd like to say this entire story is true, that would, of course, be *fiction*. So for these last few pages, I thought I'd separate the wheat from the chaff, the truth from the fiction. The three big-ticket items that became the foundation for this book concern Mormonism, early Native Americans, and our Founding Fathers. As you might imagine after reading this novel, these topics do intertwine. But I'll try to break them down as clearly as I can:

Mormonism. While I was raised Roman Catholic, I've always been fascinated by the Book of Mormon, especially by its take on early America. The specific mystery at the heart of this text is the Mormon belief that Native American clans originated from a fleeing lost tribe of Israelites. While modern DNA emphatically disputes this, pointing to an Asiatic origin for early American natives, I read a fascinating paper that can be found online, a paper that balances Mormon belief with modern genetic science: "Who Are the Children of Lehi?" by D. Jeffrey Meldrum and Trent D. Stephens.

In this book I also broach the commonality between Hebrew and Native American languages (specifically Uto-Aztecan). If you'd like to know more (I only mention a few examples in the book, but there are hundreds), check out the article that can be found online: "Was There Hebrew Language in Ancient America?" by John L. Sorenson.

According to the Book of Mormon, John Smith translated the text from a collection of gold plates written in a language called "reformed Egyptian," an advanced form of Hebrew with elements of Egyptian. I borrowed a language from the Middle Ages, named the Alphabet of the Magi, to stand in for that script, as the Magi Alphabet was also derived from Hebrew. Also caches of strange metallic plates—golden and otherwise—have been discovered throughout the Americas. Most are hoaxes, but some come with some substantial provenance. I'll leave their veracity up to you to decide.

Native American History. Segueing into this topic, I should mention that there was much friction between Mormon settlers and Native Americans in the mid-1800s, including massacres and wars. But the Northwestern Band of Shoshone of Brigham City is known for being a Mormon Indian tribe.

1. *Chief Canasatego* is a real Iroquois leader who had a profound impact on the founding of America. Many people do believe him to be a lost Founding Father. The story related about the arrows and Franklin and how it led to the bundle of arrows in our national Great Seal is true.

2. As is *Resolution 331*, passed in October of 1988, which acknowledges the influence that the Iroquois constitution had upon our own founding documents, including the Declaration of Independence.

3. For example, in 1787, John Rutledge of South Carolina read to members of the Constitution Convention from Iroquois law, words written 250 years before our constitution. Here are those words he read: *"We, the people, to form a union, to establish peace, equity, and order . . ."* Sound familiar?

4. *Caucasoid remains* from ancient America have been discovered in various regions of the United States and baffle anthropologists. A few of those are: Kennewick Man, Spirit Cave Mummy of Nevada,

Oregon's Prospect Man, and Arlington Springs Woman. And there are many more.

5. Some of the oldest petroglyphs found in America are the Coso Petroglyphs, found above the China Lake basin in California, dating back sixteen thousand years.

6. A new study based on carbon content in stalagmites suggests that the Native American population in pre-Columbian America may have numbered over 100 million. That's more people than were living in Europe at that time.

7. For more about Indian legends associated with Yellowstone, check out *Storytelling in Yellowstone: Horse and Buggy Tour Guides* by Lee H. Whittlesey and *Indian Legends from the Northern Rockies* by Ella E. Clark.

8. The disappearance of the Anasazi continues to provoke great interest and speculation. One of the newest theories is that the Anasazi discovered a new faith, and this resulted in a religious war that wiped them out. Also, it is said that the eruptions that raised the Sunset Crater also had a huge impact on their ultimate fate.

Founding Fathers. We talked about Chief Canasatego as the *lost* Founding Father. Now let's look at those who were not lost.

1. *Thomas Jefferson* was a scientist, statesman, inventor, and politician. He was unique in that he also wanted better relations with the indigenous population in America. His interest was such that he built a huge collection of Native American artifacts that he kept at Monticello. Most of it mysteriously vanished after he died, including a decorated buffalo hide (and yes, Meriwether Lewis died on a buffalo-skin robe). Jefferson also did indeed send a secret letter to Congress to admit that a major purpose of the Lewis and Clark expedition was to spy on the Indians. And yes, he did help found the mint with his friend David Rittenhouse. And he was very fond of secret codes and ciphers, inventing several himself, including a code he used with

Meriwether Lewis. And like Native Americans of the time, he had a profound interest in fossils.

2. *Benjamin Franklin* was indeed fascinated by the Laki eruption, which killed six million people and likely contributed to the factors that caused the French Revolution.

3. *Meriwether Lewis* (okay, he's not a Founding Father, but I'm putting him here because he was a friend of Jefferson's and a contemporary of the others). He was a soldier, spy, and scientist, so he would make a great Sigma Force member. He and Clark did indeed miss finding Yellowstone by a mere forty miles. Also, the quote from an early pioneer, hinting that the Indians were hiding something powerful inside Yellowstone, is a real quote. So, it's hard to believe Lewis's expedition never found Yellowstone . . . and so I wrote this story. It's also true that Lewis's death was considered a suicide, but mounting evidence now points to murder, most likely assassination. The burial site is as accurately described as I could make it.

The Great Seal. I already mentioned how the story of Chief Canasatego and the arrows is true. But so is the fact that the *olive branch* and *bundle of arrows* are the symbols representing Manasseh, one of the ten lost tribes of Israel. And it is this very tribe that the Book of Mormon suggests came to early America. Additionally, both Jefferson and Franklin had initially proposed that the Great Seal depict scenes of exiled Israelites. They lost that debate, but here are some thoughts to chew on. Could the symbols of the olive branch and arrows be a remnant of the two men's original proposals? If so, *why* were the Founding Fathers so obsessed with the lost tribes of Israel?

Science Tidbits. I try to be as accurate as possible in regard to the science in my novels, so most of the factoids are based on some manner of realistic data. I thought I'd signal a few here.

1. The *Super-Kamiokande detector* is a real facility doing subatomic particle research using a tank full of fifty thousand tons of ultrapure

water. And yes, sixty billion neutrinos pass through your fingernail every second—and those particles still remain a mystery to modern physics.

2. The novel contains much information about *volcanism*. Most of it is true, including the fact that you should be careful about drilling into geothermal levels. Explosions and lava production have resulted.

3. On a minor note, the *Underground Physics Research Laboratory* at BYU is indeed buried underground north of its science building (sorry for blowing a hole in it).

4. Evidence of ancient *nanotechnology* does exist in Damascus steel, ancient medieval glass, and some hair dyes. As to modern nanotech, I went into that at length in the foreword: all true . . . and yes, that scary.

5. *Weaponry* in the book: Taser XREP shotguns, flashbangs, up-armor kits for Humvees, and one kick-ass cattle dog. All real.

Places. We're mostly in America, so it must be real.

1. There is a *Serpent Indian Mound*, but it's in Ohio, not Kentucky.

2. *Sunset Crater* does have lava tubes that hold ice all year round in the Arizona desert.

3. *Wupatki* does have a blowhole that opens into seven million cubic feet of cavern space and gusts of wind of up to thirty miles an hour do blow through it.

4. *Crack-in-the-Rock Pueblo* is a real place.

5. The *Westman Islands* south of Iceland do have the largest orca population (so, of course, they had to play a role). Ellirey Island can only be reached by rope and does have a small lodge on its top. Heimaey Island is indeed known as the Pompeii of the North.

6. Most of the landmarks in *Yellowstone* are accurate, including *Fairyland Basin* with its scatter of geyserite cones. And yes, since the 1990s, fewer than thirty people have visited that beautiful and strange little basin.

7. And *yes*, the Yellowstone caldera is due to erupt. It's late, in fact. The geological information that Chin gave regarding an impending eruption of the supervolcano and its aftermath is *true*. So it's not a matter of *if* that supervolcano will erupt, rather of *when*.

Other Books of Interest. While a long bibliography could be given here, I thought I'd share the books that are of the greatest relevance to this novel.

1. *Solomon's Power Brokers* by Christopher Knight and Alan Butler (specifically for information about the "star families")
2. *Jefferson and Science* by Silvio A. Bedini
3. *Southern Paiutes* by LaVan Martineau
4. *American Monster* by Paul Semonin
5. *Unearthing Ancient America* by Frank Joseph
6. *The First American* by Christopher Hardaker
7. *Founding Fathers, Secret Societies* by Robert Hieronimus, Ph.D.